SHADES OF BLUE

Other Books by Kenny Ferguson

The Lost Lamb

Tariq

The Balkan Photo

SHADES OF BLUE

KENNY FERGUSON

SHADES OF BLUE

iUniverse books may be ordered through booksellers or by contacting:

iUniverse
1663 Liberty Drive
Bloomington, IN 47403
www.iuniverse.com
1-800-Authors (1-800-288-4677)

ISBN: 978-1-4917-5552-5 (sc)
ISBN: 978-1-4917-5551-8 (hc)
ISBN: 978-1-4917-5550-1 (e)

Library of Congress Control: 2014922213

Print information available on the last page.

iUniverse rev. date: 01/27/2015

To my wife, Marie, who gave me the time and space to create this story and to all the men and women in blue, who repeatedly step into the unknown to protect all of us.

PART ONE

THE CRIME SCENE

FLASHES OF RED AND YELLOW LIGHTS BOUNCED OFF THE BUILDING FACADS in lower Manhattan with a rhythmic cadence and ricochet through the quiet city streets. Those same lights pulsed on the face of Charlie Weadock as he approached the police lines. Weadock nudged a few curiosity seekers aside to reach the yellow crime scene tapes then paused to check his watch. It was a few minutes after midnight.

A group of nosey bystanders irritated Vincent Kennedy; the Detective-Lieutenant in charge of this homicide investigation but the sight of Charlie Weadock showing his Sergeant's badge to a uniformed police officer at the crime scene perimeter annoyed Kennedy a lot more.

"What the hell is he doing here?" Kennedy complained to the Night Duty Captain.

Captain Carmody twisted his body to look at Weadock. "I called the Internal Affairs Division and told them that Weadock's business card was found in the victim's pocket."

"So, why'd they send him here?"

The captain shifted his owlish eyes in thought. "Because it was his card?"

"Ah," Kennedy's naturally red face got redder as he shook his head from side to side. "I hate this son of a bitch, Captain. He's a true scumbag."

"Charlie Weadock?" The captain narrowed his eyebrows and formed a questionable expression on his face. "He seems like a team player to me. You don't like him, huh?"

Kennedy looked up at the night sky. "It's personal."

Weadock came closer to the shattered remains of a corner newsstand and the tarp-covered corpse in the street. "Good morning, Captain."

"Hello, Charlie." Carmody loosened his tie. "You know Lieutenant Kennedy?"

"I do."

"Tell me something, Weadock," Kennedy closed the gap between Weadock and himself. "How come this dead guy had your business card in his pocket?"

Weadock glanced down at the tarp. "He was an old friend."

Kennedy lifted the blue tarp to expose the upper part of the corpse. "This piece of shit was your friend?"

Weadock peeked at the body then looked up at a solo lighted window across the street before moving even closer to Kennedy. "He grew up in this neighborhood, look at us." Weadock waited until Kennedy made eye contact with him. "Some of us became cops, some became priests, some others became drunks or–"

"Junkies." Kennedy let the tarp slip from his fingers.

"I guess."

"So, which one are you, Weadock?"

"I wonder sometimes." Weadock crouched down again to get a better look at the victim. The skull was still exposed. "You don't remember this guy at all, do you?"

"Should I?"

"He lived on our block."

"What? No way."

Weadock covered the body and stood up. "That's Tommy Raffes laying there. He lived at 339 West Seventeenth Street, just across the street from you. He was your neighbor until you moved to Long Island."

Kennedy crinkled his face in thought.

"Remember those houses on the other side of the street. The ones the city ripped down to build the new high school?"

Kennedy shot the victim a perplexed glanced. "He lived there, huh? That would be right next door to you."

"Some of the guys called him Rat Face."

"Rat Face?" Kennedy registered a smirk. "I don't remember anybody named Rat Face."

"He was the skinny lefty who played first base for Saint Bernard's."

"Rat-face-Tommy, huh. Well, he doesn't have much of a face anymore. Does he?"

Weadock scanned the area again. "Any leads?"

Detective Marini, a Tony Curtiss look alike, stepped into the conversation. "Not a clue, Sarge. Just that busted up newsstand and this dead guy. This area is desolate after 10:00 o'clock at night. You know that."

"What else do you know about this bum?" Kennedy demanded.

"Before off track betting came along, he ran numbers for the local bookies."

"Then he has a yellow sheet?"

"Nothing much, a couple of short visits to Rykers Island for shop lifting. He annoyed the shit out of the local merchants but he was harmless and broke most of the time." Weadock glanced at the body again. "When he needed cash, he worked at that car wash on 19th Street and Tenth Avenue." Weadock pointed south. "And I've seen him pushing a rack of dresses in the Garment District."

"You getting this?" Kennedy nudged Marini and Marini began taking notes.

Weadock looked down again. "I haven't spoken to him in a year or two but one of my detectives recently told me he was running errands for a drug dealer up town on the west side."

"So he was a junky?"

"He may have been but I can't think of anyone who would want to do this to him. Perhaps it was a robbery?"

"It was no robbery." Kennedy insisted, "He's got money in his pockets and an expensive watch that's probably stolen."

"An attempted robbery?"

"No!" Kennedy showed his teeth, "No robbery."

"Okay, okay." Weadock threw up his hands and looked at Marini. "Are there any witnesses?"

"Not yet." Marini slid his eyes at his boss, "No witnesses."

"You want to claim the body, Weadock?"

Weadock ignored Kennedy and continued talking to Detective Marini. "His parents moved to Florida about five years ago. Too bad he didn't go with them. Look," Weadock paused to look at the body again. "He was an alcoholic and a petty thief and probably a drug addict but he wasn't a trouble maker. He kept pretty much to himself."

Kennedy came closer to Weadock and Marini. "You knew this guy pretty well, Weadock. I'll bet he was one of the rats on your payroll." Kennedy nodded at Captain Carmody.

"He was." Weadock grinned. "He was a Registered Confidential Informant for the New York City Police Department and I was his contact. But he's dead now and all that doesn't matter much anymore. Does it?"

"I'll have to see his folder."

"You can't see a CI's folder."

"What are you talking about? This is a homicide investigation and the guy's dead. I think that entitles me to see his folder, Sergeant!"

"I'll find out what I can for you, Lieutenant. But it's Department Policy, not mine. All CI folders are automatically sealed in the case of their death because their folder may contain information about active cops under investigation. I'll screen his folder for you and if there's anything in there connected to this case, I'll see that you get a copy of it."

"Excuse me, Captain," Kennedy said. "But I've got some real police work to do. Now I know why they called this dead guy Rat Face." Kennedy nudged Weadock aside as he moved around him.

Marini followed Kennedy toward the splintered newsstand.

The Duty Captain beckoned Weadock to come closer to him. "How come you guys are so fond of each other?"

"It's a long story, boss."

Captain Carmody leaned back against the fender of a patrol car. "I've got all night."

"Well," Weadock shrugged. "I dated his little sister when we were kids and he didn't like it… I also arrested his older brother, Tom, about four years ago."

The captain raised his eyebrows again.

Weadock hesitated. "Tom Kennedy was a patrol sergeant in Midtown Manhattan. It was one of the first cases I caught as a Field Internal Affairs Unit Investigator. That case ended Tom's NYPD career.

"Wow, I was working in the Bronx then."

"Tom Kennedy was the oldest of the Kennedy boys and the first of his generation to join New York's Finest. His Grandfather is a retired Sergeant and his father was a Lieutenant and still on the job when this happened. When Tom got booted from the job, his father threw his papers in and retired. The whole Kennedy family took it on the chin, including him." Weadock nodded at Lieutenant Kennedy.

"What's Tom Kennedy doing now?"

"He's a bartender at the Blarney Rock Bar near Madison Square Garden."

"I could never work Internal Affairs, Charlie. If I did I wouldn't have a friend in the department."

"You're right about that boss."

The captain stretched. "Why do you suppose there's so many screwed up cops on the job today?"

"I don't know. I guess they keep this blue wall of silence around them. They think it binds them and protects them, like doctors and lawyers. Cops will protect other cops to the death no matter what they've done wrong. That's the part I don't understand and that's why I took this job with FIAU."

"What about this dead guy?" Carmody moved a few steps and looked down at the corpse. "Was he really on the city payroll?"

"Of course."

"Working for you?"

"Yeah," Weadock nodded, "but nothing recent."

"Well," Carmody pulled a pen from his pocket. "It was nice chatting with you, Charlie but I've got to start the paper work on this incident. We have to talk again sometime, over a martini."

Yes, Sir. It was nice to see you again, Captain."

Kennedy and Marini came back to the body when Carmody walked away. They hovered around the corpse, looking at it from different angles.

Weadock joined them. "I'm not recommending an IAD complaint number for this case."

Kennedy ignored Weadock.

"Do you need me for anything else, Lieutenant?"

Kennedy still ignored him.

"Hello!"

Kennedy glanced at Carmody who was now sitting in a patrol car then moved closer to Weadock. "This guy was a big pal of yours, right? You must know where he lived."

"He had an apartment in the Chelsea Housing Project. Weadock waved at the buildings across the street. I'll look up the exact address when I get back to my office and call you."

"Call him." Kennedy nodded at Marini. "I don't want to talk to you unless it's absolutely necessary."

"Okay but you might want to send someone over to talk to Mr. Hansen. He's the guy who owns this newsstand or what's left of it. He and Tommy were pretty tight."

"Don't worry about my case, Weadock. My detectives can handle this investigation without any help from you. This is a homicide investigation. It doesn't concern Internal Affairs… Or does it?"

Weadock twisted his neck to scan the area, then looked at Marini. "Did the Crime Scene Unit leave yet?"

"I don't know, why?"

"I was wondering if they took any pictures of this tire track here." Weadock pointed a pen size flash light at the ground near the body.

"Why would they do that?" Kennedy asked. "This is not a hit and run. There is no car involved."

"Perhaps not but someone or something wrecked that newsstand," Weadock flicked a finger at the newsstand, "and there was a car parked here before the murder and now it's gone."

"You think so, huh?"

"Yes, I think so. Look, there's no blood here." Weadock pointed toward the black top again.

Kennedy and Marini looked at each other.

"Take a step back here with me." Weadock said as he motioned them to move around the body. "See how the explosion of blood forms a circle around the body. There's blood everywhere but there's none here and there's a tire print in the blood. It looks like a pizza pie with a slice missing."

"He's right, Lou." Marini stood up next to Weadock and looked down, "Look at that shit!"

"Thanks a lot, Sherlock but the Crime Scene Unit is still here," Kennedy looked around." Kennedy moved closer to Marini to speak privately. Then Marini walked away.

Kennedy looked at the ground again and shook his head in silence.

Weadock began moving away. "I was just trying to be helpful."

"I don't need any help from you or your scumbag unit."

"It's Manhattan South, Field Internal Affairs Unit, Lieutenant." Weadock objected to Kennedy's comments about scumbags but decided to let it go. He paused again. "By the way, how's the family?"

Kennedy followed Weadock and caught up to him. "What did you say about my family, Weadock?"

"I just asked if they were okay."

"My family is none of your fucking business, Sergeant. Oh, you mean, how is my sister?"

"Okay, how is she?"

"I haven't seen her in two years but it's been a lot longer for you, hasn't it, hotshot?"

"Goodbye, lieutenant." Weadock turned and walked away."

"My family is just fine." Kennedy spoke loudly at weadock's back. "And they'll stay fine as long as you stay away from them. And keep your nose out of my case too."

Weadock twisted his body under the bright yellow reflector tape that was wrapped around the crime scene and threaded a path through a maze of empty patrol cars to his parked car.

He got in and sat behind the steering wheel thinking about what had just transpired. Looking at the date on his digital watch, his thoughts faded and Theresa Kennedy's face came into clear focus. ***Don't do this to yourself, Charlie.*** **He thought.**

Weadock moved his car out into the early morning traffic and headed uptown. The area

around the Port Authority Bus Terminal was grid-locked with a taxicab accident and he became trapped in the stalled traffic. Two cabbies and a bus driver were arguing about who hit who and there was no way to back up. He put the transmission into parking gear and slumped against the backrest. He saw her face again on his windshield and remembered the first time they met.

...Theresa was sitting across the table from him at a neighborhood wedding. She was studying him when he first noticed her and she looked away when their eyes met. When she glanced back at him, he looked away. This avoidance of eye contact continued for several minutes until her bewitching blue eyes captured him. He was stunned by her aggressiveness and tried to act tough. She sensed his shyness and made the first move. She came to him, took his hand, and led him to the dance floor. He protested but couldn't let go of her hand.

"I can't dance." He pleaded.

"It's easy," she tugged at his hand, urging him to the center of the room. "It's just a polka."

They sailed around the room in each other's arms with their eyes locked together. Everyone and everything in the room faded

away. When a slow dance followed, she stepped in close to him and waited. Her scent was intoxicating. He was apprehensive and took a step back. She took a step closer and he surrendered...

The loud honking of car horns brought him back to reality as the traffic knot became undone and the noise faded, he headed east toward his office in the 17th Precinct.

An hour later, at the Midtown South Precinct Station House, Lieutenant Kennedy spread the contents of Tommy Raffes's property envelope on his desk and began examining the items.

"Carbonaro," the lieutenant called.

A chubby Italian detective in his fifties stuck his substantial nose into Kennedy's office. "Yeah, boss?"

"Let's see the DD5's on the canvass you and Marini did."

"The follow-up 5's are not typed up yet, boss."

"So tell me about them."

"Okay but so far we only did the windows facing the street."

"Well?"

"One witness, an old hag who lives over the tire shop on Thirty-Fifth Street. She heard a noise and looked out her front window."

"She saw a car, right?"

"Yeah," the surprised detective said. "She said she heard screaming about midnight and went to the window. She saw a big black limousine parked at the newsstand but she was watching a good movie on the late show and went back to the tube. How did you know about the car, boss?"

"Just a guess."

"That's why you're the lieutenant and I'm the detective, right?"

"Any other witnesses?"

"No, nobody else."

Kennedy picked up Weadock's business card and examined it. He lit a cigarette and was tempted to torch the card but tossed it back into the victim's property bag. "When you finish the canvass tomorrow, go back and talk to that old woman again. Get more details; see if she remembers the license plate number or anything about the occupants in the car. Then go interview the owner of the newsstand. Your partner took his name and address from the peddler's license at the crime scene."

"We could go over there now, boss?"

"Nah, I'm going to meet some of my Irish buddies at Morgan's Bar while it's still open." Kennedy grabbed his jacket. "Tomorrow's just fine but I want all the crime scene reports on my desk by noon."

THE TERMINAL HOTEL

IT WAS STILL DARK WHEN RAMON VELEZ PARKED LOPEZ'S limousine on a quiet street near the Terminal Hotel.

"This is stupid," Lopez wagged his distressed face. "You can't leave this car here. What happens if cops come along? I don't have a badge to show them like you."

Ramon spread his hands. "But this is where the guy lives, poppy. What would you have me do?"

"Don't you think the cops would be curious about a brand new Cadillac being parked in front of this shit hole?"

"I guess."

"There's an all night diner on Tenth Street. Park the car there and walk back. And stop calling me Poppy."

"You're the only Poppy I have now."

"Didn't they teach you anything in the army?

"Like what?"

"Like getting me too close to your repulsive work."

"You came with me to find the rat man. Didn't you?"

"That was different, Tommy was on my payroll, like you but I didn't think he would steal from me. From me!" Lopez's face turned red with rage. "Look, I don't know this news paper guy and I don't want to know him. I just want my luggage back."

Ramon drove three blocks north and parked the limousine in front of the Village Diner. He stepped out and surveyed the mostly empty diner. It reminded him of a railroad dining car. He raised the collar of his topcoat and began walking south on the Bowery towards the hotel. *…It wasn't a real hotel,* He thought *but an old clock factory converted into a maze of one-room apartments for homeless and destitute men. He had heard rumors that the hotel was named after the now abandoned Terminal Fruit Market at the end of the street but the local cops say that the staggering mortality rate led to its inappropriate title.*

Ramon sniffed at a foul odor in the air and about the same time saw a group of derelicts on the corner. Three of the local rogues stood close to a fifty-gallon drum that raged with hot flames. They also shared a common bottle. As they drank, the clear liquid in the wine bottle glistened off the fiery flames and somehow reflected the hollowness of their empty existence.

The dimly lighted hotel was a seven story stone building. Most of the two-foot letters illustrating the real name of the hotel were haphazardly hanging from the once illuminated canopy. One letter dangled precariously over the hotel's main entrance where a man crouched in a dark corner. Ramon thought this man resembled Tommy Rat Face, the man he had killed a few hours earlier.

"You have any brothers, Mister?" Ramon asked.

The bum looked up at him without answering.

"Where does Happy live?"

The bum failed to respond to Ramon's question and slammed his eyelids closed. Then he began rubbing his face hard with both hands. When he dropped his hands, a long, gooey substance dangled from his nose.

Ramon backed away and turned a nauseating sneer in Lopez's direction. He stepped to the side to go around the man but the man stretched out one hand to reach him. Ramon pushed him back with his foot and the man fell back against the wall.

"You got a quarter, mister?" The bum reached at Ramon again.

Adjusting the collar on his black cashmere topcoat, Ramon side-stepped the bum and entered the dimly lit building.

Zombies, he thought. *Filthy, dirty, zombies.*

Inside the lobby, Ramon paused in front of a large full-length mirror to comb his slick black hair. He pulled a few strands of hair loose with his fingers and let them dangle in front of his face. Then flicked at his thin mustache with his comb. He brought his face closer to the glass and studied his image in the mirror. He relaxed his eyes and for a brief moment imagined himself inside the mirror looking out.

When he shifted his focus to the filth on the mirror's frame, he backed away from his reflection. For some reason unknown to him, the sight of dirt sickened him. He thought about the drool on the face of the bum at the door and remembered how Lopez drooled over Tommy-Rat-Face at the newsstand before ordering his death.

He made his way to a half-opened French door in the hallway. The word "Office" had been crudely printed on a paper sign and scotch taped to the wall above the door. The upper part of the door was held open by a twisted wire coat hanger.

Inside, a young man sat on a barstool with his eyes glued to a television set. Ramon guessed that he was a college student, perhaps eighteen or nineteen years of age.

The young man detected a shape in the open doorway with his peripheral vision and somehow, without moving his eyes from the television screen, he knew it was a man wearing a white shirt and tie.

"Yes?"

"Detective Santos, Tenth Squad," Ramon said, "I've got a notification for a man named Happy. He owns a newsstand on 34th Street and Tenth Avenue. His newsstand was burglarized. I got his name and address from a permit on the wall. He does live here, doesn't he?"

The young man sensed that Ramon was a cop even before he flashed his phony gold detective's badge. "Happy, huh?" The young man hopped off the stool and started acting busy. He opened and closed the same desk drawer three times before unpinning a long sheet of typed paper from a bulletin board behind him. "Happy, Happy, Happy," he mumbled repeatedly with his face close to the document. "5G, Room 5G. That's on the fifth floor. His real name is Harry Hansen, you know." The young man looked up from the document to see an empty doorway. "Is there

anything wrong, Detective?" He took a few steps toward the door but his fascination with the movie he was watching got the better of him. He remounted his stool and continued watching it.

Unseen and unheard, Ramon's dark shadow threaded a dimly illuminated stairwell to the fifth floor. The smell of dried urine in the hallway almost made him turn beck. It reminded him of the hallway in the tenement building where he lived as a kid. Paper signs indicating the floor numbers were attached to the staircase walls with gray duct tape. Ramon noted similar signs above the doors to the rooms as he passed them. The first room on the fifth floor was a huge room without furniture and had no front door. He peeked inside; at least a dozen men could be seen inside sleeping on naked mattresses. He could smell their unwashed bodies and hear their difficult breathing. He felt that they were the same men who crowd the local intersections to clean car windshields with dirty rags and beg for quarters. These derelicts rarely traveled more than a block or two from the hotel. He had heard that some of them were wealthy and successful people before their demise. Now they spend a good part of the days intimidating motorists to

fill used coffee containers with enough coins to buy their next bottle.

He moved down the hallway pondering how he would separate Happy from this pile of human waste but paused in front of room 5G. Ramon resisted the loud snoring and snorting coming from the other rooms down the corridor. He donned a pair of thin rubber gloves and he twisted the doorknob in his hand. He was surprised to find it locked. He leaned against the door and jiggled the knob.

"Who's there?" A voice responded to the wobbling knob.

"Police, open the door."

Happy reached for the long cord hanging above his bed and pulled it. A naked 40-watt bulb filled the small room with dim shadows and he looked around at stacks and stacks of old newspaper surrounding him. "I've got to get rid of some of this shit." He mumbled to himself.

Happy slipped into his worn flannel bathrobe and a pair of pink bunny slippers. Then shuffled to the door and opened it. The door stopped with the snap of a short metal safety chain and he stuck his unshaved face into the four-inch gap. "Whadayawant?"

Ramon dangled his gold detective shield in the opening. "Somebody broke into your newsstand."

Happy closed the door to unlatch the chain. He let the door swing open until it hit a stack of newspapers. "Did you catch any of the little pricks?"

Ramon entered the room and closed the door behind him. "You know a guy named Rat Face?"

"Sure, everybody knows him."

"Well, he's the guy who did it."

"Who, Tommy?" Happy smiled. "Tommy wouldn't break into my stand. He watches it for me when I go to the toilet."

"He told us he gave something to you to hold for him and he was breaking in to get it when we grabbed him."

"Where is that little shit?" Happy looked passed Ramon at the closed door. "I'll get dressed and come down with you."

Ramon glanced through Happy's dirty Venetian blinds at dark sky outside. Sensing that daybreak was near, he checked his watch. "You don't have to come down right now, old man. Just give me the item and we'll release your friend."

"What item are you talking about, officer?" Happy asked. I better come and talk to Tommy."

Ramon tugged on his pair of shear plastic gloves until they were tight on his hands. He looked like a surgeon about to begin an operation. He shoved Happy against the bed.

"Just give me the bag, old man, and I'll go away." Ramon had powerful arms for his size and carried two loaded thirty-eight-caliber revolvers but in situations like this he preferred a short length of half-inch brass pipe. The only item his real father let him play with as a kid. It was twelve inches long with a coupling threaded on each end. He removed the blunt instrument from his coat pocket, screwed the two couplings onto the ends, and without warning, struck the old man on the head.

Happy fell backward onto the bed. "Oooohhh!" He groaned, "What is this?"

"Where is the fucking bag?" Ramon demanded.

"What bag? Ouch! Stop that!" He recoiled backward when Ramon hit him again. "What are you talking about?"

"The suitcase," He raised his voice. "The one that the rat man gave you."

"You're not a cop. A real cop wouldn't hit me for nothin'."

"Look, Mister Happy, all I want is the suitcase. Cough it up and I'm gone."

"A black suitcase?"

"Correct."

"Yes, there was a suitcase but Tommy told me to keep it for him."

"Where is it now?"

"Ah, the professor took it."

"What professor?"

"I don't know his name but he buys my papers."

"Aaaaahhhh," Happy screamed again as Ramon slashed at him with the brass pipe. The old man cupped his hands over his ears for protection but it was too late. Blood gushed between his fingers.

"Don't give me any of that professor bullshit!" Ramon shouted, smashing the pipe into the top of the dresser and briefly turning his eyes to the window again. "The rodent told me that you had it. Now cough it up!"

"It's true," Happy held the wooden bedpost with one hand and his painful ear with the other. "But the professor took it when I got sick." Happy looked around for an escape route. The door was the only way out and the enemy was blocking it.

Ramon hit him again and Happy remembered the Japanese interrogator who tortured him years ago in the war. He knew there was no escape from the pain. He came to attention and snapped a hand salute. "The professor will never talk." He looked straight at Ramon; "You sons of Nippon will never get the information."

Ramon formed a questionable expression on his face then hit the old man again. "Where is the bag?"

Happy ignored the pain and stood tall. "Corporal Hansen, United States of America."

"The bag!" Ramon yelled.

"Corporal Hansen, serial number 12579698."

"What's this professor's name?"

"Corp-"

"Wrong answer." The bloody pipe came crashing against Happy's head again and the old vet made an unsuccessful dash for the door. Ramon struck at him like a coiled snake and this time the thin pipe bit deeply into the old man's skull. Happy bounced off the wall and hit the floor hard. He remained motionless.

Ramon heaved Happy's heavy body, face up, onto the bed and tapped his knee joint as if he were a doctor. Receiving a negative response, he moved his face closer to Happy's face. He felt the old man's neck for a pulse but there was none.

Ramon scanned the room, toppling stacks of newspapers and furniture but the black suitcase was not there. Studying the dead body on the bed, Ramon wondered about him. How come all the other zombies are sleeping in open pens and this guy rates a private room with a lock on the door and furniture?

He crossed the room to the body and stood over it, examining the eyes. The old man seemed to be looking back at him.

"How come you got all this stuff, mister?" He questioned the dead body, "huh?" He spread Happy's lips with the end of the pipe and worked the pipe into the corpse's mouth. "Say aahhhh." Then rammed the pipe down with a vengeance.

Moments later, the dark shrouded figure moved through the quiet lobby in the opposite direction. Pausing in front of the huge lobby mirror once again, Ramon admired his perfect teeth. A flicker of light emanating from the television set in the office bounced off the mirror and into Ramon's eyes. Eyes that became prominent in the glass and for an instant they resembled the eyes of the old man he had just killed. Ramon quickly backed away from the image.

When he moved through the vestibule, a voice mumbled at him from the darkness and he stopped. The bum he had knocked down earlier was still there and reaching up at him. "Got a quarter, mister?"

Ramon pulled a few coins from his pocket and tossed them on the ground. The derelict swept them up with his hands and Ramon stepped through the open doorway.

Outside, he dropped his blood stained gloves in a corner trashcan and walked north on the Bowery.

Antonio (Lobo) Lopez was a forty-five-year-old alcoholic and cocaine addict who looked sixty. The road to riches had been long and painful for him, but now he was powerful and feared in his little area of the world. He wore silk shirts and thousand dollar suits. He liked to wear his shirts open at the collar to expose his heavy gold jewelry. He wanted everyone to know that he had made it to the top.

He kept a stable of young boys around him and bought them expensive gifts. The handsome young boys often accompanied him to the racetrack and the opera. Lopez excelled in all his vices and was truly a self-made millionaire but right now he was on the Bowery, in the back seat of a parked limousine waiting for his assassin to return. The limo's backseat ashtray was now filled with cigarette butts.

Lopez was startled when Ramon suddenly appeared at his side window. He could see that Ramon did not have the suitcase.

Ramon slid into the driver's seat.

"Where's the bag?"

"It's not there. I searched his room and questioned him thoroughly. He said he gave it to some professor when he got sick."

"What professor?"

"I don't know." Ramon started the engine. "He refused to tell me."

"And?"

Ramon drove east on Houston Street toward the FDR Drive. His silence told Lopez that the old man was dead.

MORGAN'S BAR & GRILL

LIEUTENANT KENNEDY'S HOME TELEPHONE BEGAN RINGING AT ten o'clock in the morning. His wife, Mary, stopped folding hot clothes in the basement laundry room and raced upstairs to reach the kitchen telephone.

Vincent Kennedy felt like he was submerged in a deep dark sea. Depth charges were exploding all around him in methodical order. He tried to swim away from them but the explosions followed him and became louder and closer and stopped when Mary picked up the phone. He opened one eye and tried to focus on a photo on his dresser. When he opened the other eye, his wife and kids came into the bed room and he knew he was safe at home. He tucked his head under a pillow to muffle any future detonations. The blasting had stopped but pain in his head suggested that he was wounded. He gently shifted his head to see the rest of his bed room. *How did I get here, how did I get home? How could I drive from Manhattan to Long Island and not remember any of it? I have to cut down on the booze.* Vincent Kennedy was no stranger to the pain of a hangover but he wasn't ready to spring into action either. Hoping to fall asleep again, he closed his eyes and remained motionless.

Mary Kennedy had been screening her husband's calls for ten years now and knew which to accept and which to refuse. She knew he had no intention of doing any serious work on Saint Patrick's Day. No respectable Irishman would. "Honey," Mary's gentle voice floated through his pillow and managed to penetrate into the deepest parts his brain. "Jerry Marini is on the phone, he says it's important."

Kennedy kept his eyes closed and answered through a space under the pillow. "Tell him I went fishing."

"He says Captain Shapiro ordered him to find you."

Kennedy crawled his way across the bed and reached for the bedroom telephone. "This better be good, Marini!"

"Lieutenant, you're not going to believe this. Mario and I are at the Terminal Hotel in the Ninth Precinct. You know the big flophouse near Seventh Street and the Bowery. Lieutenant, you there?"

"Go on." Kennedy groaned.

"Yeah… Well, the newsstand guy, Happy. You know, the guy who owns the… I mean the guy who owned the newsstand where Raffes was killed last night. Well, he got wasted too; his brains are all over his room here. It looks like a re-run of the newsstand homicide. The Ninth Squad's got this one. Shapiro's here too and he wants you to get down here ASAP."

Two hours later, Kennedy paused on the fourth floor landing of the Terminal Hotel to stabilize his heavy breathing.

"You all right, lieutenant?" A young female Police Officer in uniform asked him as she jogged passed him on the staircase.

Kennedy checked her name tag and her butt as she hustled around him. *I don't know her, how did she know I was a lieutenant? Without this white shirt and tie I guess I could be mistaken for one of the hotel residents.* Rubbing the stubble of his unshaved face, he continued up to the crime scene and two of his detectives.

"Are you alright, Lieutenant?"

"What…? Tell me I look like shit."

Marini nodded. "You look like shit, Lou."

"Who found the body, Jerry?"

"We did." Marini flapped a hinged hand between himself and Carbonara, "Mario and me, we got here about eight o'clock this morning. The old guy's door was unlocked, so I pushed it open. When I saw the body I backed out and called it into the Ninth Squad. We questioned some of the residents while we were waiting for the patrol sergeant and the squad to get here but most of these guys don't know their own fucking names. Nobody saw nothing and nobody heard nothing. But it's the same MO as the newsstand; this killer is a phantom.

"The squad interviewed the social worker on duty down stairs but he didn't know anything either. He came on duty at seven o'clock and said the guy on the graveyard shift told him it was a boring night. It seems like the same perp did them both but this time the killer left the murder weapon, a short piece of pipe."

"How do you know that?"

"It's sticking out of the victim's face." Marini nudged the door open with his foot. "Well, it appears to be the murder weapon anyway. The Ninth Squad found a pair of bloody gloves in a trashcan outside the building. The transparent type, you know, the kind doctors use."

"What else?"

"Forensics is here; they're bagging and tagging everything. There are no prints on

the pipe so they're leaving it in place for the Medical Examiner."

"When was he killed?"

"The ambulance attendant pronounced him DOA. He said five to six hours ago. So what do you think, boss?"

"I can't think right now." Kennedy massaged his eyes. "It seems like the same perp, doesn't it?"

Marini nodded in silence.

"Where's the Captain?" Kennedy asked.

"He was here earlier for about twenty minutes and left. He wants you to call him later. He's on the golf course with Chief Lazarus."

Kennedy continued pressing his fingers against the pain in his head. "Why would anybody want to murder these two no accounts on Saint Patrick's Day? Is either of them Irish?"

Marini stretched his neck while examining the ceiling. "Actually, Raffes was killed yesterday.

"Okay, what's the motive here?" Kennedy probed his first grade detectives. "Raffes had money in his pockets, right?"

"About a hundred bucks."

Kennedy looked around. "Was anything taken here?"

"We don't know, lieutenant." Marini spread his palms Italian style, "The Crime Scene Unit hasn't finished their song and dance yet. If it's okay with you, we'll give the Ninth Squad a hand with the search."

"Sure."

"There's money on the table over there." Marini nodded. "It's in open view."

"I can't deal with this shit right now." Kennedy put his hands on the sides of his head again. "I need a bloody Mary and some aspirin. You guys stay with this until they seal the room. Then get a copy of the complaint report and any follow up DD5's. And find out the nationality of the two victims. If you need me for anything, I'll be at the office."

Later that afternoon, Detective Marini pecked away at a DD5 in his typewriter. It read that Harry Hansen, AKA Happy, was a male, white, 71 years of age who lived at 427 Bowery, New York City, Hansen was the apparent victim of a homicide. The Medical Examiner set the approximate time of Hansen's death at 3:00 AM, Tuesday, March 18, 1992. The cause of death was a blow to the head by a blunt instrument. The 12" length of ½ inch brass pipe, threaded on both ends with couplings attached removed from the victim's

throat appears to be the murder weapon. It is the opinion of the ME that Thomas Raffes, AKA; Rat Face was killed with a similar type weapon at the 34th Street newsstand. However, the pipe recovered from Harry Hansen's body at the Terminal Hotel was not the same weapon used to kill Tommy Raffes. The two weapons may have been similar but the two victims had different blood types and only Hansen's blood was on the weapon recovered at the Terminal Hotel. It also appears that robbery was not the motive. Hansen had $54.75 on a table near his bed, $650.00 in a coat pocket hanging on the closet door and three bankbooks under his mattress containing the sum of $355,000.00. The victim also had a business card in his wallet belonging to a member of the service - Sergeant Charles Weadock, Manhattan South/ Field Internal Affairs Unit.

Kennedy telephoned Weadock and disclosed the brutal details of Happy Hansen's death. He also suggested that they meet later that day at Morgan's Bar on Tenth Avenue and 19th Street to discuss the case. Weadock agreed but got to the bar an hour late.

Kennedy had just finished his third scotch when Weadock entered the bar. The bartender, Brian, was pouring him a buy-back-drink and waited to take Weadock's order, Brian stared

at Weadock who seemed to have materialized from nowhere.

"A vodka martini, very dry, straight up with olives."

"I didn't think you scumbags drank on duty," Kennedy said.

"How about laying off that scumbag stuff while we talk like two professionals.

Kennedy nodded in silent agreement.

"What makes you think I'm on duty?"

"It doesn't matter," Kennedy took a long drink.

"Actually the rules only apply to cops in uniform."

"So, when did you start playing by rules?"

Weadock threw a twenty-dollar bill on the bar and looked around the premises. "I like your office," Weadock let his eyes survey the old bar, "you conduct all your business here?"

"Why? You going to open a case on me?"

"Look, Vinny. You invited me here. You want to talk about these two murders or not?"

"I do." Kennedy scooped a hand full of peanuts from a bowl in front of him and tossed a few into his mouth. "But let's get one thing straight, Weadock. I don't like you. I never liked you and I never will like you. This is strictly a company meeting. The only reason I asked you here was to keep you and

your IAD crew out of my office and away from my Detectives."

"I'm not with IAD, I'm FIAU."

"Same shit."

A friend of Kennedy's got his attention and Weadock had a chance to properly scan the landmark tavern. The old Irish Pub hadn't changed very much since he was a kid. Except for a new brass rail separating the bar from the dining area and a colorful new jukebox, the quaint little tavern was the same as he remembered it twenty years ago. He recalled the fluted wood panels, the stained glass windows and the five leather-lined booths against the 19th Street wall, especially the booth at the end near the fireplace. ***A long legged woman once stopped him and teased him about his good looks. She touched his face and tipped him five bucks to run back to Happy's Newsstand for a World Telegram and Sun.***

"What's going on, Weadock?" Kennedy broke the spell.

"I sold newspapers in this place when I was a kid."

"I don't mean that. The same perpetrator murders two useless human beings in different parts of the city on the same night and both of the victims had your business card in their pockets?

"Some coincidence, huh?" Weadock smiled.

"C'mon, why were they killed?"

"How would I know that?"

"Were they working some black bag case for you?"

"Tommy Raffes was a paid informant. He got a hundred-dollar bill from the city once a week when he was working a case, but he was in the deactivation file when he was killed. That means there was no contact with him for over a year. Happy was just an old acquaintance of mine. He had to be fifty years old when I bought newspapers from him for my paper route. He kept to himself as far as I know and he was never on the city payroll. My dad told me that Happy moved into that newsstand just after World War II."

"How'd he get your card?"

"I gave it to him. I used stop and chat with him whenever I visited the Midtown South Station House. The newsstand was just around the corner. He was an intelligent man, you know. He read most of the newspapers he sold. I gave him my card a few years ago but he never called me with information. I have no idea why anyone would kill either of them. Tommy led a wasted existence and Happy was a harmless cripple."

"He had a big bank account."

"Who? Happy?"

Kennedy looked down his nose at Weadock. "About three hundred grand."

"I wouldn't doubt it. The guy cooked on a hot plate every day. Who is the beneficiary?"

"I don't know that, yet."

"Are there any other victims?"

"Isn't two enough?"

"I mean in addition to them."

"No..." Kennedy ran a finger between his collar and his neck. "Well, all the facts are not in yet but I'm not aware of any others."

"I looked at Tommy Raffes's CI folder. There's nothing in it that relates to your case. I went over it several times."

"That's not good enough, Charlie boy." Kennedy grabbed another handful of nuts from the bowl in front of him. "I'm going over your head with this one." He climbed off his stool and moved closer to Weadock. "By the way, my kid brother, Michael, is on the job now. He's in the First Precinct."

"I know. I've seen his name on the pink sheets."

"Well, do you think you could keep your hands off this brother?"

"He seems like a good kid."

Kennedy moved an inch or two closer to Weadock. "Don't fuck with him the way you fucked with Tom!"

"Tom Kennedy's case is history - why don't you let it go?"

"I'll never let that go. Just don't fuck with this kid!"

"Everybody gets complaints, Vinnie. A cop who never gets a complaint is probably not doing his job."

"You mean me?" The Kennedy raised his voice a few decibels. "I never got a complaint. A cop like me, right? I'm not doing my job?"

"I didn't mean you." Weadock backed off the stool and to put some distance between him and the lieutenant.

Kennedy moved to the bar again and drained what was in his glass. Weadock followed him. "We're not accomplishing anything here, are we?"

"Tell me something, Weadock." The lieutenant leaned into him, "How does it feel to fuck a brother cop? Good? They tell me you really enjoy your work. How many cop suicides have you generated since you became the big corruption fighter? I hear a lot of cops off themselves while they're under investigation. How many have you killed? How many other families like mine have you destroyed?"

"I've got to go, lieutenant."

"Yeah, I know, you're a busy man."

Weadock glanced around at the other customers to see if any were paying attention to his conversation. There were none. He picked up his change and headed for the door. Kennedy wasn't aware of it but he did invoke a painful memory for Weadock. One that Charlie Weadock did not want to remember. He caught a case against a young cop suspected of using and selling drugs and went after him with great tenacity. Considering the details of Weadock's investigation, the Borough Chief ordered the cop to take a Dole Test. The officer knew what the results would be and hanged himself in the station house locker room. He was twenty-three years old.

Weadock's question about other victims stuck with Kennedy until he arrived at work the next day. Kennedy telephoned every detective squad in Manhattan and had them search their files for any unsolved homicides committed in the past five years with the same Modus Operandi.

A week later, Kennedy sat at his desk analyzing the results of his inquiry.

"Now I have to call that scumbag, Weadock and tell him he was right about the body count."

"What else can you do boss?" Marini said, "Seven unsolved murders in the last five years with the same MO. That makes nine

counting the two Saint Patty's Day Murders." Marini looked at the black board behind Kennedy, "Five drug dealers, a judge, a politician and our two. All bludgeoned to death with a blunt instrument. Out of the nine homicides, five identical pairs of bloody gloves and four identical size pipes were recovered and nobody spotted it."

Kennedy slammed the case folder closed. "How the fuck did this happen?"

Marini shrugged. "There could be more, you know

"C'mon, Jerry. You're the best detective I've got. Doesn't anybody check the stats anymore?"

"I don't know, boss. There's a cop or a detective in every precinct checking crime statistics but they only do their own stuff."

"Now I'm going to have to call Shapiro with this. I guess I'll have to call weadock too. Shit! Shit! And double shit. I really hate this guy, Jerry. What is he, some kind of psychic?"

"Well..." Marini checked some notes he had written on a small notepad that he always carried in his shirt pocket. "He was right about the car too. Remember what the old witch over the tire shop said."

Kennedy searched Marini's handsome face for some hidden meaning in his comment.

"Remember the old lady who saw a black limo parked near the newsstand at the time of the murder and--"

"I know about the car, Jerry." Kennedy interrupted.

Marini turned to leave and stopped. "There's one other thing, boss."

"What now?" Kennedy pushed his desk drawer closed.

"You've got to ask Weadock to check out that IAD Log."

"What IAD Log?"

"I thought you knew about that." Marini pleaded with his hands, "There was an IAD Log attached to one of these homicides. A drug dealer named Cruz, killed two years ago around Christmas time. The MO was the same."

"Do me a favor, Jerry.

Marini waited in silence.

"You call Weadock. Give him the IAD log number and ask him to check it out. They give detectives a hard time when we ask them for information but they'll give to him. And don't mention the other six homicides to him, not yet, anyway. I don't want him hanging around here."

"The talk outside," Marini glanced toward the squad room. "Is that he's one of the best investigator in the job. My friend, Detective

Webber, at Homicide told me they've been trying to pick him up for years."

"Che Webber?"

"Yeah, you know him?"

"I know of him. So what?"

"Sergeant Gill is retiring soon. He'd make a pretty good second whip for our team."

"Bite your tongue, Marini."

HECKLE & JECKLE

A WEEK LATER, WEADOCK RECEIVED A PARTIAL ANSWER to his question about similar unsolved homicides. Pressing the telephone against his ear, he listened to Detective Marini's account of the murder of Jose Cruz. Weadock doodled bits information on the large calendar pad on his desk. 'IAD log number 90-2709, 3rd Street and Avenue B, and December 1, 1990.' An IAD log number attached to any criminal case meant that some serious police misconduct was alleged during the investigation. Weadock dialed IAD as soon as Marini got off the line.

The sergeant assigned to the IAD Action Desk for the day was an acquaintance of Weadock's. He didn't hesitate reading the information on his computer screen. "The allegation was received by telephone on October 16, 1991. It came from a Confidential Informant attached to the Treasury Department's Alcohol, Tobacco, and Firearms Unit. The complaint was investigated by the IAD PI Team and closed two weeks later as unfounded."

Weadock asked for a hard copy of the investigation and the sergeant put him on hold.

A few minutes later, an administrative lieutenant came on the line. "Lieutenant Marone, here. Why do you want this information, Sergeant Weadock?"

"It's kind of complicated for a telephone call, lieutenant."

"Well, first of all your request needs the approval of the Commanding Officer of IAD. If you can obtain that, you can review the case folder here within the confines of IAD."

"Okay, can you switch this call to the C.O.?"

"Ah, you'll have to talk to the Duty Inspector first."

"Okay, can you transfer this call to the Duty Inspector?"

"Hold on."

Fifteen minutes later, a Deputy Inspector answered the telephone and listened to Weadock's request to review the case folder. He approved the request.

The next morning, Weadock parked his car on a tree-lined street in Brooklyn Heights and walked a block to the IAD building on Poplar Street. IAD Headquarters was a run-down three-story Gothic-type structure with a green copper roof. Constructed mostly of huge stone blocks and heavy iron bars. It had been the original 84th Police Precinct. The precinct numerals were deeply cut into the granite over the main entrance. Anyone in the building with a window facing Poplar Street had a superb view of the Manhattan skyline and the Brooklyn Bridge. The Internal Affairs Division took over the building in 1975 when the new 84th Precinct station house opened a few blocks away on Gold Street. This old building, frequently referred to as Gestapo Headquarters by NYC cops, had a unique architecture quite unlike the wooden row houses around it that were just as old.

At nine o'clock in the morning, Charlie Weadock dragged his fingers over the space that was chiseled in the corner stone in 1903 and rang the front doorbell.

Inside, an elderly man lowered himself in a small, cage-like elevator to the street level floor and came to the door.

The New York City Police Department's Internal Affairs Division and the Field Internal Affairs Unit in each borough conducted similar investigations but IAD did not consider the FIAU Units to be part of the Internal Affairs Community. Weadock didn't get along with most of the IAD staff either. He especially did not like IAD's practice of turning bad cops into investigators and keeping them in the fold.

The Boris Karloff look-alike who came down in the elevator unlocked the front door. "You rang?"

Weadock showed his badge. "I have to pick up something at the Action Desk."

"Sign the log book and wait there." The old man pointed to a spot on the ground then ascended alone to the second floor in his elevator. "Someone will come for you."

A dozen IAD Investigators passed Weadock as he waited in the small corridor. One of them nodded in recognition but did not speak.

Ten minutes later, a young sergeant came skipping down the stairs like a kid playing hopscotch. He led Weadock up a back staircase to the Action Desk.

"Is this the scenic route?"

"Nah," The Sergeant said. "It's like a back door entrance used to avoid exposing the investigators to outsiders."

"Is that a fact?"

"Oh, yeah."

"I guess that's why they kept me waiting there, where I could see them all coming and going."

"Yeah, right." The young sergeant flashed a confused smile.

The Action Desk was in a large, filthy room on the second floor where hundreds of cardboard boxes with faded labels were stacked against the walls. The boxes blocked out most of any day light and sealed the room in a thick odor of mildew. Another sergeant on duty there questioned him then pulled a legal size manila folder from a metal cabinet and dropped in on an unused desk near the door. "You can use that desk if you like."

Weadock sat down and attentively read through the six-page report in about four minutes. When he asked for a copying machine, the sergeant hesitated.

"This is a closed case and its department property, isn't it?"

The sergeant scratched his head. "I guess."

"So."

The Sergeant stopped what he was doing and grudgingly made one copy of each page as if he were paying for paper.

After leaving the IAD building, Weadock drove two blocks to the East River and parked in a quiet spot near the water's edge. He wanted to review the pages in his hand but the view of downtown Manhattan was too powerful. He eased his head back against the seat to absorb the awesome sight. The swift moving current of an outgoing tide mesmerized him and he let the IAD papers lay on the front seat.

He removed an old passport size photo from his wallet and studied it. He tried hard to keep her out of his thoughts but she kept pushing her way back. He remembered how they maneuvered into that small photo booth at Rockaway Play land. He wondered if she still had the rest of the four-picture photo strip. The black and white photo was as clear as the day it was printed. Her eyes penetrated his defenses, evoking powerful memories. He hadn't looked at the snapshot in a long time and wondered how much she had changed since they last saw each other. Theresa Kennedy was a beautiful girl. He could still sense her power and remembered her body close to his on that hot sandy beach. He studied the shape of her lips, her penetrating eyes, and innocent smile. Then suddenly, he tossed the photograph to the wind and it blew towards the river. *Stop it!* He thought. *Stop punishing yourself.* He slammed the transmission into reverse. The tires spun wildly against the loose gravel in the lot and the car shot backward until he slammed on the brakes. He got out, walked to the photo and picked it up.

At 10:58 AM, Weadock entered the FIAU office in the Seventeenth Precinct, signed the logbook, and poured himself a hot cup of coffee. He settled down at his desk and spread the pages of the super thin IAD investigation out in front of him. The first three pages, known as the base papers, told of the allegation. The second three were work sheets prepared by the assigned investigator, Sergeant Jeffrey Dorfman. The original allegation came from Sergeant Elizabeth Savage of the U.S. Treasury Department's Alcohol, Tobacco and Firearms Section on October 16, 1991. The preliminary investigation, conducted by Sergeant Dorfman, was closed on October 31, 1991, as UNFOUNDED, recommend FILE.

Savage reported that a Confidential Informant, known to her as CI 10837 made the allegation. He stated that he was the chauffeur and bodyguard for a drug dealer and was present at a meeting of drug dealers in December of 1990. When a driver for one of the other drug dealers engaged him in a friendly conversation. When the meeting broke up, he overheard this driver graphically described to his boss how he killed a drug peddler on the lower east side of Manhattan. The CI identified that driver who made the statement as a male, Hispanic named Ramon.

About a week later, the CI saw Ramon again. He was standing outside the Fifth Precinct in a police uniform. He reported this to Sergeant Savage.

The first work sheet by Dorfman was an interview of the Confidential Informant. That took place on October 23, 1991, at ATF Headquarters, 26 Federal Plaza. At that interview, the CI restated his allegation and said that he saw Ramon a third time a few months after the drug meeting riding in a police car on Canal Street. Again, he was wearing a police uniform.

The second work sheet indicated that Dorfman obtained a copy of the Fifth Precinct Command Roster and presented a photo array to the CI. It contained six photographs, one of Ramon Torres, the only Ramon in the precinct and five fillers.

A third work sheet indicated that the CI viewed the photo array. He was certain that Ramon Torres, a cop assigned to the Fifth Precinct, was not the person who made the murderous statements in the parking lot in December of 1990. Dorfman closed the case a week later.

Turning his chair around, Weadock gazed out the window at East 51st Street. Unlike traditional station houses, the Seventeenth Precinct was housed inside a midtown

Manhattan office building and the FIAU Office was inside the station house on the second floor. Weadock watched wave after wave of pedestrians' hurry past the police station. If not for the flock of patrol cars parked in front, no one would ever suspect it was a police facility. He reached for the telephone and dialed Sergeant Savage at the Treasury Department.

Weadock made a formal request to interview the CI and Savage agreed. She said the CI was currently involved in a deep undercover operation but she would contact him and arrange a meeting. She insisted that all interviews of the CI be conducted inside her office at 26 Federal Plaza.

Sergeant James Casey and Detective Valerie Bishop, two investigators on Weadock's team, came into the office. Dropping into her chair, Bishop reached for the telephone in the same motion. Extending her lower lip, she blew a lock of hair away from her face and began pecking a number into the telephone with her witch-like fingernails. Weadock motioned for her attention and she cupped one hand over the telephone mouthpiece.

"I want you to do a 49 for me."

Bishop pulled a yellow writing pad across her desk and waited.

"It goes to the Commanding Officer of Management Information Systems Division, One Police Plaza. Request a list of every Ramon in the Police Department, both civilian and sworn personnel. When you finish it, I want you to hand deliver it to MISD at One Police Plaza."

"Shit." She flashed her eyes at Casey; "We just came from 1PP."

Weadock ignored her comment. "I want the answer as soon as possible. Ask them to expedite it."

"Why don't you send the elephant man for it." She nodded at Casey. "He could use the exercise."

Casey held three fingers against his arm indicating that he was a sergeant and outranked her.

"Do I have to take orders from him, Sarge?" she frowned.

"He's your boss, Valerie."

"No, you're my boss!" She tried to keep an angry expression on her face as she moved her chair closer to the typewriter but she busted out with a spray of laughter. "What's that name again, Sarge - Raymond?"

"Ramon, R-A-M-O-N." He said slowly.

"I do know how to spell it, Sarge." She rolled her eyes across the ceiling.

"Do you know how to spell dimwit?" Casey asked.

"Is that your middle name, sergeant?" Bishop responded, "You ought to know how to spell your own name by now."

Pulling a crumpled napkin out of the mug on his desk, Casey headed for the coffee pot. He had a shit-eating grin on his face. His 6′7″, 220-pound frame was deceiving. Casey was one of the most amiable cops in the Department but nobody messed with him. As the only black male and female team in the office, he and Bishop caught most the observations in the black neighborhoods.

The next morning Weadock left the FIAU Office with his regular sidekick, Detective Falcone. They bulldozed their way into a jam-packed southbound subway train. Falcone squeezed himself into the crowded subway car behind an attractive female straphanger and they became locked in intimacy until the door sprang open at the City Hall Station. The girl couldn't see Falcone's face during the ride but she felt his presence and fired an angry look at him as she broke free. Subway travel was rough and cheap but also the fastest means of transportation around New York City. During the rush hours, it's an all out war just to get on and off the trains.

Weadock bought a doughnut and a container of coffee from a street vendor in front of 26 Federal Plaza and considered the hundreds of immigrant's on line outside the building.

"I wonder what they're giving away over there?" Falcone asked.

"Freedom," Weadock nodded at the girl from the train as she passed them. "They're giving away freedom, Alex."

"Hey, wasn't that the girl from the train who hates me?"

Weadock sipped his coffee. "She must have followed you. Why don't you help her again?"

"Are you kidding? I thought she was going slap my face."

"What did you do to her?"

"Nothing," he smiled. "I guess we were a little too close each other."

Weadock looked around then spilled the last inch of coffee from his container into a sewer drain. Walking away, he paused to glance back at that drain. He thought about the newsstand crime scene and remembered that there was similar sewer drain at that corner.

To avoid setting off the metal detector alarm with their guns, the two investigators approached a uniformed guard at the main entrance of the Federal Building. Falcone told the guard they were NYC cops looking

for the Alcohol, Tobacco and Firearms Unit. Without checking their ID, the guard directed them around the metal detectors to a special bank of elevators used exclusively by the FBI and Treasury Department.

A crowd of Federal employees, holding their ID cards high in the air, swarmed toward the open elevators. Weadock and Falcone did the same and a guard on duty there merely waved them into the next open elevator.

"Great security," Weadock said.

Falcone held his police ID card up so Weadock could see it. He wiggled his fingers at the top of his head and did his best Stan Laurel impersonation. "I could've had a gorilla's picture here and nobody would've been any the wiser."

"Looks like a gorilla to me," Weadock said.

Falcone considered his photo carefully then showed it to a female passenger who was listening to their conversation. "Does this look like a gorilla to you?"

The woman looked at the picture, and then looked at Falcone. She busted out laughing. Falcone reacted with an annoyed expression and Weadock erupted with laughter. Then Falcone laughed; everyone in the elevator began laughing but then someone ripped a loud, smelly fart in the packed elevator and the laughing stopped. When the doors opened on the eighteenth floor, all the passengers rushed out.

Weadock and Falcone continued snickering as they made their way down the corridor. Whenever they looked at each other, one began to laugh. They made an effort to stop cackling outside room 1810 when a leathery looking female with folded arms examined them. She was irritated but they kept laughing.

"Sergeant Savage?" Falcone asked.

"Yes." She shook her head with disapproval. "You must be Sergeant Weadock?"

"No," Falcone pointed a finger at Weadock. "I'm Detective Falcone."

Savage executed a military about face and entered her office.

They followed her to the office door and peeked inside. A chunky young man in his twenties sat in the corner. His body filled the large upholstered chair to its capacity. Weadock suspected that he was the Confidential Informant. The fat boy grinned at them as if he knew what had happened in the elevator. He rearranged his jellyroll shape into a more comfortable position.

"I'm Heckle." He raised a beefy hand to Weadock. "I'm the Confidential Informant."

Weadock and Falcone continued snickering. "I am sorry," Weadock turned to Savage, "but something funny happened in the elevator and-"

Savage, irked with the cops clowning around, turned her head away and headed down the hall.

"C'mon, Sarge." Weadock tried to control his chuckling but failed. He called after her, "We could interview him right here."

"Absolutely not," she ordered. "Follow me." She led them down the busy corridor to a small conference room.

Falcone, who was lagging behind, caught up. "Hey, didn't she ride a bike in the Wizard of Oz?"

Heckle cupped one hand over his mouth and slid his eyes at Savage. He knew that she also heard Falcone's remark about the witch.

Inside the small room, Heckle considered the two NYPD Investigators as they worked on Savage for cooperation. He liked them immediately.

Sensing that some unspoken and immediate bond had taken place between her CI and the two cops, Savage kept shifting her gaze between them.

"Heckle," Weadock said. "It is Heckle, isn't it?"

"Yeah," the CI giggled. "And my brother is Jeckle."

"I suspected as much."

"Do you have any sisters?" Falcone asked.

"Hold it, hold it." Savage scolded the CI. "Just stick to the facts of the case and tell them what you told me in October of 1991."

"Ok, like I told Sergeant Savage, here," Heckle nodded at her, "I'm a licensed locksmith by trade. I had my own store on Third Street for a while, but there wasn't enough money in it, so I took this job two days a week as a driver and bodyguard for the Chinaman."

"Heckle; leave the extraneous names out of this!" Savage ordered.

"Okay, okay." Heckle seemed annoyed with Savage's pushy attitude. "Driving the Chinaman turned out to be fun and a lot more profitable than making keys. Anyway, it was around Christmas time when I drove him to this big meeting of drug dealers on Attorney Street. There was lots of quality cars parked in the courtyard behind the building. That's where I had this conversation with Lobo's driver, Ramon.

"We talked mostly about sports. He told me that he went to P.S. 114 in the Bronx and that he was a great short stop. Almost made the pros. "Later, when Lobo came to the car. He's the dealer that this Ramon guy was driving. Anyway, Lobo asked Ramon if he took care of the business on Third Street. Ramon described how he clubbed some motherfucker to death. He told this to Lobo in Spanish but I'm Spanish. I heard every word. "Then Freddy came out. He was my boss, Freddy the Chinaman."

Savage put a hand on Heckle's arm to stop him from divulging any more information but He shook it off.

"I told Freddy what happened," Heckle continued, "Freddy said it was okay because Ramon was a cop but he was with us. So I forgot the whole matter. A few times after that I saw this Ramon guy coming out of the Fifth Precinct. He was in a police uniform. I waved to him but he didn't see me. That was it."

"Why didn't you report this when it happened?" Weadock asked.

"I'll tell you the truth, Sarge. I was hanging out with some bad people then and doing some pretty bad shit. You know, transporting the product and kicking some ass. I'd still be doing it if the Feds hadn't grabbed me. Not these guys, it was the FBI. At first, I thought my brother had turned me in because he was already in custody. I'm still not too sure about that. He was running guns into New York in his luggage but got caught by these guys." He nodded at Savage.

"When did this drug meeting take place, exactly?" Weadock asked.

"I don't remember that, exactly. It was around Christmas time, November, December, 1990."

"Where was it?"

"I don't remember that either. Somewhere on Attorney Street on the East Side. There's a Mr. Pizza on the corner. I love pepperoni pizza."

"What was the building number?"

"Sorry," Heckle offered.

"Could you get the address if you went back there?"

"I guess so."

"Would you go there and get the number for me?"

"Sure."

"Okay," Weadock nodded. "Now tell me about Ramon. What did he look like?"

"He's a Puerto Rican, 5′10″, 180 lb., straight black hair, mustache, fair skin, good build, nice looking guy."

"Would you recognize him if you saw him again?"

"I guess."

"You said Freddy is the China man?"

"Freddy Colon, yeah. Everybody knew him as the China man. He looked Chinese but I think he's a Filipino. He's in jail now."

"How do you know that?" Falcone asked.

"I put him there."

"Detective Falcone has some pictures to show you," Weadock said.

"IA already showed me pictures."

"How many?"

"Six."

"Six," Falcone repeated, "I have sixty-three photographs to show you."

Falcone began placing the photos on the table as if he was dealing a hand of solitaire. He aligned them in rows and columns until the deck was empty and the table was covered.

"Take your time," Weadock suggested and moved away from the table to speak to Falcone. "Are all the Ramon's there?"

"Yes, sir." Falcone handed him the list of names. "Fifty-nine cops and four civilian employees."

"I don't recognize anyone, Sarge," Heckle moaned, "It was a long time ago."

Weadock patted Heckle on the shoulder. "I want you to look at every picture carefully and pick up the ones that you're absolutely sure are not him and stack those on the chair."

Examining the photos closely, Heckle picked them up one by one until there were only two photos left. "I think he's one of these two guys."

Weadock flipped the two remaining photos to expose the pedigree information on the rear. One photo belonged to Detective Ramon Fernandez assigned to a Bronx Narcotics Unit and the other was Ramon Velez assigned to the Fifth Precinct.

"Did IAD show you these two pictures?"

"Nope, they showed me this guy." Heckle pointed to a picture of Ramon Torres in the stack of discarded pictures. "I see this cop around the neighborhood all the time. He's in the Fifth Precinct too but he's not the guy from the parking lot."

Savage could see that Heckle was eager to help the two investigators and made it clear to Weadock that any future contact with this informant could only be made through her office. Weadock wanted to give the CI his business card but Savage was hawking them too closely. Weadock reluctantly kept his business card in his pocket. When he thanked Heckle for helping the NYPD, he slipped him the card. "I may need to talk to you again, Heckle."

"No problem, Sarge."

"Just call me first," Savage interrupted, "and I'll set up all meetings."

Inside an empty elevator, Weadock pushed the ground floor button. When the doors closed, he turned to Falcone. "IAD fucked up. I'll bet they went down the roster until they found that Ramon Torres's name and stopped. They made up a photo array with his picture and showed it to Heckle. When Heckle failed to pick out Torres, they closed the case." Weadock flipped the pages of the roster. "There are only two names on the last page and Velez's name is one of them."

"What a blunder," Falcone said, "Guglielmo is going to love throwing this one back to IAD. He hates them."

"We're not telling Guglielmo or IAD."

"We're not?" Falcone asked.

"Once IAD realizes that they screwed up, they'll want the case back."

"They can't do that after we identified the subject."

"They've done it to me before." Weadock explained. "This is a major screw-up for them. You think they're going to sit on the sidelines and watch us play a super bowl without them."

"What are we going to do?"

"They had their shot and blew it. Now it's our turn. This is the kind of case we should be working instead of all that Mickey Mouse shit the chief sends us. You go to One Police

Plaza. Pull Velez's personal folder and copy everything. I mean everything, the schools he attended, the jobs he worked, his friends, his relatives, everything. I'm going to have lunch with somebody who might know this Police Officer Velez."

J.J. HARRINGTON

THE BULL & THE BEAR RESTAURANT is one of a few elegant eating and drinking establishments to survive in New York City's accelerating culture. Charlie Weadock entered the establishment through the Lexington Avenue entrance and paused between two marble columns to scan for J.J. Harrington. He spotted him standing beneath one of the eight huge crystal chandeliers. The Victorian style restaurant, rarely crowded, always seemed to have just the right sprinkling of beautiful young women and distinguished old gentleman.

A vintage maitre d' positioned himself at the base of the grand staircase to welcome guests. He glanced at Weadock but turned to greet some guests who were descending from the lobby of the famous Waldorf Astoria Hotel.

As usual, a number of big business deals were in progress at the horseshoe shaped bar and J.J. Harrington was in the thick of it. Wearing a dark blue, vested suit, a white shirt and an emerald green tie, he stood before two seated gentlemen like an old time elixir salesman. Harrington caught Weadock with the flick of his eyes when he entered the premises but continued his engaging conversation with the two men until the sergeant was almost standing next to him.

"Ah, Sergeant Weadock." Harrington glanced at Weadock then moved closer to the two men. "The finest of the finest has finally arrived."

Weadock had asked Harrington on numerous occasions not to mention his name or occupation in public but he did it anyway. It was part of Harrington's strategy to let his marks know that he had powerful friends in the New York City Police Department.

"Mr. Harrington," Weadock interrupted, "can you spare a few minutes for me?"

"Of course, my boy." He put his hand into Weadock's. "You may have the very blood from my veins. But first let me introduce you to these fine gentlemen from the south. Gentlemen," he turned to his prey. "This is Sergeant Charles Weadock of the New York City Police Department, Internal Affairs Division."

The two strangers were impressed and shook hands with Weadock. Harrington introduced them as a retired army colonel and a bank president from Kentucky. Then he quickly prodded Weadock to an empty stool away from the two men. Leaning close to Weadock, he lowered his voice to a whisper. "Give me ten minutes to conclude this deal and I will be totally yours."

Weadock could always gauge how inebriated Harrington was by the degree of finesse and diplomacy he displayed. When sober, Harrington was a soapbox politician with outstanding command of the English language, but the more he drank, the sloppier he got. Drunk or sober, he was always loud and Weadock could hear him telling the two men how costly it was to maintain close ties with the NYPD. Harrington felt that the image of close association with the police gave him an edge or some credibility and he never missed a chance to use Weadock for that purpose.

Harrington telephoned Weadock several times a week. Usually he just wanted companionship and used a ruse of having discovered some new information about bad cops. The problem for Weadock was that Harrington intermittently came up with some great intelligence. So he tolerated the trickery and embarrassment to acquire the information.

"Oscar," Harrington rapped on the bar with his sledgehammer hand. "Give my two friends a small libation on me."

Oscar Sanchez, one of the seasoned bartenders who supplied Harrington with insider information, wiped the bar in front

of Weadock. Oscar was a slick character with over thirty years of service at the Waldorf Bar. He had a weasel like nose and bulging eyes and whenever he dangled a cigarette from his lips, he resembled the actor, Peter Lorre.

"What is your pleasure, Sergeant?"

"A vodka martini, straight up, very dry, with olives."

Straining the cold clear liquid into a stemmed glass, Oscar waved an unopened bottle of vermouth over the cocktail with his other hand. "Very dry, sir."

Weadock had a steady hand but had to sip the drink where it stood on the bar. The surface tension at the rim of the glass made it impossible to pick it up without a spill.

"I haven't seen you in here in a long time, Sergeant."

"I've been busy with the bad guys."

"I hear yeah," Oscar pushed a bowl of mixed nuts in front of Weadock. "There's a refill in the shaker when you're ready, sir."

"You must have stock in this place by now, Oscar."

"About thirty-five years of it, sir."

"How long do you know J.J.?"

"Mister Harrington was sitting on that seat." He nodded at the seat next to Weadock. "When I came to work here in 1968. He gave

me a twenty dollar tip for one drink and I've been his business partner ever since."

"He is a man of habit. Why do you suppose he likes that particular seat?"

"He refers to it as his business chair. I have to keep a reserve stool in the back just in case it gets crowded and his chair is occupied. He watches everybody like a hungry cat."

Weadock watched Harrington as he worked the two strangers and thought about their first meeting. He took another sip of the cold clear liquid and remembered a younger Jeremiah Joseph Harrington.

...It was a rainy, November night when he answered the "Call Out" from the IAD. They ordered him to meet Sergeant Arthur Hart of the Public Morals Division at McSorley's Ale House on East Seventh Street.

Hart had reported that the elderly Irish gentleman sitting next to him at the bar had told him a story of robbery and murder by a New York City Police Sergeant. The old man said that this Police Sergeant killed a man and stripped the dead body of four thousand dollars worth of U.S. Savings Bonds. The Irishman further stated that he had the stolen bonds in his possession now.

Twenty minutes later, Hart introduced Weadock to Harrington as a co-worker then left the bar. Weadock tossed a hundred-dollar bill on the bar and made an immediate bond with Harrington. After a few drinks, Harrington told Weadock about the crime.

"Thank you, sir. Harrington sipped his drink and studied Weadock's face. My mother told me to always say please and thank you." Harrington waved a wad of money in Weadock's face and ordered more drinks. He stood a roll of hundred dollar bills on the bar to impress Weadock.

"Aren't you afraid that someone will take all that money from you, old man?"

"You have no idea how dangerous I am, do you, sergeant?"

"How dangerous are you, Mr. Harrington?"

"Well, sir." Harrington stood up to adjust his clothes, I'm sixty-six years of age and I've never been married. I've never had a girlfriend either. Do you know why?" He turned to glance at a crowd of people and raised his voice. "I hate women. Women rule the world, sergeant. My own mother told me that all women should be put to the sword before their twenty-fifth birthday." Harrington continued quoting his mother and other famous orators and his loud articulate tones soon faded into convoluted mutter. "Here," Harrington pulled

a handful of bonds from the worn brief case at his feet and pressed them into Weadock's hands. "They gave me these to fence."

"They, who are they?"

Sergeant Thomas Kennedy and his driver."

Kennedy told me that he killed some guy in the London Terrace Hotel and stole the bonds and if I didn't sell them for him, he would kill me too."

As Weadock copied the serial numbers from the bonds, it became apparent that Harrington was a man of knowledge and grit, a man who feared no one "I'm not from PMD, old man."

Harrington got up and crossed the sawdust-covered floor to one of the vacant wooden tables. He grabbed a passing waiter and ordered a platter of tomatoes and cheese and another round of drinks.

Weadock followed him to the table and sat close.

Harrington cupped one hand behind his neck for support and swallowed the remains of his drink. "I guessed as much by the tone of your questions. So what happens now?"

"I could arrest you right now for possession of the stolen property. You could also be an accessory to burglary… And murder."

"C'mon, sergeant. You wouldn't have bought me all these drinks if you were going to arrest me."

"Will you cooperate with me?"

"I like you, Sergeant." Harrington handed Weadock a business card, "You're as tough as they come, kid. I'm going to enjoy doing business with you."

Harrington went on to wear a wire for Weadock and set up Tom Kennedy for the fall. As it turned out, there was no murder. The owner of the bonds died of natural causes but stealing the bonds was enough to get Tom Kennedy fired. Weadock tried to get the case shifted to another Investigator but Harrington refused to work with anyone else…

A stinging slap on the back brought Weadock back to the present. "Do you have any idea how many assholes there are on this planet, Sergeant?" Harrington asked.

"I told you not to do that, old man!" The blow was painful but Weadock concealed his distress. When the second blow came his way, he reacted with lightning speed and grabbed Harrington by the wrist. "You're a lot stronger than you think you are old man. One of these days I'm going to forget you're an old man and knock you on your ass."

"You need me, sergeant." Harrington massaged his wrist. "Your bosses can't buy the information I give you for nothing."

"For nothing? What about the aggravation you give me? No, you're right. There are very few wealthy weasels like you who work for the FBI and organized crime and--"

"Excuse me." Harrington turned towards Oscar. "I said excuse me."

Oscar graciously spread his hands.

"Give my friend here another drink."

"No, no more drinks." Weadock felt that Harrington was quite drunk and suspected that he was going to be a pain in the ass the rest of the night. "Listen to me for one minute, Mr. Harrington." Weadock put his hands on Harrington's shoulders and turned his shoulders square to him. "Did you know Tommy Rat Face or Happy Hansen?"

Harrington nodded. "I was acquainted with them, somewhat."

"Do you know why they were killed?"

"Don't have a clue, my friend, but I will make some inquiries for you."

"Would you really do that for me?"

"I would walk on hot coals for you, my boy."

Weadock smiled. "How long will it take?"

"A couple of…" Harrington brought his face closer to Weadock's face. "Does the NYPD want to spend any money on this?"

"No."

"Ok, a week, maybe."

"Thank you, Mr. Harrington." Weadock moved to leave.

"Wait." Harrington put his hand into Weadock's hand and squeezed. The old man had the grip of a steel vise and no respect for weaklings. "Does this mean I'm back on the payroll?"

"If you come up with something, I'll talk to the captain."

"The same captain who couldn't find the parking lot I sent him to because there was no address over the entrance?"

"Yeah."

"Ask him if he wants to borrow a few thousand so he can hire me."

"Now you're a loan shark?"

"I've always been a loan shark."

Weadock rolled a vodka-soaked olive from his glass into his mouth and headed for the door. He could hear Harrington loudly reciting a poem to Oscar, the bartender. "There was an old owl that lived in a tree, and the more he saw, the less he said, and the less he said, the more he saw and…"

THE SHOW-UP

IT WAS TEN MINUTES AFTER SIX IN THE MORNING when Falcone tipped the office coffee pot to get the last few drops of black liquid. He carried two cups of coffee down the hallway, set them on Weadock's desk and dropped into the empty chair next to it. "Savage called last night after you left."

"And?"

"She said you wanted Heckle for a show-up."

"And?"

Falcone emptied four packets of sugar into his coffee and stirred it with his pen. "She insisted on bringing Heckle up here."

"No, way. I don't want this CI anywhere near a police station."

"What else could I do?"

"She turns you on, huh?"

Falcone gagged on his coffee.

"Call her back and tell her to meet us at the Gulf Station on 23rd Street and the East River. I don't want her up here either. You and Valerie pick up a surveillance van and bring it to the pier. We'll put Heckle in the back and Savage in the front.

"I don't want her sitting with me." Falcone sulked, "She's one scary bitch."

"I need to talk to the CI without her in my face. You'll be just fine. You know she likes you."

Falcone shrugged. "The body isn't too bad but she really needs a face job."

"Some guys are turned on by that."

"Not me, nothing turns me on. Ask my wife."

Weadock lifted a new case folder from the basket on his desk and opened it. He read the first page and tossed it on Bishop's desk. "What kind of surveillance van did you order?"

"Ah," Bishop perused the new case folder; "I had to go to IAD for it. The new one at headquarters was booked for the month."

"Which one did you get?"

"They said they only had one."

"They have three, two new ones and a wreck."

"Well, we shouldn't be taking a brand new van to Spanish Harlem anyway."

"Which one did you get?"

"It's perfect for where we're going."

"You know something, you're right."

Five hours later, Falcone drove the graffiti covered van to the Gulf Service

Station at the East River. Savage and Heckle were there waiting.

Sporting a flowered Hawaiian shirt and dark sunglasses, Heckle stood at the end of the pier waving at a boatload of tourists who were passing close to the pier. Several people on the boat waved back at him. Heckle struck a shit-eating grin and walked to the van. When he climbed inside, the van rocked under him like an off balanced canoe. "Nice van, Sarge."

Falcone held the front passenger door open for Savage. She ran her fingers along the rim of the door as she entered and cringed at the dirt. "Where ever did you get this piece of shit?" She wiggled her dirty fingers at Falcone.

"Hey, I had a tough time getting this piece of… This van. Everybody wants it because it blends so well with certain neighborhoods." Falcone didn't tell her that he had to charge the battery and fill the radiator just to get it started.

Weadock twisted his body to adjust the heavy black pads covering the rear windows. He repaired a torn pad with pieces of duct tape. Weadock shuffled his body closer to Heckle. "The van has one-way glass, my friend. We can see them but they can't see us."

Heckle joked with Weadock about the Spanish graffiti on the van as they bounced in and out of the potholes on First Avenue. He suggested putting the name and telephone number of his Locksmith business on the sides of the van.

"Go ahead," Weadock laughed, "bring your own paint next time."

Savage reached into the van from the front and tugged on Heckle's shirt. When he turned, she reminding him not to talk about their active cases.

"What the fuck is wrong with you, woman?" he erupted. "I don't like people pulling on my clothes! Every motherfucker on the East Side wants to kill me because I'm helping you out." Heckle looked at Weadock. "My brother and I have been on her leash for two years now and we haven't got dick to show for it." He yanked on the curtain between the front and rear compartments. "So don't tell me who I can or cannot talk to, lady. I'm not your fucking puppet."

Falcone parked the now quiet van at the curb and tossed a phony florist's delivery sign in the front window. He told Savage to crawl through a small connecting door into the rear compartment. She resisted then reluctantly squeezed through. He followed her.

Heckle continued arguing with Savage until Weadock broke up the encounter.

"All right, all right." Weadock patted Heckle on the shoulder, "settle down, big guy." Weadock nudged one of the black pads aside to peek outside. "The van isn't sound proof."

"You can argue later. Right now, I need you to be quiet and watch the people coming up this street. Look for Ramon."

"Okay, Sarge." Heckle stuck his tongue at Savage when she wasn't looking at him then focused on the pedestrian traffic.

Outside, the van appeared to be abandoned by a florist delivering flowers. Weadock and Falcone came to the area three times before selecting it as the observation point. It was perfect.

Heckle concentrated on the people approaching the van from the south. "Is that fire hydrant a prop?" Heckle asked.

"No, it's real." Falcone said. "And I'll probably get a ticket.

Weadock wanted a spontaneous reaction from Heckle. So he deliberately withheld any description of Ramon's house or car. The van was parked in the perfect position, mid-way between Ramon's house and his parked caddy. All they had to do was wait for Ramon. He was scheduled to work a four to twelve tour and had to walk right passed the van.

Heckle wiped the sweat beads from his face and neck. "It's hot in here, man."

Weadock patted him on the shoulder again. "It won't take long, buddy. Just stay alert and watch everyone who passes."

Surveillance is probably the most tedious and necessary aspect of police investigation. Heckle looked hard and long at several young men with similar descriptions but he remained mute. The large window on the side of the van gave him an excellent view but the air inside had become dense and stagnant. A small vent in the roof provided some fresh air, but body odor was becoming apparent. Heckle's asthmatic breathing became louder and more pronounced as the minutes dragged on. Ramon left his residence at 2:20 p.m. and walked toward his car. As he passed the van Heckle turned to Weadock.

"That's the guy, Sarge." He pointed at Ramon Velez. "That's the guy who bragged about the killing. That's him. The guy in the black hat and black coat, I'm sure of it."

"Well, where do we go from here?" Savage asked.

Weadock looked at her. "I needed a positive ID on the subject. Now I have it. There's a lot of other work to be done before I come back to Heckle here. I've got to talk to my boss and the DA and they have to talk to their bosses about how we're going to play this case."

Falcone wanted to follow Ramon and began crawling toward the front seat but Weadock stopped him. "Let him go, Alex. We don't want to spook this guy. He could be a real psycho. On the other hand we could have nothing. Heckle says Ramon bludgeoned a junkie on East 3rd Street. It just happens that the Ninth Squad has an unsolved homicide on East 3rd Street and the victim died from a crushed skull. Sound familiar?"

"Holy shit." Savage said.

Weadock closed his eyes and spoke. "I don't want anyone talking about this case to anyone." He opened his eyes looking at Savage. "This doesn't go back to your office. If you have to tell your chief, tell him in private and make sure he understands the confidentiality of it."

"Well, that's the guy, Sarge." Heckle repeated, "There's no mistake about that."

Weadock took another look at Ramon through the back window of the van. He was still sitting in his car then turned to Heckle.

"What else do you remember about that day on Attorney Street?"

"Like I told you before, Sarge. This guy said he did murder. It was the way he described it. I think he really killed that motherfucker and enjoyed doing it too."

"Besides you, who else was present when Ramon made that statement? Did anyone else actually hear him say anything about killing the guy on East 3rd Street?"

"Just Ramon and his boss, Lobo. The China man was there, too, but I don't think he heard anything. All the others were too far away."

"Lobo who?" Falcone asked.

"Lopez," Heckle glanced at Savage, "Antonio Lopez. They call him El Lobo -- The wolf. He's a big man now. You know, like a godfather. I drove for the China man then but he's doing heavy time now."

"What's the China man's real name?" Weadock asked.

"Freddy Colon. My brother and I testified against him last year. We put him in the slam for her." Heckle sneered at Savage. He isn't going to tell me anything now. He only wants to kill my brother and me."

"Perhaps he'll talk to me," Weadock suggested.

"Why would he talk to you, Sarge?"

"Nobody wants to stay in jail when there's an opportunity to get out. I think the DA might reduce his sentence if he gives us Ramon."

"Maybe the DA will reduce our sentences too." Heckle gawked at Savage, "My brother and me have been working for the Government for two years now and they're still threatening my brother with jail time."

"We're taking care of that for you," Savage interrupted.

"You ain't taking care of shit, lady! We got you hundreds of bad guys, tons of felony convictions. You would never have gotten those bad guys without us."

"Our territory is shrinking every day," Heckle appealed to Weadock. "The word is out on us."

When the van stopped at the 23rd Street garage, Savage got out quickly and walked to her car. Heckle, still complaining, walked behind her. When she got into her car and slammed the door, Heckle walked back to the two cops to say goodbye.

Weadock seized the opportunity and dealt Heckle a hand in the game. "Call me later on the phone number I gave you. Help me and I'll help you and your brother."

SURVEILLANCE

CHARLIE WEADOCK KNEW as he passed the mid-span marker of the Manhattan Bridge that he was inside the boundaries of the Fifth Precinct. A demolition crew whacking at the bridge's original stonework diverted him into the Chinatown area where he began navigating several narrow streets until he located Ramon's car. The black Eldorado was parked on Elizabeth Street near the station house.

On his way uptown, Weadock stopped at a red light near the Manhattan Bridge again and shook his head in disgust at the demolition workers chopping away at the marvelous old bridge facade.

Five hours later, at 11:15 p.m., Detective Falcone maneuvered his vintage Chevy station wagon between some construction equipment on Canal Street. His car didn't fit at first but it was the best spot to keep an eye on Ramon's Cadillac. He noted several ducks hanging in a restaurant's front window as he bulldozed his way into the spot. "Are those ducks dead?"

Weadock's eyes were once again fixed on the last remnants of the Manhattan Bridge Improvement Project. "I hope so."

Falcone shifted his focus to the metallic Black Eldorado. Except for the windshield, all the windows were made of black glass. "His tour doesn't end until midnight, that's forty-five minutes from now."

Weadock looked at his watch. "See if you can find us some coffee."

Falcone opened the driver's door and stepped outside. Looking around the area like a tourist, he stretched. "Want anything with it?"

"No."

Falcone's footsteps gave off a gritty crunch as he trudged through the construction gravel near his car.

Twenty minutes later, he returned with two containers of coffee and a bag of doughnuts. Falcone worked with Weadock long enough to know how he liked his coffee. With the bag of doughnuts dangling from his teeth, he balanced the two coffee containers on the dashboard and removed the lids. A steamy vapor floated up and fogged their view on the windshield. He turned the wiper blades on and off, then wiped the inside of the glass with an old baby diaper.

Weadock grinned as Falcone swallowed his third doughnut.

"I'm hungry," he said with another doughnut in his hand.

The two investigators were use to this ho-hum part of police work. As the minutes ticked away slowly, they sat quietly in the dark car listening to the sounds of the night. A domestic argument on the third floor across the street. Groups of night people walking by the car and an occasional siren from an emergency vehicle.

Falcone talked about his wife, his kids, his dog and his mother-in-law in that order but he hardly took his eyes off the Caddy.

"That's a bad car, Charlie," Falcone checked the empty doughnut bag. "There's just something evil about it."

"Evil?" Weadock was beginning to doze.

"The car, it looks evil to me."

"How can a car be evil?" Weadock took a sip from his coffee container. "Evil is a total human conception."

"What?" Falcone asked.

"Humans are the only creatures who kill for amusement."

"Is this going to be another one of those lectures about life on planet Earth?"

"It's true, Alex." Weadock looked at his friend, "animals kill to eat or protect themselves or their young or for something called territoriality, but human beings are a lot more complicated."

"I haven't had a cocktail yet. I don't know if I can handle this conversation."

"Look, machines can't think, they only do what we humans tell them to do. You think that car is evil, take a look at that." Weadock nodded at the station house.

Ramon Velez stood on the station house steps as other cops hurried passed him. Every time the front door swung open his dark silhouette loomed in the lighted portal. He was wearing his usual black cashmere topcoat and a black fedora. When the door swung open again, he vanished like a ghost into the night, only to reappear under the street lamp near his car.

Falcone slid his eyes at Weadock without turning his head. "Take a guess at his favorite color?"

Weadock nodded as he studied Ramon.

Ramon bent to open the driver's door then unexpectedly turned to look in the direction of the two investigators.

"He made us," Falcone whispered.

"You always say that when the mark looks at us."

"Some people seem to feel they're being watched."

"Can you?"

"No."

Twenty minutes passed and Ramon was still sitting in his car with the engine idling. Then he drove off toward the FDR Drive, they followed him with a long leash. At this point in the case, Weadock preferred losing him to alerting him to their presence.

Ramon drove like a student driver taking his first lesson. Once on the FDR, he moved into the center lane and maintained a constant 40 miles per hour.

Weadock felt uncomfortable trying to match the slow pace behind Ramon without alerting him, so he ordered Falcon to pass him and head for the exit near Ramon's residence. He parked on a dark street just off the highway, turned off the engine and the lights and waited.

Ramon left the highway at the predicted exit and drove slowly through the city streets to his house. He stopped at every red light and made complete stops at the stop signs. He parked in what seemed like a reserved parking spot opposite his building. Again he remained in the car for about twenty minutes before walking to his front door.

"This is a real creepy guy, Charlie."

Weadock slumped in the seat and put his head back. "He doesn't drive like a cop, does he?"

"Not any cop I know."

"So he's different, that's not a crime."

"I think he made us."

"He didn't make us." Weadock yawned, "I'm going to shut down for a few minutes. Keep one eye on the car and the other on the building."

"Right."

Charlie Weadock, like a lot of other cops, could fall asleep almost instantly. An occupational talent developed by working around the clock for long hours. Falcone's loud snoring put a quick damper on that.

"Alex," Weadock nudged his partner. "One of us has to stay awake."

"Sorry, my old lady had me painting the house early this morning."

They ended the surveillance at three a.m., drove to the office, signed the log book and went home.

THE PROFESSOR

JOE FERRERI'S PARENTS OWNED AND OPERATED a small bakery shop on Tenth Avenue and 29th Street. They were fat people and he was a fat kid. The scrumptious jelly and cream doughnuts they created were Perhaps the cause of Joe's childhood obesity and the bullying that plagued him all the way through elementary school and high school. He spent six years attending a private college and lost a hundred pounds. Then took a job teaching Chemistry at John Jay College of Criminal Justice because it was so close to home. His only true friends in the world were his mother and father and they died shortly after graduation. He adjusted to a lonely existence by spending most of his time at the college or at home and in two short years he became the head of the Chemistry Department at John Jay College. An achievement his parents would have been proud of that came too late. He remained a recluse and an isolated man with no friends and few acquaintances. Joe never learned how to drive an automobile and didn't like cabs and buses, so he walked the twenty-two blocks to school and back every day. His daily journeys to and from the Manhattan campus did have some benefits, it helped him to maintain his slim and trim 36 year old figure and brought him into daily contact with three casual friends. The owner of the grocery store on corner of his block, the proprietor of a small book store on 41st Street and the operator of the newsstand on 34th Street where he bought his newspapers and magazines.

After seven years of teaching, Joseph Ferreri's social life was a complete washout. Except for an occasional episode of *where did my life go?* Joe Ferreri led a solitary, well-regulated existence in the city that never sleeps.

On the morning after the newsstand homicide, Professor Ferreri approached a crowd of bystanders clustered around the partially destroyed newsstand. He intended to return the suitcase to Happy and slowly advanced to a barrier of bright yellow tape marking the crime scene. He tightened his grip on the suitcase in his hand and inched along the tape toward the newsstand entrance. An unknown force compelled him forward to a point where he could see blood stains in the street and a crude chalk mark outlining a spot where a human body had been. His mouth and eyes widened. 'What the…?"

The bystanders moved back when a tough looking uniformed cop ordered them to move on. "All right, people," he said, "there's nothing to see here. Don't block the sidewalk."

Nonchalantly closing his open mouth, Ferreri stood his ground, and raised his hand like a schoolboy. "Excuse me officer."

"Yes?" The cop locked eyes with the tall professor.

"What happened here?"

"Murder," the cop replied coldly, "a man was murdered here last night."

"Oh my God, I knew him."

"You did, huh? When did you last see him alive?"

"Last night, I saw him last night. He gave me a...ah..." Joe Ferreri glanced at the black bag in his hand then looked at the cop. "A newspaper. I bought a newspaper here."

"What time was that, mister?" The cop pulled out his memorandum book and a pen.

"About 10:30 last night. He was complaining about chest pains."

"Well, he died of a headache. You better give me your name and address. The detectives will want to talk to you."

"Is that necessary officer? I really don't want to. I didn't know him that well and I didn't see anything."

"Say, you look familiar to me." The officer came closer to Ferreri, "do I know you?"

"No, we don't know each other." Ferreri took a step back, "I mean… I am a professor at John Jay College and I have lived in the neighborhood for years but…"

"I took a few classes at John Jay; I'll bet that's where I've seen you. I'm very good with faces, you know."

"I really don't know anything about this, officer."

"Ah, it's just routine stuff. It helps the brains establish the time of death. You know, just routine stuff, nothing serious."

The officer tapped his pen against his memo book until Ferreri identified himself.

Looking at his watch, Ferreri rushed off toward the school. He kept looking back at the crime scene and collided with a stranger. He fell into the street and the bag slid away from him.

A strange man grabbed the suitcase and walked it back to the professor. He helped Ferreri to his feet. "Are you a tourist, Mister?" The stranger looked at the valise and Ferreri froze. He looked back at the crime scene but didn't see the cop. Something within him had seized his vocal chords. He couldn't speak. His mouth moved, but there were no words. The stranger put the valise down next to him and walked away. "Welcome to New York, buddy."

Joe Ferreri walked past the roped-off crime scene a dozen times in the next few days and each time it gave him goose bumps.

A week later, the yellow tape and blue police barriers disappeared and the corner crime scene dissolved back into a regional landscape. That night, in the sanctity of his home, Joe Ferreri broke the lock on the suitcase and examined the contents. He removed the forty tightly wrapped packages of U.S. currency and stacked them neatly on his desk. Each package had a paper band around it stamped $50,000.00. He slid his hands over the top of the money and held two packs against his chest.

This is blood money, he thought. The people who killed Happy must still be looking for this. *I could be the next victim inside those frightful chalk marks*.

Joe Ferreri had been in the habit of checking his pulse rate several times a day for health reasons, but that ended the day after the murder. His pulse was almost always high now and it went up a few more beats when Detective Marini telephoned and asked him to stop by the Midtown South Precinct Station House to give a statement.

The next day after classes he went directly to the station house on 35th Street.

Just inside the main entrance, he paused to watch two plain-clothes officers searching an irate prisoner. One officer slammed the contents of the prisoner's pockets on the main desk while the other cop slammed the prisoner against a brass rail.

A wiry desk lieutenant leaned over his desk and scrutinizes the threesome as he counted the prisoner's money. "Total funds, seven dollars and fifty-three cents."

One of the officers stuffed the money back into the man's pocket and led him away.

Writing in a huge logbook, the lieutenant glanced down at Ferreri over a pair of half moon glasses, and then continued writing.

A young female police officer sitting at a smaller desk leaned on the brass rail between them and asked if she could help.

"Detective Marini." Ferreri said, "I have an appointment with Detective Marini."

"What is your name, sir?" She picked up the telephone and smiled at him.

"Ferreri, Professor Joseph Ferreri."

She flashed a sign of disbelief at him. Keeping her eyes on Ferreri, she spoke into the phone. "There's a Professor Ferreri down here looking for Marini." She looked Ferreri over again as she waited for an answer.

"Walk straight back to those doors," she pointed. "Go up one flight, turn right. Then go straight ahead to room number 207. Have a nice day."

Ferreri's distress was clearly visible on his face as he headed for the back doors. He hadn't had a good night's sleep since the suitcase came into possession. He considered surrendering it to the detectives but finally decided that the money was now his. Joe's anxiety level went up with each step he took. The steel plated staircase reminded him of the stairs at John Jay. When he reached the second floor landing he was trembling and had to stop and calm down. Taking a deep breath every few steps, he managed to reach the squad room door and pushed it open.

Detective Marini waved him to a chair next to his desk. Marini had a friendly approach and Ferreri began to relax. That is until Marini told him that the person killed at the newsstand was not his friend, Happy.

"But I thought Happy was killed..."

"Happy was murdered too." Marini hesitated as he studied Ferreri's reaction. "But not at the newsstand." Marini waited again but Ferreri remained stunned and mute. "He was home in bed when it happened. He lived at the Terminal Hotel on the Bowery."

The professor frowned. "Kind of an inappropriate name for a hotel. Isn't it?"

"Yeah, inappropriate." Marini grinned, "Well, just tell me what you saw and heard on the night of the murder."

"We were trying to have a conversation but he kept coughing and rubbing his chest, He said there was something wrong with him."

"Were you at the newsstand when he went to the hospital?"

"Oh yes."

"Okay, continue."

"It was my routine to work at the college until eight or nine o'clock at night then walk home. I always bought a newspaper at Happy's newsstand and we chatted about current events and controversial issues. He was no dummy, you know. I think we talked about the Mayor's purchase of a $17,000.00 bedpost but Happy kept clutching his chest. I had to call 911 from the corner telephone. Happy locked up the newsstand while we waited for the ambulance to arrive. It took about twenty minutes for them to come. It was a Saint Vincent's ambulance. I remember that."

"Was anyone else there?"

"There were a few people trying to buy papers but I'm not acquainted with any of them and the police. That's all I know, detective."

"What police?"

"Two policemen arrived in a police car; they helped Happy into the ambulance."

"Did you notice their names or their command?"

"No I did not."

"Did Happy ever mention any relatives?"

"He said he was born in Colorado, but he hardly ever talked about his family. I can't remember him ever taking a day off or closing the newsstand for vacation. I know, I teach a summer class every year and he was always there. He said he opened that newsstand after the war."

"What war?"

"World War Two. He was a Japanese POW, you know. They tortured him for years. He was proud of his wounds and showed them to everyone. Especially when he drank too much alcohol. Horrible scars, I couldn't bare to look at them. He spent years in a hospital in the Philippines. He didn't come back to the United States until 1949. His ship docked right here in Manhattan. That was forty-five years ago, I don't think he ever went home."

"Sad story."

"Yes, he was a very sad but intelligent man. He read the New York Times from cover to cover every day and I enjoyed our little chats and debates. I'd like to think he did too. He kept a folding chair inside the newsstand just for me. I'm going to miss that man."

"You're a teacher at John Jay, huh?"

"I'm a professor at the John Jay College of Criminal Justice on 52nd Street."

"You teach criminal justice courses?"

"No, chemistry."

"I think the lieutenant graduated from that school. Do you know my boss, Lieutenant Kennedy?"

"I don't think so, detective."

"Did you notice any cars near the newsstand that night?"

"No."

"A black limousine?"

"Just the ambulance and the police car."

"Did any other customers hang around that night?"

"No, some people stopped to buy newspapers, but Happy was busy closing the newsstand and I mind my own business."

"Did you ever see or hear anyone threaten him?"

"No."

"What time did you leave the newsstand, Professor?"

"About ten o'clock."

"Why did he stay open so late?"

"He liked to catch the theater crowds."

"Why do you think Happy was killed?"

"Oh… I don't know."

"Did you know Tommy Rat Face?"

Ferreri looked confused.

"The guy killed at the newsstand."

"No, I didn't know him."

"Did you ever see this person there?" Marini handed the professor a mug shot of Tommy Raffes.

"He looks familiar. Is this the man who was killed there?"

"Yeah."

"I don't know him, but I have seen him there before but not that night."

Marini waited for the professor to continue.

"No. I did not know him. I think he did favors for Happy but I didn't… ah… you mean did I know this man in the photo, the individual who was killed at the newsstand."

"Yeah."

"No, I told you I didn't know him. I thought Happy was killed there. I told that to the officer on the street. Oh, I see, you thought that I knew this man." Ferreri tapped on the photo of Rat-Face, "no, I never spoke to this person."

"You didn't know Tommy Rat Face?" Marini repeated.

"That's right, when I saw the commotion at the newsstand the next day and saw the blood, I assumed that Happy had been killed and I told the officer that I knew the victim, but I really didn't."

"Did you notice anybody suspicious hanging around the newsstand that night?"

"No."

"All right, professor." Marini handed him a business card. If you remember anything else after you leave, call me."

"I didn't realize until today that the police station was just around the corner from the murder."

"Yeah, the next thing you know they'll be in here."

Ferreri looked closely at the business card. "Can I ask you a personal question, Detective…? Marini?"

"Sure."

"A friend of mine found a bag of money on a country road and he doesn't know what to do with it. Would you advise him to surrender it to the authorities?"

"How much money?"

"I don't know the amount but a lot of it."

"I wouldn't."

"You wouldn't?"

"Naaah, the government doesn't need it. They don't know what to do with the money they have now. And if they need more, they just print it."

"Really?"

"It's a fact, professor." Marini began plucking away at his typewriter with one finger from each hand. "Tell your friend to enjoy it. Live it up, have a good time. Possession is nine-tenths of the law anyway."

Joe Ferreri felt better after his little chat with Detective Marini and looked around for the young female cop who gave him directions but she was nowhere to be seen. He wondered how such a beautiful young girl could work at such a violent occupation. Contemplating his new situation, Ferreri walked home a happier man. He never had any real money or a first class vacation, but his situation has now changed.

Before the nocturnal visits with his editorial friend ended, Ferreri used to tinker in the school laboratory until nine or ten at night, but that had to end also. The twenty-block walk from the school campus to the antiquated brownstone he inherited from his parents was now too much for him to handle at night. Every time he passed the boarded up newsstand, he imagined his own body inside a chalk diagram on the street.

He couldn't get the old vet with the weather beaten face out of his thoughts and now he worried about the killers who must still be searching for the valise full of money.

He had helped close the newsstand that night before Happy went in the ambulance and remembered standing there with the mysterious valise in his hand.

"Hold on to this bag till tomorrow," Happy said. "Don't give it to anyone but me."

Perhaps someone else saw him that night. The bag was worn and heavy and he used it to rest on several times before getting home. Walking as fast as he could, twisting and looking back, he remembered successfully passing two tough-looking youths. He thought they were sizing him up for a hit. Even the familiar shadows of his own building intimidated him. Descending into the dark alcove under his stoop, he fumbled with his door keys. He had some difficulty getting his the key in the lock.

Inside, he pushed the suitcase under his desk and went to the window to look out. He saw a young couple pass under the lamppost across the street.

Every day and every night after the dreaded newsstand incident, he stared at the bag. He couldn't walk past it without stopping to examine it. He watched it from

the dinner table each night like a predator contemplating a meal. Once, he gently poked at the lock hoping it would pop open, but gave up quickly when he pondered the fate of his long-time associate at the newsstand. He was completely unaware of the contents until the moment he broke the lock and opened the valise.

Joe Ferreri was also unaware of the evil occupants of a black limousine that cruised through his neighborhood several times a week.

ACES & DEUCES

CHARLIE WEADOCK LEANED BACK IN HIS SWIVEL CHAIR against the office wall and opened Ramon's case folder to page one but his thoughts were somewhere else. He turned his eyes toward an army of pedestrians hustling to work along East 51st Street but his thoughts were about the summer crowds at Rockaway Beach.

Theresa Kennedy's image was firmly imbedded in Charlie's mind. Her strong body and robust laugh matched her inner strengths and she always seemed hungry for his touch and his opinions. Her beautiful face formed an instant smile whenever they met...

An unanswered telephone in the outer office brought him back to reality and Ramon's case folder came into focus. The telephone stopped ringing and Weadock tossed the case folder back on his desk. He tilted his chair back and faced the ceiling, "Monster stew."

Falcone and McIntosh stopped typing and looked at each other. Uncertain which one of them the sergeant was addressing; they shrugged at each other and continued typing.

"That's what we've got here, boys. Monster stew." Weadock repeated louder, "You can have all the right ingredients and still fuck up the dinner."

Falcone looked up, twisted to look at McIntosh, and went back to work again without speaking. He knew Weadock was a rebel and a loner but something was eating at him today and it wasn't the heavy caseload. It was something else, something personal. Something he hadn't talked about yet.

When Weadock left the room, McIntosh leaned on his typewriter. "Must be final exam time at school again."

"Nah, he got his master's degree last year. Remember, we celebrated at JD's Bar and we got wiped out?"

"Then how come we're getting all this outer space shit now?"

"Look at the books behind his desk. If you read all that Psycho and literary shit, you'd be talking to yourself, too."

"He reads encyclopedias, you know."

"See, who the fuck reads an encyclopedia?"

The phone rang as Weadock came back into the room. McIntosh answered it and wrapped one hand over the mouthpiece. "It's Heckle, Sarge."

Weadock picked up the extension and listened to the scratchy voice on the other end of the line.

"I need to talk to the sergeant."

"Go ahead, I'm listening."

"Not over the phone, Sarge. Can we meet someplace? It's important."

"Sure."

"No police stations, no ATF and no strangers. Some place private."

Sergeant Jim Casey came into the room with a pile of new case folders. He stacked them neatly in Weadock's already overflowing in-basket and smiled. "The Captain wants you to open these new cases, Charlie."

"Thanks. Jim."

Jim Casey smiled innocently and left the room.

"Alec, where did we have the Duck's retirement party?"

Falcone looked at the ceiling for an answer. "it was that place with the big wooden tables in the back - Aces and Deuces on 30th Street and 2nd Avenue."

Weadock repeated the name and address into the phone and agreed to meet Heckle there at noon.

Weadock and Falcone entered the Aces & Deuces bar at 12:15 p.m. and made their way to a cluster of empty barstools at the very end near the window overlooking the street. There was nothing unique about the quiet neighborhood tavern. Some of the regular customers looked them over as they entered. An old woman wearing an expensive, out-of-style, knit dress studied them more carefully than the others. She was in her late sixties and held a smoldering cigarette between her fingers. When she brought the cigarette to her lips, a long ash dangled precariously from the end. Noticing the ash, she carefully lowered her cigarette to an ashtray without disturbing it.

Two men in brown uniforms sat in the middle. One of them spoke loudly about baseball trivia while the other devoured a huge salami hero. It appeared to Weadock that the neighborhood people somehow sensed that he and Falcone were cops.

The owner, a long time acquaintance of Falcone's, filled the old woman's beer glass from a half empty bottle sitting in front of her. He acknowledged Falcone with a nod and maneuvered his portly body along the bar until he stood before him. The clientele resumed their business.

"How you doing', Alex?"

"Okay, Henry. And you?"

"Good."

"Henry, this is my partner, Charlie Weadock."

Weadock shook the outstretched hand of Henry McDonald and formed an opinion. Weadock had a sixth sense about handshakes and first impressions and he thought McDonald's handshake was disappointingly weak for a man his size.

Falcone ordered a scotch and soda and a silver bullet for Weadock. "He likes it straight up, very dry, with olives."

Weadock turned his stool slightly to face Falcone. "How is everybody at your house?"

"Great, Katie's making her first communion next month. She expects you to be there."

"She's the one who calls the office when she wants her daddy home early?"

"Yeah." Falcone smiled, "you're her favorite policeman, after me."

Suddenly two distorted faces appeared against the 30th Street window that drew the attention of all the patrons. Weadock turned to see Heckle shielding his eyes from the bright sun. Pressing his face against the window to survey the interior of the bar, Heckle searched with his eyes and smiled when he saw Weadock. He and his brother hustled

around to the front door and entered the premises.

"Hey, Sarge." Heckle extended his beefy hand to Weadock. Cupping his other hand over his mouth, he rolled his eyes upwards. "Sorry. I forgot we were undercover."

"It's okay," Weadock said. "They already know who we are."

Heckle put his arm around Jeckle and pulled him closer to Weadock. "This is my real brother."

They didn't look like brothers to Charlie Weadock. Jeckle was shorter, thinner and a lot more passive than his rambunctious older brother.

"Well, my name is Charlie Weadock." Weadock extended his hand to Jeckle. "And this is my real partner, Alex Falcone."

The informants laughed at Weadock's remark and ordered a couple of White Russians. Heckle began detailing the events that led to his involvement with Alcohol, Tobacco and Firearms. His statements were spontaneous and candid. He complained bitterly that an ungrateful Treasury Agency was now putting their lives in danger.

"Two years ago Sergeant Savage at ATF asked me to help them generate a few new cases and

they would let Jeckle go. That was the deal they made me."

When two new customers came into the bar and sat close to them, Weadock nodded at Falcone and the foursome moved to an isolated table in the rear.

When they sat down, Heckle wagged a hand between his brother and himself and continued. "We helped ATF bag a whole gang of Colombian drug dealers. We testified against them in court and they all went down, big time."

"These guys we sent to prison have a lot of friends that are still on the street." Jeckle said. "Some of them know my wife and my kids and where I live."

Heckle sat down. "We helped ATF get hundreds of felony convictions, but they still won't let Jeckle go. Whenever he mentions it, they threaten him with jail time. I've got a kid too, Sarge," Heckle grinned. "A daughter. It's time for us to leave town."

It became obvious to Weadock that Heckle and Jeckle were being abused by ATF.

Heckle studied the waitress as she sauntered passed their table. "Not much of a face but she has a great ass."

Weadock nodded in agreement and leaned closer to Heckle. "Look, I need you guys help me with this Ramon Case and I'll talk to someone who can get you out of ATF. I've got a friend at the Manhattan DA's office who can help you. I think he can cut their hold on you guys and perhaps get you some expense money."

The two brothers went to the bathroom together and came back smiling. "How much expense money?" Jeckle asked.

"Since you're helping us, Sarge. We're going to give you a cop," Heckle said. "A bad cop. This guy's been dealing drugs in the Ninth Precinct for five years."

Weadock waited.

"You know Alvin Baker?"

Falcone flashed a winning grin at Weadock and Weadock nodded. They were quite familiar with Alvin Baker's name. It was, in fact, the name of a cop who has managed to avoid capture for years; a cop with a long list of drug allegations with no convictions. There were rumors that the citizens on Baker's post disliked him and he wasn't very popular with his brothers in blue but somehow he managed to elude every IAD Investigation that was ever launched against him. Weadock saw this as a prime opportunity to get a corrupt cop off the force and signaled Falcone with his fingers to start taking notes. Weadock kept the brothers' drink glasses filled and they took turns disclosing the details of their long association with this rogue cop.

"He never spends his own money, Sarge," Jeckle said. "We give him money and he gets the product for us but he always keeps some of the money and some of the product for himself."

"Were any other cops with him when he made these buys?" Weadock asked.

"No, but I've seen him spooning with some of the brothers."

"Where and when?"

"All the time, in bars, at parties. We hang with him a lot. He throws a big, 4th of July bash every year at his house. This year it's a luau and we're invited. All his cop friends will be there."

Weadock wrote his pager number on a piece of paper and handed it to Heckle. "This pager is on twenty-four seven. Call me anytime."

Heckle ripped the paper in half, wrote his pager number on the blank half and gave it to Weadock. "We're open all night, too."

As soon as Weadock got back to the FIAU office, he telephoned Bureau Chief William Bergermeister at the Official Corruption Unit of the Manhattan District Attorney's Office.

Bergermeister listened anxiously to Weadock's allegations and insisted on an early morning meeting at his office.

THE DETECTIVES

PUSHING A SMALL STACK OF COMPLAINT REPORTS ASIDE, Lieutenant Kennedy let his eyes roam through the outer office of his squad room. *...Detective squad rooms seem to be cast from the same old mold. This one at Midtown Precinct South wasn't much different from all the others he had visited. An assortment of hand-me-down typewriters, gooseneck lamps and a pot puree of wooden and steel desks. At least I have a room facing the street,* he thought.

The Anticrime Sergeant's office was in the back facing the shithouse and the air between him and me is laced with malice and envy...

Kennedy nudged his door closed to muffle the ongoing pecking of typewriters but let his eyes wonder across the faces of his detectives.

Few outsiders know that detectives are just policemen with gold badges who are ranked in grades. Kennedy had two first graders, Marini and Carbonaro. First grade detectives were usually expert in some area of investigation, but his two were just old timers who gravitated to the exalted slot.

Kennedy resented the fact that his First Grade Detectives took home a bigger pay check than he did as a Lieutenant. And his one second grade Detective was being paid more than his second whip, Sergeant Gill but Gill was on long-term sick report and not expected to return to duty. Kennedy should have requested a replacement a month ago but had no particular sergeant in mind. The rest of the squad were third-graders who receive about a thousand dollars a year more than the white shield cops. Whatever their detective grades, they were still cops and could easily be busted back to the bag if they got into trouble. He, on the other hand, was a ranking officer. Sergeants, lieutenants and captains held civil service ranks and were almost impossible to recant. Vinnie Kennedy began studying for promotion on his first day in the police academy and hadn't stopped yet. He wanted the rank of Captain.

"Don't be boot lickers for twenty years," Joe Kennedy preached to his sons. "Study the nuts and bolts and be a boss!"

When Vinnie made sergeant, his father, Joe Kennedy used his influence to get Vinnie into the Detective Division. He prodded Vinnie every day to study for the lieutenant's test then used his influence to get him the Squad

Commander's job at the Midtown South Squad. Joe Kennedy not only drove his sons to become cops, but expected one of them to become a two-star-chief or Commissioner. Vinnie was thankful for his father's efforts. Thankful that he hadn't become a truck driver or a bank teller or bum like so many of his childhood friends. He was thirty-five years old and the Commanding Officer of a New York City Police Department Detective Squad.

Lieutenant Kennedy liked those old peel and stick white gloves that pointed at and led citizens to detective squad rooms in old station houses but he was unable to find them anywhere. So he assigned one of his junior detectives to paint some on station house walls and stairwells in his new precinct.

The Detective Zone Commander, Captain Harold Shapiro, suddenly appeared at the squad room door for an unannounced visit. The squad room suddenly came alive with a symphony of typewriters and telephone calls. As soon as Captain Shapiro entered the squad room, detectives began calling complainants and witnesses; plucking at their typewriter keys just to make noise, hiding newspapers and magazines, and shuffling case folders on their desks. Each of the brawny sleuths nodded or waved at the captain as he passed them.

Shapiro was a soft spoken man who supervised several Detective Squads in Manhattan South. He wasn't taken in by their aggressive antics and ginned and shook his head from side to side as he ambled across the room to Kennedy's office.

Detective Marini, closest to the Lieutenant's office, turned an ear to listen to their conversation.

"I can't understand how you missed this one, Vinnie."

"My best team is on it, boss."

"Two men?"

"My best two men."

"Who?"

"Marini and Carbonaro."

"You've got to put more people on this."

"C'mon, Harold," Kennedy sulked. "The Ninth Squad has four detectives on this and they should. Most of these pipe murders happened in their precinct. The Fifth and the Seventh have two guys assigned like us, that's ten detectives."

"It's not enough."

"Why? Most of it's in zone two. That means its Captain Potter's problem, right?"

"Wrong, I came here straight from the chief's office. He briefed the Police Commissioner and the Mayor this morning and they want this matter cleaned up ASAP!" Shapiro crossed the room to look at Kennedy's FBI Academy Diplomas hanging on the wall. "I can't believe you missed this," Shapiro slammed the palm of his hand against his face. "I can't believe that I missed this. You've got to get this guy fast and keep this quiet, too!" He whipped Kennedy with a pointed finger. "Make sure your men keep their mouths shut, no leaks and no press!"

"Don't worry, boss." Kennedy reassured him.

Shapiro moved to a chair and sat down. "One other thing, send a copy of all the DD5's on the Raffes homicide and all the other unsolved homicides to Sergeant Weadock at the Manhattan South FIAU."

"Why would I do that?"

"He thinks the perpetrator's a cop."

"That's bullshit!"

"Perhaps, but the chief said Weadock has a possible perpetrator and the chief wants you to cooperate with him."

"I didn't know that." Kennedy stood up. "Who does he suspect? What's the cop's name?"

Rubbing the back of his neck, the captain looked down at the floor. "I don't know."

Kennedy turned an angry face at his FBI Diplomas and walked over to level one of the frames.

"The Chief doesn't know either," Shapiro said. "At least that's what he told me."

"That's fucking great. What kind of cooperation is that? Internal Affairs gets all our files just for the asking, but they won't give us the name of the fucking murder suspect."

"It's confidential."

"Confidential! Everything we do is confidential."

"The PBA would be up the Commissioner's ass if IAD gave up the subject of an internal affairs investigation. They just can't do it. It against Department Policy."

"You want me to work around them?" Kennedy offered.

"The Chief wants you to coordinate your investigation with Sergeant Weadock."

"No way," Kennedy laughed. "No fucking way! Get someone else to do this." Kennedy's face reddened as he moved toward the door. "Get the Ninth Squad Commander to do it; he has most of the fucking DOAs anyway."

"C'mon, Vinnie. Be a Squad Commander. Don't blow this and embarrass the Chief and me by being unprofessional. There are hundreds of lieutenants in the Department who would love to have your job and Chief Lazarus would cut your balls off in a second if he ever heard what you just said."

"You don't understand, boss. I can't work with this guy. He locked up my brother."

"I don't care if he locked up your mother. The Chief knows that this sergeant uncovered most of this information and he likes him. He's in charge of this special FIAU Team and you're running our team. That's the way the Chief wants it. He wants you in charge of the Detective Division's part of this case, not me."

"He does?"

"Yeah, but if you side-step this one, you can kiss this command and your career goodbye. Is that what you want?"

Kennedy sat quietly.

"Look, you're the youngest squad commander in the city and you've got a chance to make a name for yourself with this case. Don't blow it. If you need anything, call me. I'm creating a small task force for this case. Two detectives from each command in Manhattan South. That'll give you twenty men."

Kennedy continued to sulk without answering.

Shapiro closed the door but opened it again and managed a smile. "Task Force does sound better, doesn't it? Don't let the press gets wind of this and touch base with the other squad commanders. Be nice to them and they'll help you get this perp. This could be the big one for you and me."

When the Zone Commander left the squad room, all fell silent again and Marini stuck his head into Kennedy's Office. Kennedy turned his chair to admire his FBI Diplomas and Marini waited quietly for his boss to acknowledge him, but Kennedy remained still. Without turning around he spoke to Marini.

"Put Martinez and Wong on the plumber case. Send them out to canvas the areas around the newsstand and that fleabag hotel in the Ninth. I want the four of you on this case."

"Martinez is in court all next week with the Brown Case and Wong picked up a shit load of new cases when Leroy retired."

"I don't want to hear any of that negative shit, Marini. Just do it! Tell them to walk and talk with their Puerto Rican and Chinese buddies. I want some facts."

"Martinez is Cuban and Wong is Korean… Boss."

"Same shit. Look, I don't give a fuck what they are, just get me some results!"

Kennedy finally turned his chair around and sent an icy glance at the First Grade Detective. "Well?"

Marini's eyes rolled upward and he left the room in a huff.

Ten minutes later, Kennedy walked out of his office into the squad room and stood in front of Marini's desk. When Marini ignored him, he leaned on the desk with both hands. "Have you read all the new cases?"

"Yes, sir, Lieutenant," Marini answered with cold efficiency.

"Did you read all the Fives on the Raffes Homicide?"

"Yes, sir. Lieutenant."

"What do you think, so far?"

"There's not much to go on."

"Well, you're a First Grade Detective, Marini. That's why they pay you the big bucks. Find something!"

Marini had the feeling that his peers were watching and headed for Kennedy's office. He held the door open until Kennedy followed him inside then closed it.

"If you want to discipline me, Lieutenant, do it by the book. In private."

"Okay, okay, I didn't mean to come down on you in front of the others but Shapiro is breaking my chops."

Marini didn't respond.

"He's dumping the plumber case on us and he wants us to work with those creeps at IAD."

"I'm sure we can handle it, Lieutenant."

"Of course we can handle it; the victims are all dirt bags."

Marini didn't answer.

"Just send Martinez and Wong down the street to canvas the newsstand area again. Then send them over to the Bowery. I want 'em to talk to the bums over there, they'll blend right in with them."

"Not for nothing, boss, but everybody's busy with active cases."

"I don't need you to tell me that, Marini. You saw Shapiro in my face, didn't you? Well, it isn't going to stop with him. Next thing you know, the chief will be here. The pressure isn't going to stop until we get this piece of shit in handcuffs."

"Okay, boss."

Marini opened the door but paused when Kennedy raised his hand.

"When your pizza-face partner comes back, I want you to re-interview all the witness in all the unsolved homicides."

"All of 'em?"

"Isn't that what I just said?" Kennedy looked around the office for some imaginary person to verify his statement. The detectives in the outer office took note of the tension. "All the witnesses in all the cases. Find something that may have been overlooked."

Five minutes later, Kennedy walked into the outer office and stopped at Paula Ferguson's desk. "You hungry, detective?"

"Starved."

Kennedy walked back to Marini's desk. "Where's the new girl, what's her name? The one with the big tits."

"You mean Detective Napolitano?"

"Yeah."

"She's at BCI running prints."

"When she gets back, tell her to make up one of those little pin maps showing the locations of the pipe murders, something with lots of colors. It'll give Shapiro something to play with when he comes to visit us again. Fergy and I are going to meal."

THE INVESTIGATORS

THE NEW YORK CITY POLICE DEPARTMENT MAINTAINED SIX FIELD INTERNAL AFFAIRS UNITS, one in Brooklyn, the Bronx, Queens. Staten Island, and two in Manhattan. Every Investigator at the Manhattan South unit was aware of the unsolved pipe murder cases and that Charlie Weadock was pursuing a New York City Police Officer for committing all the brutal unsolved homicides.

On the morning of April 16, 1992, Weadock waited in his Commanding Officer's office for the Captain to finish a phone call.

Ralph Guglielmo was a short, skinny, Italian man who lacked all of the aspects of a formal education. At age fifteen, he dropped out of high school to work at the family fruit stand. He acquired an equivalency diploma during his two-year hitch in the Army and became a cop in 1949. Patrolman Guglielmo pounded a beat for thirty-three years before passing a sergeant's exam. Cramming the nuts and bolts of police work into his head for two more years, he haphazardly passed the next two more promotion tests. His seniority and

veteran status points catapulted him from police officer to captain in six years. He never opened a police manual again and never missed an opportunity to rub his lack of a formal education into the wounds of any Police Officer attending college.

"Charlie," Guglielmo turned to Weadock and lowered the telephone with two fingers. "You gotta forget all that psychology crap they taught you in college and dog this motherfucking cop until he drops."

"I followed Velez several times before the District Attorney asked us to hold up on the surveillance. This guy goes straight home after work."

"What?" Guglielmo ignored Weadock as he searched for a match to light a cigarette.

"The DA has ordered us to suspend any surveillance until he interviews the China man."

"What China man?"

"An inmate at Bay view Prison. Our CI says that this China man may have been a witness to the Cruz murder."

"We don't work for the DA, we work for Chief Whalen and he wants us to dog this motherfucker. Those were his exact words and he wants an update every day. I have to report to him at the Borough Office right

now. He wants the SIU Team on this case around the clock."

"We don't have the manpower to do that and what about the other fifty active cases we have now?"

"I don't want to hear any excuses. Just bring me up to date so I can go talk to the Chief."

Weadock opened the manila folder in his hands and quickly closed it. "All we have here is an unsubstantiated allegation made by a CI who is working for Alcohol, Firearms, and Tobacco. They say he's reliable. They've made over a hundred felony arrests and convictions based on his undercover work and court testimony."

"Then he must be telling the truth. Do you think he's telling the truth?"

"Yes, I do. But you have to understand that there is no hard evidence here that actually connects Velez to these unsolved homicides." Weadock tapped on the case folder.

"But I thought there was?" The captain's eyes narrowed into thin slits. He rotated his head from side to side looking for someone to confirm his suspicions. "Wasn't there something about a Black Camaro and a high school in the Bronx?"

"That's just bits of hearsay, Captain. Unsubstantiated remarks made by the subject to the CI in a parking lot in 1990. It's not evidence. The CI also said he overheard Ramon say that he killed someone on East 3rd Street and Avenue B in the Ninth Precinct, but that's not on tape either. It's all uncorroborated testimony. All we know for sure is that a drug dealer named Jose Cruz was killed at that location around Christmas time 1990. We know that this homicide took place on or about the same day that the CI reported it. We also know that Jose Cruz, Harry Hansen, Tommy Raffes, and perhaps a dozen other victims of unsolved homicides were all killed in the same manner. The murder weapons recovered in four of the incidents are exactly alike, a twelve inch piece of half inch brass pipe with couplings on each end. A pair of cheap plastic gloves was also recovered at three of the crime scenes. They were identical but none of that proves anything."

"Why don't you come down with me, Charlie?"

"I can't, I have things scheduled, and the chief and I don't get along."

"Nonsense, if he didn't like you, you wouldn't be running his SIU Team and you certainly wouldn't be investigating this Ramon business."

"Perhaps."

"Just think about it, Charlie. I've got five lieutenants in this office and a sergeant runs the most sensitive team. Why is that?"

Weadock waited in silence.

"Okay." Guglielmo put on his jacket to leave, but stopped in the doorway. "Why use a pipe to kill when you have a gun?"

"I don't know." Weadock looked at the case folder. "Actually it's a smart weapon, a little crude, but smart. You can buy one at any hardware store, it's legal to carry and you throw it away when you're fin-"

"Anything else?"

"There were no prints found at any of the crime scenes. Once he gets rid of the weapon, he's clean. Even if he's stopped while escaping. However, there may be a few witnesses."

"Go on."

"There was a witness to the Cruz murder. A girl actually saw the murder. She stated that the perpetrator was a male Hispanic and he left the scene in a black camaro. How she could tell the car was a Camaro from the tenth floor beats me but that's what she told the detectives at that time. I'm going to interview her again as soon as possible. It might be just a coincidence that Ramon owned a black Camaro in 1990. He reported that the car was stolen a week after the murder. It was never recovered."

"Maybe you should talk to the Chief, Charlie."

"I can't." Weadock moved to pass Guglielmo. "Falcone and I have a heavy GO15 hearing to do right now on another case. Oh, there's one more thing."

"What?"

"The CIs want some expense money from us."

"They do, huh? Well, fuck them!"

"C'mon, Captain. They're giving us some bad cops."

"I say fuck 'em!"

"When Alvin Baker gets busted, you're going to look awful good."

"We'll see."

"They're asking for five hundred up front, two-fifty each. You know, just to show good faith."

"No fucking way, Jose. Ask the DA for the money when you see him."

"These guys have agreed to wear wire and make cocaine buys from Baker for us. Then go into court and testify against him. I'm sure the city can invest a few hundred dollars to rid the Department of a few drug dealing cops."

"Aren't these guys criminals themselves? Aren't they working off time for crimes committed?"

"They don't have to do this for us, captain. They're already getting fucked by one government agency."

"Shit." Guglielmo looked at the clock on the wall and hustled out to the administrative office. "Now I am really late.".

Weadock followed Guglielmo to the exit door and watched him leave the office. "It's only money Captain. We give them money and they give us Baker."

"Fresh coffee, gentlemen?" Detective Bush stuck her head between Weadock and the Captain and smiled.

Guglielmo checked his watch again and smiled at Detective Bush. "Shit!" He said and ran back into his office.

Detective Bush backed away with a shocked expression on her face.

Leaning over his desk, Guglielmo pulled three case folders from the top drawer. "I almost forgot. The chief wants you to look at these cops. They made a lot of money last month."

"Captain, I'm up to my ass in bullshit overtime cases. Take them back to the Borough Office and give them to an accountant."

Guglielmo ignored Weadock and raced out the front door.

Weadock made his way into the SIU room and dropped the three case folders into McIntosh's in basket. "Work on these when you get a chance."

McIntosh fingered the folders. "I've done a dozen of these, Sarge. The cops are making good felony collars and earning lots of overtime in the process. They're making lots of money because the system sucks."

"Just give them case numbers and put them on the back burner for a while."

Falcone came into the SIU Room with a huge stack of case folders balanced in his arms. He bounced off the doorjamb and knocked Detective Bush on her ass. "Sorry Ada, I didn't see you." He lowered the pile on his desk and helped her to her feet. Falcone began dusting her off with his hands but she stopped him.

"Watch those hands, Alex. This is my body." She pointed at her breasts with two fingers. "You're not supposed to touch a girl's body unless she asks you." Bush nudged him aside and left the room.

"Sorry." Falcone followed her down the hallway with his eyes then turned the palms of his hands towards his team. "I said I was sorry."

Weadock grinned. "She goes out of her way to make you a fresh pot of coffee and you knock her down and feel her tits."

Falcone also grinned. "She only makes coffee for the captain, Sarge. If he had stayed here in the office, we would have gotten zip."

"Well, the captain's gone to the Borough, so get us a cup that coffee and we'll try to make some sense out of this pile of shit."

McIntosh put two hands on the stack of unsolved murder cases. "There must be a hundred DD5's in each one of these."

"Well, take one and start reading."

Falcone came back with two mugs of hot coffee and sat down next to Weadock. "Why is it that all detective squad's have two bosses and twenty detectives and FIAU Units have twenty bosses and two detectives?"

Weadock sipped his coffee. "I guess you guys need more supervision."

"He's right, Sarge." McIntosh said. "How come we have so many sergeants and lieutenants?"

"Because the Detective Division investigates crimes committed by civilians and FIAU investigates crimes committed by cops. Only a Sergeant or above can prefer charges or arrest a Police Officer."

McIntosh began to laugh. "What kind of parents would name their daughter ATE HER BUSH?"

"It's Ada Bush, dummy," Falcone, said.

"That's what I said." McIntosh left the room laughing. "Ada Bush."

THE DISTRICT ATTORNEY

THE NEW YORK STATE SPECIAL PROSECUTOR'S OFFICE came into existence in the early 1970's as direct fallout of the Knapp Commission Investigation on police corruption. When the Special Prosecutor's Office closed its doors on March 31, 1981, the District Attorneys in all five boroughs moved quickly to establish their own corruption fighting units.

William G. Bergermeister, a soft-spoken family man with an uncompromising disposition, was selected as the Anti-Corruption Chief in Manhattan.

It was 8:30 AM when Weadock passed an empty secretary's chair at the front door and made his way through a labyrinth of small corridors to reach Bergermeister's office. He paused in the doorway and Bergermeister waved at him to enter. Weadock dropped into an empty chair opposite the District Attorney and gave Ramon's case folder a slow deliberate push across the desk.

Bergermeister opened it as if it were the first page of an incredible story. With his eyes glued to the first page, he felt for the coffee container that Weadock had placed in front of him and peeled off the lid. He shifted his gaze to Weadock when the sergeant began reciting some facts of the case from memory.

Leaning back in his comfortable swivel chair, he listened to Weadock's account of the story.

The sergeant flipped a photo of Ramon Velez into the open case folder as if he were dealing a poker hand. Bergermeister picked it up and spun his chair around to face his computer. Perching the photo high on his keyboard, he took the first sip of coffee. "Velez?" He brought his face closer to the photo. "V-E-L-E-Z."

"Yeah, Ramon Velez, DOB 06-21-66."

"How do you feel about the 'CIs, Charlie?"

"I think they're basically telling the truth."

"I have to meet them."

"They won't come here. Too many cops around."

"Can I bring TJ?"

"Are you picking up the tab?"

"Of course."

"Then bring anyone you like."

"There are two things that this office has in abundance, money and arrogance."

"How about lunch?" Weadock suggested.

"Today?"

"The sooner the better."

"Where?"

Weadock described the Aces and Deuces Bar & Grill on 2nd Avenue and 30th Street as a quiet place with large tables in the rear.

"You said something on the phone about cops and drugs?"

"Alvin Baker." Weadock flipped Baker's photo on the desk.

Studying the grin on Weadock's face, Bergermeister picked up the picture. "What is this?"

"He's a Police Officer in the Ninth Precinct with a long list of drug allegations and no hits. When I told the CIs that you would help break ATF's hold on them, they gave me this cop. They have been buying and using cocaine with this cop for years. According to them, he transports a major shipment of cocaine from Florida to New York once a year in his car and celebrates by throwing a party at his house. All his drug dealing cop friends will be there and now we're invited."

"Holy shit!"

"That's what I thought," Weadock said. "Both CIs will wear a wire and testify in court for us but they want a favor."

"What exactly do they want?"

"They've been working for ATF for the past two years. One is working off a felony conviction. The other is just helping his brother, but they want out. I told them you could arrange it."

"You did, huh?"

"I knew you'd go for it."

Bergermeister studied the two photographs. "My main interest is this Ramon character, but this drug allegation could lead to a rat's nest. Let's do them both."

Weadock and Bergermeister huddled in the back room as the legal system at One Hogan Place slowly came to life.

"When and where is the party?"

"The CIs tell me it's a Hawaiian type luau this year at Baker's house in Staten Island on July 4th weekend. I'd like to crash that party."

"So would I." Bergermeister turned in his chair again. "You say we can wire the CI's?"

"Of course."

"Will they make a couple of buys prior to the party?"

"You get them out of ATF and they'll do anything for you."

"I guess I could do that."

"Are you kidding me? You pull this off; you could run for congress and you should." Weadock smiled.

"I'm not a politician."

"You should be one."

"How many cops will be at this party?"

"I don't know, but the CI's are dropping a lot of names."

"How many names?"

"Five or six on the job, and two who were fired last year for dealing drugs. The common denominator seems to be cocaine."

Bergermeister leaned back in his chair. "What can I do to help your case?"

"You're the prosecutor, it's your case."

"Wrong, my friend. I'll help you all I can, but it's your investigation. I can't trust anyone around here. I'll supply you with resources, check the Tolls & Ludds to find out who's calling who, but you have to build this case."

It was 10:00 a.m. when the two men walked the length of the long corridor from Bergermeister's office to the front elevators. Waiting for the elevator doors to open, Bill held up a photo of his two boys. "The big guy is five and the baby is one."

When the doors opened, Weadock backed into the crowded elevator. "One o'clock."

"I'll be there."

Weadock acknowledged with a nod as the doors closed.

It was 2:30 p.m. when Bergermeister and his chief investigator, Tommy Johnson, entered the Aces & Deuces Bar. Heckle and Jeckle were already three sheets to the wind. Falcone told them that the DA was paying the bill, so they each put away a half dozen White Russians waiting for him to arrive.

TJ and Weadock nodded at each other. There was no handshake. They had been rookies together in the Brooklyn South Task Force but never became friends. TJ was injured on the job and retired on a medical pension. His uncle got him the job in the DA's Office.

When the introductions were over they all moved to a picnic size table in the rear. Heckle pulled the window shade down to eye level.

The waitress remembered them from the first visit and expected another amusing comment from Weadock, but it never came. She flirted with him, but he ignored her and she shifted her attentiveness to the young attorney. She leaned against Bergermeister when she took his order for a turkey sandwich and a club soda but he failed to sense her body language.

Heckle nudged Weadock. "My father told me not to trust a man who doesn't drink."

Weadock inched away from Heckle. "My father said that the guy paying the bill can order whatever he likes."

Heckle mutely agreed.

"All you need to know is that this man," Weadock identified Bergermeister with his eyes, "is going to get your ass out of ATF's frying pan."

"You're right, Sarge." Heckle put his arm around Weadock indicating that he understood. Then he drained the last drops from his glass with his free hand. Heckle filled an empty chair next to Bergermeister and began telling him about Ramon. Heckle had a good head for details and gave a good account of his relationship with Ramon. When the subject of Alvin Baker came up, Heckle beckoned his brother to join the conversation and the brothers took turns talking. While one brother ate, the other spoke and vice-versa.

TJ moved his chair closer to the conversation, listened for a while, then touched Jeckle's arm. "How do you feel about wearing a wire?"

Jeckle shrugged.

"And testifying in court?"

"It's like this, man. We know this cop Baker a long time and he trusts us, but we don't like him anymore." Jeckle grinned at

Weadock. "We like the Sarge because he's a straight guy. So we're giving him Backer."

"Tell me more about Alvin? Baker." Bergermeister said.

Heckle wiggled his empty class at the waitress. "He's got a nice house in Staten Island, we've been there. A good looking wife, two kids and a big fish tank full of tropical fish."

"This dude is a party animal." Jeckle said. "He loves drinking and snorting with strange broads but sometimes he gets wild with his hands. So we don't like him anymore."

"He takes a vacation in Florida every summer," Heckle said, "and comes back with huge load of coke. He told us that he hides the product in his spare tire. His wife doesn't know shit about it. He gives himself a flat tire before he picks up the product and gets a bill to show that the tire was repaired at a Florida gas station. He even hides a sample at the tire shop in case he gets caught. Then he can play dumb and blame it all on the gas station attendant who doesn't know shit about it. He never told us where he gets the product or where it goes, but he always has a big chunk of coke and money when the trip is over."

"You know about the party, right?" Jeckle asked.

"We know," TJ answered and flicked a look at Bergermeister.

"Do you know that he calls us twice a month for a blow?"

TJ looked at Bergermeister again.

He's always broke when it comes to paying for the product. We give him money, he picks it up and we all get a blow, but he keeps most of the product for himself."

Bergermeister was generous when it came to spending the City's money on corruption fighting, but didn't miss a trick. He asked a lot of specific questions and laid out the precise procedures he wanted the CIs to follow. Once he had all the answers to his questions he took the fun out of the party by asking for the check.

Bergermeister insisted that all future telephone conversations with Alvin Baker be recorded.

The two 'CIs nodded in harmony. Heckle handed a micro tape to Bergermeister. "He called me twice this week."

TJ stood up and leaned toward Jeckle. "Remember, you agreed to wear a wire when the time comes."

"I've been wired more times than Frankenstein."

When TJ headed to the bathroom, Jeckle expressed his disapproval. "It walks like a cop and talks like a cop, but it ain't a real cop."

TJ overheard Jeckle's comment and hit him with a hard look.

"I don't like that motherfucker." Jeckle turned to Falcone. "You like him?"

"Me?" Falcone shrugged. "I hate his guts."

Jeckle laughed at Falcone's answer, then they all laughed.

TJ stepped out of the little boy's room with a little boy lost look on his face and they laughed louder. Even the waitress laughed.

When the laughter quieted down, Bergermeister leaned in Weadock's direction. "My office will supply the money for the buy."

Heckle heard what Bergermeister said and placed his hand his shoulder. "What's in the pot for us?"

"What do you mean?"

"We need money too," Heckle nodded at his brother. "We're out of work and we've got to eat."

"All right, I'll give you three hundred for the buy and a hundred a week for as long as you work this case."

"That's a hundred each, right?" Jeckle asked.

"Okay, a hundred each."

"When do we get the money?"

"The day the buy goes down."

The waitress put the check down in front of Heckle. He looked at it and dropped it as if it had a roach on it. Jeckle glanced at it and slid it across the table to Bergermeister. The DAs eyebrows curved somewhat when he looked at it, but he handed it and a credit card to the waitress.

"Better leave a good tip," Heckle said. "We might want to fuck her later."

Weadock could sense TJ's irritation with the CIs and tried to calm him down while walking to the exit. He talked about the old days they spent together in Brooklyn.

Bergermeister paid the check and joined them.

"Where the fuck did you find those two idiots, Charlie?" TJ spoke loud enough aid for Bergermeister to hear him. "I don't like the whole deal and I especially don't like those two clowns."

"Tom," Weadock said, "sometimes you have to bury your personal feelings to get the job done. There's no way we can make this case without them."

Bergermeister picked up on the hand job Weadock was giving TJ and played along. "Some CIs are worse than the perps, Tom, but in this case, Charlie's right. We have nothing without them."

Weadock looked at TJ "I think we should use your recording equipment. It's better than ours."

"Well, we finally agree on something," TJ. responded. "Okay, we'll use our Nigra tape recorder, our Kel transmitter and our cell phones."

When TJ left to get the car, Bergermeister turned to Weadock "You could have been a great attorney, Charlie."

"You have cell phones?"

Bergermeister nodded.

"He can't be your best investigator."

"He's related to Uncle Henry."

"The Manhattan DA?"

"Okay but IAD is full of guys like him. That's why we're in so much trouble."

"I don't do the recruiting," Bergermeister frowned. "But we'll make it work."

Weadock returned to the back room and sat down opposite Heckle. "I want you and your brother to stay clear of TJ."

Heckle walked to the bowling machine and dropped two quarters in the slot. "That guy's a piece of shit, he doesn't scare me."

"Just avoid him, okay?"

"Whatever you say, Sarge. What do you say to one last championship game?" Heckle slammed the puck against the backboard of the machine and all ten pins flew up. He waved his empty glass at the waitress and waited for Weadock to shoot. "Jeckle and I always seem to be on a losing team. We grew up in the South Bronx. There was no choice there, you either got into trouble or you got into trouble. It was the only life we ever knew, but I think things are changing for us. Now, we wanna be on the good guys' team."

"I doubt that," Weadock grinned. "You guys will always be bad."

Heckle laughed. "Maybe we can be professional informants. You think we can make a living at this?"

"No, I think you should get into another line of work and soon. You're a licensed locksmith. You can set up shop anywhere in the country. Your brother, the arms dealer, will have to be retrained."

"He's a good driver, Sarge."

"Look, Bergermeister said he'd get you guys off the hook. He will probably put you and your brother into the Federal Witness

Protection Program. If you help him get these bad guys, I know he'll do the right thing for you. He's a good guy and he won't lie to you. You pull this case off for him and you'll both be able to make a clean start somewhere."

"Sounds great, Sarge." Heckle looked towards his brother. "Especially for my brother, he has a family."

"What about you? You're the older brother." Weadock threw another strike on the bowling machine.

"Aahh!" Heckle threw his hands up in resignation. "I can't beat you, Sarge. Where'd you learn to play this game?"

"Squandered youth in a place called Chelsea. You're not married, are you?"

"Tried it once," Heckle answered with a shrug as he headed for the men's room. "Didn't work out."

Standing alone at the window, Weadock thought about his younger days in old neighborhood.

He played the bowling machine and other games for money and drinks. Charlie Weadock wore a black motorcycle jacket and ran with a pack of wolf cubs' known as the Royal Kings. A naked skeleton shooting hoops adorned the back of their jackets. Survival on West 17th Street meant gang membership. Young Charlie

Weadock had his share of dumb exploits and close encounters with death but he also had something the other kids didn't - luck. Not that he won prizes or anything, but Charlie could run like the wind and people liked him and watched out for him. People helped him grow.

Nora Campbell, an eighth grade school teacher, was one of those people. She saw great potential behind the tough facade that young Weadock carried in front of himself as a shield.

There was something noble in his leathery manner that she admired. He was tough and gentle at the same time and had an engaging smile that made people like him instantly.

During that school year great changes took place in the wiry youth. His failing grades changed to straight A's and a new name appeared on the super honor roll at PS 3. His friends in the gang came back to school with him and his parents were completely overwhelmed.

Little Miss Campbell made Weadock aware of his own untapped abilities. She tutored him in the subjects he avoided for years and enlightened him in a number of other subjects. He was a frequent visitor at her apartment on Bleeker Street where she taught him to focus his own destiny. When the eighth

grade ended, he went on to High School and Miss Campbell took a new student under her wing.

Heckle finally abandoned the idea of beating Weadock at the bowling machine and sat down at the table next to his brother. "Whattya' say we tell Savage to go fuck herself?"

"That's easy for you; she doesn't have you by the balls."

Weadock watched the two brothers quibbling. He thought they were immature and risky but he needed them to capture Ramon and the Baker gang and would tolerate their foolish antics until the case was over. They were showing signs of uneasiness and fear for themselves and their families and it wasn't just due to the undercover work they did for ATF. They had fingered lots of bad guys in federal court. Some of them received long sentences. Others were already back on the street and spreading the word about them. They both knew it was only a matter of time before a guy like Ramon paid them a visit. Heckle had worked for drug dealer, Freddie Colon. Colon was no killer but he knew guys like Ramon and the more time he spent in prison, the more time he had to think about getting revenge on the guys who sent him there.

Weadock walked to the table.

Jeckle looked up. "I hope you're right about this District Attorney, Sarge. There's no place for us to go anymore. We're marked for death and we can't afford to just pack our bags and run."

"I still get some locksmith work from people in the neighborhood," Heckle said, "and Jeckle used to come as a helper. Now he comes for protection. Now, we're always together."

Weadock went over Bergermeister's instructions again so there would be no errors.

Picking up the empty glasses, the waitress bent over to expose her frontage and flashed her puppy dog eyes at Weadock once again. "Would you like anything else, sir?"

"Yes." Weadock hesitated. Heckle, Jeckle and Falcone waited for him to continue. "Give these two gentlemen another drink and bring the bill to me."

THERESA IS BACK

WEADOCK HAD NO IDEA WHAT HE WAS LOOKING FOR when he returned to the 34th Street crime scene. He parked and sat in his car near the boarded up newsstand and reviewed Detective Marini's account of the Raffes homicide.

He cranked his window down and studied the area. His eyes brushed the store fronts and apartment windows above them. *Why would a big shot drug dealer like Lopez send out his top assassin to kill a drudge like Tommy Raffes, and why here? Why was he killed here?*

Climbing out of the car, Weadock considered the One-Eyed Jacks Bar, a local police watering hole on the next corner and reviewed the facts in his mind. *Any cop stopping for a drink would have to pass this place. If Ramon Velez is the killer, he took a big chance doing it here and why did the killer plunder the newsstand? What was he looking for?* Weadock leaned against his car. *Then he travels all the way across town to kill the owner of the newsstand in his bed, a harmless old man, but doesn't take the old guy's money which is in plain view on the night table. The killer was searching for*

something other than money, perhaps drugs? The killer was searching for drugs?

Weadock walked along the curb to the spot where Tommy Raffes was killed. The crude chalk lines that surrounded Tommy's frail body had already vanished but he remembered the exact location of the body.

The gutter drain on the corner was unnoticed during his first visit but clearly visible in the light of day. He stepped back behind an empty beer can and booted it. The can flew about ten feet, bounced off the curb and went down the drain. *Score! If the New York Rangers could sink pucks like that, they'd have another Stanley Cup this year.*

Heading downtown, Weadock passed Morgan's Tavern on 18th Street, the Irish pub so often frequented by the nefarious lieutenant Kennedy. He thought the lieutenant might be there conducting business, he parked his car. He knew that the Detective Lieutenant would be under lots of pressure to solve the pipe murder cases. No matter how he felt about Vincent Kennedy personally, he respected his position as a squad commander and decided to bounce a few notions off the sleuth.

Weadock strongly felt that some type of "gone sour" drug deal was the motive for the

murders and wanted to share his theory with the Lieutenant.

A shock wave of nostalgia rushed at his senses when he stepped inside the smoke filled pub. He let his eyes rake over the crowded bar. As he turned to leave as an unfamiliar voice called his name.

"Sergeant Weadock?"

Weadock considered the young Irishman who called his name.

"Yes?"

"You probably don't remember me. Mike Kennedy."

"You're right, I don't remember you. So, how is it that recognized me?"

"Big brother pointed you out to me the other day at that newsstand crime scene."

"Vinnie pointed me out?"

"Yeah."

"I have some information that I wanted to share with him and I thought he might be here."

"He was about an hour ago."

"Well, I'll call him tomorrow." Weadock turned again to leave but stopped when Mike continued talking.

"How is the great big homicide case going?"

"I'm afraid there aren't very many great big leads."

"That's too bad. Vinnie said you suspect a cop."

"Vinnie has a big mouth."

Mike Kennedy nodded in agreement. "Got time for a drink?"

"I thought I was on the family's shit list."

"You are, but that's not my shit list. I knew what my brother Tom was doing long before you bagged him. The whole family knew." He shrugged. "But Irish family ties are strong. It's so much easier to blame an outsider than yourself for mistakes by the family."

"Sort of like the Corleons."

"Well, I wouldn't go that far, but you're right, they still hate you."

"All of them, huh?"

Michael shrugged again.

The bartender came over and waited. He remembered Weadock's first visit. "Vodka martini with Olives. Shaken, not stirred."

Michael looked around the room and back to Weadock. "I understand you used to date my sister."

"That was a long time ago, Mike."

"She's here, you know." Michael nodded at a group of attorneys in the rear.

When Weadock focused on Theresa, she was already looking at him, but she was far away and unsure. She suspected that the man talking to her kid brother was her old flame and she took a few steps closer to them. When she recognized him and understood that he was also looking at her, she turned away quickly and engaged a friend, who wasn't listening or looking at her. She engaged that person in a one-way conversation. When she glanced back at him, he turned his face to Michael. An instant replay of their first meeting as kids was taking place but this time the looks were cold and hard and neither made an effort to break the icy analysis of the other.

"Thanks for the drink, Mike." Weadock backed away from the full glass in front of him and turned to leave but hesitated. "Oh, ah, thanks."

For what?"

"For being a decent human being, I owe you one. Kid."

Weadock could feel her eyes on him as he moved toward the exit. An uncompromising anger swelled up inside him and forced a quick retreat. Fifteen years of torment flashed before his eyes in a single instant. In two seconds of time she had ruptured his shell of invincibility and his brain flooded with all kinds of distressing thoughts from the past. All the agonizing pain came back to him. Uncertain what he was feeling, he kicked at the exit door and rushed out into the evening air.

"Why should I feel bad?" he asked himself out loud. "What did I do?"

A pedestrian with an open umbrella took a wide path around him.

"I didn't do anything wrong!" he spoke at another passersby. "It was her. She did everything! She caused all this fucking trouble!" A clap of thunder rumbled in the darkened sky and downpour of cold rain hit him as walked to his car. He never looked back at the tavern and the icy rain ran down his face as he fumbled for his keys.

He sat in the car a long time thinking that she might follow him outside and beg for forgiveness. *What's the matter with me? All this was over a long time ago. Why should I feel bad? Why should I feel angry? Why should I feel anything? Why am I doing this?* He looked back at the tavern and considered going back to confront her, to finally get it off his chest, but he turned the ignition key and drove off.

Inside the bar, Theresa's steamy expression did not change as she moved toward her brother sitting high on a barstool.

"Do you know who you were talking to, Michael?"

"Yes, big sister. He seems like a nice enough guy to me. How come you Kennedy's hate him so much?"

"Aren't you a Kennedy?"

"That I am."

"We don't hate him, Michael. It's just that he arrested your brother and caused the family a lot of grief. Tommy lost his job and his family because of it."

"You don't really believe all that bullshit. Do you, big sister?"

"Of course, don't you?"

"No," Mike raised his eyebrows. "I don't."

Theresa turned to glance at the exit then turned her angry expression at her youngest brother.

"Weadock was just doing his job and I hear he's pretty good at it." Michael turned on his seat to face his sister. "Tommy was a bad alcoholic, big sister. He was a bad cop, a bad husband, and a bad father. He was doing drugs and prostitutes long before Weadock came along and caught him. He never gave one shit about *his* family or ours."

"You don't know what you're talking about, Brat. You're drunk." Theresa Kennedy crossed the room to the jukebox draped herself over the record player and fed the machine a dollar bill. Before she realized it she played an old record that belonged to her and

Charlie Weadock. "Only you," a song by the Platters. She remembered Rockaway Beach and a chill came over her. *He was weak and deserted me when we were kids. When I needed him. My dad is my real strength. It was dad, who kept me out of trouble then, and dad who set me on the right course, and dad who watches over me now.* She looked at the other attorneys with her and speculated that all things turned out for the best. *I'm a successful lawyer now and have a great career with a prominent law firm. I have everything a girl could want. An expensive Manhattan apartment, a new Mercedes Benz, distinguished friends and associates, money and status. Things I would never have gotten... with him. If Charlie Weadock had any feelings for me,* she mused, *he would have come after me a long time ago. I would have never made it through college and law school. I'd be a fat wife with fat kids in a fat house on Long Island like my brother Vinnie. I have every right to hate him. He abandoned me when I needed him. I do hate him. Why is it easier for a man to walk away then it is for a woman? All that suffering and pain I felt may very well have been the fuel that drove me to finish law school.*

Michael Kennedy noticed the dazed look on his sister's face and made his way across the room to her. "I heard you and Weadock were a hot item once upon a time. You wanna talk about it?"

She turned and dropped her head gently on his shoulder. This was the first sign of physical affection Mike had ever received from his sister and it surprised him. "Wow." He lifted her head. "Tears from the iron princess?"

"It's just the cigarette smoke in my eyes, stupid," she snapped. Drying her eyes on his shirt, she turned back to the jukebox.

"You still have the hots' for him, don't you?"

"For who? What are you talking about?"

"Weadock, big sister. Charlie Weadock. You know the guy who left here a few minutes ago."

"You're out of your mind, Michael! That was just kid stuff."

"Well, kid stuff or not, you really rang his bell. You should have seen his face up close when he first saw you. He still cares about you and its heavy stuff too."

"Why don't you mind your own business, brat?" She hardened her eyes and took a few steps backward. "You were always a little brat!"

"Why do you keep avoiding each other?" Michael spilled his beer on her.

She came back at him. "Because I hate his guts, that's why."

"Well, you certainly fooled me, counselor."

"Just leave me alone." She pushed away from him. "Stupid cops, you're all alike."

Michael followed her toward the coat rack. "We cops are not all alike and I'll tell you something else, big sister. Our brother, Tom." Michael waved a finger between them, "cut his *own* throat, so you can't use that as an excuse. I talked to a lot of cops who knew Tom back then. They'd never talk to outsiders like you, but--"

Theresa steadied her brother when someone bumped into him.

"You know, code blue and all that shit, but they talked to me."

Struggling with her coat, she listened.

"Nobody wanted to work with Tom because of the drugs. He was a user and a dealer. I mean, he's all right now, but back then he was a junkie in uniform. If you're holding that against the sergeant, you're making a big mistake."

Theresa took a deep breath and smiled at him. "It's not just that, Michael. It's complicated." She put her hands on the sides of his face and kissed him on the head. "I have to work this out alone."

"Okay, okay." He made a wobbly turn to leave.

"Michael." She stopped him. "Why did he come here?"

"He was looking for Vinnie."

"Vinnie. Why?"

"They're working on some murder case together. You should hook up with Vinnie, he hates Weadock more than you."

THE FIRST EIGHT BALL

THREE DAYS LATER, WEADOCK WAS STILL AGONIZING over his encounter with Theresa Kennedy. Keeping his head as steady as possible, he slowly moved past an empty vodka bottle in his kitchen sink and ignited a flame under a pot of water on the stove. Charlie Weadock was a complete failure at brewing coffee and became accustom to drinking instant coffee at home. He eased himself into a soft sofa chair and sipped the hot coffee. The television set was on. It had been on all night. The original addition of The Day the Earth Stood Still was playing so he left it on. Just as Michael Rena was solving some professor's math problem in the movie, Weadock's pager on the kitchen table began beeping. He ignored the pager and waited for the commercial break before struggling out of his chair. He shut off the pager without looking at the number then headed for a shower. His two day binge was still dulling his senses, but that's what he wanted, he couldn't have fallen asleep if he was sober. After the shower, he looked at the pager and recognized Heckle's home phone. He dialed it. Someone picked up the receiver but did not speak.

"Heckle?"

"Sarge?"

"What's up?"

"Baker wants to party on Wednesday afternoon but he claims to be broke. He wants me and my brother to meet him and his friend, Cholo, at the Sportsman's Bar on 5th Street and 2nd Avenue at 12 o'clock and we should bring the money for the buy."

"Did you tape the conversation?"

"Yeah, I got it all."

"Okay, on Wednesday morning, you and your brother will meet me at the Gulf Gas Station at 23rd Street and the East River at 10:00 AM. Bring that tape."

"We're going to need money, Sarge."

"How much money?"

"Two hundred for the product and some expense money for us, we're broke too."

Weadock telephoned Bergermeister at home and made arraignments for the money and equipment he needed for the Wednesday buy. Then he telephoned the rest of his team at their homes. One by one, he told them they were working a day tour on Wednesday. Then he watched the rest of the movie.

On Wednesday morning Detective Bishop and Sergeant Casey headed for headquarters to pick up a surveillance van.

Detectives' Falcone and McIntosh followed them out the door, but they went to Bergermeister's office to pick up the money and equipment.

At 9:00 AM the SIU Team crowded together at the Madison Restaurant on 54th Street and 1st Avenue to hear Weadock's plan for the operation.

"Jimmy McIntosh, Jimmy Casey, and Valerie will take the Buick and sit on the La Bamba Restaurant. Right here." Weadock drew a circle on the precinct map and waited until they all looked at it. "If any of you get a notion to follow someone, call me first. I'll be in the van. This is just the beginning of this case. I don't want anyone blowing it unnecessarily. At this point, I'd rather lose the subject under surveillance than get spotted. Alec and Brigitte will be in the van with me. We'll park near the Sportsman's bar, here." He drew another circle. "Alex will run the video camera and Brigitte will operate the 35. We'll all leave here together and go directly to the Gulf Service Station at the East River and 23rd Street. We'll meet in the rear parking lot."

The huge, but secluded parking lot on the eastern edge of Manhattan Island was an excellent location to prep the CIs. The lot filled up early and was usually void of people until the evening rush hour. The SIU Team watched as the two informants emptied their pockets on the hood of the Buick. Falcone patted the brothers down and nodded to Weadock that they were clean. Weadock swept their money into a plastic sandwich bag and left the rest of their property on the hood.

"Alex will keep your money until we return. We don't want to mix it with the buy money."

"That's easy for me, Sarge." Jeckle pulled his pants' pockets inside out.

Falcone switched on the video camera and Casey counted out ten marked twenty-dollar bills like a bank teller and handed them to Heckle. The serial numbers were prerecorded.

Neither of the two female detectives flinched when the CI's dropped their pants. McIntosh installed the recorders and wires. The Nigra tape recorder on Heckle and the Kel transmitter on Jeckle.

Weadock loudly identified all present and a synopsis of the case, then Falcone stopped recording. "Okay." Alex will switch on the Kel and the Nigra for you guys just prior to the action, then you guys can forget that you're wearing a wire and try to act natural."

Jeckle shot an anxious look at Weadock as he climbed into the auto.

"Don't worry," Weadock said. "We'll be listening to every word. If there is any sign of trouble, we will rush in."

The two CIs drove out of the parking lot.

Twenty minutes later, Falcone backed the surveillance van into a spot directly in front of the Sportsman's Bar. A convenient fire hydrant gave them a perfect angle to video tape the premises. Falcone climbed into the rear compartment through a small door in the partition and fumbled his way to the back windows. A small air vent in the ceiling provided the only light - It was dark. He climbed past Weadock and over Brigitte Brigiere to reach his video camera.

"Alex! That's not part of the camera!"

"Sorry, Brigitte."

"Sorry?"

"Well, I can't--"

"Stop fooling around, Alex," Weadock insisted, "and get the camera going."

"I'm trying, but Miss America here--"

"The subject is out *there*, Falcone. He's out there now."

"Where?"

"There." Weadock peeled one of the black leather pads away from the window. "He's down the block talking to another cop."

"Where is he?" Falcone floundered with the camera.

"There stupid!" Brigitte moved the video lens away from her body and steered it toward the two cops. "Where did you get this fool, Sarge?"

Falcone giggled. "Sorry, but this equipment is old and bulky."

"You're old and bulky, Falcone."

"C'mon, Alex," Weadock urged, "get the camera on him. There isn't any time for retakes."

"I'm on it, I'm on it." The red light came on, but Falcone and Brigiere continued to snicker in the dark.

"C'mon guys," Weadock whispered, "that giggling will be part of our evidence."

When the conversation between Baker and the unidentified cop ended, Baker walked past the van and into the bar. He sat next to the two brothers.

The transmitter inside Jeckle's shirt was operating better than Weadock expected, but it was also picking up a lot of useless background noise. Most of the conversation concerned Heckle teaching Baker how to unlock doors without a key. Baker was eager to learn the craft of lock picking and urged Heckle to teach him the trade.

Weadock had cautioned the CIs not to talk about the narcotics until Baker brought it up. Any suggestions on their part to buy narcotics could be interpreted as entrapment and used as a defense at the trial. They were warned that Baker's defense attorneys would have access to all the tapes. The brothers didn't have to wait long; Baker made the move before they finished the first drink.

"You bring the blow money?" he asked.

"I've got a deuce," Heckle answered.

"That'll do, man."

Baker backed off his stool and the three of them left the bar together. They walked south on 2nd Avenue.

Falcone snaked around Brigitte to the front of the van. Keeping the three men in sight, he inched the van down 2nd Avenue behind them.

"Rubber-two?" Weadock spoke into the radio.

"Rubber two," McIntosh acknowledged.

"They're coming your way, Mac."

"10-4."

At Third Street, the threesome entered the La Bamba Restaurant and Falcone nudged the van to the curb. He crawled pass Brigiere again to get to the video camera. She was

busy snapping shots with the 35mm camera and made no objections.

Inside the restaurant, Baker introduced the two brothers to Cholo, a short Hispanic man with dark eyes. Cholo untied his apron and waved at the woman in the kitchen. All four left the premises and crossed 2nd Avenue to an apartment building on the opposite corner. Cholo was the only one of the four who eyeballed the van as the group passed close to it. He was a burned out junkie in his late thirties, thin and shallow in appearance. Both he and Baker wore t-shirts and sneakers.

Cholo stopped to peruse his reflection in the van's rear window. His dark, untrusting eyes alarmed Brigiere. She sat motionless until he moved on. Cholo stopped again on the stoop of the building and scanned the neighborhood like the rear guard for a platoon of soldiers. He let his eyes slowly rake the area. He looked long and hard at the Buick down the street.

Heckle noticed Cholo's uneasiness and cleverly drew his attention from the vehicle with a question about the building.

Weadock brought the radio to his lips. "Jimmy."

"Yo."

"Move the Buick now! Go around the block and find another spot."

The Buick moved and the foursome vanished into the building.

Fifteen minutes later, Baker came out and walked to the bodega on the corner. He bought two six packs of beer and returned to the apartment house. A garbled, but steady flow of conversation came over the Kel transmitter during the next hour.

Without warning, Cholo appeared once again in the doorway of the building. He glanced at the Buick's vacated parking spot and crossed 2nd Avenue and headed east on 3rd Street. Bishop followed him on foot and Casey followed her. Cholo hiked two short blocks to Dalia's Bodega on East 4th Street between 1st and 2nd Avenue and went inside.

Bishop entered the bodega behind him. She would later report that Cholo was not visible in the front of the store. She rummaged around, finally purchasing a soda and leaving the premises.

Five minutes later, Cholo came out with a brown paper bag. This time Casey followed him back to the apartment building; Bishop followed Casey. Cholo looked around again but ignored the van.

Ten minutes after that, Falcone shattered the silence in the van with his loud snoring.

"Do you believe this guy, Sarge?" Brigiere whispered in the dark. "He's out cold."

"He does that quite often and he never says goodnight."

Falcone's behavior was not that unusual for a seasoned investigator. Most teams assigned to a long surveillance welcome a chance to catnap. It was all right as long as someone stayed awake to watch the subject. Falcone had been moonlighting as a house painter to make ends meet and often fell asleep at his desk.

"Is the video camera off?"

Brigiere moved her face out of the darkness and examined the camera. "Yeah." She massaged her neck with two hands. "This is uncomfortable and boring. You ever get used to it?"

"No."

"I like working with SIU," she said. "Is there any space on your team for me?"

"Not right now."

"Well, keep me in mind. I wanna be a good investigator and the guys in here seem to be the best."

Weadock considered Brigiere's face. She had magnetism and he felt the attraction. "You could be a fashion model, you know. They earn a lot more money than cops. You should exploit your assets."

Brigiere was radiant and hungry. She was already exploiting her female assets. The top four buttons of her blouse were open as she shifted closer to Weadock. "But I like being a cop."

"So do I." He checked her advance by concentrating on the entrance to the building.

She became moderately unsettled when Weadock failed to hit on her. "You think I should be a model, huh?"

"I do."

Her body stiffened with disappointment as she pointed the 35mm camera down the block at the unmarked Buick.

Weadock studied her profile when she looked away. "You remind of someone I used to know. Someone very beautiful."

"I'll bet." Brigiere felt indignant about Weadock's fatherly touch. This wasn't what she wanted. She knew she had turned him on. She had charisma. She dripped of it and Weadock was tempted to hit on her, but his latest encounter with Theresa Kennedy invaded all his thoughts.

"How long have you been on the job?" he asked.

"Six years."

"You made detective in six years? That's impressive. There are a lot of old timers in anti-crime and narcotics with ten years on the job and still waiting for that gold shield."

Buttoning her blouse, she ran her teeth over her lower lip. "I just know a lot of high ranking bosses." Falcone awakened with a violent, gagging snort and Brigiere jumped toward Weadock. They came close together for a moment but in that moment she detected his unwillingness to move on her and she backed off. She hid her face behind the 35mm camera.

"Sorry about that." Falcone slapped the side of his own face. "I must have dozed off."

"Don't you ever sleep at home?" Brigiere scolded him and moved away.

"Sorry."

Falcone ran his fingers rapidly through his curly black hair. "What's the matter with her?"

"She's bored." Weadock checked his watch and the building before looking at Brigiere again. She was hard to resist but he remembered what his mentor, Sergeant Donato, told all the young cops about romancing with coworkers. *Never eat where you shit.*

Two hours and twenty minutes later, the foursome under surveillance emerged from the building in an extremely cheerful state. The two brothers shook hands with their two friends and headed north on 2nd Avenue. Baker and Cholo returned to the La Bamba Restaurant.

Weadock removed one of the black pads covering the windows and held a portable radio to his lips. "Rubber One to Rubber Two."

"Rubber Two."

"Stay with the subject. Don't spook him. Lose him if you have to, but don't spook him. I'm going back to the garage."

"Ten-four."

When the van pulled out into traffic, Weadock could see the unmarked Buick about two blocks north of the restaurant.

Ten minutes later, they met the CIs behind the Gulf Service Station.

"Should I kill the tapes?" Falcone asked.

"Just the Kel, let the Nigra run." Weadock helped Heckle remove his equipment. Pointing at the tape recorder to remind Heckle that it was still running, Weadock began his debriefing. "The time is 16:10. CI 10837 and 10838 are present at the starting point with Sergeant Weadock and Detectives Falcone and Brigiere. Tell me exactly what happened inside the apartment building."

Heckle flashed a baffled look at his brother. "Baker asked me for the money. He said he was going to buy an eight ball. He took the money from me, counted it and handed it to Cholo."

"You saw him give the money to Cholo?"

"Not really," Jeckle said, "they kind of huddled at the door."

"What happened next?"

"They never left us alone," Heckle said. "Cholo was with us when Baker went out and Baker hawked us when Cholo went out. Cholo came back with the product about a half an hour later. Baker unwrapped it."

"How was it packaged?"

"He had it in a brown paper bag. He gave me back a twenty-dollar bill and said it was change. The product was rolled in tin foil. Baker told us it cost a hundred and eighty bucks, tax and tip included. He did two spoons in front of us, Cholo did one, and I did one. Jeckle was able to fake it, but I had to join the party. They were watching me."

"Anything else?"

"Cholo has a lot of roaches in his apartment," Jeckle cringed his nose.

Holding the Nigra recorder in one hand, Weadock verbalized the serial number on the returned twenty-dollar bill and described the package of alleged cocaine. He shut the tape recorder off with a loud click and patted Heckle on the shoulder. "Well done." He handed the brothers an envelope marked Heckle and Jeckle. "Sorry that there isn't more here, guys. You deserve more."

Heckle weighed the envelope in his hand and raised his eyebrows to his brother. "How 'bout a little party, Sarge?"

"We have too much paper work to do, some other time, perhaps."

Twenty minutes later, the SIU Team was back at the FIAU Office. Some of the other investigators pitched in to help with the dreaded paper. Detective Bush volunteered to go for sandwiches and everyone on duty crowded into the back room to watch the videotape. The captain thought the tapes came out fairly well, but he didn't care much for Brigiere and Falcone's grab-assing in the background.

The unused cocaine was packaged and sent to the police lab for analysis. Both the Nigra and Kel transmitter tapes were understandable, but would require enhancement before prosecution. The original tapes were

sent to Bergermeister's office. Weadock telephoned the DA with the results. He was ecstatic and suggested that a second buy would cement the criminal case against Alvin Baker.

Guglielmo rushed out to the Borough Office to suck up to the chief.

Later that day, Guglielmo told Weadock that the Borough Commander, Chief Whalen, telephoned the Chief of Inspectional Services Division, Chief Brennan and Brennan issued an order to have Weadock and Guglielmo report to him in his office at 9 o'clock the next day with the Baker and Velez case folders."

It was after midnight when the paper work was finally done. Weadock thanked everybody who helped in the operation. He and Falcone were the last to leave. They walked east on 51st Street toward their cars. "Will IAD take the cases from us now?" Falcone asked.

"I don't know," Weadock shrugged. "Maybe I can convince them to leave it with us."

"How you going to do that?"

"I'll make them an offer they can't refuse."

IAD

THE NEXT MORNING, Charlie Weadock entered his parked car, put the key in the ignition, and paused to look back at the three bedroom row house he had bought from his old friend, Sergeant Peter Donato. When the Don, as he was known, retired and moved to Florida, Weadock lost his best friend and confidant. Donato was a vast source of experience and integrity. Something that Weadock now lacked in his lonesome job as the team leader of the Special Investigations Unit. He started his car and wondered as to how The Don would have handled these two major cases but driving through the streets of Brooklyn's Park Slope, he knew that the outcome of the Velez and the Baker cases were his alone to resolve.

Division Headquarters for the Internal Affairs Division is located on a quiet, tree-lined street in Brooklyn Heights. Captain Guglielmo waited outside in his car until Weadock arrived. They entered the building together.

Deputy Inspector Gregory Jones, the ranking officer present, was a tall, lanky man with a straight nose and a full head of black hair. He sat at one end of a long wooden conference table toying with an ashtray.

Captain John Fox sat next to him. He was drumming a tune on the table with his fingers.

Guglielmo and Weadock took seats and waited. It was 09:10 a.m.

"What are we waiting for, John?" the Inspector asked.

"The Chief isn't coming."

Fox waved at an empty chair next to the Inspector. "Marone."

Just then Lieutenant George Marone entered the room and sat next to Inspector Jones like a missing bookend. Marone had an ape like walk and an ape like attitude to match. He came on like a two-star general. "Alright, let's get started."

Captain Fox tilted his head around the Inspector to examine Marone's mismatched blue suit. "Nice suit, George."

When Marone jerked his head at Fox's remark, Marone uprooted his cheap hairpiece and Fox snickered.

The other four men in the room grinned as Marone nudged it back into place. Marone was eager to get going and fired the first question at Weadock. "Sergeant, what makes you so damn sure that our Ramon, Police

Officer Ramon Velez, is in fact, Ramon the hit man?"

"I don't have any factual proof but the CI positively identified Velez as the subject." Weadock tapped his finger on the case folder. "He picked him out of a photo line-up and later identified him in an actual show up. The informant also stated that he heard Ramon Velez tell a drug dealer that he killed a drug addict on 3rd Street and Avenue B in 1990. The CI is sure about this and I believe him."

"Based on what evidence, sergeant?"

"I have no evidence, lieutenant."

"Ha." The lieutenant stood up and walked away from the table. He glanced at a piece of paper in his hand, and then spun around. "This CI is a paid informant who works for money. Actually, he's a criminal who works for money and he's getting away with other crimes by snitching on his criminal buddies. So, why the fuck should we believe anything he says?"

"Well, Lieutenant. It's my understanding that you have several criminals, right here in this building who are wearing badges and receiving city paycheck for informing on their brother Officers. Why do you believe what they say?"

Marone sat down again. "What are you talking about?"

"Don't you have cops here who were caught committing criminal acts? Who were flipped and are still on the job because they turned in other criminal cops to save their own asses and you use them here as Investigators."

"We've got some of the best investigators in the business here."

"I doubt that."

"What?"

Can we stick to the issue, gentlemen?" Captain Fox interrupted.

"Right now, this is my investigation." Weadock appealed to Fox. "My gut feeling is that this cop and the pipe murderer are the same person. Whether or not I can prove that will be determined by the results of my investigation."

"We can't do much worse than you guys," Captain Guglielmo interjected. "You had this case before us and dropped the ball."

"What do you mean by that, Captain?" The Deputy Inspector asked.

Marone turned to face Inspector Jones. "He means that we had the case some months ago. Sergeant Dorfman in the PI Unit did a preliminary on it. He closed it as unfounded, but due to the nature of the allegation it was sent to FIAU for a routine follow-up."

"In other words, Lieutenant," Guglielmo interrupted, "IAD fucked up!"

"Listen, Ralph." The lieutenant stood up again, planted both his fists on the table and leaned toward Guglielmo. "I run the show here and I can take that case back anytime I want it."

Guglielmo moved his chair back and stood up. "Hey, I'm Captain Ralph to you, Lieutenant."

"Lieutenant! Captain!" The Inspector motioned with two hands for them to sit. "Nobody's taking the case from FIAU."

"But Inspector," Marone pleaded.

"But nothing, George." The Inspector shook the gold oak leaf on his collar to remind the lieutenant that he was the ranking officer in the room. "The sergeant is doing an excellent job with this investigation and we have no intention of taking the case back. At least that's what Chief Brennan and I agreed on yesterday. The Internal Affairs Division will monitor these cases closely and assist FIAU."

Marone dropped into his seat with a huff.

"Now," the Inspector looked at Weadock, "what can we do to help you?"

"Well, to start with, I'd like to get a new 'C' number for the Baker case."

"No good," Marone argued. "That's against Department policy, Inspector. We don't split cases."

"You may have to change Department policy, Lieutenant," Weadock said.

All the other faces turned to Weadock.

"Look, it doesn't work in this situation. The only relationship between Ramon Velez and Alvin Baker is that the allegations are coming from the same source.

"When I arrest Baker and his associates, they will all be charged with the Criminal Sale of a Controlled Substance and this case folder will become a public record. Once that happens," Weadock flipped the folder open, "the contents of this folder must be, according to law, turned over to their defense attorneys. Attorneys from the PBA. How long do you think it will take them to alert the other subjects in this case?" The Inspector and the Captain looked at each other.

"I'm merely suggesting that we separate the two investigations now and avoid compromising either case down the road. I already have two additional subjects in the Baker case and a high probability for more."

The Inspector leaned back in his chair. "I'll talk to the chief about this later today."

Marone smirked as if he had swallowed a tasty goldfish.

Captain Fox raise a hand, "You mean additional subjects in the Baker case?"

"Yes, sir," Weadock replied. "Baker has bought. Sold, and used quantities of cocaine in the presents of our informants. His career as a Police Officer is over."

"I'm aware of that," the captain said, "but I haven't seen the details yet."

"Well, just prior yesterday's drug buy, Baker had a ten minute conversation with another Ninth Precinct cop. This little chat had nothing to do with the actual drug buy, but our CI identified this other cop. Later, he told us that he saw this other cop and Baker together on a prior occasion and they were both high on coke. The cop's name is David White."

"Go on."

"We also have a separate and independent allegation made by a field associate in Baker's command. The field associate says Baker and a third cop named Keith Suggs are asshole buddies. They often work together as partners in a radio car and like Baker; Suggs also has a dozen unsubstantiated drug allegations against him."

"You want us to give new corruption numbers to all the new subjects?" Fox asked.

"No, sir. I just want to separate the Velez case from the Baker case. That's not an unreasonable request, is it, Captain?"

Fox glanced at Marone.

"It's against Department policy," Marone argued.

"These rules are not written on stone tablets,' Jones said, "Perhaps they need to be changed."

"Perhaps," Fox said.

"Listen, Ralph," Jones stood up and moved closer to Guglielmo. "The Chief wants these two cases to stay in the hands of FIAU. I'll speak to him later about the C numbers and get back to you."

THE C I ATTACK

ON MAY 18, 1992, SERGEANT WEADOCK AND DETECTIVE FALCONE ENTERED THE NINTH PRECINCT DETECTIVE SQUAD ROOM. Lieutenant Kennedy arranged for them to interview the Detective who handled the Cruz Murder, Joe Levine.

Detective Levine, like a lot of other cops, disliked and feared IAD investigators but Lieutenant Kennedy told him to be a professional and deal with the situation. Levine reluctantly handed the case folder to Falcone and walked away. "Help yourself."

Shuffling through the hefty folder, Falcone stopped to read one of the Detective's follow up reports, a DD5. He waved it at Weadock. "It looks like they did a pretty good canvass of the murder scene but they came up with nothing."

Weadock handed his clipboard to Detective Levine when he came back. "I'd like to interview Maria Ramos. Your report says she actually saw perpetrators."

Levine glanced at the report and saw his name on it. "She was a long way from the scene, Sarge. "She saw three men and a black Camaro."

Levine handed the DD5 back to Weadock. "I had the original investigation and interviewed this broad three times. She was waiting for her sister and looked out the window to see if her sister was coming. She was ten floors from the street when the crime went down. I took her to Central Photo and she looked at a million mug shots. She was very cooperative, but couldn't ID the killers. The results were negative. She didn't mind the inconvenience at all; she thought we were on a date."

"You think she still lives at this address?"

"Why?"

"I'd like to talk to her."

"You'd just be wasting your time, Sarge."

"Look, she saw enough to know that there were three men, Hispanic men, and she identified the model of the car. Perhaps she'll remember something else."

"What does this have to do with the Plumber Case?"

"Is that what they're calling it now?"

"Yeah, me and my partner are assigned to the Task Force."

"So are we," Falcone said.

The telephone rang and Levine picked up the receiver. "Ninth Squad, Levine." He handed the receiver to Falcone. "It's for you."

Falcone listened and lowered the telephone. "It's Brigitte; she says Heckle and Jeckle were beaten up. They're at Memorial Hospital."

"How bad?"

"How bad?" Falcone repeated into the phone. "She doesn't know."

Weadock carried the case folder to the door and turned. "Levine."

"Yeah, Sarge."

"Find out if Maria Ramos still lives at that address."

"Okay, Sarge."

Twenty minutes later, Weadock and Falcone elbowed their way through a crowded hospital emergency room.

"Must've been a plane crash or something," Falcone said.

"You've been living in East Cup Cake too long, Alex." Weadock took out his shield and clipped it on his vest pocket. "It's always like this in the big apple."

Weadock gently nudged a nurse aside as he made his way through the jammed corridors.

She turned and put her hand on his badge to slow him down. "What can we do for you, Sergeant?"

Weadock looked her in the eyes. "You have a busy shop here. Looks like lots of people waiting for treatment." He stretched to see around her. "And lots of people waiting for people waiting for treatment," He looked down another corridor. "And lots of people… Just waiting."

Falcone put his hand on the nurse's hand which was still on Weadock's badge, "We're just looking for a beat up Laurel and Hardy team." Falcone turned his head to watch a berserk woman attacking an out of service soda machine.

The nurse looked at Falcone's Detective shield. "You mean the two detectives who were in a fight?"

Weadock and Falcone looked at each other.

"They do look like Laurel and Hardy, don't they?"

"Yeah."

The nurse grinned and pointed a finger. "The last room on the right down there."

The two brothers smiled from ear to ear when Weadock moved the curtain aside to see them. An overweight nurse, wrapping Jeckle's arm, turned to look at Weadock and Falcone over her shoulder.

"This is our sergeant, big nurse." Heckle pointed a closed fist at Weadock.

The nurse lowered her eyes to the gold shield hanging from Weadock's pocket then continued attending to Jeckle's wound. "Do these two wise asses belong to you?"

Weadock nodded.

"He's our boss, big nurse." Jeckle and Heckle said together.

"Well," the nurse smiled at Weadock. "they look like they have the same last name."

Heckle and Jeckle turned, looked closely at each other then screamed, "Aaahhhh!"

"Are they okay, Nurse?"

"Mentally or physically?" The smile vanished from her face. "They've been a big pain in the ass since they got here. You can get them the hell out of here now."

As soon as they hit the street, Weadock stopped them. "What happened?"

"We went to Houston Street on a lockout and these four Cubans jumped us," Jeckle said.

"They were Dominicans," Heckle argued.

"Cubans."

"Dominicans."

"Stop," Weadock said. "What's this detective bullshit?"

"Detective bullshit?" Jeckle repeated.

"You guys are the detectives." Heckle waved a hand between Weadock and Falcone.

"You told these people you were detectives?"

"If we didn't do that, Sarge, we'd still be in the waiting room bleeding to death."

"And they believed you?"

"Sure." Jeckle flashed a detective's badge.

Heckle folded his lapel like Jackie Gleason's Poor soul to expose his badge.

Inside the police car, Jeckle told Weadock about Miguel Ramlochan, a Brooklyn metal worker who makes and sells police badges. "This guy's got uniforms too, guns, whistles, badges. You name it, he has it. We paid fifty bucks each for these badges."

"They look real to me." Falcone said.

"This guy has everything, Sarge. He gets lots of other stuff from his cop friends. Thirty-five bucks for a cop's badge, fifty for a detective. We had to be detectives." The brothers smiled at each other. "The girls love detectives."

"You wanna be a captain, Sarge?" Heckle said. "We'll pick one up for you."

"Whatever you do," Weadock shot them with a flinty expression, "don't wave those at any cop. Understand?"

"We won't, Sarge. We promise." They turned, licked their forefingers and touched them together as if they were ringing each other's doorbell.

"All right, tell us what happened."

Falcone scratched out the details on a piece of paper as the two brothers took turns giving their account of the incident.

"We came home from a locksmith job," Heckle said, "I was removing a bag of tools from the trunk of our car, when they jumped us."

Jeckle held up his injured arm. "Yeah, they were waiting for us. One of them whipped out a blade and backed big brother against the car and the others began beating on me."

"Yeah," Heckle said, "that's when I dropped the tool bag on one guy's foot, the one with the blade. When he hobbled away, I charged the others."

"You should have seen him, Sarge." Jeckle patted his brother on the back, He was like a raging bull. He knocked one guy over the car and slammed another into a wall. They were calling us rats."

"We get that all the time," Falcone said.

"Yeah, now we're like you," Jeckle said.

Heckle nudged Jeckle aside. "That's when I grabbed a tire iron from the car whacked the guy who was holding the blade. He dropped it and ran away crying like a baby. Then I whacked this fat guy. He has to be in a lot of pain. I caught him in the ear with that tire iron. They all ran through this vacant lot."

"We were bleeding." Jeckle lifted his arm. "So we came here, then we called you."

"You guys have a car?"

They both grinned and looked up into space.

Weadock was somewhat suspicious about the story they told because they were laughing too much as they told it. He nudged Falcone into the hall. "Their perpetrator descriptions are pretty vague and there are no witnesses. Make up a regular complaint report but leave that detective badge business out of it."

Later, at the FIAU Office, Weadock telephoned a new log report into the IAD Action Desk. It concerned the manufacture and sale of bogus police badges in Brooklyn.

J.J. REPORTS

AT ABOUT ONE O'CLOCK IN THE AFTERNOON ON WEDNESDAY, Charlie Weadock received a fishy, yet interesting telephone call from JJ Harrington. He left his office and wormed his way through the 17th Precinct Station House to the door on 51st Street. Some of the cops nodded at him, some turned away, but all of them knew him by his resolute reputation. Weadock glanced up at a cloudy May sky then headed west. Checking his image in a store-front window reflection, he decided he needed a new sports jacket. The small vest-pocket park on the next street was loaded with brown-baggers. A positive sign that summer was here.

Weadock visualized an intoxicated Harrington waiting for him at the Parkside Hotel bar and got the urge to return to his office but the promise of new corruption information implored him on-ward. He paused again before the hotel's strange façade to consider the four metallic rats attached to the cables supporting the marquee. Harrington once told Weadock that merchant seamen financed this hotel when New York City was a bustling seaport. The hideous creatures seemed out of place above the entrance to a hotel and had been painted over several times to make them almost unnoticeable.

Harrington slipped off his strategic bar stool when he saw Weadock and beckoned the sergeant forward with his hand. The old man always positioned himself where he could watch people entering and exiting the premises. An ambiguous entrepreneur, Harrington, waved his money in public like a red flag. He never left his hotel room with less than a grand in his pockets. The seventy-one year old tough guy had a handshake like a steel vise.

Weadock suspected that Harrington had been some kind of liaison between the Irish gangsters and the Italian Mafia in the old days. Harrington's confidential informant folder suggested that he had definite links with organized crime and he frequently dropped the names of Irish and Italian racketeers as if they were his close friends, He knew all their first names and aliases. Only a few First Grade Detectives in the NYPD had comparable knowledge in this area.

Loan sharking had been Harrington's bread and butter for over thirty years and Weadock knew he could not have operated all that time without mob approval. But Harrington furnished him with free intelligence information. He did it regularly and for strange compensation. All Harrington ever asked was for Weadock to meet him at various times and places, usually bars and restaurants, where he could demonstrate to his clients that he had close ties with the NYPD.

Harrington was an ingenious swindler who had been arrested only once in his life. During World War Two, Corporal Harrington was caught stealing eleven tons of butter from a military warehouse and spent one night in the brig. A week later, he left military service with medical discharge. Harrington was extremely alert and had the charisma of a talk show host. He waited patiently until Weadock was standing next to him at the bar. His eyes blazed with alcohol.

"I hate everyone." Harrington slid his eyes from side to side, waiting for a response, but Weadock ignored him. Harrington continued. "I hate niggers, spics, wops, kikes and women, especially women. But I don't hate you, Sergeant Weadock." He turned his stool to face the barmaid and ordered a martini for Weadock. When she returned with a shaker of vodka, he leaned into her. "You know something, darling," he said softly, "I'm seventy-one years of age and have never been married. In fact, I've never had a steady girlfriend."

The barmaid shot Weadock a skeptical glance before locking her eyes on Harrington. "I don't believe that, sir."

"It's true, darling," he said, "My very own mother told me never to trust a woman - any woman."

Weadock sipped his martini but reacted like a gunfighter to stop Harrington from slapping him on the back. He caught Harrington's hand in mid-air and stopped him cold. "I told you not to do that, old man." Weadock forced Harrington to lower his arm. "Don't fuck with me today; I'm not in the mood for it."

Sweeping the room with his eyes, Harrington spilled his drink on the bar. "Sergeant Weadock, you're my only true friend."

"You're drunk."

"I've never been drunk."

"You've never been sober."

The barmaid mopped up the spill.

"That's Absolute, orange juice and ice." Harrington touched the three glasses in front of him like the tooth fairy. "And give the sergeant here another drink."

"I'm fine, Miss." Weadock waved his hand over the martini. "Just take care of him."

"Excuse me darling. I said excuse me!" Harrington raised his voice when the barmaid failed to acknowledge him.

The attractive brunette stepped back with her hands on her hips, examining the two individuals before her. Cocking her head to one side, she smiled.

Weadock was not quite sure what her smile meant and pretended not to notice her great body as she walked away.

Harrington liked Weadock from day one of their relationship. Charlie Weadock was the only noble part of his lowly existence. He trusted him. It was Harrington who helped Weadock set up the arrest of Sergeant Thomas Kennedy for stealing U.S. Savings Bonds.

Weadock never saw Harrington use or sell drugs, but he couldn't forget that Harrington once told him that Tom Kennedy asked him for a kilo of cocaine a few days prior to the arrest of Kennedy. That statement is still recorded in the Kennedy arrest tape.

When the young barmaid returned, Harrington took her hand and softly folded a fifty-dollar bill into her palm. Her eyes widened to explore Harrington's huge diamond pinky ring. "Is that real?"

Holding her hand, Harrington examined her face. "You have a vivacious smile, young lady. Who is your favorite poet?"

She flashed a "What should I do?" glance at Weadock, and then looked back at Harrington as he leaned closer to her.

"My name's Amanda and I'm not into poetry."

"Life *is* poetry, Amanda." Harrington released her hand as he slid off the barstool. "I'm a poet. Shall I compose a poem for you? I wrote one for the Sergeant here.

There was an old owl that lived in a tree
And the more he saw, the less he said
And the less he said, the more he saw—

Excuse me." Harrington wavered towards the men's room.

Weadock watched the old man shuffle away. Drunk or sober, Harrington had an agile mind. He moved big money around with finesse and shrewdness. He read several New York newspapers from cover to cover every day and was a walking encyclopedia of street knowledge. Law enforcement officers from a dozen agencies often sought him out and paid him big bucks for his underworld knowledge and contacts. Harrington thought nothing of giving a hundred dollar tip to a maitre d' or twenty dollars to a doorman for a taxi.

"It's all an investment," Harrington once told Weadock. "Sometimes it comes back, sometimes it doesn't." Once, when he was exceedingly drunk, Harrington disclosed one source of his cloak-and-dagger incomes. He said that he had been receiving weekly paychecks from two West Side trucking companies for twenty-five years and never worked a day for either of them.

"Sergeant," Harrington stumbled against Weadock. "I think I'm in love again. Do you think this young lady would join me at my hotel for a late supper or something?"

"Perhaps," Weadock began to leave. "show her your bank roll and see what happens."

Harrington patted his pockets to make sure he still had his money. "Why don't you stay and get drunk with me, lad?"

"I can't, Jay." Weadock emptied his glass. "I have a lot of work at the office."

"Why don't you come to work with me?"

"You called me here and I came. Do you have anything for me?"

"Piney, a good friend of mine on the lower East side, told me that Lopez likes cops and even has a few on his payroll. He gets huge, regular shipments of cocaine, and supplies a lot of other dealers in the outer boroughs and New Jersey. He owns the Kit Kat Klub on Broadway and 62nd Street. It's a class restaurant, a hangout for the Lincoln Center crowd. He bought the building and the restaurant about three years ago. My friend, Piney, said that Lopez likes to keep society people around him. He gives them a lot of free and discounted coke just to get them into his place. He has superb seats at the Met and attends frequently. A lot of his regular customers have money and make their purchases right there at the tables during dinner. Oh, one other thing, an Irish inspector from your department spends a lot of time at his club. White hair, red face, about sixty. He's probably dirty. The bartender at the restaurant is an acquaintance of mine. So I will make some discreet inquiries for you if you like."

"Anything new on Ramon?"

"No."

"Watch yourself, old man. This Lopez character is dangerous."

"Dangerous!" Harrington became angry. "You don't know what a dangerous man I am, do you, sergeant?"

"Just be careful."

"Listen, lad." Harrington tugged on Weadock's tie like a pull chain, "Why don't you quit your job and come into business with me? I'll make you my partner. You're my only real friend. I have a good Jew lawyer, but he's not my friend. When I die, you can have all my money."

"Don't you have any relatives, Jay?"

"I do, I do, I have a brother, but I haven't seen him since he went to sea in 1955. Do you think your captain would give me five hundred for expenses at the Kit Kat Klub?"

"I'll ask him."

"I cannot understand why the Police Department is so cheap. All the other agencies are throwing money out the window at me. Maybe I should lend the NYPD some money."

"Don't do it," Weadock urged. "I'm not asking you to spend a nickel of your money or even go there. I just asked for some information. I don't expect you to spend your money or put yourself in any kind of jeopardy for a bunch of assholes who don't appreciate you."

"Okay, I'll just act like an inebriated fool and keep everyone under high surveillance."

"You don't have to *act* like a drunk, J.J. You're a natural."

"You just think I'm drunk, sergeant. That's merely a subterfuge that I use to attain my goals." Harrington tapped on Weadock's chest with a finger. "Listen to me, my confidant. I know this chap, Lopez. He's a foul and immoral son-of-a-bitch. They call him Lobo, you know. The wolf."

Weadock took a step back. "Anything else?"

"Everybody knew that Tommy Raffes was a runner for Lopez, and there was a definite friendship between Tommy and Happy. Happy fed the kid like a lost puppy. Tommy would baby-sit the newsstand for hours."

"Anything else?"

Harrington wanted Weadock to stay. "Happy was never involved with drugs. I'm sure of that."

"Anything else?"

"No, nothing else."

"Thank you, but I must leave."

"Harrington headed for the toilet again. "My pleasure kid. I'll call you later."

"Excuse me, miss." Weadock moved back to the bar and waited until the barmaid came closer. "Don't be afraid to take this guy's money. He's a millionaire and just throws it away."

She licked her lips and Weadock departed.

THE SHOE BOXES

LUGGING TWO FAT ENVELOPES AND A BULGING BRIEFCASE, Theresa Kennedy struggled to turn the key to her apartment door. She could feel the warm bath water and clean sheets as she grappled with the lock.

Still holding her work, she flopped back on her sofa with a sigh and closed her eyes. She released her briefcase, took a deep breath and relaxed for a few brief minutes. When she opened her eyes she saw a flashing light on her answering machine and reluctantly reached for the message button. As she removed her jacket and shoes, a series of insignificant messages erupted into the room. Then the melancholy sound of Jennifer Coyle's voice caused her to stop and listen.

"Hi T, it's your cousin, Jenny. I'm afraid it's bad news. My mom passed yesterday. The wake is Friday and Saturday at Farrell's Funeral Parlor, 281 Bay Avenue. I hope you can make it. I really need your support. We're staying at my mother's house until the funeral on Sunday and there's something else, sweetie…" Jennifer hesitated for a long time. "I found something in the house that you need to see. It's very important that you come to the Funeral."

The next morning, Theresa tossed her bloated briefcase, an overnight bag and a few case folders into her Mercedes Benz and left New York City. She had become a pretty good attorney and detected some urgency in her Cousin Jennifer's voice. She took the fastest, most direct route to Boston.

Jennifer Coyle was not just one of her many cousins; she was the best friend that Theresa Kennedy ever had. They shared Jennifer's large bedroom in Boston and drove to and from the college every day. They studied together and shared each other's secrets. They remained close friends long after Jennifer became pregnant and dropped out of college to marry John Coyle.

John Coyle graduated a year ahead of Theresa. He wasn't an especially brilliant student, but he had a charming mannerism and became an instant success with a local law firm. Jennifer was content to be a wife and mother and help John with his cases. She was the only child of Stephen and Shirley Flaherty. Stephen Flaherty, a member of Boston's finest, was killed in the line

of duty four days after Jennifer's tenth birthday.

The Coyles' had just finished lunch and were walking back to their car for a return trip to the funeral parlor when Theresa pulled into the driveway. After an emotional embrace, Jennifer asked John to drive ahead with the kids so she and Theresa could talk.

"So, how is the big shot attorney doing?" Jennifer beamed.

Theresa nodded at the thick briefcase on the back seat. "Not such a big shot, I brought my office with me."

"Well, you wanted to be in the fast lane, honey."

"How are you holding up, Jen?"

"Okay." Jennifer began to weep, "I found her, you know. In that rocking chair my dad gave her. She loved that chair."

Theresa made an attempt to stop the car, but Jennifer urged her on. "She was facing the window and I had to walk around the chair to see her face. I thought she was sleeping. She scared the shit out of me. All I could think of was that movie, *Psycho*. Remember when Janet Lee's sister approached that old woman in her rocking chair."

"How terrible for you."

"Ah." Wiping her face, Jennifer forced a smile. "It wasn't really that bad." They didn't speak for a few blocks. "Farrell did a nice job on her. Wait 'til you see her, she never wore make-up when she was alive. She was a real piece of work but you knew her as well as me. I think she scared me more when she was alive."

"C'mon, Jen. That's just nerves talking."

"Yeah, you're right, you're right." She began crying again. "Just stay behind John and I'll tell you the heavy stuff."

"The heavy stuff, huh?" Theresa scrunched up her eyes. "Are you in any trouble?"

"No, no, no. I thought about not telling you, but you know me. I couldn't live with that."

Theresa's smile faded and a silent concerned expression formed on her face.

The traffic light changed from red to green and Jennifer nudged her cousin to catch up to the other car. "I was searching mom's bedroom for insurance policies when I came upon these three shoe boxes. They were high on a shelf in her closet." Jennifer hesitated. "They were full of sealed envelopes, hundreds and hundreds of envelopes. They're all addressed to you."

"What?" Theresa's lips parted.

"It's true, they've never been opened."

"I don't understand." Theresa began gnawing at her lower lip.

"When you first came to live with me, you talked a lot about a guy named Weadock, Charlie Weadock." Jennifer's eyes widened as she waited for Theresa's reaction. "They're all from him, every one of them. The postmarks go back to our days in high school, they must be ten or twelve years old or more."

"This is a joke," Theresa grinned. "Isn't it?"

"It's no joke, honey."

"Why would your mother hide letters that were addressed to me?"

"I don't know, T." Jennifer pressed her lips together. "I guess we'll never know the answer to that question. If you don't want them, I'll dump them in the trash. That was my first inclination but I couldn't do it without first telling you." Jennifer began to whimper. "I thought about those nights when you first came to live with us. When you tossed and cried a lot at night."

"I don't understand, Jen."

"I don't either, but what else could I do?"

Theresa stared into empty space at the next traffic light and failed to follow John when the light changed. The motorist behind her sounded his horn, prodding her through the intersection. Her eyes were now glued to John's taillights, but her thoughts were far away in space and time. Approaching the funeral parlor, Theresa broke the silence. "I saw him recently, you know."

"Who?"

"Charlie."

"Really," Jennifer raised her eyebrows. "I want full details."

Theresa grinned. "He's still handsome and pompous."

"What did he say?"

"Nothing, we still hate each other."

"Really, what are you going to do?"

"Nothing, I guess. I always thought that he abandoned me without a word but now… What do you think?"

Jennifer shrugged.

"Should I read them? It was so long ago."

"They're yours, you know. It might be fun."

"I don't think so, Jenny."

"Watch the road!" Jennifer clamored when Theresa's concentration drifted off. "Just follow the gray Caddy, honey."

Later that night, at the Flaherty house, Theresa Kennedy paced around the three shoeboxes stacked on the floor, grilling herself over and over in courtroom fashion, and answering her own questions. *Why would*

Aunt Shirley do this to me? She was a hard woman, but she wouldn't have done this on her own. She must have had orders from New York. Daddy was her favorite brother; she would have done anything for him. It was easy enough for her to do. Theresa mused. *The mail only came on weekdays while we were at school. But why did she keep them all these years?*

Theresa moved close to the boxes, touching them softly. *Why didn't she just destroy them? Perhaps she felt guilty about it?* She carried the three boxes to the bed and popped the tops. Running her fingers through the letters, she scanned the dates until she located the oldest one. It was postmarked September 27, 1977, four days after she left New York City. Her father had ordered her to live with her cousin in Boston and attend Boston College the following year.

She thought the envelopes and papers would crumble in her hands like the Dead Sea Scrolls, but they were in remarkably good condition. There were five pages of script in the first envelope. She separated them and began reading. After reading the first letter, she read it again. She had completely forgotten what a wonderful poet Charlie Weadock was and wiped the tears from her face. The words "I love you" on the last page burned their way into her heart as she recalled the last days they had spent together. She spoke the words, "I love you," over and over again. This delicate and beautiful segment of her life had been ripped from her, stolen forever.

She was compelled to read on and she did. Letter after letter like a chain smoker until the bed and the floor were covered by half of the first box. Fatigue and heartache eased her into a restless sleep.

The morning sunlight flooded Theresa's bedroom but the bed was made and the room was empty. Her bags and the three shoeboxes lay on the back seat of her Mercedes Benz. Theresa sat at the kitchen table sipping a hot cup of tea as she waited for her cousin to come down. Stress and rage were apparent on Theresa's face as her cousin came into view.

"I have to leave, Jen."

"What's wrong?"

"I have serious questions about what happened to me and I need immediate answers."

"You read his letters?"

A lone tear ran down her cheek. "Some of them."

"Will you see him again?"

"Perhaps. He's a cop now, you know."

"Isn't everyone?" Jennifer looked upward. "Well?"

"Well, what?"

"C'mon, you're not going to leave me here with my tongue wagging, are you?"

"What?"

"What'd they say? What are you going to do?"

"Nothing, I'm not going to do anything. I'm just going home to find out how this happened to me."

"What about *him*?"

"What about him?" She began to cry. "He hates me and he has damn good reasons for it. A couple hundred of them." Theresa turned. "It's all out there in those boxes. My whole life is out there."

"Oh, sweetie." Jennifer put her arms around Theresa and began crying, too. "I guess I should have dumped them, huh?"

"No, no. I'm glad you didn't."

"When are you leaving?"

"Right now. I was just waiting for you."

"Okay, but call me when as soon as you can. Keep me posted."

"I will."

The two women walked to the car.

"Hey, this is some car." Jennifer opened the door for her cousin. "Nice to have money."

"It's nicer to have a family like you."

"Nobody's stopping you, Sweetie."

"Yes, somebody stopped me and I'm going to find out who and why."

"Well, that was wrong, but your life isn't over, T. You're a good looking woman with talent and money. You must have a ton of guys eating their hearts out for you right now."

"You don't really know me, do you Jen?"

"Look, I'm sorry for what my mom did to you, but She's gone now. Try to forgive her, will you?"

Theresa answered with a weak but affirmative nod. "I wanted to spend more time with the kids' but--"

"Next time."

"I'll call you when I get out of this coma." Theresa glanced at the shoeboxes on the rear seat and started the car.

"You going to be all right?"

Theresa forced a smile and drove out of the driveway.

About an hour later, she pulled into a roadside rest area overlooking the Atlantic Ocean and read a few more letters. Many of them were written on stationary from the Hotel Windsor where Charlie Weadock worked as a teenager. Some were on plain paper, others were on lined loose-leaf paper, but all were

bursting with passion and desperation. Every letter, with a few exceptions, contained lines of original poetry. His passion and torment jumped off the pages and ripped at her soul. The more letters she read the less passionate and more tortured the letters became. They read like the chapters of a novel and she could sense the changes in him as the letters spanned the years. All this pain and agony written years ago erupted from the pages before her, and only now, all these years later, she absorbed it all like a dry sponge.

THE SECOND EIGHT BALL

THREE WEEKS AFTER THE FIRST COCAINE BUY Mother Nature unleashed a preview of the coming summer. The hottest day of the year so far had little effect on the Morales brothers as they strolled down Second Avenue from their drop off point. Dressed in casual street garb, Heckle and Jeckle joked about getting paid for sniffing free cocaine.

"People don't lock their doors in Wyoming, you know." Jeckle said. "So people there really don't need locksmiths, how about California?"

Heckle paused in front of the Second Avenue Deli and stopped Jeckle with his hand. Watching the chef slice through an overstuffed corn beef sandwich, Heckle rolled his eyes. "I hope they have delicatessens in Wyoming."

"What's all this Wyoming shit, anyway?" Jeckle tugged at Heckle's sleeve. "The Sarge says we can pick any state we want."

"Don't you watch television? Everyone involved in the witness protection program goes to Corn Town, USA."

Jeckle frowned as they continued walking south on Second Avenue toward the La Bamba Restaurant. "We aren't going' there, are we?"

Five blocks away, Alvin Baker sat at a window table in the small corner restaurant with his ankles crossed. Nursing the last drops in his bottle of beer, he let his eyes follow a young girl with green hair as she ambled passed him. He massaged the mouth of the bottle with his thumb between sips.

"Want another cerveza, man?" Cholo asked as he set a hot bowl of arroz con pollo on the table and sat down opposite Baker.

Cholo dug a piece of chicken out of the rice with his fingers and sucked on the meat until the bone was exposed. He cleaned his fingers by running them in and out of his mouth. "Want some?"

"How can you eat that shit, man?" Baker stretched his neck to look for the two fraudulent brothers.

"This is good shit, man. You should try the Mondongo."

"What?"

"Beef tripe soup."

Baker looked around the greasy spoon restaurant with a nauseous expression on his face before walking to the door.

The La Bamba Restaurant was on the rim of the East Village. Most of the business was take-out. The food was cheap and the portions were large. The eight dilapidated iron stools bolted to the floor in front of a small counter left little space for seating. A huge, out of place, oil painting hung on the back wall. It portrayed the goring of a picador's horse by an enraged and dying bull. It had an enticing and frightful quality to it. Without its yellow frame and years of accumulated grease, it could be hanging in the Prado Museum.

A block away from the restaurant, Heckle began to sweat and scratch at the wires under his shirt. The transmitter was performing perfectly except for Heckle's irritation with it.

"Stop that!" Jeckle smacked Heckle's hand.

"It itches me, man."

Inside a surveillance van parked opposite the restaurant, an anxious SIU Team watched the Morales brothers perform their Laurel and Hardy act on the street. The conversation was comical and scratchy and no one had any idea what would happen next.

"Stop fucking with the equipment!" Jeckle smacked his brother's hand again. "If they see you doing that and find the wire, they're going to kill us both."

Heckle put his finger to his lips as they entered the restaurant.

Sergeant Scarlet O'Hara, a newly assigned FIAU Investigator, sat in the back of the van watching as Weadock supervised the operation. "How'd you find out about this?" She asked.

"The subject, Alvin Baker, invited the CIs to this drug buy and they invited us. This is the second buy with this cop. The DA wants us to buy larger and larger quantities of cocaine. This time the CIs will ask the Baker to buy two eight balls. They told him that they're dating a couple of sex-starved females from New Jersey and need the extra coke for them -- A fairy tale that almost caused us a problem because Baker wanted them to bring the girls to this buy. You might have made your acting debut here today, O'Hara."

O'Hara turned her attention to the restaurant.

"Do you like Spanish food?" Weadock asked.

"Love it."

"Good." Weadock looked at the restaurant. "Why don't you join the lunch crowd?"

"Me?" O'Hara's smile faded.

"Just walk in and order some takeout food."

O'Hara raised her eyebrows.

"You don't have to take any action. Just look around and listen."

"What?" she objected. "You want me to go inside the restaurant?"

"Sure, you're a new face. Nobody's going to make you as a cop." *Nobody's going to make you as a female either*. Falcone whispered.

"I don't think that's a very good idea," O'Hara argued.

"You have a problem with that?"

"I didn't volunteer for this, you know."

"Well, I did." Weadock raised his voice.

The other investigators in the van were drawn into the conflict.

"What did you think you were going to do here, Scarlet?"

"I was forced to take this assignment."

"Okay, but you're here now. The Captain insisted that we bring you along because he thought you might learn something. I really don't give a rat's ass what you do in the office but you're out with my team today. I have people out here who could get hurt if you fuck up. So if you don't want to help, don't get in the way. Just sit there and watch and don't cause any problems."

"I heard about you," O'Hara said after a long silence. "Long before I came here."

"Is that a fact?"

"Yes, that's a fact. They say you go for the throat every time."

"What can I say? I'm unscrupulous." He looked up and down the avenue for the unmarked car. "It's a flaw in my character, I know. And I keep all my cases open too long. Perhaps I'm just a prick like you say."

"I'm sure you're right." She smiled.

A long silence took place in the dark van before Weadock nudged one of the black curtains to peek out. "You see that black guy over there?" He nodded at Alvin Baker sticking his head out of the restaurant door. "Do you really believe that I'm going to enjoy walking that cop through the system in handcuffs?"

O'Hara looked at Baker in silence.

"This is a police officer," Weadock said, "who buys and sells drugs. He transports drugs interstate by using his wife and kids for cover. He has twenty-seven previous drug allegations but he's never been caught. You know why?"

O'Hara shrugged again.

"Because the cops and bosses who work with him never took him down. They know what he's doing and they look the other way because they refuse to rat out another cop. That's why the Department needs pricks like me. I've already got him for one felony and he's about to commit another. This is my case and I'm going to take him down. And you know what else? I'm going to enjoy it. It's a shit job like you say, but I love it."

O'Hara studied Baker leaning against the restaurant door and rolled her eyes at Falcone.

"Sarge," Falcone said, "they're leaving."

The curious foursome exited the La Bamba Restaurant and ambled to Baker's red Toyota. Cholo sat next to Baker and the brothers climbed into the rear. The Toyota moved six blocks, directly to Dalia's Bodega on East 4th Street.

The conversation inside the Toyota came over the Kel Transmitter loud and clear. Baker asked for the money and Heckle counted the three hundred dollars in loud, audible tones, as Weadock instructed. He gave the money to Baker. Baker spread the fifteen twenty-dollar bills like a poker hand, counted them and gave it all to Cholo. Cholo went in and came out with two brown paper bags.

Falcone stopped the van a half block away and wedged a seat cushion into the doorway between the front and back compartments so Weadock could see out the front windshield.

"Who's the guy who went in the grocery store?" O'Hara asked. "A drug dealer?"

"His name is Oswaldo Urena," Weadock said. "He's got a long yellow sheet."

Baker was the first to pop a can of beer. As he drove around the neighborhood, he pressed the brothers for information about the two sexy females that Heckle mentioned. He wasn't paying attention to his driving and had to slam on the brakes twice. Both times he incited an uneasy reaction from his observers in the van but he never once suspected that he was under surveillance. He adjusted the rear view mirror to comb his hair.

Heckle twisted in his seat to look out the back window.

Jeckle was afraid that Baker would notice Heckle looking and tapped his brother on the arm to stop him.

A few minutes later, Baker parked on a quiet street opposite an elementary school and opened one of the two foil wrapped packages. As he peeled away the foil, exposing the product, his eyes broadened like a birthday boy. The package contained ten

smaller packets covered with tin foil and pink tissue paper. Baker and Cholo snorted one spoon each and passed the open package to the rear. The two CIs later reported that they had faked using the drug.

The four men in the Toyota each drank a can of beer before leaving the school area.

Due to the loose surveillance and Baker's reckless driving, Falcone lost and reacquired the Toyota several times. When the voices on the Kel transmitter became weak, Falcone turned the van until the voices became stronger again. Every once in a while the brothers gave a hint about their location by mentioning a street or landmark as they passed it. After sharing a quantity of cocaine and consuming the rest of the beer, Baker parked his Toyota on the corner of Avenue C and 13th Street, and the foursome entered Caesar's Driving School.

O'Hara continually shifted her body in a hopeless attempt to find a more comfortable position in the crowded van. "Does this cop use drugs on duty?"

"We don't know," Weadock answered. "Nor do we know how many cops are involved. We believe there are ten or twelve more."

"No shit?"

"The only thing we know for sure is that he bought felony weight cocaine three weeks ago and he has twice that amount now. Last time, he used the drug and took some with him after the sale. He'll probably do that again."

Keeping her eyes on the driving school, O'Hara brought her two fists up under her chin to rest her head on them.

Inside the premises, Heckle excused himself with a feigned attack of diarrhea and rushed to the bathroom. Something had gone wrong with the transmitter and it began burning his skin. He found a piece of hard cardboard in the bathroom and shoved it down between the hot spot on the recorder and his jellyroll belly.

The rendezvous at the driving school lasted an hour and fifty minutes. The Nigra tape recorder and the Kel transmitter continued to work perfectly. Baker's tongue wagging about his upcoming Fourth of July party was now a matter of record.

"You gotta' bring those sex kittens to the luau," Baker said.

"They might not be in the city then," Jeckle replied.

"Make sure they come, this is my party."

"I'll persuade 'em," Heckle said.

"Cholo's coming," Baker announced, "and the brothers are bringing all their beautiful sisters and there'll be enough product to blow your mind."

"I'm sure they'll come," Jeckle said.

Afraid that the transmitter might explode in the store or the car, Heckle claimed to be getting sick. Baker took his cut of cocaine and handed the rest to Heckle.

Baker and Cholo exited the building with the brothers, but stood near his red Toyota until the brothers were out of sight. Baker was glassy-eyed and euphoric. Cholo lit a cigarette and scanned the streets as if he was waiting for someone. He looked at the van several times.

"He made us!" O'Hara said.

"Have you been hanging out with Falcone?"

"Look at him; he's looking right at us!"

"He's looking at her." Weadock nodded at a girl in tight Capri pants standing next to the van. "But you're right; we don't want to get caught."

"What happens now?"

"These two guys are dead meat. We just sit back and wait for the luau."

Baker and Cholo, oblivious to the net that was about to fall on them, sauntered back into the driving school.

The Morales brothers hustled two blocks to the public telephone booth on 11th Street. Faking a telephone call, Heckle talked directly into the transmitter.

"Pick us up fast, Sarge!" Heckle urged, "There's Something wrong with the recorder, it's cooking me, man!" He ripped the transmitter from his body.

Falcone looked to his sergeant for instructions.

"Go! Go!" Weadock pulled one of the black window pads off to let some light in the rear. "Could you walk away from this, Scarlet?"

"I guess not."

"But you could walk away from a cop who accepts a free meal?"

"It's not the same thing. I mean, you're confusing me."

"You can't be confused. You're a supervisor, you have to decide whether a cop goes to jail or not. Your bosses can be confused when they read your work sheets the next morning, and the attorneys and judges can be confused months later when they prosecute these cops, but you have to make your decision while the gun is in your hand."

"What does that mean?"

"Let's say you see a cop getting a free ice cream cone. You decide it's harmless and walk away, right?"

"Right."

"Wrong, you have a lot of discretion, but you can't walk away unless you're alone. You can't put it on paper or tell your partner or anyone else."

"This is very confusing."

"Okay, let's say that you're alone on surveillance and watching two cops. They beat up a local drug pusher and toss his drugs down the sewer but they keep his money. You hate drug peddlers, so you drive away and say nothing. The cops committed an assault and robbery, but there's no crime unless you do something about it. Only you can make it a crime."

"I don't want to think about that right now."

"Why not?" Weadock swung the side door open to pick up the brothers. "You think I'm a prick, right now."

"I never--"

"But that's what you think, isn't it?"

"You haven't changed my mind about IAD. Everybody thinks you guys are scumbags."

"Frankly, Scarlet." Weadock used his best Clark Gable impression and moved his finger in a circle to emphasize that everyone in the van was in IAD. "Everybody thinks that *we guys* are scumbags."

Back at the parking lot, O'Hara leaned against the empty van. She tried to understand what Weadock meant as she watched him debriefing Heckle and Jeckle. The two informants had tremendous confidence in Weadock. He had a way of making people trust him. The CIs felt good about their part in this dirty business, and it wasn't the money they earned or the fact that they were bringing down a bad cop, it was him. It was Weadock. He had offered them a way out of the sewer and right now they wanted that more than anything else. She tugged on Falcon's jacket. "This is easy for him, isn't it?"

Falcone glanced at Weadock before turning to O'Hara. "Just being a cop is tough work but this is harder. When you take down a cop, you take down his whole family. A cop's family puts up with a lot of shit. The danger, the hours, cops are almost never home when they're needed. They work crazy shifts, all through the night, holidays. It isn't easy for any of us."

O'Hara leaned toward Falcone. "Would you give charges to a cop for accepting a free cup of coffee?

"I don't have that problem, Sergeant. Only supervisors like you can arrest a cop or prefer charges against them. Thanks to him," Falcone nodded at Weadock, "I'm just a First Grade Detective collecting Lieutenant's pay." Falcone walked away.

CORRUPTION ON ICE

DAYLIGHT FADED QUICKLY when Charlie Weadock parked his car outside Bergermeister's White Plains home and turned the engine off. He remained in his car for a few minutes to absorb the country like silence that surrounded the house. A row of old fashioned street lamps slowly came to life and an unseen door slammed shut. He could hear a youngster pleading with his mother to stay outside a while longer. The two corruption fighters had been acquaintances for over two years now but this was Weadock's first visit to the District Attorney's home.

Weadock never met Bill's wife, but sensed that she was the woman sitting on the front steps with her arms clasped around her knees. She fit the mental picture he had formed of her.

As he ambled up the sixty-foot walk to the house, she began toying with her long blond hair. Encouraging a few short strands to hang in front of her face, she cocked her head to the side and announced Weadock's arrival to her husband. Then stood up and moved to open the screen door.

Standing three steps above Weadock, Deborah Burgermeister acknowledged her guest with an uncomplicated smile. She guessed he was about Bill's age and liked the way he walked. She also had a feeling that he was checking her out with his eyes. "You're Sergeant Weadock?"

He looked into her eyes as if he could see her thoughts. "I am."

"I wasn't sure." She sighed, "I'm Bill's wife, Debby."

He grinned. "I was thinking it might be Rapunzel."

Fussing with her hair again, she pursed her lips. "You know your fairy tales, Sergeant?"

"Yeah," He handed her a bag with two bottles of wine, one red and one white. "I investigate hundreds of fairy tales every year."

"Hey, Charlie." Bill came to the door and shook Weadock's hand like a used car salesman. "Come in, come in. I'm glad you're here." Bergermeister led Weadock through the house to his den. "How about a couple of martinis, Deb?"

"You're having a martini?" She asked.

"Ah, they're for Charlie, honey."

"This is my *real* office." Bergermeister flopped on a leather sofa, waving at the books covering all four walls. "Sit here." Bill pointed to a comfortable looking chair near him.

Debby returned, balancing a tray of frosted glasses, a bottle of beer and a shaker of martinis. Tilting Bill's beer glass like a barmaid, she poured a perfect head, then dropped three olives into a cold martini glass and filled it to the rim. Without speaking a word, she left the room.

"She have any sisters?"

Bill laughed and flicked a glance toward the kitchen before leaning forward. "Wait until she has a glass of wine and starts asking questions. She's a better interrogator then me."

The two men discussed the details of the first and second drug buys and Bill indicated that he was happy with the tape recordings and amount of cocaine recovered. Bill had a childhood habit of rubbing his hands together rapidly in front of his face when he was excited. "That's it." He rubbed. "We've got 'em." He slouched back on the sofa and grinned. "Now we just wait for the Fourth of July fireworks."

"Baker expects the CIs to bring a couple of sex starved females to that party. Since he has never met these girls, we have an opportunity to send a couple of gorgeous police officers in with the boys."

"Great," Bill wiped his lips with the back of his fingers, "Baker has also bragged on tape that all his cop friends are coming to the party."

"Yeah." Weadock sipped his martini, "He mentioned David White and Rudy Suggs, and another cop named Lenny."

"Lenny who?"

"That's all we have right now."

"Where are we getting the girls from?"

"IAD, I guess. Unless your office has--"

"Wait" Bill jumped up and moved to a huge oak desk, made a note about the girls and locked his hands behind his neck. "Maybe we can hide a video camera in a purse or something. I'll get us some rooms at a nearby Staten Island motel where we can interrogate the prisoners." He began writing again. "We're going to need a city bus to transport them all. We don't want any marked police cars or uniform cops anywhere near them until they've been debriefed. We don't know where we're going with this until we find out who all the players are. We don't want anyone to know who we grabbed, including the press. Maybe we can turn some of them to get bigger fish. This is a major case, Charlie. Who knows about the party?"

"Me and my team, the CIs, Captain Guglielmo, Chief Whalen, IAD, the PC, the Mayor."

"Anyone else involved?"

"Heckle ran into Baker on the street the other day. He wasn't wired when Baker told him about two ex-cops who are coming to the party. William Lee and Tyrone Butler, were both fired from the force last year for drug related incidents."

"Have you been to Baker's house?" Bill shook the last drops from his bottle into a glass.

"I have a diagram and some photos. It's in one of those cul-de-sacs, you know. One road in and one road out. Looks like there's an empty house across the street. We might be able to use it."

The excited DA rubbed his hands in front of his face again. "We're going to need warrants." He began writing again. "For their houses, their cars, Department lockers, everything." Bill looked up. "I have to discuss this with Hank, you know."

"Why?"

"Protocol."

"You're never going to get his job if you let him take the credit for this."

"He's my boss, Charlie."

"I know the routine. You and I do all the work and our bosses take the bows. By the way, you look like shit lately."

"I didn't shave today."

"You could run for office after something like this."

"You think lawyers and politicians are all liars, don't you?"

"I guess."

"Enough of this." Bill clasped his hands around his knees and began rocking slowly in his seat. "What's doing with Ramon?"

"You told me to hold--"

"Right, right." Bill rolled his empty beer bottle between his hands. "I think you have psychotic cop on your hands."

"Could be."

"Well, don't do any surveillance until TJ gets back from Attica. He's going up in the morning with Valentine to interview this China man character. We don't want Ramon to know that he's a murder suspect."

Weadock told Bergermeister about the homicide task force that was formed to solve the plumbing murders and pressure from Kennedy to get Ramon's name. "He says I'm protecting a serial killer and maybe he's right. Ramon could have done all these killings. He was off duty every time a murder was committed. I checked."

"That doesn't prove anything, Charlie." Bergermeister began wiggling his empty beer bottle. "Maybe something will turn up at the prison."

When Bergermeister went to the kitchen for a beer, Weadock's eyes focused on a photo of Bill and his son. The picture invoked a painful memory and it registered on Weadock's face.

"Are you okay, sergeant?" Debby appeared suddenly. She considered his expression.

"Oh yeah, I just remembered something that I wanted to forget."

"What was that?"

"You don't want to know."

"Yes, she does." Bill flopped on the sofa next to his wife. Both waited for the bedtime story.

"It's the Mickey Mouse shirt." Weadock tapped on the photograph of him and his son. "I was on patrol in the 71 Precinct and took a *Call for help assignment in* another precinct because no one acknowledged the run at 04:30 in the morning. It took us twenty minutes to get there with lights and sirens. We passed two other radio car crews who weren't on assignment. They could have gotten there sooner.

"The kid was about your son's age and wore a Mickey Mouse shirt similar to this one. It was a poison case. I found him on the floor in the kitchen. He was unconscious but alive. The mother was in shock. When I scooped the kid up, he doubled up in pain. I left the mother there, she was out of her mind and too big to carry. My partner grabbed the bottle that he apparently drank from and we raced for Kings' County Hospital. The kid went limp in my arms before we got there. I felt the life force leave his little body and I didn't want to be a cop anymore.

Debby excused herself to check on dinner, but went to her son's bedroom where she dried her face. Moments later, she appeared in the doorway to signal that dinner was ready.

THE NIGHT STALKER

SCUTTLEBUTT ABOUT A SERIAL KILLER who poses as a plumber to kill his victims with a pipe was floating through every station house in the city.

When Ramon heard this rumor, he telephoned the Midtown South Precinct Detective Squad and asked for the name of the Detective in charge of the Raffes homicide. He claimed to be a morgue attendant who had some autopsy reports to send him. After making several such inquiries, he was sure that Detective Marini had the case.

When Ramon was certain that Marini had gone home for the day, he visited the squad room in uniform. Using the ruse of delivering some erroneous precinct mail to the First Grader, he simply asked one of the other detectives to point out Marini's desk so he could leave an envelope.

Sometime after midnight that night, Ramon parked his car opposite Midtown Precinct South Station House where he could observe the Detective Squad room. He knew if there was any information concerning Lopez's black bag would be in Marini's case folder and the names of any suspects in the homicide investigation would be in there too. The lights inside the second floor squad room went out at 11:50 PM, but he waited in the darkness of his car.

Ramon turned off the pocket pager vibrating against his body. He knew at a glance that the ten flashing sevens on the top of his pager meant that Lopez wanted an audience. He continued watching the station house until all went quiet for the night. Ramon was aware that the bulk of detectives worked Monday to Friday, 8 to 4 and 4 to 12 shifts, leaving only two detectives from one of the borough's squads to cover the 12 to 8 shift and weekends. Ramon needed to know what the detectives knew about the Raffes and Hansen murders and the rumors about the plumbing murders.

At 2:05 a.m., Ramon walked into the Midtown Precinct South Station House wearing a white shirt, tie and sports jacket. He flashed his phony Detective's badge at the desk officer on duty and claimed to be Detective Santos from the Bronx. He told the young sergeant that he was in the squad room earlier and left his arrest reports on Detective Marini's desk in the squad room. He needed them for a court appearance in the morning.

"The squad room is closed."

"I don't want blow this case, Sergeant" Ramon pleaded. He sensed that the young inexperienced sergeant wouldn't give him any trouble. "I know exactly where my papers are, Sarge. I'll be in and out in five minutes."

"No problem." The sergeant launched his swivel chair across the station house floor toward an open metal box of keys. The keys clicked and dangled on coded tags as he fished through them, finally tossing one key to the pseudo detective. "That's the only spare key to the squad room door. Make sure you bring it back here when you're finished."

Ramon penetrated the station house like a stealth bomber, he was tempted to spread his arms and fly silently through the corridors, but his mission required a low profile. The possibility of being caught, however, excited him and made him stronger. He felt invincible as he moved up the stairwell like a flurry of snowflakes.

Rays of obscure light flooded into the dark squad room from an outside street lamp, guiding him to Marini's desk. He sat in the detective's chair, analyzing it, absorbing its power. He pulled the chain of a gooseneck lamp and a small, but intense light filled the office with dull shadows. He let his eyes survey the room before focusing on the case folder. It was right where he did not expect to find it, in the center of Marini's desk.

He thought about the flamboyant detectives; how they often got drunk on duty and slept in the squad room dormitory. He considered checking it out, but somehow, he sensed that no one else was there with him, and if there were, who would hear his swift fingers quietly flipping through the pages? After all, he grinned, who would expect the perpetrator of a murder case to come into the station house and read his own investigation.

Most detectives are sloppy, he thought. But the cops in this unit deserved the label, pigs. Unlocked file cabinets, confidential folders left out on desktops and dust everywhere. The smell of uneaten food was in the air and he could hear the frantic attempt of a mouse trying to escape from a corner wastebasket. He skimmed through the unimportant DD5's and took photos with his small spy camera and made important notes on a handy yellow pad. Tearing his notes from the notepad, he returned all of the items he had moved to their original positions and locked the squad room door.

Downstairs, the muster room was void of personnel. An unmanned Teletype machine produced page after page of useless data. The information folded neatly into a cardboard box under the machine. A male voice could be heard coming from a squawk box on the wall giving out job assignments on the base radio. When he did not see the desk sergeant, he placed the key in the center of the main desk and left.

He lingered, feeling his omnipotence at the front door of the station house. He knew things now that made him powerful. He knew the name and address of a professor who had been questioned as a witness in the rat man murder. He knew the name of a girl who witnessed the Cruz murder two years ago and he knew that the rat man had been a confidential informant for the NYPD for over five years. He knew that Tommy Raffes and Happy Hansen had business cards belonging to Sergeant Weadock of Manhattan South, FIAU, and he knew that Weadock suspected that the pipe murderer was a cop.

Ramon went out of his way to stop at the shattered newsstand at 34th Street and 10th Avenue and unfolded the yellow piece of paper in his pocket to consider his notes. Then sat in his car in the darkness behind the black

glass and watched two kids removing the tires from a new car up the block. He remained there until the kids left with the tires. He thought of his own troublesome youth.

Ramon grew up in an area of Manhattan known as Spanish Harlem. Public School was within walking distance of his house and his attendance was good until he reached the fifth grade. He had a vague, but fond memory of his father and remembered him as a compassionate and caring man who had hacked out a paltry existence as a plumber's helper. He remembered that this man struggled to help him with homework assignments. His father was always angry with himself because he couldn't master the English language. There were frequent and violent fights between his parents.

One day just prior to his eighth birthday, his father left in a furious rage and never returned. His mother told him that this man was not his real father. That he was a drifter and a womanizer who lived with them for a long time. She said his real father was a secret agent for the CIA.

Ramon was one of those boys who needed a father figure to emulate. Instead, he became a devout admirer of a tough drug peddler

named Antonio Lopez and a secret agent known as 007.

His mother left the apartment as soon as he went to school and often came home late with a drunken stranger or not at all. She haphazardly provided her only child with the basics of life and frequently ignored him to the point of pure neglect. His pleas for affection became an annoyance to her and she never hesitated to use the strap on him. As she disappeared for longer and longer periods of time, he learned to survive on his own.

He took up with a wolf pack of rascals like himself and hastily became involved in a number of violent criminal incidents. His quick wit and fleetness of foot helped him avoid apprehension. In fact, he got away every time. His successes only reinforced his feeling of invincibility. He felt comfortable in the dark, frequently prowling the neighborhood back yards like an alley cat, peeping and snooping into the windows of strangers.

By the age of thirteen, he had become a talented thief and a skilled burglar who could pick any lock with the ease of a magician. He often entered his mother's bedroom while she slept, toying with the idea of killing her to avenge his father's banishment. A year later, he bludgeoned his mother's cat to pieces with a twelve-inch piece of brass pipe that his father had left behind in the family tool bag. As tough and streetwise as he became, he never saw Antonio Lopez as his evil mentor.

Antonio Lopez liked young boys and Ramon became one of his favorites. Ramon liked Lopez and often slept at his mentor's apartment, often sharing the same bed. Ramon was somehow unaware that Lopez was sexually victimizing him. He felt safe with him, and Lopez became his guru and friend. Ramon could have paid for his own home on the money he earned as a runner for Lopez, but he continued to live in the unkempt tenement apartment with his mother.

Two years later, while burglarizing an apartment on the first floor of his building, he became trapped and killed the old male resident when he returned unexpectedly. Unable to escape, Ramon concealed himself in a clothes closet and watched the old man for a long time. He was a big man, but he was old and slow. Ramon slid the weapon that his father left him out of his pocket and waited. He waited until the old man turned on his television set and eased himself noiselessly out of the closet. He intended to slip silently past the old man and out the door, but the floorboards squeaked and the old man turned in his chair. Ramon attacked him from the shadows, striking the harmless victim several times in quick succession until he slumped to the floor. The old man was stronger then he suspected and resisted. He sent agonizing screams through the quiet neighborhood. Ramon slipped out a rear window and made his way through the open backyards to the front of his building. There he stood in the middle of a crowd of bystanders innocently asking what had happened. His cruel act of violence barely distressed him until he learned that the old man survived and might identify his attacker.

That night, Ramon walked east through Central Park pondering his fate. Tossing the family weapon into a lake, he continued into midtown Manhattan. Any dignified secret agent would have done the same thing.

He washed his hands and face in the bathroom of a 42nd Street porno movie house and then watched the movie. It was late when he left the movie house. Times Square was still bustling with people. He found himself standing in front of a marine recruiting *station, facing a sign of Uncle Sam pointing a finger at him.*

Ramon's mother, Nelda Velez, eagerly signed the papers, allowing her son to join the U.S. Marine Corps as an underage candidate. Two days before Ramon left for basic training, his mother vanished.

All Ramon's early leaves of absence were spent in his old neighborhood. He liked poking around the local bodegas, drinking beer and playing dominos with the old men. He enjoyed lying to them about his military exploits around the globe and the old men and kids respected his uniform but feared Lopez's black limousine when it came around for him. Lopez provided Ramon with an apartment, transportation, and anything else he wanted when he was in town.

Lopez became a wealthy and powerful individual in the drug trade and now kept several layers of insulation between his new respectable image and the street level business under his control. He was well aware of Ramon's dark side but protected him and nurtured him to keep him out of trouble. Lopez encouraged Ramon to study for his GED Diploma. He showered the marine with

gifts and encouraged him to take the NYPD's test to become a police officer during his last months in military service. When Ramon came home to New York City he became a cop, Lopez's cop.

THE CHINAMAN

DETECTIVE ROBERTO VALENTINE'S FIRST LOOK at Attica State Prison came when he began descending a high mountain road. It was off in a distance and intermittently shrouded in a light fog. The ominous complex reminded him of ruins of a Moorish castle that he once visited as a child. The long drive had relaxed him to the point of highway hypnosis, but the sight of the dreaded prison on the horizon gave him a second wind and he nudged his sleeping partner. "That has to be the worst nightmare for a cop."

TJ opened his eyes. "What's that?"

"Being locked up with the same animals you put here."

"Yeah, right."

Valentine stopped the car at the main gate and identified himself to a uniformed guard.

Inside the prison, Valentine and Johnson identified themselves again as they reluctantly surrendered their weapons. A lanky guard with a dismal grin on his face led them through an endless number of corridors to a heavily barred, cage like section of the prison. Once there, they identified themselves again to a second guard and restated their business. That guard summoned a third guard who arrived wearing a sweat-stained gray tee shirt and uniform pants. He ushered them to a small 12′x12′ interrogation room and locked them in it. He snickered as he disappeared down another dimly lit corridor.

Valentine flicked his head at the guard. "It seems like the deeper you get into this place, the harder it is to tell the guards from the inmates. It's a good thing the guards wear uniforms."

"I guess," TJ replied with a shrug of indifference. "The guards do spend a lot of time with the inmates. Perhaps they exchange more than just words."

A 3 foot by 6 foot oak table with four chairs occupied the center of the room. Valentine moved one of the four straight back oak chairs out placed his tape recorder on the table.

TJ slid one of the other chairs away from the table and sat on it. He glanced under the table and let his eyes rake the room before looking back at Valentine. "Good setting for a horror movie, huh?"

A single 60 watt light bulb set into the ceiling with a heavy wire cover provided the only source of light. It cast distorted shadows on the prison floor. When TJ stood up, his shadow appeared on the wall and followed him to the door where he bent his body down to see through a two inch wire mesh covered peephole into the corridor. "What happens if Igor doesn't come back?"

Valentine looked at TJ as if he didn't know him.

"There are no windows in here. You can't tell if it's night or day and we're locked in here without a key." TJ began nibbling on his fingernails. "You think these guys give a fuck about us?" TJ was beginning to reveal his claustrophobia. "Seems like we're the prisoners now."

Valentine removed several pieces of paper from his jacket pocket and began reviewing the questions he wanted to ask Colon. "Are you okay?"

"No, I'm not okay. Maybe… Ah, I mean… yeah. I'm okay. I just don't like the idea of being confined in here." TJ lightened up when the guard turned the key in the steel door and swung it open. He beckoned with his hand and the prisoner reluctantly appeared in the doorway.

Freddy Colon was much shorter than the two cops suspected. The runty, middle-aged Hispanic with straight black hair entered the room. Valentine greeted him with a Spanish phrase and an outstretched hand. Colon ignored Valentine's gesture of friendship and lowered himself into one of the end chairs as he inspected the faces of the two cops. He rolled his eyes from one detective to the other. "I hope one of you cops has a cigarette."

"You speak pretty good English." TJ said.

"Why shouldn't I? I was born in New York City. I'm an American Citizen."

Valentine tossed Colon a half-full pack of Camels and offered him a light. Colon lit the cigarette in his mouth and put the rest in his pocket. He took a long drag on what appeared to be his first cigarette in a long time. "What do you want with me?"

"I'm Detective Valentine and this is my partner, Detective Johnson. We're not cops. We work for the New York City District Attorney's Office."

Colon leaned back in his chair. "Same shit."

"My boss thinks that you know something about an old unsolved crime that he's trying to figure out. If you help him solve this old mystery, he'll cut you a new deal."

"Who is he, Monty Hall? What kind of deal, man?"

"Information for time served," TJ, said.

"How much time?" Colon fingered through the pack of cigarettes and lit another one from the one smoldering in his hand.

"That depends on what you know and what you're willing to tell us." TJ said, "You interested?"

"You think I like this shit hole?"

"Why do they call you the Chinaman?" Valentine asked.

"I dunno," Colon coughed. "My father was a Filipino or something. That's what my mother--"

"Wrong answer, my man," TJ interrupted. "wasn't that your street name?"

"Right, my man." Colon gave TJ a hard look. "That was my street name."

"Look," Valentine said, "it's our job to determine if the information you have has any merit. We did not come here to hurt you. We can only help you if you cooperate with us."

"When I got here last October, I didn't have these marks on my face. This is a bad place, man. If you can get me out of here, I'll tell you whatever you want to know. I have a wife and a kid back in the city. They're living with her mother and it's tough going."

"Okay," Valentine moved to the chair next to Colon. "Tell me only the truth. The minute I think you're lying, I'm out of here."

Colon nodded. "Right."

"What were you arrested for?"

Colon was an old man at thirty years of age. He lit his third cigarette from the stub he was smoking and coughed again. Colon's deep hacking cough caused TJ to move to the chair at the other end of the table. Colon's left eye had an ugly red clot that expanded whenever he looked to the left. Colon spun a sad but familiar tale of poverty and drug abuse that began in childhood and ended twenty years later when he was grabbed for the big one. He said his main area of operation was the Lower East Side of Manhattan, but he had a small piece of the Green Point section of Brooklyn. "Selling drugs is like having an ice cream route," he smiled. "You got to meet your customers every day or they buy from someone else. There's a lot of competition, but if you stay in your own territory, you can make a bundle and live to enjoy it. I started using the product when I was nine. When I couldn't steal enough money to buy it, I began selling it. I moved up to distributor when I was twelve. For me, there was no other way to go. It was easy, but I got stupid and got caught. I did some time, got out and started again. I couldn't get a driver's license so I bought a limo and a driver. We went to Atlantic City every weekend with different broads. It was nothing to blow ten or twenty grand in one night."

"Who was your boss in 1990?" Valentine asked.

"My boss?" Colon shifted his glanced between TJ and Valentine. "Fat Al." Colon displayed a puzzled expression. "But you already knew that, right?"

No response.

"Fat Al had the whole top floor at 770 Grand Street. I think he owned the building too. There was a party there every night. Plenty of booze and women, but no drugs. He never allowed drugs in the apartment. Whenever I had to conduct business, Danny Green Eyes brought it to me. He brought me the product and I gave him the cash. I guess he took it back to Fat Al or some accountant. Nobody on the street ever dealt directly with Fat Al."

"Did you have a regular driver or bodyguard?" Valentine asked.

"I used different guys."

"Name some of them," TJ said.

Colon turned his face down and away.

"Talk or we walk."

"Pedro Perez, Chico Vargas, Big Heckle, Jose and Angel Rivera, they were brothers." Colon rubbed his chest. "What else, man?"

"Did you ever attend meetings with other drug dealers?"

"I was a drug dealer, man. Whattaya think?"

"Did you?" TJ prodded.

"Of course, man."

"Name some of the locations where these drug meetings took place," Valentine said. "Remember, I'll know if you're lying."

"Who knows that I'm talking to you?" Colon looked at the small porthole in the door.

"The three of us and the DA," Valentine answered.

"If it gets back here, I'm a dead man."

"Everything you tell us is confidential."

"The agency," he mumbled.

"What?" TJ asked.

"The travel agency at 13th Street and Avenue A had a big conference room in the back. Henry's Diner in the Bronx, Sometimes we'd meet in Atlantic City or in the Poconos."

"Anywhere else?" TJ leaned into him.

"Lots of places, but usually--"

"Did you ever meet at a location where all the cars could park in the rear lot?" Valentine asked.

"Attorney Street?" Colon focused on Valentine.

"How often did you meet there?"

"I don't know, sometimes."

"Do you know any cops who are on the pad?"

"All of 'em." Colon grinned.

"What are their names?"

"Hold it." Colon began tapping the fingers of one hand into the palm of his other hand as if he was asking for a time out. "I'm telling everything and getting nothing. What's in this for me? Do I get out?"

Valentine got up and walked to the door. "So far we're not convinced that you have anything worth trading."

Colon lowered his eyes. "Whattaya mean?"

"Tell us about the meetings at Attorney Street," TJ said.

"What about them?" Colon reacted.

No response.

"Could you check the door," Colon twisted in his seat. "Just see if anyone is out there."

TJ walked to door and looked out. "It's clear."

"It used to be some kind of famous restaurant, but it's closed. Been closed for twenty years or so. It's got a big parking lot in the rear."

"What about cops?"

"You want crooked cops?"

"Yeah."

Colon gave them detailed scenarios on several corrupt cops like the Irish guy, the black guy, etc. but no names. "When this DA puts it in print, I'll give you names, dates, and places. Sort of fill in the blanks. Get me out and I'll give you the Narc cop who picks up from Danny Green Eyes. They meet every Saturday afternoon at a Spanish Restaurant in the village. And there's a cop in the Fifth Precinct on Fat Al's payroll. Another one in the Ninth, and two more in the 88th precinct in Brooklyn and a lot more.

"There's a narcotic detective who gets a thousand a week because he works at police headquarters and warns Fat Al when a raid is coming. The others get a couple of hundred a week. Danny Green Eyes makes all the payoffs."

"This is all great stuff," Valentine said, "but it's not what we came for."

"The DA wants the cop who's making the hits."

Colon looked down for a long time before raising his head and answering again. "I don't know any cop hit man."

"Do you know any cops who are chauffeurs for drug bosses?"

Colon got up and walked to the door. He peeked through the mesh. He turned, lit another cigarette and peered through that small mesh again. This time, without turning around he answered. "No, man. I don't know any cops who do that."

"You don't have to give me the cop's name right now but tell me something." Valentine urged, "Give me something to bring back to my boss."

"I can't help you man." Colon avoided eye contact. "Don't you think I would, if I could? I could tell you anything. I could be lying my ass off and you wouldn't know it. But that's not what you wanna hear and that's not going to get me out of here."

Colon went on to give a physical description of the narcotics cop as a male, white, Irish, about 40 years of age, 5′ 10″, blue eyes, salt & pepper hair. "That's gotta be worth something, man."

"How do you know this guy's a cop?"

TJ asked.

"How do I know you're a cop?" Colon frowned.

Valentine smiled for the first time.

Colon said that Danny Green Eyes took him to this restaurant a few times. While we were there Danny went over to another table and talked to this cop for a few minutes, then Danny gave him a fat envelope. When Danny came back to their table, he said he met the narc every Saturday for the pay off. Colon went on to give skimpy descriptions of four other uniform cops but no names.

"Every junky on the street knows the names of the cops who break their balls," Valentine said. "But I'll pass what you said to the DA. If he wants it, and uses it to convict a cop, he'll reward you with a reduced sentence."

"That's it? That's all I get?"

"You didn't tell us what we came here to learn." TJ shaped his hand into a gun and waved a finger of disappointment at Colon.

"See what you can do for me, huh?" Colon pleaded to Valentine. "You're a brother."

"I have no brothers, man!" Valentine nodded at TJ and held out his business card. "He's right. You didn't give us what we came for."

"What am I supposed to do with this?" Colon waved the business card.

"My boss has a lot of power and he wants this cop who does the hits. The other stuff you gave is shit. It's not going to get you out. Perhaps you'll remember something after we leave or you might talk to someone who knows something. You have lots of time to work on it. If you come up with the answer, call me."

TJ rapped on the steel door and it swung open. The guard nodded and Colon sauntered towards another steel door with the guard in tow. Colon looked at Valentine's business card again and feigned a laugh. At the end of the hall a steel door slammed shut behind him.

THE REPLY

WHENEVER FIAU INVESTIGATORS LEAVE THE SEVENTENTH PRECINCT IN GROUPS, it was news. A coded message, alerting all cops on patrol in Manhattan, usually followed them out the door. The one exception was the five o'clock dinner bell. Somehow it became routine for the FIAU Team working the 4PM to midnight shift, to leave the station house for dinner at 5PM, today was no different. A few heads turned as Weadock and his team filed out of the station house and headed for one of the local restaurants. No alert was sounded.

Papparazzi's on 51st Street was a weekly dinner stop for the team. The Italian restaurant made their own pasta and offered all customers a 20% discount between 5:00 and 6:00 PM. The SIU Team habitually sat at the one big table in the corner and talked shop. Weadock encouraged his team to discuss cases openly, but this week he was preoccupied with personal matters and was little help to anyone. After dinner, he left the group and walked north on 2nd Avenue to 57th Street, east for a block, then south on First Avenue.

This was the third night in a row that he had taken the same route alone. He paused near a brightly-lighted store window and unfolded the letter he received five days ago from Theresa Kennedy.

The letter was a reply to the hundreds of letters he wrote to her when they were teenagers. The light blue envelope was mingled with several days of junk mail just inside the entrance door of his house. It was hand written and had a distinctive fragrance. Somehow he sensed it was from her and dropped it; face up, on the patio table and walked to the refrigerator. He had several bottles of wine and beer but selected a cold bottle of vodka. He switched on a string of Christmas lights in the yard. The lights cast a dull illumination on the letter. *Why would she write me now?* He poured two inches of vodka into a shallow glass and gulped half of it. As he poked the envelope around the table with his finger, a flash of lightning ignited in the night sky. Then a long rumble of thunder followed by a slow cracking sound like the splitting of an iceberg. Draining his glass, he looked up at another lightning bolt and poured another drink. *It must be a sign.*

He paced around the unopened letter for a long time. The sky rumbled again and a heavy rain began tapping on the green plastic overhang that he put up five years ago. It was cheap stuff, but it provided a dry shady spot for the barbecues. He poured another drink and opened the letter.

Dear Charlie,

A few days ago I learned that my family and I were responsible for causing you several years of distress. I want to apologize for them and me. I hope you will accept my apology at this late date.

My Aunt Shirley passed away last week and my cousin, Jennifer, discovered the letters that you wrote to me. She found your letters, hidden in three shoeboxes in my aunt's bedroom closet. They were unopened. I never answered these letters because they were kept from me. All the letters that you wrote to me when I left New York City to live with my cousin in Boston are now in my possession.

I don't know why she kept these letters from me or why she took them in the first place. I may never know. The sealed letters were given to me two weeks ago and I read all of them.

You probably don't remember what you wrote on those pages but the words were sincere and beautiful. So I had to reply. Only to thank you for them and apologize for what happened to you. I wanted you to know that I finally received them. It may not be of any importance to you now, but I can imagine how terrible it must have been for you then. For that, I am truly sorry and hope you will forgive me at this late date.

I know now why you looked at me with such hatred when our paths crossed last week. If you want your letters back, drop me a note and I'll send them to you.

Sincerely,
Theresa Kennedy
85 E. 56th Street
New York, N.Y. 10022
(212) 555-1272

Standing on the corner of 56th and First Avenue, watching people enter and exit Theresa's apartment building, he tried guessing their occupations. It was like matching a dog to its owner but twenty minutes of idle game playing was all he could handle and he began walking again.

Suddenly, a taxicab came menacingly close and screeched to a halt. He wanted to say something particularly nasty to the driver but the rear door opened and Theresa Kennedy climbed out.

"Charlie Weadock?" She looked at him with a serious face then turned to pay the driver. She looked back again. "Wait right there, Mister!" she ordered as she fumbled with money and bags. After paying the driver, she walked toward him. She moved quickly at first, then slower as they made eye contact. "Did you get my letter?" Switching a weighty attaché case from hand to hand, she searched his eyes for some sign of acknowledgment. "The letter. I sent you a--"

"I got it."

"Good." She managed a slight smile before glancing at a group of people entering her building. "So you know what happened?"

He studied her face in silence.

She put her heavy case down and glanced up at a skyscraper. "I'm sorry." She spread her palms apart. "But I didn't know about them. I mean I didn't receive your letters." She looked deeper into his eyes.

"I understand, Theresa." He looked up at the same skyscraper. "It was a long time ago in a far off place."

"Still the poet, huh?"

"And you? I hear you're a big shot attorney now. Your family must be proud of you."

"Well, I'm not so proud of them right now." She wanted to touch him, but she held back.

"It's okay." He turned to see a full moon trying to hide behind the towers of the 59th Street Bridge. "Everything is okay with me right now."

"I hope we can still be friends, Charlie."

"Is that possible, now?"

"It wasn't my fault entirely, you know." She took a defensive stand. "I thought you abandoned me."

"How could you have thought that?" He looked at the moon again.

She dropped her head with a deep breath and resigned. They stood there in utter silence, avoiding eye contact, as the lights and shadows of moving vehicles shifted around them.

She lifted her heavy brief case and he instinctively took it from her hand. There was only the slightest touch in the exchange but it was powerful. "C'mon." He looked around. "Let's take a walk. I'll buy you some coffee or something."

She smiled. "We use to walk a lot, didn't we, Charlie Weadock?" She bit her lower lip as they walked. Pieces of the past flashed through her mind as they crossed the busy street. "You think I can I have a sandwich with that coffee? I'm awful hungry."

He spontaneously slipped his free hand into hers. "You can have anything you want, T."

Crossing First Avenue, he tightened his grip to stop her from walking into a wild taxicab. She was reminded of his strong but gentle touch. She sensed something else about him. Something electrical -- something that told her that he still cared for her.

Inside the railroad-shaped diner, they slid into a booth. The restaurant's black and silver decor was overdone. Weadock did most of the talking, filling in some of the gaps in their lives. He made her laugh and she flushed with warmth. Warmth she hadn't felt in a long time. Warmth that traveled over her body like a hot sunny day after a cold swim. It became clear to her that Charlie Weadock was willing, right then and there, to let all the agony of the past slip away.

"I never thought you'd become a cop, Charlie."

"Neither did I."

"You still go to Rockaway Beach?"

He shook his head in the negative. "I did interview a witness out there last year. It's not the same place."

"Do you see any of the old crowd?"

"No. Do you remember Tommy Raffes?"

"No."

"A tall, blond kid with a hook nose. Everybody called him Rat Face."

She nodded as she considered his face.

"He was murdered a couple of months ago in our old neighborhood. Your brother, Vinnie, and I are sort of collaborating on this investigation."

"Vinnie?" She sat back. "You can't be serious? Vinnie hates your guts. My whole family hates you."

He brought his coffee cup to his lips, but didn't drink. "Your brother Michael talks to me and you don't hate me anymore. Do you?"

"I don't hate you, Charlie and I'm truly sorry for what happened, but I've had a rough week at the office and I don't want to impose on you."

"You're not imposing on me, T." He patted her hand. "I came here looking for you."

"I know." She leaned back; closing her eyes for a moment then sat up. She wiped her teary eyes with a paper napkin. "I've got a lot of homework to do."

Outside, they waited to cross the busy avenue. "Are you still angry with me?" he asked.

"No." She shook her head. "I'm angry with my family."

"Am I going to see you again?"

"A lot of things have happened to us since -- then."

"Okay." He nodded and looked away.

"No." She raised her voice. "It's not just okay. I need time to work on this, Charlie. I don't hate you, I never hated you, but you hurt me just the same." She raised her hand between them when he tried to respond. "Even though it wasn't your fault, I thought it was your fault and it still hurts. Does that make any sense to you?"

"Yeah, I know all about pain. I'm an expert on the subject."

They stood in front of her building talking for another thirty minutes, but it was a useless attempt to hide their true feelings. Their eyes betrayed the true feelings raging within them.

"My office is only a few blocks from here," He said, "Perhaps we could have dinner some time and talk about the old days."

The day they said goodbye flashed in her mind and a single tear appeared on her cheek.

"What?" He noticed that she was becoming emotional.

I never get confused, she thought, but her head was spinning with confusing thoughts. *She did hate him for not coming after her, but that wasn't his fault. Still, she agonized over it and her emotions raged as she thought about the rest of the Kennedy Clan who plotted to steal her youth.* "I've got to go, Charlie." She started towards the building.

They both turned to walk away, but she stopped him by reaching for her brief case. "My case, Charlie."

Their hands touched briefly as the case was transferred.

"Yes," she said.

"Yes, what?"

"Call me; my number is on that letter. Please call me."

THE WITNESS

WAITING FOR THE COPS TO ARRIVE, Maria Ramos danced close to her living room window. Every so often, she'd lean toward the glass and peek into the street below. Her body was in complete sync with the cha-cha music coming from her radio and her rhythmic glimpses out the window failed to slow her movements. *What a body.* She thought as she paused in front of the large mirror on her dresser. *A body built for dancing*. The music ended and she returned to the window. "*Where are these guys? I have to get going...*"

Maria went to the front door and looked down a dim hallway toward the elevators. The twenty-four story housing project had an atmosphere of its own. Vandals and destitute tenants often stole the light bulbs for their personal use. It was an uncomfortable and scary place to visit, even the cops were cautious.

Maria moved into that bedroom apartment six years ago with two children and a younger sister. Hundreds of families lived in the building but she only knew a handful of tenants on her floor and a few others in the

building. She had a hot date to go dancing and was sorry she made the appointment to talk with Weadock. Then a new song flooded out into the hallway and she began dancing again.

Weadock spotted Maria as soon as he stepped off the elevator. Her petite silhouette formed as a dark figure in her lighted doorway. As he and McIntosh approached apartment 10E, Maria geared down her dancing to slow motion. She shaped her mouth into a slight frown. "Sergeant Weadock?"

Weadock held up his gold sergeant's badge.

Maria retreated into the apartment, leaving the door wide open for them to follow. Her red party dress had shifted up and she tugged it down with two hands. It was two sizes too small for her. "Can we make this quick?" she pleaded. "My date is waiting downstairs in his car."

"This is Detective McIntosh." Weadock nodded at his partner as he quickly scanned the apartment. McIntosh held his ID card up so she could read it.

Maria glanced at his card with complete indifference.

"We'll be brief," Weadock said. "Just a few questions about the homicide you witnessed last year."

"It was two years ago, Sergeant."

Weadock noted her impatience. "Which window was it that you looked out of then?"

McIntosh glanced into a bedroom and Maria responded.

"It was this window, Detective." Adjusting her lips to form an irritated kissing shape, she tapped on the windowsill. "I was waiting for my sister to come home when it happened. She watches my kids, you know."

Weadock could see a young girl in the bedroom. "Is your sister here?"

Her eyes moved from Weadock to her sister. "She doesn't know anything."

"Did anyone interview her?"

"No, but she would have told me. Ask her yourself."

Weadock motioned and McIntosh disappeared into the bedroom.

When Maria bent over to put on her three-inch red heels, she revealed some of her other charms. The shoes made her look much taller and she ambled toward Weadock, searching his face for a sign of interest. When he failed to respond to her allure, she began her account of the incident. Her statement was an exact rendition of the DD5 report of the murder. She could have been reading directly from the police report he held in his hand. He could sense her eagerness to leave and asked her a few quick questions. "How many people actually attacked the victim?"

"I only saw the one guy. He hit the man with the yellow shirt."

"What was the killer wearing?"

"Dark clothes. Black clothes." She displayed her impatience again.

Weadock held out the DD5. "This report says there were three people in a black Camaro.

"Well, I saw someone's arm hanging out of the back window and somebody else drove the car away."

"How did you know it was a Camaro?"

"One of my boyfriends had one, we washed it every day. I loved that car. Believe me, it was a Chevy Camaro, a black one."

"Detective Joey, the good-looking one who talked to me that night, he thought the killer drove the car away, but the killer got into the front seat on my side. I could see him when the car drove away."

"Did anyone else see this car?"

"I don't know what anyone else saw. That's what I saw. That's all I know. Can I go now? I really have to go." Maria became insistent. "You know, I wouldn't have been a witness to this shit at all if it wasn't for that good-looking detective. He's the most handsome cop I ever saw. I wanted to marry him."

McIntosh came into the living room. "The sister doesn't know anything, boss. The radio cars were already on the scene when she got home." McIntosh bumped into the statue of a large plaster dog and had to grab it to keep it from falling.

"Hey!" Maria yelled, "Watch out for my dog, man. I won that dog in Coney Island. You ever go to Coney Island, Sergeant?"

"When I was a kid." Weadock continued asking questions as the threesome descended in the graffiti covered elevator. A choking odor of dried urine and pine cleaner lingered in the air of descending the cubical.

The abused elevator seemed to stop at every floor and a ten-year-old black kid with a stone cold face entered on the sixth floor. He stared at McIntosh until the elevator bounced to a stop on the third floor. No one smiled.

"What a piece of shit," McIntosh said. "We could have walked down faster."

"Not down these stairs," Maria warned.

McIntosh nodded at her shoes. "Too far to walk in ruby slippers, huh?"

"It's okay for you guys, you have guns."

"Yeah, but you've got the ruby slippers. All you gotta do is tap 'em together."

The elevator came to a grinding halt on the main floor and the door opened slowly. Maria Ramos darted into the warm night air without saying goodbye.

CORRUPTION IN THE RANKS

DETECTIVE MARINI LEANED ON Lieutenant Kennedy's desk with both his hands. Then lowered his head and whispered. "Carbonaro and I can handle this case."

Kennedy leaned back in his chair and waited for Marini to straighten his body. "Is that a fact, Detective?"

"Of course, you don't have to tie up the whole squad with this investigation. It's not going anywhere anyway."

Kennedy glanced around Marini to look at the other Detectives in the outer office.

"There isn't enough work here for the two Detectives, let alone a task force."

"Are you done?"

"Yeah." Marini shrugged.

"Okay, now you can assign our two new detectives to that Task Force."

"You're joking?" Marini stepped back as if a mild electric shock hit him. "The two girls?"

"It'll be good experience for them."

Marini nudged the door closed with his foot. "You better be careful, boss."

Kennedy raised an eyebrow. "What does that mean, Detective Marini?"

Marini lowered himself to Kennedy's level by sitting on the edge of a chair. "It means that everybody in the squad knows that you're balling Ferguson. She came here six months ago with a white shield. You recommended her for the gold shield and she got it. Now you're pushing her for Second Grade."

"Who said that?"

Marini turned to face the Detectives in the squad room. "You know how it works here, Lieutenant."

"Fuck them!"

"All right, you're my boss and I'll follow your orders, but I've been in the Bureau a lot longer than you. I worked with your father and I'm telling you, you're making a big mistake. The old timers here really don't like taking orders from a baby-faced lieutenant and you haven't exactly been Mister Clean. You can't break their balls unless you're willing to do straight eight's. Somebody's going to drop a dime on you."

"Okay, okay, I get the message." Kennedy lowered his eyes. "Now I gotta kiss everybody's ass, huh?"

"No, but you have to show some respect to the senior detectives."

"Alright, Jerry. I'll follow your advice.

Marini smiled.

"Is everyone here for the meeting?"

"Everybody is outside."

"Okay, usher them in and I'll give them all a big kiss."

Marini shook his head.

Kennedy followed Marini to the door and motioned Detective Ferguson into his office to a ringside seat. "We're having a task force meeting."

She hunched her shoulders. "Should I be here?"

"You're on the case now, you and Napolitano."

"But we're only rookies."

"You're not going to become a second grader by brewing coffee or filing thousands of complaint reports. You gotta' get your name on a major case."

"Vinnie, everybody thinks I got the gold shield for-"

"You earned it." He grinned and raised his eyebrows.

She rolled her eyes. "Most of the anti-crime cops in the precinct have great arrest records and they've waiting years--"

"Did someone say something to you?"

"No, but--"

"But what?"

"I have to work here, you know."

"Don't worry. If anybody annoys you, I'll transfer 'em."

"Great," she sulked. "Just great."

Kennedy pulled a fifth of scotch from his bottom desk drawer and dumped two inches into his ceramic coffee mug. "Pay attention to Marini's run down and don't ask any stupid questions." He wanted to tell her she could learn a lot from Marini and Carbonaro, but Martinez and Wong came into the room and took seats in the rear.

Napolitano wormed her way past the others to sit next to Ferguson as the detectives from outside commands filed into the crowded room.

Marini and Carbonaro characterized the brains and brawn myth that surrounded the detective culture for so many decades. Every member of the squad came to them for advice. Marini moved to the front, raising a dark green window shade and exposing a collection of statistics on the blackboard.

"We don't have much," he commanded their attention, "but this is what it looks like. Lieutenant Kennedy," Marini nodded at his boss, "has found a connection between the Hansen and Raffes homicides and these other seven unsolved homicides." Marini tapped on the chalkboard with his knuckles to get Wong's attention. "All nine murders occurred in Manhattan over a six year period and there may be others. None of them appear to be random killings and they all have similarities. None of the victims were robbed. All nine of these murders occurred at night and a similar weapon was used in every case. They appear to be some type of ritual executions. There's no information on the perpetrator." Marini glanced at Ferguson and Napolitano. "We believe the killer is a male, Hispanic using a black limo. The surgical gloves and pipes are the connecting links.

"In every case, the M.E. reported that death was caused by a blow or blows to the skull by a blunt instrument. The pipe and gloves found at the Terminal Hotel homicide match the physical evidence from many of the other cases but there is no way to trace them. The kid at the newsstand was also bludgeoned with a similar weapon. Apparently, the perpetrator has an unlimited supply of these weapons and accessories."

"Maybe he's just a plumber, Jerry." Martinez said.

"Thanks." Marini waited for the laughter to stop and shot Martinez an irked stare. "Can I continue? There are two witnesses to the Raffes murder. A school teacher who saw him alive at 11:30 PM and an old lady who saw a black limousine leave the scene around midnight. So far, there are no witnesses in the Hansen homicide. There was a desk clerk on duty at the hotel, but he didn't see or hear anything."

"Somebody wake up Wong," Kennedy said.

"Okay, look at this." Marini drew their attention to the next blackboard. "Angel and Julio Perez, two Hispanic brothers, ages 19 and 23, were killed in their apartment on Halloween, 1987. Both were drug dealers in the 7th Precinct. Angel was beaten to death in his bed and Julio was attacked in the same manner when he walked through the front door two hours later. Presumably, the perpetrator waited for the second victim to come home.

"The murder weapon was recovered at that scene. It was a twelve-inch long piece of half-inch brass pipe with a coupling screwed on each end. It was a replica of the pipe found at the Hansen homicide. No money taken, no witnesses, no prints, and no arrests, no anything.

Hector Santos, male, Hispanic, drug dealer, age 27, murdered in his car outside his residence on 13th Street and Avenue D on August 18, 1988. Cause of death: a blow to the back of the head with a blunt instrument. The killer was most likely sitting in the rear seat of the car. No money taken, no weapons recovered, no witnesses, no prints, and no arrest, 9th Precinct.

Carlos Fernandez, male, Hispanic, 43, struck on the side of the head with a blunt instrument while exiting the subway station at Union Square on July 7th, 1990. This one caused an uproar in the community. He was an up and coming politician making a lot of noise about neighborhood drug sales. Again no money taken, no weapons, no witnesses, no prints, and no arrests, 13th Precinct." Marini moved a few feet.

"Jose Cruz, A.K.A. Tony Boy, male, Hispanic, drug dealer, 28, murdered on 3rd Street and Avenue D on December 1st, 1990. Struck in the head several times with a 12-inch length of brass pipe. The weapon was recovered at the scene; it had the same measurements as the other pipes. A female Hispanic actually saw the murder from the tenth floor, but she was too far away to make any identification. She said she saw two male Hispanics leave the scene in a black Camaro. No money was taken, no prints left behind, no arrests, 9th Precinct.

"Rafael Santiago, male, Hispanic, age 17, drug dealer, killed in an alley on Delancey Street by one blow to the head, September, 1991. This guy had money and drugs in his possession and nothing was taken. No weapons found, no witnesses found, 5th Precinct.

His Honor, Judge Jason Spodek, male, white, 58 years of age, struck in the head by a blunt instrument while leaving night court, 100 Centre Street on November 26th, 1991. No money taken, no witnesses, no weapons, no arrest, 5th Precinct."

Marini moved to the last blackboard. "Thomas Raffes, AKA, Rat face, male, white, drug dealer, age 35, murdered at the newsstand around the corner. March 17th, 1992. Again, no money or property taken, no weapons, no prints, no arrest, Midtown Precinct South.

And… Harry Hansen, AKA, Happy, male, white, age 72, the owner of the newsstand where Raffes was killed. He was murdered in his bed at the Terminal Hotel. This time the weapon, a 12-inch of brass pipe was left in his throat."

"At least he buys brass, Jerry," Martinez said. "None of that cheap galvanized stuff for him."

"That's a good point," Kennedy said. "He does seem to prefer brass."

Marini waited to make sure Kennedy was finished with his comment, then continued. "Again, No prints, no witnesses, no money taken, 9th Precinct. Any questions?" Marini looked at Martinez, and then continued around the room until he reached Kennedy. "Oh, yeah." Marini glanced at Kennedy. "There's one other thing. There's a team of Investigators from Manhattan South IAD also working this case and we will coordinate our investigation with them. That order comes directly from the Chief of Detectives."

A soft rumble of whispers floated through the room.

"Thank you, Detective Marini," Kennedy said as he walked to the blackboard and corrected a misspelled word. "It's a team from FIAU, not IAD. Any other questions? Does anyone have anything worthwhile to say?"

"How come Internal Affairs is on this case with us, Lieutenant?"

"An allegation made a few years ago by a criminal who suggested that a cop was involved in one of the murders. That allegation proved to be unfounded but the Police Commissioner wants a second look at it."

"It look like everybody killed by same perp," Detective Wong snickered. The rest of the Detectives laughed at Wong's abuse of the English language.

"Excellent, Mister Chan," the lieutenant smiled at Wong. "Anyone else?"

Detective Ferguson waved her hand like the smartest kid in the class.

"Paula."

"Is there any way to trace the weapons, sir?"

"Good question." Kennedy turned to Marini for an answer.

Marini pulled a 12-inch piece of brass pipe from a brown paper bag and dropped it on Kennedy's desk with an attention-getting thud! "I bought this pipe and the two couplings yesterday at a hardware store on 2nd Avenue. It cost six dollars and ninety-five cents. These short lengths of pipe are already cut in most hardware stores and I doubt very much that our perpetrator buys all his weapons at the same store."

"Did the perp take anything from the victims?" Ferguson asked.

"You didn't listen to the briefing, Fergy. I just told you that nothing was taken from the victims."

"How do you know what was taken if it's already gone when you get there?"

Marini raised his two hands. "This briefing is now over."

"This is bull shit!" Kennedy stood up and all eyes focused on him. He twirled a business card between his fingers like a card sharp. "This guy is not telling us everything."

"It's the best I can do, boss," Marini answered.

"Not you, Marini." Kennedy turned the business card so everyone could see it. "This scumbag sergeant from FIAU knows a lot more about these killings than he's telling us. He has the name of a possible perpetrator and won't share it with us. So when you're out there doing your jobs, watch your back too."

Later that day, Lieutenant Kennedy and his zone commander, Captain Harold Shapiro visited Captain Guglielmo at the FIAU front Office in the Seventeenth Precinct.

Falcone rapped on the doorjamb of the back office and waited for Weadock to look up. "The brains are in the captain's office and he wants you in there."

Weadock grudgingly made his way to the Captain's office and found a sixty-year-old, obese man in a cheap tan suit sitting between Kennedy and Guglielmo. He was finishing a humorous story and reached over Guglielmo's desk for some matches to light his pipe. Still laughing at his own joke, this man turned to look at Weadock. "Ah, Sergeant Weadock." Shapiro sucked on the pipe stem until the tobacco glowed red. "Lieutenant Kennedy tells me you have a possible perpetrator in the pipe murder mysteries. Is that correct?"

Pausing in the open doorway, Weadock looked at Shapiro then moved his eyes past Kennedy to Guglielmo and back to Shapiro. "I don't know you, sir."

"This is Captain Shapiro, Charlie." Guglielmo gestured with his hand.

Weadock stepped into the small office and closed the door. He looked at Shapiro. "Captain, I'm sure that you and the Lieutenant know that we are not allowed to discuss active cases with anyone outside the internal affairs community."

"Hey," Shapiro kept laughing. "We all have our jobs to do but we're all cops, right?" He looked at Guglielmo for support. "Sometimes we have to work together to get the bad guys. This guy has committed nine murders in six years and those are only the ones we know about to date. There must be a way to get around this red tape?"

"None that I'm aware of, Captain."

"What do you think, Ralph?" Shapiro pleaded with Guglielmo. "Captain to Captain?"

"I dunno?" Guglielmo appealed to Weadock. What do you think, Charlie? It's up to you."

"It's not up to me, boss. I think the lieutenant and the captain here are out of line. They're asking us to compromise an FIAU Investigation."

"No, we're not!" Kennedy snapped. "We're asking for some cooperation, sergeant."

"This is an active case. We're not allowed to reveal the subject of an active investigation."

Looking at Weadock, Shapiro put his hand on Kennedy to calm him. "Can you tell us anything?"

"Yes." Weadock opened the door to leave. "We have an unsubstantiated allegation against a member of the service by a confidential informant. The informant stated that he overheard this officer brag about committing a murder. That's all we have. This statement was made about two years ago on an unknown date at an unspecified location and involves an unknown victim. Since we opened the case two months ago, not a single piece of evidence has surfaced to substantiate that allegation. We have an obligation to the officer and the Department to conduct a complete and confidential investigation." Weadock turned to Guglielmo. "They'll have plenty of opportunity to review this case when it's closed."

"Do we have to go to the Police Commissioner on this?" Kennedy threatened.

"Good idea," Weadock said, "but I don't think he'll give you the name either."

Shapiro leaned towards Guglielmo. "Ralph, can you help us out here?"

"I'll have to talk to the Chief first. Then I'll call you later," Guglielmo stood up.

"I don't understand why the sergeant is so set against us." Shapiro said.

Weadock shifted his glance between the two captains and the lieutenant. "This case is being monitored by ADA William Bergermeister at the Manhattan District Attorney's Office. Why don't you call him and ask for the subject's name?"

Kennedy waved his hand in frustration. "You know we can't do that."

"That's right, you can't ask him, and you shouldn't have asked us either."

"What exactly does that mean, Sergeant?" Kennedy came closer to Weadock.

"It means that we're not going to let the Detective Bureau compromise an active FIAU Investigation."

"You don't like me, do you, Sergeant? Kennedy took another step closer to Weadock.

"I'd rather not debate that issue right now, Lieutenant."

"Gentlemen, Gentlemen." Guglielmo moved between them.

"Look, Captain." Weadock turned to Shapiro. "I'm not trying to give you a hard time or anything but the DA, the Chief of Inspectional Services and the Police Commissioner know the name of our suspect. Why don't you ask your Chief to call one of them for the name? It's really not fair for you to dump this on us. We're just mere investigators."

"Maybe we should've helped 'em, Charlie." Guglielmo swung his head from side to side.

"If we gave them the name, Bergermeister would put us both on trial. We can't accommodate them until our case is closed. They're the Detectives. This is a criminal case you know. They should have solved it six years ago."

"But the PC."

"If the PC gives them this information, the PBA will be up his ass and if that happens, who do think he's going to pin it on?"

"How could the PBA ever find out?"

"If they ask me, I'll tell them."

THE KENNEDY CLAN

ELIZABETH KENNEDY'S EYES AND MOUTH WIDENED as she spotted her daughter's 5'8" frame at the front door but her huge smile faded when she sensed that something was very wrong. "So, what brings you here on a Saturday afternoon?"

"Mom." Theresa pushed pass her mother and flopped on the sofa. "We have to talk. Where's Dad?"

"Why? He's down at McBear's Pub with your brother, Michael. They'll be home for dinner, I'm sure. I made a corned beef."

"Did you and Dad go to Aunt Shirley's wake?"

"Of course."

"Did Jenny tell you about the letters?" Theresa squinted.

"Letters?" Mrs. Kennedy winced. "What letters?"

"The letters that Aunt Shirley hid from me when I lived in Boston. My letters. Didn't you know?"

"I don't know what you're talking about, Sweetheart."

"Didn't Jennifer tell you anything?"

"No, but I'm sure you will."

Theresa placed her two hands over her eyes and rubbed gently. She took a deep breath.

"Why don't we have a nice cup of tea and talk about this?"

Jumping to her feet, Theresa followed her mother into the kitchen. "I don't want any tea, Mom. I need a drink."

"You'd better tell me what this is about, dear."

Theresa Kennedy was ready for a fight, but her rage turned quickly to sniveling sobs as her story about Weadock and the shoeboxes unfolded.

Elizabeth Kennedy listened carefully as she massaged her daughter's hands. When it was over a bond emerged between mother and daughter that had not existed before. Theresa was certain that her mother knew nothing about Charlie Weadock's letters.

"I can't believe that your Aunt Shirley would do this to you. She loved you so."

"She wouldn't have done it on her own, Mom." Theresa's expression hardened again. "But she'd have done anything for her brother."

"I can't believe that your father would--"

"Oh, Ma!" Theresa clenched her hands into fists and moved to the front window. A huge ocean liner was being nudged into pier 46 by several tugboats. Watching it calmed her down and she changed the subject. "I suppose you thought Tom was innocent, too."

"I -- I thought Tommy was innocent. I don't know what I thought." She began sobbing.

Now it was Theresa's turn to comfort her mother. She massaged her shoulders and neck. "I'm sorry, Mom. I didn't mean to upset you. None of this was your fault."

"It's all my fault." She snapped. "I'm the mother, I'm responsible for everything that happens to my children -- all my children. And you're right about your brother."

Mother and daughter sat close together. Elizabeth Kennedy's voice was almost a whisper. "I spoiled Thomas the most," she said. "I always called him Thomas when I was angry with him. He was such a weak kid, afraid of everything. The neighborhood boys used to run after him and beat him up. He was chunky and timid and the other kids bullied him for it. Every time he passed Kelly Park they chased him. I can still hear him calling my name as he ran for the house. Your father rejected him for that weakness and favored Vincent. Vincent was a tougher cut of meat and stood his ground against the bullies. The last thing in the world your brother Thomas wanted was to become a cop, but your father pushed him into it. He wanted the boys to follow him on the force, just like he and his brother did for his father. Vincent and Michael wanted to be cops, but not Thomas. It's amazing he didn't try to pin a badge on you."

Suddenly, the front door swung open and Joe Kennedy filled the doorway with his presence. He spotted the mother and daughter in each other's arms as they looked up with wet faces.

"What's this? The daughter finally comes for a visit and everyone is crying?"

"We have to talk, Dad." She wiped her eyes.

"Sounds serious," he shrugged. "I better have a drink."

"You've had enough drinks," she said, placing her palms on his shoulders and pushing him down into his favorite chair.

Joe Kennedy leaned sideways to gaze around his daughter at his wife. "What?"

Theresa turned, moved away, and then turned again as if she were attacking a hostile witness in the court room. "What do you know about the letters?"

"Letters?" He looked at his wife again.

"Three shoeboxes full of letters that Aunt Shirley kept hidden from me in her bedroom closet. You know, the ones she stole from me."

"My sister stole letters from you? My sister?" he raged, elevating his voice several decibels. His voice bounced off the walls. "You accuse my dead sister of larceny and her sweet soul just gone to heaven? Have you no shame, girl?"

"Jenny found them. She was looking for insurance papers and found the letters in Aunt Shirley's closet. They were there, Dad. That's an established fact."

"Don't lay any of that legal shit on me, girl. I'm not responsible for your letters or any mess you got yourself into when you were a kid."

"So you did know." She squinted.

"What are you talking about?" He threw his hands up and walked to the bedroom where his wife had already gone to avoid any involvement in the dispute. "What is she talking about, Liz?"

"Dad," Theresa followed her father. "I never said they were my letters but you already knew that, didn't you?"

"I think Shirley did mention something about letters coming from that person, but it was a long time ago. I don't remember what she said about it."

"You remember everything, pop. You have a memory like an elephant. So don't tell me you don't remember."

"True, true, true…" Michael Kennedy entered the kitchen and headed for the coffee pot.

"All I want to know, dad." Theresa tried to look her father in the eye, "Is why?"

Joe Kennedy didn't answer. He sat on the edge of his bed with his back to his wife and his arms folded in defiance. He stared into space for a long time. Massaging the corners of his mouth with his thumb and forefinger. He quietly explored the depths of his flustered mind for an appropriate answer and found none. He turned to Elizabeth, but she mutely raised her eyebrows above an already perplexed expression.

"Is she staying for dinner, Liz?" He asked with his back to his daughter.

"Why, Dad?" There was no benevolence in her voice. She waited for an answer.

"You have to understand something, daughter. My concern was for you. When Shirley told me that the Weadock kid was writing letters to you, I told her to burn 'em."

Michael and Theresa looked at each other.

"She thought he was a New York hoodlum trying to get you into trouble, and he was."

"Why would she think that?"

"Because it was true and I told her to protect you from him anyway she could."

"You liked Charlie Weadock, didn't you dad?"

Joe Kennedy looked at his younger son for sympathy, but Michael turned his face.

"That was long before the thing with Tom," she said. "Why did you hate him so much then?"

"I don't have to answer to you or anyone else for my actions." Joe Kennedy's Irish Brogue became heavier and more pronounced in his defensive mode. "I did what I thought was best for you. The truth of it is I like the lad. He reminds me a lot of his leathery father who was a good man, a scraper. Young Weadock was a tough kid who respected his elders, but it didn't trouble me any to break up your little romance. When Vincent told me about drunken orgies on Rockaway Beach, I saw red. I had no choice but to do what I did."

So Vinny was the stool pigeon. Theresa backed away from her father and leaned against the wall. "You could have talked to me, dad. You could have asked me if there was any truth to it."

"No matter!" Joe Kennedy shouted. "I'll never forgive the Weadocks, any of 'em and that, young lady," he pointed a jerking finger at his daughter, "is what I call an established fact!"

Theresa threw up her hands. "You still think Tommy was innocent, don't you?"

"Tommy made sergeant in six years. He'd have been a chief in twenty years if not for Weadock. He went after Tom to get back at me for what I did to you and him.

"Dad," Michael tried to intercede. "Tom was as guilty as sin."

"Tommy was framed, he never stole a thing in his life," Joe Kennedy rebutted. "Charlie Weadock retaliated against me for breaking up her little romances on the beach." He wiggled a finger at Theresa. "And he waited like a snake in the grass to get back at me. When the opportunity came, he struck with vengeance. Sometimes I think he only joined the force and IAD to get his revenge on me. He really wanted to get me. When that failed, he went after my first born."

"What?" She put one hand over her heart and tried to laugh. "I always knew you were self-centered, Dad, but I didn't realize until today how really demented you are." She knew her stabbing words were cutting into her father like a dull knife but she couldn't stop. "When Vinnie came to you years ago with that bullshit story, why didn't you ask me about it? What did you think? I was prostituting myself at the beach? You must have believed what Vinny told you."

He lowered his eyes.

"And why did Vinny spin such a nasty lie about me in the first place? She argued. "He was probably afraid to tell you the truth. You never listened to any of us. Look at Mom; even she's afraid of you."

Joe Kennedy kept his eyes glued to the floor "I'll thank you to be leaving my house now. Right now, daughter."

"When was the last time you went to confession, Dad?"

"You know," he looked up to face her, "you can still get your head handed to you, young lady."

"Are you threatening me, father?"

"Get out!"

Theresa turned to leave. Her mother stood up and moved toward her daughter, but stopped in her tracks when Joe Kennedy raised his pointed finger at her. "Let her go, Lizzy. She has no respect for the parents that raised her from a baby."

Theresa took her time leaving, she wanted to stay and have it out. She had come for a fight, but her courtroom training taught her not to argue with an irate judge. She walked to the front door and stopped. *Telling him that she had a date with Weadock tonight would have really flamed his ass.* A spark of humor flashed on her face. She knew that her mother and Michael would catch his rage when she left. Still, she could not resist taking a parting shot. "If you really want to know the truth about your son, Tom. Just ask Michael, but then, you already know the truth, don't you dad?" She grinned and shook her head as she walked away. "You're really quite an asshole. Aren't you?"

"Get out!"

Theresa made her way down the squeaky old staircase. How often she counted the seventeen steps on each flight, some steps had a familiar squeak. She paused in the narrow foyer at the front of the building and looked around as if it were her last look. The piece of octagon floor tile she had kicked out as a child was still missing and the mailbox was still ragged with age.

Outside, she looked at the new high school. The main entrance arched on ground where Charlie Weadock's house once stood. As she walked east to Eighth Avenue, she felt as if some terrible burden had been lifted from her soul.

THE ARREST ORDER

WEADOCK WALKED THE LENGTH OF THE FIAU OFFICE holding a note from Heckle that was two hours old. He rapped once on the Captain's door jamb and waited for the Captain to finish his phone call.

Guglielmo raised one hand to stifle Weadock and continued his pleading to someone on the telephone. He was engrossed in some serious sucking up with the person on the telephone and fanned at Weadock with his free hand to get him to leave but Weadock failed to retreat. Guglielmo cupped one hand over the mouthpiece. "What?"

"Baker wants more cocaine."

Guglielmo held up five fingers and turned his back to Weadock. He continued his phone call in muffled whispers and loud outbursts. Weadock drifted into the clerical office in the next room.

"The Chief's not in his office." Guglielmo called out after hanging up the telephone. When Weadock failed to reappear in his doorway, The Captain followed Weadock into the clerical office. "You think I ought to call him at home?"

"I wouldn't."

"Okay, waddaya got?"

"Heckle called this morning." Weadock held up the note, "He said Baker wants to make a larger buy."

"When?"

"Thursday."

"Do we need this?"

"No, but we don't want to make him suspicious either."

"So?"

"Bergermeister wanted us to go for a larger quantity, so let's do it."

"I'll have to clear it with the chief."

"I don't want any loose cannons on this one, Captain. My team can handle this alone."

"Charlie, you gotta take the new people out with you. They ain't learning anything here in the office."

"Let 'em learn somewhere else, boss. This is a dangerous situation with real guns and real cops. It's risky enough for my team and they know what they're doing." Weadock stood his ground and waited.

Guglielmo's telephone rang and he retreated to his office.

"This guy carry's two loaded guns," Weadock trailed after the Captain. "And he's high on drugs and alcohol most of the time."

"All right, all right." The captain cradled the telephone in his lap and shooed Weadock out of his office.

An hour later, Guglielmo ambled into the back room and plopped his bulk down in an empty chair near Weadock's desk. He had a twisted grin on his face. "The chief wants Baker arrested."

"He will be arrested."

"On Thursday."

"No way," Weadock said.

"Chief Whalen wants Baker in handcuffs on Thursday." Guglielmo broadened his smile. "Those were his exact words."

Falcone, McIntosh and Bishop stopped typing. Detective Valentine's face cringed with confusion.

"Captain." Weadock nodded at Valentine and the civilian sitting next to him. "This is Senor Vargas. He's the complainant in the Delancey Street case, and this is Detective Valentine from the Manhattan DA's Office. Vargas doesn't speak English so Valentine volunteered to be the interpreter. They were just leaving." Weadock thought Valentine was a top-notch investigator who could be trusted, but noticing Valentine's reaction to Guglielmo's remark about arresting Baker before the house party, he quickly escorted Valentine and the civilian out of the room.

Weadock came back and sat next to Guglielmo. "You said something about arresting Alvin Baker on Thursday."

"Yup, you heard it right. The chief wants Baker taken into custody when he makes this buy."

"Why?" Weadock turned a baffled glance at his team.

"I dunno, that's what he wants."

"Well, that's dumb, isn't it?" Weadock leaned toward the captain. "Tell him he has to wait."

"I can't tell a chief what to do."

"Sure you can," Weadock urged, "you're the captain of his FIAU. He expects you to stop him from making dumb mistakes."

"You don't know this chief, Charlie."

"He's just a man like you and me, Captain. You're his top advisor on corruption; he has to listen to you."

"He won't."

Weadock rubbed the cobwebs from his eyes and leaned back in his chair. "He must. He has no experience in these matters. He's an administrator. He's never been out on the street." Weadock flapped his hand between them. "We're the experts."

"Maybe so, but he was adamant about this. He wants this cop taken down before an incident occurs." Guglielmo leaned toward Weadock and tapped an administrative finger on Weadock's chest. "Baker in handcuffs on Thursday."

"You're pulling my chain, right Captain?"

McIntosh erupted in a burst of laughter then slapped his own face.

Guglielmo was annoyed with McIntosh's laughter and held Weadock responsible. "You see?" He gestured at McIntosh with his hands, "There's nothing funny about orders." He rubbed his hands together briskly. "Now, we'll use your team and the team on duty. I'll ride in your car as commander of the operation." He moved toward the door. "FIAU will arrest Officer Baker on Thursday, June 17th, 1992, and this case will be history."

"What about the party, Captain? What about the other cops involved?"

"The chief knows everything and he doesn't want to wait any longer."

"IAD won't sit still for this."

"Whalen has already conferred with Chief Brennan and that's the way they want it."

"They're going to run like roaches when Baker goes down," Falcone said.

"That can't be helped." Guglielmo looked at Falcone.

"Maybe the chief isn't aware of the full potential of this case."

"We're taking him down on Thursday. Whattaya need, a telegram?"

Weadock followed Guglielmo into the next room. "Captain, Baker's been carrying a gun and sniffing cocaine for eleven years. Why the big rush to grab him now?"

Guglielmo turned to face Weadock. "Why can't you just follow orders like the rest of us?"

"Because this is wrong."

"The Chief knows what he's doing, Charlie." Guglielmo pointed an accusing finger at Weadock again. "Remember, he's a chief, I'm a captain, and you are a sergeant."

"Captain." Weadock grabbed for one last straw. "Can I talk to the chief?"

"No, you can't and I don't want to hear anymore about it."

"I can't believe IAD is buying this bullshit." Falcone began typing again.

"I can." McIntosh spun around in his swivel chair. "Remember Slovak? He worked here for a couple of years before he went to IAD. Well, we're pretty good friends and he told me that IAD has eight investigators on every team and his team handles about twenty cases a year and that's five less than I handle in a year by myself."

"Slovak's an asshole," Falcone said. "Is he really your friend?"

"Ah, they're all assholes over there, but Billy's a nice guy."

"Isn't Slovak the guy who was dumped for the one photo lineup?" Falcone asked.

"Nah that was Zuckerman."

"What's a one photo lineup?" Bishop asked.

"You show one picture to a witness and asked if that's the guy."

"What are we going to do, boss?" Falcone appealed to Weadock as he entered the backroom.

"I don't know." Weadock flopped into his swivel chair and turned it to face the window. "Bergermeister will call me as soon as Valentine gets back to his office. If the DA can't stop it, we'll make the collar on Thursday."

Falcone crossed the room and filled the chair vacated by Guglielmo. "Can you work the Hernandez case with me tomorrow night?"

"I'm over my cap for the month."

"How about Jimmy or Valerie?"

"No, you need to have a boss with you. I'll ask one of the other teams."

Falcone frowned.

"Wait." Weadock stood up and walked the full length of the office and once again stood in Guglielmo's doorway. He waited until the captain looked at him. "I need another sergeant on my team. My detectives need a supervisor with them on all heavy cases. Falcone has to do surveillance on Hernandez tomorrow night in Suffolk County and McIntosh has to follow a cop in the 34th Precinct that could lead to an arrest."

"What the fuck's going on?" Guglielomo said. You're out of the city on one case and out of the borough on the other. The 34th is in Manhattan north."

"We've gotta follow Hernandez to his drug selling location. That happens to be in Suffolk County and O'Rourke works in the 9th but lives in the 34th"

"The chief promised me six more sergeants. When I get 'em, you'll get one."

"I need a sergeant now, Captain. I'm capped out on overtime. How about giving me Casey back?"

"Noooooo, he's the only sergeant on team two with experience. You do whatever you have to do to get the job done. I'll approve the overtime."

"I can't cover two cases at the same time."

"Everybody's got problems, Charlie." Guglielmo widened his eyes. "If you would

close some of your damn cases, you'd have more time to go out with your team." Guglielmo stopped Weadock as he turned to leave. "Did you know we were rated number one again? We are the best FIAU in the City of New York. I might get promoted out of this shit hole yet."

The next night, Weadock handed a precinct roll call to Falcone. "You, Valerie and Sergeant O'Hara will pick up Hernandez at his precinct. Follow him home. If he goes to the bar, you and O'Hara go inside with him. You might have to mush it up with her, for cover."

"Ugh, I'd rather eat lima beans." Falcone spit in the wastebasket.

"C'mon, Alex. You know she likes you. When she found out you needed a supervisor, she volunteered."

"What am I supposed to do while the two love birds are having cocktails?" Bishop sulked.

"You observe," Weadock said.

"He has all the fun and I just observe?"

"You don't think he's going to enjoy himself boozing it up with city money, do you?"

Bishop sat stone faced until Weadock told her she could do the bar scene next time out. She grinned from ear to ear.

"Jimmy, you and I will follow O'Rourke. You'll probably lose him right away. The guy drives like a maniac. Once we put O'Rourke to bed, we'll hook up with Alex in Suffolk.

When Weadock left the room, McIntosh turned to Falcone. "What's he mean I'll lose him right away? I never lost a subject in my life. I used to drive a cab, you know."

"Five bucks says you lose him in the first twenty minutes."

"You're on."

Weadock returned to his office at 10:30 PM and found two notes taped to his telephone. Both were from Theresa. He called her immediately. "Sorry to call so late but I just got to work."

It's okay, Charlie. I had a big fight with my father today and now I can't fall asleep. I keep thinking of what he did to you, to us and I wanted to apologize to you for being such a weakling. I should have had more faith in you. I was dumb and blind and angry about everything back then. How could I have been so stupid? You were the only dependable person in my life and I turned my back to you. I'm a totally lost soul."

"You're not a lost soul, sweetheart. You were just a confused kid, like me."

"You can call me sweetheart after all this?"

"Nothing has changed for me, I still carry your picture in my wallet, the one we took at the beach, remember?"

Calmness came over both of them as he reminded her of the old times they shared. He made her laugh and her laughing made him feel good.

"The beach!" she cheered. "Let's ride the A train to Rockaway Beach like we did when we were kids. We'll go on a Sunday. This Sunday."

About an hour later, McIntosh positioned his car on a dark street near the 34th Precinct. He could see Police Officer O'Rourke's sports car rudely double-parked about a hundred feet in front of him.

Watching the front door of the station house, Weadock sunk down into the car seat. Now he carried Theresa's picture in his shirt pocket and hit it with a pen light. *Am I rushing her? Should I have waited a while longer? Perhaps I should have let her make the first move. But she did, she answered my letters. Several years after I expected her to but…*

"There he is, Sarge!" McIntosh jolted in his seat, knocking Weadock out of his deliberation.

"Where?"

"There. The chubby guy with the green jacket. He's in his car already."

O'Rourke started his car and backed up in one motion. The car shot backwards against the flow of a one-way street and into an intersection. He took the red light on the next corner and vanished in a cloud of smoke.

"I don't believe this fucking guy," McIntosh took a second look at the empty street. "He's a god dammed psycho."

"No problem, Jim." Weadock glanced at the notes in his hand with the aid of his pen light. "The allegation is that he is shaking down drug peddlers near Sixth Street and Avenue B. in the Ninth Precinct. Let's see if he's over there."

"It looked like he was headed for the Bronx, Sarge."

"Let's check the 9th Precinct location first, and then we'll go to the Bronx. If we don't find him, we'll go to Suffolk County and hook up with the rest of the team."

An hour later, when they failed to spot O'Rourke's sports car at either of the two locations, Weadock and McIntosh headed east on the Long Island Expressway.

It was 2:20 AM when McIntosh pulled into the sparsely populated mall parking lot in the Town of Wyandance. He quietly eased his car up next to Bishop's car. Her body was slumped over the steering wheel on folded arms.

Cranking his window down, Weadock listened to Bishop's loud, rhythmic snoring.

"She must have asthma or something," McIntosh said.

Weadock summonsed up his best Bogart impersonation. "In all the gin joints in all the world, she's gotta pick this one to fall asleep in. What's happening sweetheart?"

"Aaaahh!" Bishop snapped to attention in her seat, "You scared the shit out of me, Sarge."

"Sorry, but you're supposed to be watching your partners."

"I'm supposed to be home in bed." She lowered her voice to a little girl whimper. "It's creepy out here."

"What's going on, Valerie?"

She rubbed her eyes with clenched fists. "Well, Hernandez went straight home from the station house. He crossed 34th Street to the

Queens-Midtown Tunnel. Then took the L.I.E. to Exit 47. We lost sight of him a few times but his car was outside his house when we got here. We waited down the road for an hour, when he didn't come out; we came down here for a look. "The love birds went into the bar and left me out here alone."

"You're a cop, ain't ya'?" McIntosh asked.

"Hey," She frowned at McIntosh, "This is one scary place. There are things moving in the bushes over there." She shifted her eyes to the side.

"All right, all right. Weadock urged her to Continue."

"O'Hara and Falcone were inside the bar about fifteen minutes when Hernandez showed up. He went into the bar and came right back out with some guy. Male, white," she looked at her note pad, "curly blond hair, about twenty-five. They got into a black Jeep and drove around behind the building. They stayed back there for about ten minutes, and then came back to the parking lot. They remained in the Jeep for another five minutes, then Hernandez went back in the bar and Curly-locks and left in his Jeep. I walked over to that phone booth," she pointed, "and got the license plate number of the Jeep but I couldn't take any movies because this piece of shit didn't work." She held up the night camera.

"Let me see that." McIntosh reached over Weadock for the night scope, "I've seen this thing in the Army Museum." The camera came apart in his hands as he maneuvered it up to eye level. "This is trench warfare stuff, Sarge. World War One. I'm in the reserves, I know."

"Hernandez is out, Sarge," Bishop said.

They watched as the subject walked to his red Firebird. He left the driver's door open and stretched over the seat to the glove compartment.

McIntosh touched the keys dangling from the ignition, but waited. He knew the sound of the Buick's engine would carry the full length of the quiet parking lot.

Hernandez slammed his car door closed and drove off.

"We'll take him from here," Weadock said. "Listen to the point-to-point radio. When Alex and Scarlet come out of the bar, tell them to wait here until I get back."

Weadock and McIntosh followed the subject home. Thirty minutes later, they returned to the mall parking lot and ended the surveillance. By the time the team got back to the office, it was daybreak.

PART TWO

A VIEW OF THE CITY

THERESA KENNEDY CLOSED THE LEGAL FOLDER IN HER HANDS and settled back against her soft, black leather sofa. *I must be going nuts, My family hates me, I can't concentrate on my work, my apartment looks like shit and I'm addicted to teenage love letters.* She looked around her apartment. Letting her eyes brush over the stacks of legal documents growing like plants against the walls. She reached for the three shoeboxes on the sideboard table but stopped. *And it's not just these letters -- it's him.*

She struggled to her feet and crossed the living room to the terrace door. Nudging it open, she stepped out into a city of blazing lights. Her thoughts floated toward the red, white and blue lights on the Empire State Building. Then shifted to the solitary flame held by the Statue of Liberty in the harbor. *Status,* she could hear her father's voice, *status is everything. He drummed those words into my head until I thought the idea was mine.*

Theresa turned to contemplate an expensive oil painting on her living room wall. *And why did I buy that? I don't even like it. Is this it? Is this the end of my ten year struggle for Status?*

She looked down and her eyes followed a lone emergency vehicle-racing south on the FDR Drive. *Why are all the men in my life so involved with danger? Thank God Daddy didn't force me to become a cop.* She watched the vehicle with the red and yellow flashing lights until it stopped near the Brooklyn Bridge. It continued sending its signal. "Crises, crises, in the night."

The cool night air forced her inside and she reached for her half-empty glass of Cabernet Sauvignon. Theresa noticed that she had absentmindedly put out two glasses for dinner and a sense of loneliness surrounded her again. The empty glass annoyed her and she was sorry that she hadn't been more receptive to Weadock's advances. She knew now, deep down, that she wanted him back in her life but was too afraid to reach out for him. She didn't want to experience that agonizing pain again. She fondled her empty glass and remembered some of the fun times she had with Charlie Weadock. *It seems like the only true happiness I ever had was with him. He always held my hand. He held doors open for me. He cared about me. He was my noble knight. Ah, all that time lost. Well, I can't think about that now. I have to figure a way to get him back? Somehow, someway, I have to do it.*

Her old flame had excited her the other night when they met. The mere touch of his hand had ignited that old blaze of fire in her gut. She knew she wouldn't be able to trust her emotions around him ever again, and somehow she didn't care. She picked up the phone and dialed the 17th Precinct.

"You have reached the 17th Police Precinct," a recorded voice uttered. "If you have a police emergency, please hang up and dial 911. Otherwise this call will be answered in the order it was received."

She slammed the phone into its cradle and locked up her eyes. *You're doing it again,* she thought. *What a coward you are, T.* Then she grinned and popped her eyes open. *Well, at least I called Daddy an asshole and got away with it. That took guts, and writing that letter to Charlie. That took guts. Perhaps I'm not the big scaredy-cat I think I am.* She poured another glass of wine and started reading the last of the shoebox letters.

In the morning, dripping wet, Theresa stepped from the shower and paused in front of the full-length mirror on her bathroom door. She let the towel slide off her body like Gypsy Rose Lee and considered her slender frame. *Not too bad*, she stooped to retrieve the towel, *low mileage, minor damage and a high performance engine.* She moved closer to the glass to survey her fatigued face. Suddenly, the radio alarm clock came into focus and she was late for work again.

A week of restless nights was becoming more and more evident on Theresa Kennedy's face but those signs were invisible to doorman, George Valdez. At fifty-two years of age, Valdez considered himself to be a Latin lover of vintage quality. He had never married but boasted of fathering a kid in every port. He and Theresa Kennedy were about the same weight but she was nine inches taller than him. George got the hots for Theresa the day she moved into the building.

"Miss Kennedy, wait." George waved an attractively wrapped package in the air as he chased after her. Attempting to determine the contents, he shook the box with gentle vigor. He caught up to her at the front entrance. "This came for jou last night, but my cousin Jose, the night man, didn't want to bother you." She examined the box while he examined her body.

When she noticed George's probing eyes, she snapped the gift from his hands. "Thanks a lot, George."

"Jou are a lawyer, jes?" He followed her to the sidewalk.

She surveyed First Avenue for a cab and he surveyed her tight skirt. "I'm late for work, George."

"I know but my nephew got busted for riding in a stolen car with his friends and he didn't do anythin. Anyway, he needs a good lawyer. I thought--"

"Sorry George, but I'm not that kind of lawyer." She waved at a sea of taxicabs. "You need a criminal lawyer."

George began jumping and flapping is arms up and down like a fledgling bird trying to fly. He insanely waded into the snarl of morning traffic. "I'll get you a cab, Miss Kennedy."

Theresa had to laugh at George's bizarre antics.

George turned to face her, but continued his jumping jacks in the street. "Could - jou - rec - o - mend - a - law - yer - for - me?"

A cab screeched behind him and he hopped onto the sidewalk. He took her package back and held it until she slid into the cab. Her skirt rose up and he rolled his eyes across the sky. She laughed again and offered him a dollar bill.

"No, no, no." He objected with his fingers locked on her money.

"Okay, George. I'll ask around for you." She let her head drop back on the seat.

George hesitated to close the cab door so he could get a last ogle at Theresa's legs.

"You are quite a slime ball, Mister." She shifted in the seat, forcing a smile at the driver.

"What was that, lady?" the driver asked.

"Not you," she apologized and gave the address of her job.

The cab lunged forward, crossing five lanes of traffic and causing Theresa to slide across the seat. Horns sounded, tires screeched and the driver lowered his window to yell something in Arabic at another cab driver. He flashed a repentant smile at Theresa her and continued driving.

She pulled Weadock's business card from a small envelope attached to the package and flipped it over. "How about dinner tonight?" was written on the back. The box held a cuddly brown and white teddy bear, eight inches tall with a button nose, two captivating black eyes and a sad but charming expression on its face. The words *I Love You* were printed on the bear's red tee shirt.

It was another tough day at Simon, Simon and Starky, but Theresa plunged into the backlog of bankruptcy cases the instant she sat at her desk. Firing orders at the legal secretaries, sorting briefs and organizing caseloads, she seemed to extract some magical strength from the furry creature perched on her desk. She was lighthearted and zippy and her seldom seen joyful behavior did not go unnoticed by her secretary, Joanne.

"Cute bear." She nodded at the furry creature on Theresa's desk. "What's his name?"

"Charlie."

Joanne raised her eyebrows with a smile.

"Sergeant Charlie Weadock, one of New York's finest. Remind me to call and thank him for the gift."

"Wait a minute." Joanne lowered her head to peer over her glasses. "I want full details."

"It's a long story, Jo-Anne."

"So, we'll take a long lunch."

Joanne had been with the law firm for six years when Theresa came on board last year. They became good friends and spoke on a first name basis when no one else was around them. Joanne dropped some finished reports on

Theresa's desk and yanked her coat from the closet.

"I guess you're not going out for lunch."

Theresa tapped on a pile of papers with her pen. "I have to knock this stuff out today."

"You seem… happier since the bear arrived, but you look so worn out, honey."

Theresa shrugged. "I know."

"Tuna salad on whole wheat and a diet soda?"

"No, Today I feel like a ham and Swiss cheese on rye with Russian dressing and a diet soda."

"Wow. This sounds serious." Joanne paused at the door. "I want all the details and don't forget to call Charlie Bear."

Theresa *did* forget, or resisted until Joanne cued her a few more times. She and Charlie talked for twenty minutes and agreed to meet at the San Goulash Restaurant on Second Avenue.

It was 7:30 p.m. when Theresa peeked through the front window of the secluded Hungarian restaurant. Only the bar was visible from the street. Seven of the ten barstools were empty. A smartly dressed couple sat facing each other at one end, and Charlie Weadock sat alone at the other.

The bartender, a distinguished older gentleman standing behind the bar and Charlie Weadock were engrossed in a three-way conversation. All three men greeted her like the homecoming queen.

Theresa's eyes widened in awe as she ogled the exquisite décor of the bar and restaurant. The bar was twelve feet of Italian white marble set between two fluted oak columns. The couple at the bar retreated to a white leather sofa in a hidden alcove and a young, handsome maitre'd rushed at her from the restaurant.

"May I take your coat, Miss Kennedy?"

Theresa smiled, and the face of an obviously inexperienced youth, flushed red.

The older gentleman pulled out a barstool for her and waited.

"The firm I work for is just around the corner. I've been there for a year, and never knew this place existed.

"This is my friend, Bruno Zyskowski. He's the owner. The charming young man with your coat is his youngest son, Alfonso. And this handsome devil here," Weadock motioned at the bartender, "is Homdia, the best bartender in the City of New York and perhaps the world."

Homdia was neither handsome nor adept. In fact, everything about him was odd and clumsy, but he was a kind and gentle soul and Weadock liked him. Some years earlier, Homdia spilled a pitcher of beer on a group of football players. Weadock stepped between Homdia and the angry men and identified himself. He settled the dispute with an offer of drinks on the house. He and Homdia became instant friends.

About a month later, an unscrupulous building department inspector tried to shake down Bruno. Homdia went to Weadock and Weadock came to the restaurant. He identified himself to the inspector and told him that he had the restaurant under surveillance in order to catch a cop who was getting free drinks. The inspector never returned.

Homdia shook Theresa's hand as if he was jacking up a car but Bruno nudged him aside and cradled her hand as if he held a small bird. He kissed her fingers softly before clicking his heels like a German Corporal.

Theresa knew she was a long way from Morgan's Bar and liked Weadock's friends immediately.

"Homdia," Bruno dipped his head, "a glass of champagne for the lady. Compliments of the house." Bruno excused himself and disappeared into the restaurant.

Every time Bruno passed the bar, he wondered why the young couple was not drinking. What he didn't know was Homdia was topping off their glasses every time they took a sip. Theresa was having fun and laughing about everything. It was almost nine o'clock when Alfonso led them to a corner booth. Theresa felt important. Every waiter in the place knew her name and stopped to check on them. She couldn't believe the attention they were getting. Even the chef, Otto, came out of the kitchen to inquire about the food. "Try this appetizer." He waited for her reaction.

"Scrumptious," she said. "What is it?"

"You don't want to know." Weadock stared at Otto, "It's some kind of chicken, I think."

Dinner was a filet of red snapper in a mouth watering, spicy red sauce with shrimp, clams and mussels. The wine was a smooth Merlot. Otto came to their table several times and sat down with them after the main course. He ordered Puszta, a Hungarian cocktail, for the three of them and began a narration of his escape from Russian-occupied

Hungary but stopped when Bruno urged him to return to the kitchen.

"The next time you come to the restaurant," Otto said, "I will make Kocka. I only make this for Mayor Koch when he comes here but I will make it special for you because you are the woman of Sergeant Weadock and because you are so beautiful."

Theresa was no slouch when it came to alcohol but even she started slurring her words. "You better get me home, Charlie." She pointed her thumbs at herself and laughed.

"Who's going to get me home?" Weadock waved at Bruno for the check. Stooping to kiss her hand again, he bowed at the waist. "You cannot be leaving so soon?"

Weadock waved his hand for the check.

Bruno waved his palms at Weadock. "There is no check for you, my friend."

"There better be a check for me if you want to see me in this joint again."

"This is not a joint, Sergeant." Bruno scratched out a check for twenty dollars, slid it under Weadock's dish then reached for Theresa's hand again.

"Hey, that's enough with the hand." Weadock shooed Bruno away and dropped a hundred-dollar bill on the table.

"That is too big a tip for these guys, Sergeant." Bruno raised his eyebrows. "You're spoiling them."

"They'll know what to do with it." Weadock shook hands with the waiters as if they were good friends. Theresa had kicked off her shoes earlier and just shoved them into her large bag. She went barefoot to the street.

The night air made her woozy. She steadied herself by leaning on Weadock. "I could take a cab, you know."

"I know." He moved closer to her. "You're very beautiful and very independent, but my car is right here." Weadock opened the door with a sweeping dip and assisted her into the car.

"What's Kocka?" She stared at Weadock when he climbed into the car next to her.

He began laughing.

She began laughing too. The fallout from a week of sleepless nights fell upon her like an anvil. "What the hell is Kocka?" she slurred. "I hope it doesn't taste the way it sounds."

"You're going to like it, but right now I'd better get you home."

They didn't speak during the short trip to First Avenue and Fifty-Sixth Street. Weadock parked his car in the bus stop in front of her building and turned to look at her. He thought he might have to carry her upstairs but she slid over to his side of the car and used him as crutch. The light from the lobby fell on her face in perfect harmony. He smiled because he was with her again. He felt that they belonged together. Nothing could change that now. She moved against him with her eyes closed like a little girl falling asleep. He wanted to kiss her sculptured face. "You'll always be beautiful, T." He whispered. "No matter how old you get, you'll --."

"What?"

"We're home." He took her bag.

"We're where?"

"Don't you live here?"

"How did you know where I live?" She opened one eye.

"I'm a cop."

"Isn't everyone?" she stumbled.

"Would you like me to carry you?"

"No but you can carry my books."

"You don't have any books, sweetheart."

She studied his mouth when he talked. She liked the soft sound of the sweetheart remark and felt safe with him.

A middle-aged Hispanic man spotted them and darted for the front door. "Miss

Kennedy." He was surprised to see her in an unprofessional manner. "Are jou alright?"

"I'm fine Jose." She attempted to stand on her own, but couldn't. "This is Sergeant Weadock. He's a policeman; he's here to talk to *jou* about stealing that car." She turned to Weadock. "Now, I'm beginning to talk like him."

"Angel stole the car, Miss Kennedy. My nephew, Angel."

"Okay." She examined his face with her eyes. "I thought you were George."

"George is my cousin, he's the day man."

They stepped into the elevator.

"Do you have to deal with this stuff at *your* apartment house?"

"I don't live in an apartment house."

"George is a slime ball doorman, you know. He's been bugging me to defend his nephew in a criminal case."

The elevator door sprang open on the 16th floor and she pointed in the direction of her apartment door.

"He'd be better off with a legal aid attorney."

"Who?"

"Your friend down stairs.

"Is that right?"

"I'm sure you're a great attorney, T." He noticed her pursed lips, "but these legal aid guys deal with street level crimes every day. I'll advise this George character for you. Would that be okay?"

She paused in the gap of her half opened apartment door and smiled. "Thank you for a wonderful evening, Sergeant. Everybody calls you Sergeant. Don't they?" Weadock took that as a goodnight and turned to leave.

"Wait!" She kicked the door opened wide. "I want you to see my apartment. You have to see the view."

In almost a single move, she slipped out of her tweed business jacket, opened a few buttons on her blouse and yanked the window cord. The terrace curtains flew open exposing a grand view of lower Manhattan. As she reached back to put her hair into a ponytail, her breasts crowded against the few remaining buttons of her blouse.

"That is a magnificent view." Weadock walked pass her to the terrace doors and stopped. "This is nice too."

Theresa moved to the sofa, patting the seat next to her. "Sit here; it's the best seat in the house. Look, you can see the old Con-Edison clock tower from here. You do remember that clock tower, don't you, Charlie?"

"I remember the clock. I didn't own a watch then." He explored her body with his eyes as he approached her. He saw through the facade of small talk she was putting between them and made his move. He brought his lips precariously close to her and whispered in her ear with eagerness. "I remember everything."

She detected his urgency and moved away. She propped her legs up between them as a barrier. "I had a super time tonight, Charlie." Her toes touched him as she twisted into a cat-like stretch. "Your friends were nice to me, the restaurant was wonderful, and the food was wonder--"

He began massaging her feet they way he used to on the beach at Rockaway.

"And my little bear is wonderful. I have to think of a name for him."

He moved his hands from one foot to the other, gently massaging them. His strong, but delicate touch moved to her ankles. "Oohhh," she moaned, "you don't know how good that feels but… She couldn't stop him. Where did you learn to do that?"

"Remember Rockaway Beach?" He shifted his hands from one ankle to the other, kneading the kinks and pains in her feet. "My hands are yours." He manipulated her calves and shins like a professional masseuse. Her eyes widened when he reached her knees. When he passed them, she became anxious but didn't stop him. He moved both hands up one leg to her thigh, squeezing, gently massaging. The aches and pains turned to pleasure. He switched from leg to leg. She didn't want him to stop, but she didn't want him to think she was easy either, and slid off the sofa with the ruse of making some coffee.

"Uh--how do you like your coffee?"

"You're very tense, aren't you?" He followed her into the kitchen, "But you were always a little nervous. I made you nervous, didn't I? I'm sorry about that but I couldn't keep my hands off you then and I'm having a problem with that now. I wanted to be with you all the time. I guess I always wanted too much, too soon."

"It's been a long time, Charlie." She tried to move away, but his hands were on her shoulders, massaging the knots in her neck and shoulders. His hands were warm and gentle. She swung around and collapsed into his arms. Their lips met for what seemed to be the first time, the innocence was still there and they both knew it. Her tongue shot into his mouth and he answered in a burst of passion. His hands moved down her body pulling her close to him. Sliding his fingers under her blouse, around her bare waist, moving and massaging, his hot hands moved up inside her bra. Massaging her breasts with the same gentle touch, her nipples hardened under his fingers.

"Wait!" She broke free and backed away. "Wait." She threw her hands up between them. "I don't know if I'm ready for this, Charlie. This is all happening too fast."

He backed up against the wall and dropped his hands to his sides. "How can it be wrong when it feels so right?"

"It feels right but I'm--I'm tired and you're tired and we drank a lot of wine and my family hates--"

"So that's it." He pushed off the wall and walked to his jacket on the sofa.

"No, that's not it." She followed him.

He walked to the door and turned. "All your problems are somewhere else, sweetheart." He put his hands on her shoulders and gently pulled her against him. Her lips and face were hot and wet. They kissed again. "I love you, T." He looked deeply into her eyes. "I loved you from the first day I saw you."

She put her fingers on his lips. "People change."

"Nothing can ever change that for me. I loved you when you when we first met and I love you now. We can have a good life together, you and me. But it has to be only you and me, and it has to be now. We let other people take all those years from us. We lost all that precious time we could have had together. You can see that and you must come with me now."

She wanted to say more but couldn't find the words.

He backed up to the door and left.

She called after him. "Charlie." She closed her eyes. Charlie, can you ever forgive me?"

THE ARREST

ON JUNE 17, 1992, two and a half weeks before Baker's house party, Weadock sat in an unmarked police car with Captain Guglielmo trying to rationalize the stupidity of arresting Baker. He twisted his body to face his commanding officer who was sitting in the rear seat. "Are you sure you want to do this, Captain?"

Guglielmo answered Weadock's question with a cold stare.

"I mean, this is such a dumb move."

"If you're having a problem following orders, Charlie. I can get someone else to make this collar."

"No sir, it's my case. If it has to be done, I'll do it."

The Morales brothers waited outside Caesar's Driving School in a rented Lincoln Town Car. Jeckle sat behind the wheel toying with the new car's digital gadgetry and Heckle spread his bulk across the back seat. They talked openly, with total disregard for the recording devices taped to their bodies. Anthony scratched at the wire taped to his waist. "This thing is a pain in the ass, man."

Jeckle glanced at his brother in the rear view mirror. "Yeah, it's against our constitutional rights too."

"True, Bro, but it's a payday."

"Did you tell Savage about the extra money?"

"No, did you?"

"Me?" Jeckle spun around in his seat. "You're the one with the big mouth."

"All right, all right." Heckle pointed at his microphone and leaned forward, "Would you fuck her?"

Jeckle glanced around at his brother. "Who? Savage… No way."

Heckle hesitated, "Why not?"

"Cause she's a pig, man. She has a pig's mind and a pig's face."

"I could fuck her without looking at her face."

"Ugh!" Jeckle faked a barf. Then he laughed.

Guglielmo leaned forward in his seat. "Didn't you advise those idiots to be careful about what they say on tape?"

"I did."

"Well?"

Weadock shrugged.

"They use too much profanity and all they talk about is pussy. These tapes will probably be heard by a grand jury."

"Perhaps they'll get a laugh at it, too."

"That's not funny, Charlie and it's all your fault."

"I can't hold their hands every minute, boss." Weadock turned to face forward again. "And without them, there is no case."

"What time does all this bull shit go down?"

"Right now." Weadock glanced at his watch; "We'll know the drugs are in the car when Jeckle starts singing about Gloria."

"Who the fuck is Gloria?" Guglielmo asked.

"Some girl that Jeckle knows," Falcone looked at Guglielmo in his rear view mirror. "He said this girl had her tits removed but he fucked her anyway."

"I hope that disgusting story is not told on the tapes."

"It was Jeckle's idea, Captain. He wanted to say something clever that would alert us and not tip off Baker."

Guglielmo put on his glasses to read his newspaper. "What happens then?"

"When Baker gets into the Town Car, Jeckle will drive north on the FDR. When he starts singing that song from the movie Gloria it means the drugs are in the car."

Guglielmo lowered his newspaper. "Is that song about the girl with the small tits?"

"No, captain," Falcone twisted in his seat to check the surrounding traffic. "The girl didn't have any tits, she had them removed surg--"

"Okay, okay." Guglielmo wiggled his fingers in front of his cringing face.

Weadock held up a local map. "McIntosh, Bishop, O'Hara and Bags are in car number two. They'll get in front of the Town car and stop on that narrow exit ramp at 42nd Street. We'll come up behind Baker and trap him on the ramp. Valentine, Johnson and Bond from the DAs office are in car number three."

"Is that 007?" Guglielmo grinned.

"His first name is Rudyard." Falcone said.

Twenty minutes later, Baker arrived and parked his red Nissan behind the Town car. He walked up to the Town Car and crouched down near Jeckle. The conversation was brief. Heckle leaned forward and handed Baker six hundred dollars in marked money.

Baker stuffed it into his pants pocket.

"Aren't you going to count it?" Heckle asked, "That's a lot of money."

I trust you." Baker said, "Meet me at Second Avenue and Fifth Street in ten minutes. Baker was smiling from ear to ear as he walked back to his Nissan.

Jeckle repeated Baker's instructions into his transmitter.

"Rubber One to Rubber Two." Weadock grinned at the Captain as he spoke into one of the new cellular telephones provided by the DA's office.

"Rubber Two," McIntosh acknowledged.

"Jimmy, you follow the Town Car. I'll stay with the subject. Do you read me?"

"Rubber Two to Rubber One," Jimmy laughed. "Loud and clear, boss."

"Rubber Three, You stay behind me."

"Rubber three, 10-4," Valentine acknowledged.

"Great equipment. Huh?" Weadock held his cell phone up so the captain could see it. "Once these babies are set to a three-way conversation, we can go anywhere in the city and talk without static or interference. They're a lot better than anything the NYPD has."

Jeckle parked the Town car at the corner of Fifth Street and Second Avenue as instructed. Heckle began talking about a very tall girl he met and the problems they had in bed.

McIntosh double-parked on the West side of Second Avenue opposite the Town Car to avoid being blocked in by a sudden swarm of delivery trucks in the area.

"Jimmy."

"Yeah Sarge?"

"The subject left his car in the precinct parking lot. He's now walking west on Fifth Street toward you. He's wearing a white tee-shirt, jeans and red sneakers."

"I've got him, Sarge."

"You stay with him until I catch up with you on the next block."

"10-4."

McIntosh was familiar with this leapfrog type of surveillance. After a few blocks, he would drop back and change positions with Weadock then switch again with someone else.

Baker went directly from his car to the Town Car and climbed into the front seat with Jeckle. He never looked around when he tossed the brown paper bag over his shoulder into Heckle's lap in the back seat. "That's five hundred dollars worth of product, my man." Baker then twisted around and handed Heckle fifty bucks, "I had to give the man a tip. If you don't tip 'em, you can't come back for any more product."

"No problem, bro." Heckle accepted the money.

Jeckle drove south on Second Avenue and made a left turn on Houston Street.

"Stop here," Baker ordered.

Jeckle thought Baker had spotted the tail and preparing to run as he pulled to the curb, but Baker wanted a pint of vodka and ambled into a local liquor store. When Baker entered the store, Jeckle spoke into his transmitter. "We have the product, Sarge. It's in the car. The product is in the car now!" he repeated. "I hope these fucking guys are listening?"

When Baker returned to the car, Jeckle headed east on Houston Street towards the FDR Drive. He was anxious and Baker slowed him down. "Where you going in such a hurry, bro?"

"Uptown, I gotta talk to this chick, Gloria."

"I don't want to go uptown right now," Baker said.

"But this is--"

"Not now, man." Baker raised the open pint of vodka to his lips. "Let's do a few spoons by the river. Then we'll pick up Gloria."

"Sure thing." Jeckle pulled the Town Car to the curb at Mangin Place and Houston. "But I've got to call this bitch and tell her I'll be late. He got out of the car and walked about thirty-five feet to a telephone booth on the corner. He picked up the receiver and faked a phone call. "The product is in the car, Sarge." He repeated. "The product is in the car."

It was obvious to all the investigators that Baker either made the buy in the liquor store or he already had the drugs in his possession when he arrived. Weadock turned in his seat to face Guglielmo. "Is there any possible chance of putting this arrest off a couple of weeks?"

"No."

Weadock brought the cellular telephone to his lips. "This is a better location. I'm going to take him here. You read, Rubber Two?"

"10-4."

"Rubber Three, you read that transmission?"

"Go for it, Sarge"

At 1300 hours, the three police vehicles converged on the Lincoln Town car. Weadock opened Baker's door and leaned into the car. "Don't move, Baker!"

Baker did move and Weadock seized him, twisting his shirt into a knot, he gave it a quick tug to get his attention. "I said don't move, Mister!" Their eyes were inches apart.

"You know the routine, Baker. Just do what you're told and you won't get hurt." Weadock reached into Baker's waistband removed his weapon. Then pulled him out of the car.

"What's this all about?"

"You know who I am." Bending Baker over the frame of the car, Weadock pulled one arm back and snapped a steel bracelet on one wrist. Baker was a powerful individual and resisted but Falcone jumped into the struggle.

The final ratchet click of the handcuffs made Baker stand up straight. "You have the right to remain silent…" Baker wrenched his neck around and gave Weadock a hard look when he heard the Miranda warnings, but Weadock continued telling him about his rights.

Once the situation was stabilized, Weadock moved Baker to the rear of car number one then told McIntosh to handcuff the other prisoners and paraded them past Baker so he could see them in cuffs.

Ten minutes after the initial stop, all evidence of their presence at that location had vanished. This is what Bergermeister wanted. No one except the thirteen participants in the confrontation was aware that it ever happened. All involved went directly to the Lexington Hotel on East 51st Street where they waited for the district attorney to arrive. Bergermeister was ready to cut a deal with Baker if he gives up all the other cops.

Still wearing handcuffs, Baker was isolated in one of the bedrooms. The gravity of the situation hadn't sunk in as he shifted to avoid a beam of light edging around a closed window blind.

Heckle and Jeckle waited in a second bedroom. As soon as their handcuffs were removed, Jeckle telephoned room service and ordered lunch.

Weadock and Falcone entered Baker's room and urged him to cooperate but he just ask for more water.

Falcone opened one of Baker's handcuffs and snapped it shut around a steam pipe so he could sit in a chair.

Weadock asked Falcone to leave the room then sat on the bed facing Baker. "This is the situation, Mister Baker. You are under arrest and charged with a serious felony, but nobody knows that except the people here. I can't save your job, only the Police Commissioner can do that, but I may be able to keep you out of prison. And that depends on what you know and what you're willing to tell the District Attorney when he gets here.

If you agree and tell him about your cocaine business, you could walk out of here a free man. Well, not absolutely free. You'd have to wear a wire for a while and cooperate with this investigation. Down the road you might have to testify against some of your drug buddies."

"Can I have some more water?" Baker rubbed his neck as if he were dying of thirst.

"You might also be able to save your pension. Some of that money belongs to your wife and kids. The PC has allowed some criminal cops who cooperated to remain on the job as Internal Affairs investigators but if he fires you, your pension goes down the toilet."

Baker turned his face to the window and Weadock cracked the door open to summoned Falcone.

Falcone came into the room and got Baker another glass of water. He guzzled it down and asked for more. "That won't help, you know." Falcone said. "You could drink ten gallons of water and the Dole Test results will be the same."

"Can I have some more?" he pleaded.

"Listen, Mister." Weadock rapped his knuckles on a table. "Whatever happens...? It will happen here and now, before anyone finds out that you've been arrested."

Baker turned his attention to Falcone and wiggled his hand around an imaginary glass for more water. Falcone looked at Weadock.

"Once I walk out that door it's over between us. I'm your arresting officer and I'm giving you a chance to save your own ass. You won't be able to approach me on this subject again. Don't tell me tomorrow or an hour from now that you've changed your mind. It'll be too late."

"Can I have some more water?"

"Don't fuck with me, Baker!" Weadock ordered. "You have a family. Think about them."

Baker pointed at the empty water glass on the table and Weadock left the room.

"You're being an asshole, man." Falcone said. "He's the one guy you could've counted on to be straight with you. Prison is a bad place for cops."

"I don't know anything!" Baker implored. "I didn't know what those guys were doing in the car. I'm innocent, completely innocent."

"Last chance." Falcone walked to the door and paused. "I can still bring him back."

"I want to see a PBA Delegate now. You can't hold me here. I didn't do anything. What am I charged with anyway? What did I do?"

Ignoring Baker's plea for more water, Falcone left the room.

Weadock sent McIntosh into the bed room to watch Baker when Falcone came out.

Bergermeister arrived and went directly to Weadock. "Is he going to play ball with us?"

"I made him an offer and he refused."

"Okay, TJ and I will take a whack at him now." They entered the bedroom and McIntosh came out.

"Did he say anything?" Weadock asked.

"He wants more water."

Bill Bergermeister was an ominous figure in his red tie and blue pinstriped suit. He was the image of a tough prosecutor. He picked up a straight-backed chair, reversed it and set it down close to Baker. He glanced at his reflection in a wall mirror and brushed at the gray streaks on the side of his scalp.

"Officer Baker." He focused on the prisoner. "I'm Assistant District Attorney William Bergermeister. This is my associate, Detective Johnson. We're from the Manhattan District Attorney's Office." Bergermeister straddled the chair. "Sergeant Weadock told me that you have refused to cooperate with this investigation and that you prefer to go directly to jail. Is that correct?"

"Can I have some water?"

Bergermeister nodded at TJ and TJ got Baker another glass of water. "You're

facing twelve counts of Criminal Sale of a Controlled Substance. All felonies. You have some options but you really can't afford to be a tough guy."

Baker stood up and tugged at the handcuffs binding him to the pipe.

"If you agree to cooperate, I have the power to make you a deal."

"What kind of deal?"

"You walk out of this hotel room with no criminal charges, but you must wear a wire for me. You'll wear that wire to work, you'll wear it every day, and you'll wear it during the Fourth of July party at your house."

Surprised that Bergermeister knew about the party, Baker dropped his eyelids.

"You will record every conversation, gather evidence and testify at a Grand Jury Hearing when it's over. You do this for me and I will drop all the criminal charges against you."

"What about my job?"

"That's up to the Police Commissioner."

"Can I have some more water now, sir?"

"Do we have a deal?"

"Can I talk to a PBA Delegate?"

"No," not until my case is closed and then you won't want to talk to the PBA and they won't want to talk to you." Bergermeister leaned close to Baker. "Would you like to consult with another attorney? An attorney

not associated with the Police Department, someone you trust. I'll give you time to do that, but that's all."

An hour later, a slim black attorney with iron rimmed glasses and a mismatched suit appeared at the hotel room door.

Bergermeister shook hands with the young attorney and explained the situation. Detective McIntosh led the young attorney to Baker and allowed them to talk in private with the door ajar.

Twenty minutes later, the attorney came out shaking his head. He paused next to Bergermeister. "He's a putz. I told him that he didn't have a chance in hell of beating this wrap. I told him his co-defendants are CI's who have been wired for months but he still thinks he can beat this."

"And what do you think, Counselor?" McIntosh asked.

"He certainly needs an attorney but it won't be me." The attorney shrugged and headed for the exit.

"Anybody get his name?" Weadock looked around the room before nodding at McIntosh.

McIntosh ran after the lawyer and returned quickly with a prodigious grin on his face. You're not going to believe this."

"What?"

"Algonquin J. Calhoun for the defense."

"You're a funny guy, Jimmy," Weadock motioned to see the card.

McIntosh held up the business card so that Weadock could read the name on it.

All attempts to turn Baker resulted in failure. At 6:00 PM Weadock re-cuffed Baker's hands behind his back and he and Falcone marched him across Fifty-First Street to the 17th Precinct Station House.

A young, attractive, female lieutenant on desk duty studied them as them enter the station house. She was hoping they would pass her by and go upstairs but they stopped directly in front of her at the main desk.

Weadock asked the lieutenant if there was a PBA Delegate on duty in the precinct.

She picked up a copy of the roll call with two nervous hands and scanned the names.

Weadock sensed that she was intelligent but too inexperienced be in charge of a police precinct. They had passed each other a few times in the hallway with nothing more than a nod of the head or a short greeting.

She knew his face and his reputation. Turning to face an even younger female officer on telephone switchboard duty, she snapped out an order. "Burns, give sector David a 10-2, forthwith." She leaned forward to confirm that Baker was in handcuffs and get a closer look at Weadock's shield. You're Sergeant Weadock?"

"Charlie Weadock and this is Police Officer Alvin Baker. He's assigned to the 9th Precinct. I'm his arresting officer, shield number 1065, Manhattan South, Field Internal Affairs Unit. The charged is Criminal Sale of a Controlled Substance, Third Degree, 220.39 of the Penal Code. I'd appreciate it if you would note his physical condition and personal property in your log book."

Weadock did the traditional search in the presence of the desk officer and placed Baker's personal property in front of her. Her trembling hands gave away her uneasiness as she wrote in the police blotter. Internal Affairs investigators made most field supervisors fidgety and she was no different.

"Lieutenant," Weadock said as he walked around the brass rail with a forefinger in the air. Stepping up on her platform, he came up behind her and reached over her shoulder to tap on the money. "Is this your money?" he asked Baker.

"Yeah."

"All of it?"

Baker looked at the money. "Yeah."

Weadock pushed five hundred and fifty dollars from Baker's money with his finger. "This money is evidence. Would you be kind enough to note the serial numbers in your entry, lieutenant? Also note that it came out of the prisoner's right front pocket and that the prisoner admitted that it was his money."

"Anything else?"

"I need four blank property vouchers for his guns, the drugs, the buy money and his shield and I.D. card."

"Anything else?"

"Can you send the PBA Delegate upstairs?"

"Sure."

"Thank you, Lieutenant." He grinned; directing Falcone to march the prisoner passed a huddle of stunned cops.

Traffic in the FIAU office got heavier and heavier during the next few hours. Everyone but the Police Commissioner and Chief who ordered Baker's arrest crowded into the small office, including two ranting delegates from the Police Benevolent Association.

"You're not taking the poor guy's car, are you, boss?" One delegate argued.

"The car was used in the commission of a crime and the DA wants it. Take your argument to him."

One delegate leaned into Falcone. "You guys are being a little pricky about this, aren't you?"

Weadock stopped typing to lock eyes with the irate delegate. "You are a police officer, aren't you? Well this guy is a drug dealer in a cop's uniform. He committed twelve felonies and he likes to snort his drugs on a block where children go to school. I'd be surprised if the PBA provides him with any legal representation at all."

Falcone urged the delegate to back off and he backpedaled to the door.

The PBA Delegate took a few steps toward Weadock. "Well, the PBA hasn't denied him an attorney yet. You know, he's not guilty until you prove it in court. Even criminals get that much!"

"You're right, Officer." Weadock stood up. "He is a criminal and he has rights. You can wait outside now." When the delegate left the office, Weadock walked over to a new member of the FIAU who was helping with the arrest paper work. "Brigitte, there's a small address book in Baker's personal property envelope. I want you to make a copy of it, every page. Leave the copy on my desk and put the original back in the property envelope."

CENTRAL BOOKING

AT 11:30 PM THAT NIGHT, WEADOCK AND FALCONE abandoned their unmarked police car in a bus stop and escorted Baker, single file, into the basement of One Police Plaza.

"What a dumb place to put police headquarters." Falcone's voice bounced off the quiet street facades. "I must have come here five hundred times and I've never found a legal parking spot."

The uniformed cop at the entrance booth glanced at them with indifference and continued reading his newspaper. Falcone flashed his Detective's shield at the cop near the entrance door and the threesome ambled through an open portal into the area of Manhattan Central Booking.

Inside, the same cop inserted a flat key into a heavily barred Iron Gate and it swung open on steel rollers. *The job was changing,* Weadock thought, as a young looking officer examined the gold sergeant's shield dangling from his vest pocket. These "tit jobs" as they are known in the trade were usually given to old timers, cops with over twenty years on the force that for one reason or another preferred not to retire.

When the heavy Iron Gate slammed shut behind them, Baker snapped his head at the clamor. He must have come through that gate hundreds of times in his career, but this time, *he* was the prisoner. This time, he would not be leaving when the paper work was done. His eyes searched Weadock's face for a sign of sympathy, but none was there. He wondered why this Sergeant pursued him with such passion. After all they were both cops.

A stout, red-faced sergeant at the arrest-processing desk grinned at Weadock. He was Arthur J. O'Connor, a former police officer in Weadock's last command, the 84th Precinct. Before his promotion to sergeant, O'Connor had spent the first thirty-eight years of his career on foot patrol. He lowered his head to peer over his half moon glasses at the three individuals standing before him. "Waddaya got kid?"

"Is it Sergeant O'Connor?" Weadock asked.

"Aye," O'Connor moved closer to Weadock, "it is." O'Connor moved around the desk to the front. "I was fine in the old neighborhood, had everything under control. Then all of a sudden I'm a boss like you. They must have made a mistake or something, kid."

"There's no mistake, Arty. If anybody in the job deserved the stripes. You do."

"Ah, I'd still be walking my post on Fulton Street if the wife hadn't pushed me to take that promotion exam."

Weadock touched Falcone's arm. "This is my partner, Detective Falcone."

They shook hands and Falcone excused himself when he spotted an old friend of his in the computer room.

"And this is Alvin Baker. He was a police officer for eleven years, now he's under arrest. The charge is 220.39 of the Penal Code. Think you could expedite his papers for me?"

Sergeant O'Connor looked Baker over and shook his head with a frown. "This fellow was a cop and he was selling drugs?"

Weadock nodded

"Well, fuck 'em then. He's no better than the other shit over there." The old sergeant dipped his head at the other prisoners in the main holding pen.

"He wasn't always a drug dealer, Arty. He was a cop first.

"Okay, kid. If that's the way you want it. That's the way you'll get it. I'll keep him away from the general population. Sweeney," he yelled. "Officer Sweeney!"

A tall, slim Irish cop with gray hair and a red face ambled into the room.

Sweeney looked older than O'Connor and limped across the room on a bad leg. He rolled up his magazine, stuffed it in his rear pocket and stood before O'Connor with a sign of irritation on his face.

"Sweeney, my friend. I want you to walk this prisoner through the system. Do it yourself. Do it as fast as possible and when you're finished put him in a solo cell and bring me his papers. Now, do you understand my instructions, Officer Sweeney?"

Sweeney snapped to attention like a British Private and threw one finger over his upper lip in a Nazi like gesture. "I understand completely, my Sergeant." Sweeney lead Baker away.

"I'd like to get that kind of reaction from my troops."

"Sweeney and I came on the job together in 51."

"I thought you retired."

"I did but the wife drove me nuts. Two months at home and I pulled my papers to come back to the job. Then, somehow I got promoted and my friend, Chief Mulvey, got me transferred here. Its okay, I couldn't catch anyone with these legs anymore. So, what's the story on this cop?"

"He went bad five or six years ago, but he's been careful. He's only here now because a CI snitched on him."

"Well, I'll tell you, kid. You're not going to make night court. The prints will take three or four hours, so you might as well go home. Pick up the papers in Room 241 after eight o'clock and draw your affidavit."

Weadock waved at the old timer on his way out. O'Connor was one of the few cops whose respect Weadock wanted.

Outside, Weadock navigated around the patches of broken sidewalk to reach the public telephone on the corner. He dialed Theresa's number and got an answering machine. He started to leave a message when she picked up the phone.

"Hi," she yawned.

"I didn't mean to wake you but I had to talk to you."

"Charlie? Where are you?"

"Downtown, I was busy arresting a police officer today and I just finished the paperwork."

"What time is it?"

"About midnight, I've have to be back here by six and-"

"Why don't you come up here?"

"It's pretty late."

"It's okay. I need to talk to you, too."

"Are you hungry? I can bring you something."

She laughed.

"Pizza, Chinese, bagels, take your choice."

"Nothing for me," she laughed again, "but I want you to come here."

"I'll be there in twenty minutes."

Unlike Charlie Weadock, who often worked in the dead of night, Theresa Kennedy was a nine-to-five girl and had second thoughts about this late meeting when she looked at the alarm clock. She ran her fingers through her hair and headed for the bathroom.

Falcone thought about Baker as he waited in the dark car for his boss. The red and green traffic lights at the intersection reflected its colors on his face. Kneading the back of his neck with one hand, he turned to look at the Central Booking facility. When Weadock got in the car, Falcone turned his head to look at his boss. "He screwed up his whole life, didn't he?"

"Baker? He was already screwed up. If we hadn't stopped him, he would have really hurt someone sooner or later. Maybe he'll change now."

Falcone drove uptown toward the FIAU office, but he couldn't shake the image of the broken cop he left back at Central Booking. He shook his head. "How does a cop become a drug addict?"

"I don't know. Why are so many cops alcoholics?"

"Are we alcoholics?"

"Perhaps. We drink a lot."

"I don't consider myself an alcoholic."

"Most alcoholics don't. Look, Baker worked in a toilet bowl for ten years. He was supposed to arrest those drug dealers on his post not make friends with them. It's not our concern how he became a drug addict or a pusher. Our job is to take him down and we did it. Maybe he had too much on his plate. Who knows? The job pushes us all to our limit."

Falcone drove off the FDR and stopped at a red light. "Do you take it home with you?"

"I guess but I don't have anybody at home."

"I do. I tell Lori everything. I'd go nuts if I didn't tell someone about the scary stuff."

"If we were mechanics, we wouldn't be having this conversation, but we're not mechanics. We're cops. Cops who are fed a daily diet of human tragedy. Most of us leave after twenty years."

"I never spent a day on patrol."

"You're lucky; I don't think I could go back to patrol. Those guys really earn their paychecks. They're the real cops. Everything else is just back up. We're back up."

They stopped at an all night bagel shop on 57th Street. Falcone bought a huge salami hero and a quart of beer for the ride home. Weadock bought two bagels with lox and a smear of cream cheese.

"You're not going home, are you?"

"No."

You didn't sell the house in Brooklyn, did you?" Falcone drove Weadock to First Avenue and 56th Street.

Weadock opened the car door to get out. "I'm visiting a friend."

"You want me to pick you up here in the morning?"

"Thanks but I'll walk to the office tomorrow. Hey, it's already tomorrow."

When Falcone left, Weadock entered the lobby of the upscale apartment house. The night porter stood up at the front desk and waited for Weadock to reach him.

"Hi, I'm visiting a friend, Theresa Kennedy."

The porter introduced himself as Juan Valdez. He said that Miss Kennedy called down and told him that a police sergeant was coming to see her. Juan led Weadock to the elevator.

Weadock saw the light from Theresa's apartment as he stepped off the elevator.

She swung the door open wide when they made eye contact. "You look beat."

He handed her the bag of bagels. "You look great."

When he was inside, she closed the door and leaned against it.

"I shouldn't have called you so late. I was going to call you again when I realized what time it was but…"

"I know something about cop's hours. I come from a whole family of policemen."

He shrugged.

She sniffed at the bag. "Mmmmmm." Rolling her eyes, she headed for the kitchen. "What would you like with this?"

He looked into the bedroom through the open door and smiled. "What are my options?"

She thought about the question for a while before poking her head out of the kitchen. "Scotch, vodka, beer, or coffee."

"Vodka."

"Stoley?"

"Fine." He flopped on the sofa.

She brought him a glass of ice and a bottle of vodka. He poured an inch, stirred it with his finger and swallowed it down.

Theresa was eager about going to Rockaway Beach on Sunday and kept talking from the kitchen. She brewed a fresh pot of coffee and set a fancy tray, but stayed a little too long in the kitchen. Weadock was sound asleep and still in a sitting position.

"I don't believe this," Theresa whispered as she put the tray down on a table. She draped a blanket over him and stepped back to study his face. *How can anyone sleep like that?*

The chime on Weadock's alarm watch awakened her, but she pretended to be asleep. She heard him fumbling around in the dark until he found the bathroom light switch. She closed her eyes when he came into her bedroom and stood over her in silence. She could feel his eyes moving over her body. He reached down and moved her blanket up to cover her bare shoulders.

When he pulled the apartment door closed, she felt a kind of emptiness in her stomach. Theresa wanted to run after him, but it was too late. She was sorry that they didn't make love and went to the terrace window. She saw him outside the building and watched him as he crossed First Avenue and walk South. He paused for a moment on the corner of 54th Street and looked up at her window. She wanted to wave to him, but he turned the corner and was gone. Somehow she could feel his power from that long distance and she knew that he cared for her more than anyone else in her world.

THE ARRAIGNMENT

WEADOCK AND FALCONE WAVED THEIR BADGES at a token booth clerk and made their way down to the IRT Subway platform. At 6:45 AM a southbound number 4 train, bulging with passengers, labored into the Lexington Avenue Station. The doors sprang open and hordes of straphangers poured out onto the platform. Hundreds of people without faces squeezed onto two crowded escalators that took them to the surface. The two cops stepped into an almost empty subway car and the doors closed with a familiar chime.

Suddenly, they knew why the car was so empty. A bag lady, cowering in a corner seat with a death grip on several shopping bags, studied the trapped passengers with equal suspicion. Patches of aged dirt crusted on her hands and face and her foul, choking stench drifted at the other straphangers and the two cops. All were anxious to change cars as the train slowly jerked its way south. The old woman managed a frightened smile as the two cops raced out of the car at the next station. They muscled their way into another crowded car and continued downtown to City Hall.

Charlie Weadock waited in front of the Criminal Court Building at 100 Centre Street while Falcone bought a newspaper and Lotto ticket. As they climbed the seven concrete steps leading to the main vestibule, Weadock pointed to a damaged façade. "See that?"

Falcone looked at the crumbling wall of syrupy green bricks.

"If you're going to paint bricks, at least paint 'em red."

Anticipating one of Weadock's usual lectures about the city's neglected historic buildings or mankind's failure to mature, Falcone merely nodded in empty anticipation.

They made their way through the weather-beaten main portal to a second floor complaint room. The grand corridor was pigeonholed with rooms. The small cubicle size rooms ran the whole length of inner wall and were crowded with baby-faced attorneys, aging typists and disheveled cops. The attorneys listen intently to the cop's telling their stories and transform the cop's street lingo into legal poetry for typist who completed the affidavits.

All the cops waiting for available attorneys were crammed into a big room at one end of the corridor. Some cops were watching the morning soaps on a twenty-four-seven television set; others were sleeping on chairs and tables or just talking with other cops they knew. A stack of cardboard boxes with faded labels prevented most of the daylight from entering the room and a crudely hand printed sign hanging over the door read *POLICE OFFICERS ONLY.*

"Kramer?" Weadock draped his shield from his jacket pocket poked his head into the first room. "ADA Kramer?"

"Last stall." A somewhat juvenile looking attorney jabbed his pen to the right.

Weadock turned to his partner. "The wheels of justice seem to be in motion here."

A small man with a fatigued face stood in the doorway of the last cubical watching Weadock approach. He turned his face to cover a chesty cough then spoke with a raspy voice. "Sergeant Weadock, I presume?"

Weadock nodded.

Jerking his head at Weadock's shield, Kramer yawned. "There aren't many sergeants making arrests these days." Kramer gave his head a wakeup massaged. "Bill called me at home last night and asked me to take good care of you. By the way, how is Bill?"

"He's all right, but you look like shit, Counselor."

"It goes with the job. Well, give me the details."

Kramer was a rising star in the DAs office. That is, if he didn't snap under the heavy workload dumped on intake supervisors at criminal court. Weadock liked him immediately, but couldn't help feeling sorry for the guy. No one knew better than Weadock how the system uses you and unloads you when you're spent. Kramer listened carefully as Weadock narrated the details of the Baker case. The lean attorney went on to ask a lot of spontaneous questions. Kramer scratched the wording for the complaint affidavit at computer speed, looking up only once to ask Weadock if the prisoner gave him any trouble. Then handed his clipboard to a typist and she cranked out the affidavits.

Downstairs, the two investigators navigated their way through a bustling hallway to reach Part 1A. The courtroom was packed with perpetrators, friends, relatives, attorneys, victims and cops. They elbowed their way to a half-empty "Police & Attorney Only" bench up front.

"Take seats!" An overweight court officer ordered. "Put all newspapers away. No talking!"

People responded by crowding six or seven on a bench built for five. The whispering continued.

"All rise!" The Court Officer bellowed. "Manhattan Criminal Court, Arraignment Part 1A is now in session. The Honorable William J. Artz presiding. Take seats!"

A short, Asian man in black robes made his way to the judge's chair and disappeared behind the huge desk. All of a sudden his head popped up and he surveyed the courtroom in stern silence. He seemed irritated with the large crowd but manufactured a three-dollar smile for the audience. Proving to be an experienced jurist, he dispensed justice swiftly and by the book. With the aid of his fierce looking bridge man, the judge handed out fines with rapid-fire consistency.

The bridge man read dozens of names out loud; tossing affidavit after affidavit into a basket as the defendants answered their names. The potpourri of charges ran the gamut from disorderly conduct and theft of services, to smoking on the subway. The perpetrators came forward to form two ranks in front of the judge. They stood wall to wall across the front of the courtroom.

The bridge man stepped up next to the judge and the judge leaned forward. "Is there anyone pleading not guilty?"

One man raised his hand. He was told to step aside.

"The rest of you plead guilty to a violation of section 240.01 of the Penal Code." Moving his gaze from side to side, the judge eyed them with an angry grin. "The fine is fifteen dollars or five days in jail. Does anyone want the five days?

No response.

"Okay." He leaned back. "Pay the cashier."

When the group moved off, the bridge man asked the lone cast-off if he needed time to get an attorney. The man changed his plea to guilty and followed the others.

Uniformed cops and PBA delegates in the courtroom took notice when the bridge man signaled the sergeant in plain clothes to bring his prisoner out. Weadock opened a heavy oak door on the side of the court room and vanished down a hallway that led to the Department of Corrections holding pens.

Weadock brought his prisoner into the courtroom and they sat on a side bench. Ana Buonacore, one of the PBA's most intelligent attorneys came forward and asked the judge is she could confer with her client, Alvin Baker. He agreed and Weadock moved back to his seat next to Falcone.

Falcone nudged Weadock and dipped his head at the well dressed woman sitting in third row. "Baker's old lady."

Weadock exchanged glances with Melissa Baker. She was an attractive woman who showed no signs of weakness. Somehow Weadock knew that she didn't blame him for this. "She looks like she's dressed for high tea.

"Not a bad looking broad," Falcone whispered. "I'm surprised she didn't bring the kids."

"She will. This is only the arraignment."

ADA Kramer walked into the courtroom and the case was called immediately. The bridge man read the charges aloud and everyone involved approached the bench.

"Can we have less people up here?" Judge Artz waved at the PBA delegates like a group of annoying flies and the bridge man backed them to their seats. The judge turned to Kramer. "You first, Mr. Kramer."

"Thank you, your Honor. The defendant is a suspended New York City police officer. I will ask a grand jury to indict him on twelve counts of Criminal Sale of a Controlled Substance. However, for the purpose of this arraignment, he is charged with one count - 220.39 of the Penal Code."

The judge's eyes floated from Kramer to Buonacore and she instinctively began.

"Good morning, your Honor. Ana Buonacore, Law Offices of Curshack, Curshack and Simms, 555 Broadway, New York City. I represent the defendant for arraignment purposes only."

"Good morning, Ms. Buonacore."

"Your Honor, the defendant has been a New York City Police Officer for eleven years and has no prior criminal record. He resides in Staten Island with his wife and two children. He's a homeowner and has roots in the community. I enter a plea of not guilty to all charges at this time and respectfully request that he be released in his own recognizance pending trial."

"Any objections, Mister Kramer?"

"No, your Honor."

"The defendant is released of his own recognizance. Return date is July 20th, pending any indictment."

A DAY AT THE BEACH

WHEN THERESA KENNEDY AWAKENED EARLY SUNDAY morning, the remnants of a marvelous dream were still in her head. The fine points were gone, but somehow she knew it was a wonderful dream about her and Charlie. Today, she expected everyone in the world to be wearing a holiday face. Today was her day. Today she would end any and all methodical routines in her life. She unfolded the exercise skier that stood idle in the closet for a year and worked up a thirty-minute sweat before heading to the shower.

Theresa paused in front of her large mirror to examine the fit of her new swimsuit. She was pleased with the image in the glass. "How old are you, anyway?" She walked away but backed up to see herself again. "Not bad for an old woman." Moving from room to room, Theresa continued talking to herself in childlike fashion, as if some imaginary friend was there with her. "Do you think he truly loves you?"

She removed an aging breakfast drink from her refrigerator and sniffed it and chucked it down the drain. "Of course he does. You know it and I know it." She walked to the terrace door and opened it wide. Looking out at the city that never sleeps, she thought about Christmas morning and Ebenezer Scrooge and began laughing uncontrollably. Yelling to the wind, she threw up her arms. "I don't deserve to be so happy."

An hour later, Weadock entered Theresa's apartment house and asked the man at the security desk in the lobby to ring Miss Kennedy's room and inform her that Mr. Weadock was here.

"She's coming down, sir." The little man leaned over the desk to get a good look at Weadock. He fumbled putting the telephone back in its cradle. "Jou must be the cop, huh?"

"You must be George."

"That's right, I'm George." He took a defensive stance. "George Valdez, I am the head doorman here. Miss Kennedy told me what jou said about legal aid attorneys and I told my cousin, Miguel. Jou know, the one who is still in jail."

"That's good advice."

"What?"

"It didn't cost him any money, did it?"

"No but he's still in jail, man."

"Does he have a record?"

"Of course."

"Chances are he'd still be in jail if he had an expensive attorney. Tell him to stick with the legal aid lawyers. They're in the courts every day and they know the judges."

"He wants to get out, man."

Weadock came closer to George, as if he wanted to transfer some secret message. "Tell Miguel that he could have paid thousands of dollars to a big shot lawyer and he'd still be in jail. This way he gets to stay there for free and doesn't have to pay those high priced legal fees. He's saving lots of money because the odds are he'd be in there anyway."

George grinned. "You're right, man."

Weadock's thoughts drifted from courthouse politics to how to apologize for falling asleep on Theresa's sofa the other night but his mind cleared when the elevator doors opened unexpectedly and Theresa stepped out.

Two women, talking nonsense, stopped chattering and fixed their envious eyes on the woman from the 16th floor.

George's lower lip dropped.

Theresa wore a white wrap around blouse faded blue shorts and white sneakers. Her hair, except for a few loose strands dangling in front of her face, was tied in a ponytail.

He could sense the urgency in her manner as she sauntered towards him.

"Good morning, sergeant."

"You look great, Counselor."

"Good morning, George."

George still had his mouth open. "Ah, good morning, Miss Kennedy."

Theresa bent over to adjust her socks and George's mouth opened again. Theresa had a small waist, rounded hips and long, contoured legs. Weadock wanted to say "Tennis anyone?" but waited silently while she maneuvered her shopping bag size backpack to her other shoulder. She slipped her weak hand under his arm and hit him with a smile of confidence. "I'm ready, Charlie."

The lack of traffic was notable and pleasant as they walked toward the subway station at Third Avenue and Fifty-Third Street. Theresa got a lusty look from two passersby and wondered about her outfit. "Am I dressed okay, Charlie?"

He took her bag from her shoulder and pulled her close with his other hand. "You look wonderful."

Theresa began firing miscellaneous questions at him to ease her nervousness. "What happened to us, Charlie?"

"I don't know." He lifted his face toward the sun. "When you didn't answer my letters, I thought it was over for us. So I ran away. I ran as far from New York as I could get. But it didn't help. I began writing to you from boot camp. Every now and then, when I was feeling low, I'd write another letter. You never answered them but none of the letters ever came back."

"I know, I'm sorry about that."

"It's okay. Everything's okay now. When my hitch ended in '83, I came home. The old neighborhood had changed a lot in four years. Many of the old tenements were gone. The kids I grew up with were all gone. My family had moved to Brooklyn. My Dad encouraged me to take the police test."

They walked a half block before Theresa broke the silence. "I waited a long time for you to call or write, but nothing came." She looked at him. "I cried a lot, too, but someone told me you had a new girlfriend and I…"

"I wonder who that someone was."

"Then I got wrapped up in school work and time just slipped away. When I came back to New York, a new high school had been built where your house once stood. The old gang said you joined the Air Force to see the world."

At the subway entrance, Weadock undid his tie and spread his shirt collar. A combination of cool air and dried urine rushed up to meet them as they descended. She tightened her grip as they navigated past the sleeping bodies of a growing number of underground residents.

He bought ten tokens at the change booth and they rode a noisy, two hundred-foot escalator, into the underbelly of the earth. Eight stories down, they stepped into a deep subterranean chamber. The subway platform, almost empty, had a tomb-like atmosphere. Their voices echoed softly off tunnel walls.

Twenty minutes later, an eight-car southbound E train roared into the station pushing a gust of cool air in front of it.

Inside the train, a homeless man stretched himself across three seats and snored in a loud, semi-comatose condition. Several pair of wool pants partially covered the ugly wounds on his two stumps and a pair of badly cracked shoes capped his sock-less feet. Oblivious to his location in the subway or the galaxy, the man winked at Theresa. Then he turned peacefully in his tightly wrapped cocoon of grease-stained clothing and went to sleep.

A huge black man sitting opposite them had the crazed look of a wild animal on his face. He had a death grip on the two broken and frayed cardboard boxes between his legs. They obviously contained all his worldly possessions. The handles were reinforced many times with cord and tape.

"Wonder what's in the boxes," Weadock whispered.

Theresa nudged her date to be quiet and the black man smiled, revealing a single gold front tooth.

"He shouldn't be flashing that tooth down here."

"Charlie!" Theresa nudged him again and he laughed.

She laughed back.

He slipped his hand into hers and they changed trains at Times square, crossing the platform to catch a southbound A Train. It was a new train with more light and less aroma.

Five minutes later, Theresa yanked her New York Ranger's sweatshirt out of the sack and covered her legs. "Why was that man smiling at me?"

He was just happy to be out. Don't let it bother you."

"Happy to be out of what?" Theresa tilted her head like a puzzled puppy.

"Look around you," he whispered. "See anyone else smiling?"

She let her eyes peek at the train's passengers without turning her head. "Oh shit!" She flashed an apologetic smile for the profanity. "I didn't go to mass this morning. Did you?"

"Uh… I forgot… I mean… actually I haven't been to church since I made my confirmation."

"You've been a bad boy, Charlie Weadock."

"No, I've been a good boy, Theresa. But I'm not twelve years old anymore. I'm more aware of the world around me now."

He caught her off guard and she was unsure how to respond. So she didn't. She hadn't realized how complicated and intense the man sitting next to her had become. She wasn't super religious, but she was brought up to be a good Catholic and made all her required appearances at church. She still had the fear of God in her and sensed, as she watched him scan the strangers in the subway car, that he had no storybook fears. She wondered what he was looking for as his gaze moved from face to face. She feared that he might have changed too much since they were kids, but then she wasn't the same either. She hoped that the simple, shy, little boy she fell in love with so many years ago was still inside Charlie Weadock. She resisted the temptation to ask any more dumb questions but had to ask one. "You ever get married?"

He chuckled.

"What?"

"You know I could never do that."

They changed trains again at the Euclid Avenue and boarded the S train to Rockaway. "How's your family?" she asked.

"My father died about five years ago. He was fifty-nine years old."

"I'm sorry, he was a nice man."

"Yeah, he worked two jobs for as long as I can remember. Always trying to give his family that little something extra that he never had. He was a simple man and the glue that held our family together. He was my friend."

Theresa responded to his distress by rubbing the back of his neck and shoulders.

"My brother Arthur's dead, too. Drank himself to death. What about you?"

The subway train clamored out of the dark tunnel and climbed an elevated track like a slow rollercoaster approaching its summit. It leveled off and started across the water. Bright sunlight flooded the car with warm rays and passengers put their newspapers and books away to absorb the sights.

"My parents still live on 17th Street with my grandfather. I tried to get them to move, but my dad is a bullheaded Irishman. I guess you already know that. My brothers all became cops."

"I'm sorry about Tom. I didn't want to be the one to-"

"It wasn't your fault. Michael told me."

The train rumbled across Beach Channel Inlet Bridge into Far Rockaway and came to a halt. "Michael's a smart kid."

Suddenly the train lunged forward, switching from the new track to the old Rockaway line. Shrieking its steel wheels along an old elevated track that resembled a Roman aqueduct, it headed toward the end of the line.

A swarm of beach dwellers rushed from the train toward the beaches. Theresa and Charlie turned and strolled west, through the old section. This was their private route to the beach. They passed a number of familiar buildings that were still standing. Some of the huge single-family homes and bungalow complexes built before World War II were still occupied. Others were vacant lots. The two "birthday cake" hotels on the corner of 116th Street were still standing. Deserted and boarded up, but still in place. Weadock talked about the fluted columns and ornate moldings like a seasoned carpenter. When they reached the Ocean Promenade, they turned east and walked along the boardwalk. There were hundreds of brand new benches anchored to the old thirty-foot wide boardwalk.

"These are new," she said.

"They're nice." Weadock looked at the Manhattan skyline off in the distance. "But they're in the wrong place. Only a few of these are ever used. They should have put these at the city bus stops so the old timers could rest easy while waiting for a bus."

She looked at the thousands of unoccupied benches. All were facing the ocean, and all empty, but one. A lone resident from one of the nearby old age homes sat motionless, staring out to sea. "You're right, it's a waste."

Theresa glanced at a vacant lot where one of her favorite majestic homes once stood. She tugged at his arm and they walked past an abandoned amusement park. It was ragged and deserted. "It's not the same. Is it?"

He nodded in agreement and they ambled through the shade of a boardwalk underpass to the beach and continued, arm in arm, along water's edge.

Scavenging for their next meal, a flock of fearless sea gulls staked a claim near the incoming tide and refused to give any ground as Theresa and Charlie approached. The birds fought fearlessly for scraps. Picking away at washed up shells, the rugged gulls honked aggressively at the passing couple.

Theresa picked a spot, spread a thin blanket on the sand and fell on it. Pushing out the corners, she strategically weighed the blanket down with her sneakers and bag. She patted the blanket next to her. "C'mon, sit for a while."

Weadock stripped to his swimsuit and dropped on the blanket. He was no weight lifter but he was lean and strong. He covered the remaining edge with his shoes and took a sly peep at her legs. "Well?"

"What?"

"What's to eat?"

"Oh." She grinned and dumped the remaining contents of her tote bag on the blanket. A small portable radio, two towels, two apples, Oreo cookies, a bottle of baby oil, sunglasses and a wallet. She wiggled out of her blouse and shorts. Fidgeting with the radio, she propped herself up on her elbows. "What do you like?"

"Pavarotti."

"Really?" She raised her eyebrows.

Weadock turned his gaze to the ocean and pointed. "See those jetties?"

"Uh huh." She looked at the lopsided poles running down the sloping beach into the rough sea. They disappeared under the water, only to reappear further out as a group of wooden pylons strapped together with cable.

"Don't ever swim near them. There's a very strong undertow there. It pulls you down and you become fish food."

Theresa had no intention of going in the water, but studied the dark ocean-soaked jetties as Weadock talked. Green slime, algae and broken seashells covered the slick planks. The dark jetties vanished under each incoming wave and reappeared as they ebbed out to sea again. Bursts of foam hit the beach with steady, unbinding thrusts. Each wave caressing the shore with a watery kiss and receding.

Raising one hand to shield her eyes from the sun, Theresa gazed at the Manhattan skyscrapers off in the distance. "We've come a long way, Charlie Brown."

Yes, my love, he thought as he poked at a broken seashell with a stick. *A very long way.*

Theresa spread some baby oil on her arms and legs. "If memory serves me right, you burn easily, Sergeant." She turned on her knees to rub the clear liquid on his back and shoulders.

The oil felt good, but her hands felt better.

She rubbed the remaining oil on her face and flipped over on her tummy.

Mesmerized by the breakers hitting the beach, Weadock recalled the nights his father took him and his brother's to fish for striped bass on a beach much like the one he was on right now. They also sat on a blanket and waited for the sun to disappear. Charlie's father liked to fish at night. He would attach a live eel to each hook and cast the lines into the rough surf. Brass tubes buried in the sand held each of his three long fishing poles at attention and warning bells attached to each line would alert him of a strike. His father would settle on the blanket and tell fish stories to his sons. Charlie didn't like fishing, but he idolized his father. The old man was able to pull the answers to his son's perplexing questions out of thin air. He had few things of material value but shared everything he had with his family. He knew the value and wonders of life and never asked for more.

Charlie wanted his father to be proud of him and hoped, one day, to do something for him as payback, but that day never came. Arthur J. Weadock Sr. died at an early age.

Charlie picked up Theresa's portable radio and examined it. "My dad used to bring me to the beach to fish at night. He had this neat little radio that looked like a small suitcase. He always gave it to me to carry. He said it was my responsibility."

"You miss your father, don't you?" She watched his blue-green eyes focus on a far off ship.

"Yeah, I do and I missed you too. More than you'll ever know."

She didn't answer.

Reaching to drop her sunglasses into the tote bag, she touched his body with hers and their eyes met.

"I love you,T."

"I know." She couldn't turn away. "I've always known."

His open declaration of love urged her to slam on the brakes, but her emotions wouldn't allow it. She moved closer to him. "I was the insecure one, wasn't I? She twisted until her back was to him. "How did I ever survive without you?"

"Now who's getting burned?" He poured an ounce of baby oil into a cupped hand and gently brushed it on her milky back.

"Oooohh." She moved her hair away from her neck.

Using both hands, he massaged her back with light pressure, applying just enough force to her achy muscles. Her low cut swimsuit provided easy access to her spine.

He began at the shoulders and worked down to her hips. Then up again to her neck. Most of her tension seemed to be knotted there. She moaned with pleasure every time his hands moved. Every muscle and fiber seemed to need his therapy.

"Guess you don't have a regular masseuse."

"I do now," she sighed.

He moved his fingers up the back of her skull, through her hair, and down the sides, soothing and caressing the pressure points near her ears and eyes. "Where did you learn to do this, Charlie?"

"I just made it up," he continued. "It just feels right."

"Oooohhh, it does, it does," she moaned. "You could make big money with those hands."

With a fresh supply of baby oil cupped in one hand, he applied it one finger at a time to the calves of her legs.

"Oooohhh," she moaned.

He reached her ankles and feet, compressing them to some indistinguishable point between pain and pleasure. Then he moved to her calves. When she thought it couldn't get any better, it did. His hands inched upward slowly. Using both hands to massage each leg, he alternated from one thigh to the other. His fingers slid under her shorts to her buttocks. She was totally out of control now and didn't give a damn who was watching. She didn't want him to stop.

"Am I doing this right?" he asked.

Theresa responded like a starved boa constrictor, wrapping herself around him. She buried her face against his body, avoiding eye contact, touching, and probing until her lips found his mouth. Her tongue snaked into it, searching, pulsating. He sensed her seriousness and responded. He held her tightly in his arms. They exchanged long wet kisses. She knew this was no passing fascination. She dropped her head on his chest with a sigh.

Thirty minutes later, they rushed out of a Rockaway Beach Car service limo into Weadock's Park Slope house. He led her to the bathroom and went for towels. When he came back, she was in the shower. Her discarded swimsuit lay in a trail to the open bathroom door.

Inside, hot misty air steamed the mirrors and hit him full in the face as he tried to see her.

"Towels are on the sink," he called into the gray vapor and retreated quickly to the kitchen for a look in the refrigerator. A half-gallon of burgundy wine, five bottles of Beck's Dark, and an assortment of cheeses. "Ah -- we have dinner."

When he returned to the bathroom, Theresa was standing in the doorway wearing a towel. "I left the water running for you."

He hesitated a long time then moved around her and into the running shower.

Theresa leaned back against the door watching him. She wanted him to take her, but somehow she knew it was her move. He waited at the shower for her to leave. When she didn't, he stripped, revealing all his charms to her. He heard the bathroom door close and stepped into the shower, rinsing the sand from his body. Suddenly, she was in the shower with him. The soap moved from his body to hers. Her eyes riveted on his. The intensity of her desire overwhelmed her and she moved against him. When their bodies touched it was magical. Her lips moving, seeking, she was compelled to touch him. Her soapy hands moved over his body. He wanted to look at her body, but he couldn't break the spell. Water was everywhere. Her lips moved over him and his hands touched her in places he had not touched before. His lips seeking, probing, devouring her. Her mouth came up and found his lips. They embraced. He pinned her against the shower wall and she responded. Her feet left the ground and she straddled him with powerful legs. They completely ignored the water bouncing off their bodies and flooding the bathroom floor. His body was erect with power. He probed at her until he found an entrance. She was boiling hot and needed the cool water on her body to delay explosion. She moved her knees higher and he pushed harder, deeper and faster. Their bodies locked in electrified lust. Just before she reached her point of detonation, he filled her to her deepest point. Her scream was a combination of pain and pleasure and he exploded with endless pleasure. Keeping her locked in his embrace, he slowly lowered her legs and they both sank to the shower floor, kissing again and again. When their breathing slowed, they washed each other slowly. Wrapped in dry towels, he led her up the stairs to the bedroom where they made love again. Naked and nestled in warm sheets, they stayed riveted to each other until the light of day disappeared.

CHOLLO'S ARREST

IN THE MORNING, Charlie and Theresa drove across the Manhattan Bridge into the Chinatown area of Manhattan. Then turned north and headed up town passing most of the fleabag hotels on the Bowery. As they pass the Terminal Hotel, She was daydreaming about their possible future and he was thinking of Happy Hansen. Theresa snuggled against Charlie and felt warm and safe; she wanted him to stay with her. When the car stopped in front of her apartment house, she began a giraffe like nibbling at his ear in an attempt to prolong the best time of her life and it took them almost twenty minutes to finally detach from each other. A light misty rain began to fall. It obscured the car windows and gave them some privacy. "God, you have great lips," he said. "I guess I'm going to have to marry you now."

"You don't have to—"

"Yes I do. I want to be with you until the end of my life."

She kissed him one more time and ran for the building.

In the FIAU office, Detective Woody heard the front door open and close. He popped his head out of the computer room to see Charlie Weadock sign his name in the command logbook. "The DA wants you to call him right away, Sarge."

Sergeant Bobby Gill echoed the message as Weadock passed him in the next room. "Call the DA, Charlie."

"Bergermeister's looking for you," McIntosh repeated as he entered the rear office.

Falcone came into the back room a step behind Weadock. "Bergermeister--"

"He knows, he knows," McIntosh said.

Waiting for Bergermeister to answer his phone, Weadock balanced his telephone receiver between his ear and his shoulder and shuffled through the in-basket on his desk with both hands.

"The Colon interview was for shit," Bergermeister said. "Nothing went our way. Valentine and Johnson also visited Colon's wife. They told her my deal and she went to the prison the next day. I thought she might push his buttons and get him to testify against Ramon for an early release, but nothing has happened."

After a short silence, he continued. "Ramon is coming up squeaky clean on everything. Even his telephone records, the Tolls and Ludds are clean. We went back three years on his telephone records. Not a single phone call to or from Lopez. So we have nothing, zilch, and a goose egg and... Not a shred of real evidence to connect Ramon to Lopez, or to any of the homicides. Now would be a good time to start hawking him."

"Okay, maybe I can push a button on Lopez."

"Watch your ass with that guy, Charlie. Lopez is bad news."

"What else can I do?"

"I don't know. If we don't come up with something soon, I'll have to drop the investigation."

"Maybe the magpies are lying," Weadock suggested.

"You think?"

"No, but it is a possibility."

"Shit! I didn't consider that."

"Do you know Lieutenant Kennedy?"

"Midtown North Squad Commander?"

"Yeah."

"I've met him."

"He's been pressuring my boss for the name of our subject."

"Why?"

"He doesn't have any leads either, but he knows we have a suspect in the Cruz murder and all the plumbing victims were killed the same way."

"He's getting a little out of line but you can't blame him for trying."

"It's the Bureau; they're pushing him for results."

"Oh, one other thing. Sally Ginsberg, an assistant counsel with the Mollen Commission, will call you. I told her about the Baker Case and she wants to use it in her presentation."

"I don't want to talk to her right now."

"She can subpoena you."

"Okay."

"She's a straight shooter, Charlie, and I owe her one. Talk to her for me."

"I can't do that without the PC's approval."

"Can you arrest Urena without the PC's approval?"

"Sure."

"Then, do it. Same charge as Baker. After he's in the system, I'll indict him as a co-defendant."

"Okay."

Weadock picked up the phone to call Theresa, but Guglielmo came into the room and he put the phone down.

"How's my best team?" Guglielmo began laughing. When no one responded to his question, he continued laughing.

"C'mon, Charlie. You know you're my number one guy." The Captain flopped in an empty chair near Weadock.

"Bergermeister called. He said I was going to be subpoenaed to testify at the Mollen Commission."

Guglielmo's three-dollar laugh vanished. "Why, you?"

"They're going to put the Baker Case on TV"

"Holy shit, why? Ahh… What are you going to' tell them?" Guglielmo manufactured a totally blameless expression. His eyes raced around the room from face to face.

"I'll just tell 'em the truth, Captain."

"The truth about what?"

"They wanna know why we stopped fishing after hooking Baker. When the fishing was good."

"I knew this was going to' happen. I ask the chief not to do it. What are you going to' say?"

"I'll be sworn to tell the truth. I'll tell them what you told me. The Chief said Baker was too dangerous to be left on the street."

"Yeah, yeah, that's good."

"I hope he backs you up, boss."

Guglielmo waited silently for clarification.

"Well," Weadock waved his hand to include the rest of the team as witnesses. "We don't talk to the Chief directly. We get our orders from you."

"Well, I only relay the… They don't want to talk to me, do they?"

"Nobody mentioned your name yet."

"Does the Chief know about this?"

Weadock shrugged. "Bergermeister wants us to arrest Chollo today as a co-conspirator."

"So do it." Guglielmo slipped two new cases into Weadock's in-basket and left the room.

"You want the collar, Alex?"

"Sure."

"We'll do it tomorrow." Weadock examined the two new cases. He kept the one on the sale of phony police badges and tossed the other into Falcone's basket. "Look at that when you have some time."

"When am I going to have some time to do these?" Falcone patted the dozen other folders on his desk.

"C'mon, Alex. Those cases are a piece of cake for a top-notch detective like you.

And you," Weadock turned to look at Bishop. "You type a 49 to Management Information Systems Division. I want a list of all the

Miguels in the Department. Civilian *and* sworn members and I want it yesterday."

Turning his chair, Weadock picked up the telephone and dialed Theresa's telephone number. "C'mon! C'mon!" He waved at his team's reflection in the window. "Get your asses into gear."

"Not you, sweetheart," Weadock whispered into the phone. "I was talking to the troops."

"Oh, I keep thinking about yesterday. I can't get any work done."

"I know a nice Italian restaurant-"

"No, no, no, no. I'm cooking for us tonight."

"You can cook?"

"Of course I can cook, Sergeant. Seven o'clock, my place."

Later that day, Theresa Kennedy dumped two Chicken-Licking' Gourmet take-out dinners into a pan, shoved it into a warm oven, and uncorked a bottle of red wine. At about 6:50 PM she put the heat to a small electric steam table to warm the quart of brown rice she picked up at the Chinese take-out store and lit the solo candle in the center of the table. It all looked perfect as she leaned against the refrigerator. *What am I doing? He was right; I can't cook to save my ass.* She became mesmerized by the flickering candle on the table and recalled some of her agonizing memories of the Kennedy house. How her mother suffered every time her father failed to come home on time. Elizabeth Kennedy always seemed to know the exact number of years, months and days her husband had to go for retirement. She knew it better than him. Most cops, if they lasted twenty years would retire but not Joe Kennedy. He stayed for thirty and would have stayed a lot longer if his son hadn't been busted. Every time the radio or TV flashed the story of a fallen cop, she ran for the rosary beads.

Theresa was well acquainted with the problems of having a cop in the house and swore it would never happen to her. When the doorbell rang, she ran for the door. "I lied," She tugged on his tie to pull him close, "I can't cook."

"It's okay, sweetheart, everything is okay."

"I love the way you say that. She kissed him hard. "How did you get pass security?"

"They all know me now."

Her eyes focused on the single long stemmed rose in his hand. "Is that for me?"

"I passed this flower shop on my way here." He lifted the rose with two hands and sniffed its bouquet. "And this flower lured me into the shop. I had to buy it for you."

She moved against him like a missing puzzle piece.

"I could get used to this," He said.

"Why don't you? Why don't you move in with me?"

His eyes followed her as she walked to the table. She had a great body. Everything was perfect.

"You want to, don't you?"

"I do, but…"

"But what?" She frowned.

"Don't you think we ought to get married first?"

"First, we eat dinner." Theresa was quiet during dinner. She kept thinking about his proposal. Charlie did most of the talking; she just listened and watched his mouth. He knew a lot of interesting things. She knew their conversation would never be dull or boring. He seemed to get angry when he talked about the job. He talked about the Ramon case but she was in another world wondering if their children would have his cleft chin. *He has nice lips,* she thought, *a great body and most of all; he's a good listener.* Theresa avoided people who tried to overpower her in conversation. Charlie gave her space and time to respond to him. They had a lot in common.

"I want you to live with me now!" she blurted out.

Weadock stopped in the middle of a sentence and stared at her. He was intrigued by her demand. "It's what I want too but it's not going to… Sit too well with your family."

"You're my family now, mister."

"Excellent dinner, sweetheart. What's for dessert?"

She stood up and let her dress slide off her body.

At ten o'clock the next morning, Weadock and Falcone entered the La Bamba Restaurant and sat at an empty table. Actually all the tables were empty. One customer wearing a badly stained sweatshirt sat at the counter stuffing his face with rice and beans. He kept his head down and his eyes turned up. Chollo approached the two cops with suspicion. "You guys wanna eat?"

"Ormelio Urena?" Weadock asked.

Chollo began tapping a pencil into the order pad in his hand as he looked around for a possible escape route. His first tendency was to run like hell, but resigned when Weadock pulled out his shield. The word was out that Baker was busted and these cops knew his name.

"They call you Chollo, right?" Weadock nudged a chair away from the table with his foot. "I'm Sergeant Weadock. This is my partner, Detective Falcone. "Sit down and talk to us about Alvin Baker."

"I don't know anything about Baker, Sergeant." Chollo began to walk away but stopped and dropped into a chair when Weadock wrapped on the table with his knuckles.

"Tell us what you do know about Baker."

"I don't know nothin about him. He had this post a lot. He came inside, sometimes to eat, sometimes just to sit."

"You know he's not a cop anymore?"

"I heard."

"That's right, I arrested him and the two Spanish brothers last week for selling cocaine. Detective Falcone, here," Weadock nodded at his partner, "came here to arrest you on the same charges, but the District Attorney told us we could offer you a deal."

Chollo began searching his pockets for something. When he couldn't find what he was looking for, he focused on Weadock and waited.

"He wants us to let you walk away. You walk away clean, no arrest, no jail time, and no nothing. He said if Chollo tells everything he knows about Baker and Baker's buddies and agrees to testify against them for us, he goes free."

"But I don't know anything, sergeant." He squirmed in his seat. "And I didn't do anything either."

"You have a family, don't you?"

"I don't know nothin."

"Look, I told you the deal. You're not going get another chance like this, my friend."

Chollo looked around silently.

"Is there anyone here who can take care of the restaurant?"

"No, I'm alone."

Weadock stood up. He walked to the kitchen door and looked into an empty room. "Once he puts the cuffs on you, it's over."

Chollo pleaded with his eyes.

Weadock's eyes roamed slowly around the restaurant and stopped on Falcone. "Cuff him and read him his rights."

"Hey!" Chollo protested.

"Put your hands on the counter and keep them there," Falcone ordered.

"Hey, I had nothing to do with that Baker shit."

"Toss him."

"But I didn't do anything. You're busting me for nothing?"

"Did you ever buy drugs at the Bodega on East 4th Street?"

Chollo looked toward the ceiling and took a deep breath. "Can I make a phone call? I am entitled to a phone call, right?"

"You can call from the station house."

Watching Chollo and Falcone, Weadock maneuvered himself to the pay phone in the rear of the restaurant and dialed 911. He told the dispatcher his name and that he had a person under arrest. He requested a patrol sergeant. The customer at the counter left without a word or paying his bill when he heard the ratchet clicks of Falcone's handcuffs.

Chollo sat in the SIU room with a distant stare on his face. Every once in a while he would tug on his handcuffs and take a peek out the window.

"Take a good look," Falcone suggested. "You're going to be inside for a long time. On the other hand, you could still do what the sergeant asked and maybe." Falcone was an expert interrogator. If anyone could turn Chollo, it would be him, but the prisoner was well seasoned and knew his constitutional rights better than most cops.

Chollo finally made his telephone call and waited patiently for his attorney to arrive.

SURVEILLANCE ON RAMON

WITH A TELEPHONE RECEIVER CRADLED between his ear and shoulder and Ramon's case folder open in his lap, Weadock meticulously flipped through the investigative pages as he waited for a Department psychiatrist to answer his call. When a firm female voice answered, he switched the receiver to his other ear and began doodling a drawing of Ramon on the case folder jacket.

"Doctor Austin."

"Is this the Health Services Division?"

"Yes, it is."

"Sergeant Weadock, Manhattan South, FIAU."

"Yes, Sergeant?"

"I have a complicated investigation, Doc. You may be able to help me with some of it?" He waited for her response.

"I'm listening, Sergeant."

"I'm investigating a police officer who I believe has committed murder."

"I'm still listening."

"Perhaps several murders."

"What is the officer's name, sergeant?"

"I can't give you that information over the phone, but I will meet with you."

"Is there any hard evidence?"

"If I had any hard evidence, I wouldn't be talking to you. I'd be talking to the District Attorney."

"What particulars can you give me over the telephone right now?"

In substance, he told her about Heckle's allegation and the nine or so identical homicides.

"This Police Officer works in Manhattan?"

"Yes, in a precinct close to your office."

"Where is your office located, sergeant?"

51st Street between Third and Lex,"

"I live in that area, I can stop by your office after lunch. Say around two o'clock. Is that all right, Sergeant Weadock?"

"Today?"

"Of course, today."

"Thank you, Doctor Austin." Weadock lowered the phone and turned a poker face at his team. "Anybody here think Ramon is the wrong guy?"

No one responded.

"The guy has an impeccable record." Weadock widened his palms. "He goes straight home every day after work."

"That's just it, Sarge," McIntosh stopped typing. "He's not a normal cop. Most cops stop for a drink or two to unwind."

"Okay, he's a little strange but he has no CCRB complaints, he's never been accused of using excessive force. He's not a rum head or a pothead and he gets great performance evaluations."

"There you go" Falcone leaned forward, "I never got great evaluations."

"Sure you did," Weadock frowned, "How do you think you went from third grade to second grade? In two years?"

Falcone shrugged, looked down then up again. "So why is this guy clubbing perfect strangers to death?"

Weadock turned his swivel chair to face the street. "Perhaps he just enjoys killing people."

Bishop turned her chair to face Weadock and raised her hand like a school kid. "Are these people he's killing just targets."

Sarge." McIntosh scratched his head. "Dead people don't file complaints. Remember the Boston Strangler? He went home to his wife and kids after killing people; nobody knew he was doing it."

He had a split personality. One side didn't know what the other side was doing. He didn't know he was doing it."

Falcone looked at McIntosh, "You think this guy's psychotic?"

Weadock walked to the window and looked down at a crowd mismatched commuters on East 51st Street. "No, this guy's aware of everything he does. I can feel it. I agree with Alex. He's a very lucky and a very clever assassin. He has his own set of rules. One, he never takes anything from the scene in case he is ever stopped and searched. Two he never leaves anything at the scene that he brought with him. Except perhaps the weapon and the gloves, or he dumps them at the first opportunity. The pipe with no fingerprints and rubber surgical gloves are impossible to trace back to him and he does it alone."

Falcone turned his chair to face Valerie Bishop. "I read something about a rapist who hacked off a woman's arms, legs and head before he fucked her." Falcone moved closer to Valerie and stuck his Tung out sideways "Scary shit, huh?"

"Alex!" Bishop crunched her eyelids together and widened her lips.

"It's true and he only did black girls with big butts."

Valerie swiped at Falcone with her two-foot ruler. Then ran after him when he darted out of the room.

Massaging his frontal lobes, Weadock closed his eyes and ran the details of the case through his head in fast forward. "We should be on this guy every day." He pushed a stack of bullshit cases aside.

"Why don't you talk to Guglielmo, boss? Ask him to leave us alone for a while?"

"Sure." Weadock shot a glance at McIntosh. "He wants us to finish the year with sixty completed SIU cases. He says the chief won't get his raise if we don't do it."

"What does our case load have to do with the Chief's salary?"

"Somehow he gets a cut."

Bishop and Falcone were laughing loudly as they came back into the SIU room.

"Guys, guys." Weadock focused on McIntosh, "Ramon is on his regular day off for the next two days. You and Valerie take him tomorrow. Alex and I will cover him on Friday. I don't care if you lose him but I'll be pissed if he spots you."

That afternoon, Weadock wanted to review several case folders for closing but found himself doodling cartoon sketches of each of the murder scenes at his desk. A habit that helped him put the loose ends of investigations into perspective. With his back to the door and his feet on the windowsill he sketched the newsstand scene.

Police Department Psychiatrist, Sally Austin, noted Weadock's artwork as she came up behind him. "Am I disturbing you, Sergeant?"

He saw her reflection in the window. The clock on the wall behind her also came into view. It was two o'clock exactly. Spinning his swivel chair around, he locked eyes with the psychiatrist. "Doctor Austin, I presume?"

The Department's head shrink was younger and shorter than he pictured her. She had a Prince Valiant hairdo and bulging fish eyes. He guessed she was a spinster in her mid-forties.

"I'm the chief of Psychological Services for the New York City Police Department."

"Right." Weadock raised his lower lip with an impressive nod. "I didn't know that. I just asked for a shrink and… I mean…"

"Well, this is your lucky day, Sergeant. You got the chief shrink."

"Would you like a cup of coffee, Doc?"

"Yes, I would love a cup of black coffee with sweet and low."

Weadock nodded at Falcone.

"Yuck," Falcone stretched his lips. "How about a nice glazed doughnut with that, Doc?"

"No, thank you. Just the coffee."

"You sure?" Falcone paused in the doorway. "We get a lot of free doughnuts around here. The attorneys bring 'em like Greeks bearing--"

Weadock waved Falcone away.

Doctor Austin listened carefully as Weadock narrated the details of the Plumbing murders. She wanted to take notes, but became entranced by Weadock's analysis of the crimes. She tapped her pen against her blank notepad with periodic rhythm as Weadock unraveled the Ramon mystery. His one or two glimpses inside the case folder told her he was extremely familiar with every detail of the case.

"This is an active investigation, Doc. everything is confidential."

"Of course, I wouldn't have it any other way."

"So, what do you think?"

"I have to check his psychological profile, but he sounds ominous."

"Can you help me?"

"You seem to have some reservations, Sergeant. You hint that he's the beast, but you think he could be innocent, too."

"You can analyze me some other time, Doc. Perhaps after we have a few martinis but right now I need input on this guy."

Doctor Austin let her eyes float around the SIU room. "I'll do what I can."

"Look, I don't know if this guy's a Jeckle and Hyde, but now you know what I know and you have access to those private Department files that I can't get, maybe there's something there already." He raised his eyebrows. "Something I don't know. Something only you can discover. If this guy is the killer, you have to help me bring him down."

"I'll do what I can, Sergeant." She stood up.

"Thanks for coming here, Doc." Weadock stood, rubbed his hands together and extended one hand to the doctor. "I'll keep you up to date."

She considered the cartoon sketches on Weadock's desk, shook his hand, and smiled. She didn't expect his hand to be so warm.

Two days later, Weadock and Falcone sat in Falcone's vintage station wagon opposite Ramon's apartment house. They had a clear view of Ramon's residence and car. They sat like mannequins in a store window trying to look inconspicuous in the predominantly Hispanic neighborhood.

"Surveillance is a bitch. Isn't it?"

"Yeah." Falcone dozed off.

Weadock squinted in the light of a nearby streetlamp to read McIntosh's work sheet from the previous tour… *The subject officer exited his residence at approximately 7:10 AM. He was alone and went directly to his auto, a 1984 Black Cadillac Eldorado, license #ITT927/ NY. He idled the engine for fifteen minutes before driving south on Lexington Avenue to 65th Street, west on 65th Street through Central Park to 11th Avenue then south to 30th Street. He parked on a hydrant between 10th and 11th Avenues, remaining in his auto for forty-five minutes (07:30-08:15).*

At 8:15 he proceeded north on 10th Avenue. The auto was lost in heavy traffic. Investigating officers went directly to the subject's residence and discovered that the auto had returned. At 10:30 the subject failed to reappear and the surveillance was terminated.

"Hello," Weadock said as his 35mm camera focused on Ramon's face. He snapped two quick photos as Ramon checked the mailbox in his vestibule. Weadock nudged Falcone back to reality.

Falcone awakened himself with a loud, jamming snort. "What! What!"

"Shh." Weadock tilted his head at the subject walking to his Cadillac. When Ramon started his engine, Falcone turned his key in the ignition. A much-neglected muffler was now hindering the tail. "I think you need a new muffler, Alex."

"My wife says that all the time, Sarge."

They stayed back as far as they could without losing sight of the Cadillac. Ramon took the exact same route that McIntosh described in his report. A radiant morning sun reflected off the glass storefronts along Central Park West and temporarily blinded Falcone. He lost sight of the Caddy.

"Take 65th Street West." Weadock looked at McIntosh's report again. "Then go south on 11th Avenue to 30th Street." Weadock wasn't surprised to find Ramon's car parked in the same spot described by McIntosh the day before. Ramon drove away at 8:15 AM and headed slowly up 10th Avenue, they followed.

Ramon drove past the boarded up newsstand without a pause and continued uptown to his residence. An hour later, the two investigators ended the surveillance and headed back to the barn.

Weadock wanted to put a team on Ramon over the weekend but Guglielmo wouldn't approve the overtime.

McIntosh and Bishop continued the surveillance on Monday. When they came back to the office Bishop said the tail had been blown. "Jimmy got too close," Valerie rolled her eyes, "but someone else was closer."

Weadock waited for her to continue but McIntosh answered.

"The brains were there. We lost him in the uptown traffic so we went to the 30th Street location. He was there again, in the same spot, but the brains were there too. They were up his ass the whole time."

"You sure it was them?"

"Yeah, I ran the plate through Motor Transport. Midtown South Squad."

"Great, fucking great. Did they talk to him?"

"No, but they left with him and they were really close."

"Okay," Weadock gave the time out hand signal. "I want you to keep this to yourselves." He pointed his pen at Bishop. "Don't tell anyone you saw the squad there and don't put it on paper."

McIntosh glanced at Bishop, "Okay Sarge but there's one other thing."

Weadock waited.

"I think the squad made us, too."

From that day on Ramon began taking the Lexington Avenue Subway to and from work and traveling just about everywhere by subway and bus. He became extremely difficult to follow and the case against him slowed to a crawl. He was never again spotted at the 30th Street location and Guglielmo was pushing Weadock to close the Roman case. Weadock closed dozens of other cases attempting to pacify Guglielmo but it didn't help. The Captain was insistent and threatened to remove Weadock as the team leader of the SIU Team if he did not comply. Weadock countered that District Attorney Burgermeister has ordered the investigation to continue and the captain backed off.

Charlie Weadock reviewed Ramon's case folder every day. Over and over, he thumbed through the pages of work sheets and DD5's looking for something, anything to keep the case open. He was sketching a picture of the crime scene on his large desk calendar when an idea suddenly jumped off the page at him. He looked at all the empty chairs in his office but his team members were all on assignments. He reread the DD'5 report concerning Detective Marini's interview of Professor Ferreri, picked up the weighty case folder and headed for the captain's office.

The captain was on the telephone when Weadock entered his office and turned his back to Weadock.

Weadock waited thirty seconds then dropped the case folder on the captain's desk with a thud.

"I'm on the telephone, Charlie."

"Velez is stalking one of the witnesses, Captain."

Guglielmo ended his telephone conversation and turned his chair, "How do you know that, Charlie?"

"This witness," Weadock tapped on the case folder with a finger, "lives at 428 West 30th Street. Our boy, Velez, has been sitting in his car in front of this professor's house every day."

"So?" Guglielmo widened his eyes. "Is it illegal to park there?"

"Actually it is but I'm not interested in that." Weadock pulled the DD5 from the folder and turned it around so the Captain could read it. "Detective Marini at the Midtown South Squad interviewed this guy on April 13th, 1992." He pushed the report at Guglielmo. "Professor Joseph Ferreri stated that he saw the victim, Harry Hansen, alive at the newsstand at 11:30 PM. That was about an hour before Raffes was murdered."

Guglielmo stretched and yawned with apathy. "You think there's a relationship here?"

"If you close this case now and the professor gets whacked you, me and the Chief will be in some deep shit."

"Okay, I'll report this to Chief Whalen tomorrow. You can keep your case open until then."

Weadock returned to the SIU room to find Falcone at his desk. He tossed the DD5 report on Falcone's desk. "Get this guy on the phone."

"What guy?" A perplexed Falcone asked.

"The guy on that DD5, Professor Joseph Ferreri. We have to talk to him fast. If he isn't home, call his school."

An hour later, Falcone was showing his badge to a uniform guard at John Jay College of Criminal Justice. He and Weadock made their way to a laboratory on the sixth floor. The professor was alone and preoccupied with an experiment.

Weadock held up his shield.

"NYPD," Weadock said. "I'm Sergeant Weadock, and this is my partner, Detective Falcone. We need to talk to you about Tommy Raffes and Harry Hansen."

Reaching to extinguish the flame on a gas burner, Ferreri knocked over a jar of brown liquid and the two investigators took a step backward.

"It's only coffee," Ferreri blotted up the spill with a sponge. "I like to make my own coffee. Would you gentlemen care for a cup?"

"No thanks, Professor. Weadock removed a piece of paper from his jacket and the Professor walked away to his desk and sat down.

"I told your Detective Marini everything. I don't know what else to say."

"Did Mr. Hansen, Happy, give you anything that night?" Weadock watched the professor's face for a reaction and got one.

"Ah…" Ferreri shook his head in thought, "Just… Just a newspaper."

"Just a newspaper?" Weadock glanced at Falcone, "was anything in that newspaper?"

"No," Ferreri glanced at Falcone. "Is there something missing?"

"A package perhaps?" Falcone asked.

"I don't understand." The professor began moving items from one side of his desk to the other and back again. "What? ah... Is something really missing from the newsstand? Why are you asking me these questions now?"

The two sleuths looked at each other and began firing questions at the unstrung professor. Ferreri floundered under the verbal assault, but failed to make any admissions.

"Look, professor." Weadock sniffed at the jar that spilled on the lab table. "It appears that the people who killed Tommy Raffes at the newsstand and Harry Hansen at his apartment were searching for something. Something that wasn't found at the newsstand or later that night at Happy's apartment. The killer ransacked the newsstand and the apartment but didn't take money or valuables that were in plain view."

"We think it might be drugs," Falcone said. "And they're still looking for it."

"Drugs?" The professor bit his lip. "You think I sell drugs?"

"No, we don't think you sell drugs, professor." Weadock smiled in an attempt to calm him down. "Do you still have that newspaper?"

"No," Ferreri walked to the window and looked down at the street below. "I bought a newspaper and that's all I bought. Are you going to arrest me for buying a newspaper?"

"Of course not," Weadock joined Ferreri at the window. "Did you happen to notice a black Cadillac limousine in the area when you bought this newspaper?"

"Detective Marini asked me that same question when I met him at the precinct."

"Well?"

"No. I did not notice any particular car that night."

"Okay, professor." Weadock held out a business card. "I was a student of yours once. Biology 101. You gave me a C."

"That's unfortunate, Sergeant." The professor responded with his eyes glued to Weadock's business card, "but a C is a pretty good grade in my class. I'm sure you deserved it."

The professor walked over to a large glass display cabinet on the wall and surveyed the contents. His eyes moved slowly over the geological objects and back to Weadock. He lifted the business card to look at it again. "Sergeant Weadock, am I in any danger?"

"I hope not, Professor."

"This is very scary stuff, murders, black limousines, etc. I'm not usually confronted by these things."

"This is a scary town, professor," Falcone said as he moved to the classroom door. "You have to be alert and protect yourself at all times."

Weadock pointed to his card in the professor's hand. "You can call me at anytime." Their eyes met. "Everything you say to me is totally confidential… Everything. Please call me if you remember anything else about that night or something new develops."

The professor moved to the window again and looked at the fast moving tide on the Hudson River. He summoned up his memories of that night and considered surrendering the money or at least telling Weadock about it but he waited too long. When he turned around, the two policemen were gone.

THE MOLLEN COMMISSION

CHARLIE WEADOCK PARKED HIS CAR on a cobblestone street in lower Manhattan and crossed the roadway to number Seventeen Battery Place. The 15-story brick structure, dwarfed by the nearby World Trade Center's twin towers, still had a commanding view of the New York City harbor. The weather-beaten building with a history of shady deals had endured a century and a half of salt water assaults. It was the perfect location, Weadock thought, for an inquiry into municipal corruption.

He identified himself to an elderly female at a third floor reception window and a seasoned detective immediately responded through a self-locking security door. He introduced himself as Matt Ward.

"Sarah is finishing another interview right now so she asked me to take you up to the penthouse."

Riding up in the elevator, Ward told Weadock that he was a retired NYPD Detective hired by the Mollen Commission for one year to do investigations. Ward dropped a few names, inquiring about mutual friends in the NYPD but the names didn't ring any bells for Weadock.

The penthouse conference room was a perfect observation deck for watching ships entering and leaving New York Harbor. Weadock walked to a westerly window and saw a partially visible Statue of Liberty through a skeleton of metal framework. She was undergoing her first face-lift in two hundred years.

"Magnificent, isn't it?" A short, blond woman dressed in a tailored business suit came up next to him and extended her hand. "You're Sergeant Weadock, right?"

Weadock turned to face her, noticing several paintings strung around the room between the windows. "Yes. You're Sarah Ginsberg?"

She followed his gaze at the paintings and turned to stand shoulder to shoulder with him. "Dead Sea captains who worked for the Cunard Line." She walked to a conference table in the center of the room. Weadock let his eyes roam from painting to painting. Brass plates affixed to the bottom of each painting had a name and year. The dates were decades apart but the paintings could have all been done by the same artist.

"Nice table." Weadock ran the palm of his hand over the smooth oak surface. "It must be as old as this building." He tapped it with a knuckle and scanned the room. "This table is a solid piece of wood. It must have been brought in during the initial construction."

She adjusted herself in one of the huge conference chairs like a child in an adult's seat and stretched her neck to examine the tabletop. "That is an interesting thought." Plopping her shapeless satchel flat on the table, she pulled out some papers and scanned them with tired eyes. "Bill told me about the Alvin Baker investigation. He said a lot of bad cops got away when IAD closed the case on you."

"I'm not sure who gave the order to close that case." Weadock nodded and waited for her to continue.

"The Commission is going public next week and I want to use the Baker Case as an example of IAD's ineptness. What do you think about that?"

"I guess it's good to shake the tree once in a while but it's going to upset a lot of cops and their families."

"Does that bother you?"

"No, but I have to tell my boss what this meeting is about and he's going to tell his boss, the chief of Manhattan South Area, and he is going to tell the chief at IAD and the Commissioner."

"I have no problem with that."

Weadock shrugged.

"Right now, I need to ask you a few basic questions."

"Shoot."

"Tell me about this Luau party. How many other bad cops could have been there?"

"I don't know how bad they are, but I figure five to fifteen of his police buddies, perhaps twenty."

"Wow," she said. "Who gave you the order to make the arrest?"

"My commanding officer, Captain Ralph Guglielmo."

She noted the name on her pad. "Do you think he acted on his own initiative?"

"He never has before."

"You think he was acting on orders from above?"

"Absolutely."

"Who, exactly?"

"Well, he reports directly to the Manhattan South Borough commander."

"Who would that be?"

"Assistant Chief Patrick Whalen."

"Do you think the Chief acted on orders from above him?"

"I suppose."

She didn't like that answer and waited.

"I guess you will have to ask him that question."

"What does that mean?"

Weadock stretched his body. "I take orders directly from a captain, who takes orders from a two star chief, who takes his orders from the Police Commissioner, who takes orders from the Mayor. It's interesting that a lowly sergeant like me is permitted to conduct highly sensitive investigations a mere four supervisory levels from the Mayor's Office."

"I don't think you should mention the Mayor."

"Why not?"

"I work for the Mayor, too."

"So, no one is immune. Are they?"

"This commission is investigating police corruption."

"Why stop with the police?"

She studied his face for a long time before continuing with the next question. He had thrown her a confusing question she couldn't answer. "Did you agree with the decision to arrest Alvin Baker before the party?"

"No."

"Did you make your objections known?"

"Yes."

"To whom?"

"Captain Guglielmo and ADA. Bergermeister."

"How did Bill, I mean ADA. Bergermeister, respond to the decision to arrest Baker before the party?"

"He was furious."

"What reason did Captain Guglielmo give for his order to arrest Baker?"

"He said that the chief didn't want a cop who was high on cocaine walking around with a gun in his hand."

"How did you feel about that?"

"I wanted to wait for the party. So did everyone else who cared about the case. Baker carried a gun around the city for eleven years without any problems. I think we could have waited another two weeks to wipe out that whole nest of drug dealing cops. It was a stupid and irresponsible decision."

Ginsberg covered her lips with her fingers and rolled her eyes upward in deep thought. She focused on him. "Would you be willing to repeat what you just said at an official hearing?"

"I can't appear without the Police Commissioner's permission."

"I'll subpoena you, of course, for your own protection."

"Whom do I need protection from?"

"Well, you wouldn't want the other cops getting angry at you?"

"They're already angry at me."

She cocked her head in a confused pout.

"Don't get me wrong counselor, I work just as hard to prove a cop's innocence as I do to prove their guilt, but they don't see it that way and I really don't give a rat's ass how they see it. When you handle as many corruption cases as I do, your name gets inscribed on a lot of station house walls." Weadock moved to watch an ocean liner entering the Hudson River. "Most of my old friends in the NYPD abandoned me when I joined the Internal Affairs Community but it was something I had to do."

Ginsberg fired several more questions at Weadock concerning the Baker case, but stopped to silently collect her thoughts. "Will the CI's talk to me?"

"They're still working for the Feds, but I'll ask them."

She leaned back in her chair. "How do you feel about IAD?"

"What do you mean, exactly?"

"What kind of working relationship does your unit have with them?"

"None. They run a kind of cloak and dagger operation at Poplar Street and they scare the shit out of every cop in the department.

That's why cops in the field don't go to them. Cops shouldn't be afraid of Internal Affairs; they should be a part of it. They should be totally aware of the goals of Internal Affairs and support them. What is happening now is the good cops are just turning a blind eye at the bad cops. All cops are afraid of IAD but the good ones will not rat on a brother officer no matter what he does wrong. That's what you have to change. If you don't change that now. You'll just need another commission every twenty years."

Ginsberg tried to write what Weadock was saying but he spoke too fast. She just stopped writing and listened.

"I don't care how many commissions you come up with, you'll never change the system until you change the system."

Ginsberg checked her watch. "I have an appointment at Ryker's Island today. Can we continue our talk at another time?"

They rode down in the elevator together. Before getting off, she asked him to put his suggestions for improving IAD on paper and he agreed.

Weadock found a pay telephone in the lobby when his pager went off and called his office, Detective Bishop answered.

"JJ called, Sarge. He sounded drunk, but said it was important. Something about Ramon."

"Where is he?"

"The address he gave is 25 East 114th Street."

WEADOCK AND THE WOLF

TWO OLD MEN SITTING ON EMPTY SODA CRATES in front of a corner bodega briefly looked up from their domino game to analyze the man approaching them. Somehow they knew that this man, dressed in a jacket and tie, was a cop and three young bucks sitting on the steps of a nearby brownstone sipping beer from cans covered by brown paper bags also watched Weadock with suspicion. Their eyes followed him as he crossed 114th Street and disappeared into a ground floor social club.

JJ Harrington waited inside the social club doorway and stepped out to meet Weadock. He led Weadock down a short, dark ground floor corridor to a large room in the rear. The back room had a forty-foot bar with red leather bar stools and dozens of liquor bottles on shelves behind it, many of the bottles had handwritten labels taped to them.

"Take a look at this, Sergeant." Harrington ushered Weadock to an oak pool table in the center of the room. The aged pool table had hand carved panels and leather covered pockets. "My friends here tell me that Minnesota Fats shot pool on this antique table for a thousand dollars a point." Harrington slid his hand across the green felt. "Imagine the stories this old table could tell if it could talk."

"I hope you didn't bring me here just to see this pool table, did you?"

"Patience, my boy, patience." Harrington staggered as he ushered Weadock toward the bar. "First, I want you to meet my new girlfriend, Carmen." JJ's use of princely hand gestures divulged his degree of drunkenness. "This is my very good friend and associate, Sergeant Charles Weadock of the New York City Police Department." He turned to Weadock. "Sergeant Weadock, this is Carmen Fuentes, the love of my life."

Weadock's first impression of the girl behind the bar was that she was a prostitute, but he smiled at her for Harrington's sake and Carmen smiled back. Nobody tolerated Harrington's shenanigans for very long without an ulterior motive. Weadock admired the old man when he was sober, but refused to tolerate his drunken antics unless it meant getting some information on corrupt cops. Carmen, he thought. had to be in it for Harrington's money.

"Okay." Harrington rubbed his palms together. "This is the plan. We'll have two small libations and shoot a few games of billiards with these boys." Harrington nodded at the two young Hispanics at the end of the bar. "Then we'll all shuttle over to the Kit Kat Club for lunch."

"What's going on here, Jay?"

"Why, what?"

"What is this urgent matter that needs my attention?"

"Ah, you're always in a big rush, lad." Harrington placed a hand on Weadock's shoulder brought his lips close to Weadock's ear. "You have to trust me on this one, my friend. I have time and money invested here."

"Jay--"

"Just indulge me for a few moments, sir. I've got some good stuff for you. Carmen, give this man a glass of vodka. Unless you prefer the local favorite -- scotch and pineapple soda."

"Ugh."

"The two gentlemen over there are drinking it."

Weadock turned to look at the two men as JJ spoke.

"Eduardo and Americo." Harrington dipped his head in their direction then turned back to Weadock. "I challenged them to a match." Harrington moved closer to Weadock and lowered his voice. "We'll let them win a few games for drinks then we play 'em for the big bucks."

"Jay." Weadock stood up. "I haven't got time for this bull shit."

"Yes, you do." Harrington moved next to Carmen and she put her arm around him. Harrington lifted his drink and paused. "Americo knows the wolf and the rat." A huge conceited smirk appeared on Harrington's face.

Weadock looked Carmen over when she moved through the opening in the bar. She didn't have any visible needle marks but he suspected she was a junkie just the same. "Okay, we'll shoot a few games." He swallowed the vodka in his glass and Carmen refilled it.

Harrington moved to the pool table and Weadock moved closer to Carmrn. "How old are you?"

"I'm nineteen," she said.

"Are you really his girlfriend?"

"Sure." She licked her lower lip as if she were everyone's girlfriend. "I suppose."

Harrington stretched to light the dim lamp above the pool table and Americo crossed the room to him. They talked for a moment then Americo racked the balls and Harrington came back to the bar. "They want to play eight ball for twenty bucks a man."

"Do they know I'm a cop?"

"They love cops. They think I'm an Inspector. I already bought them three drinks each. Shoot pool and talk to this Americo guy. He's okay and he knows both Lopez and Ramon. I don't think we're going to lose, but if we do, I'll pick up the tab."

After five games, Americo threw two hundred dollars on the bar and quit. Weadock refused the money and bought him a drink. It was a good investment. Americo admired Weadock's table skills and generosity. He spoke openly to his new friend about the notorious Lobo.

He told Weadock that Lopez began his career right there on Lexington Avenue. His mother and father were junkies who actually sold their son to a drug dealer named King Cole. The king's real name is Hector Coleman; it was Coleman who first tagged Lopez with the name, Lobo.

Americo was a lot older than he looked. He was thirty-nine years of age and told Weadock that Lopez began running for King Cole when he was in elementary school. "When Lobo was old enough to get arrested," Americo slurred, "Cole kept him inside. Treated him like a son. Some people say he is Cole's son, but I do not believe that." Americo suggested that Cole and Lobo were lovers. He said Lobo became Cole's driver and bodyguard. They were very close, they went everywhere together. Then about ten years ago, Cole took a header off the roof of his apartment building. The word on the street was that Lobo did it over a woman named Magda. She disappeared the same day. Americo also said that Cole kept a lot of cash in the apartment, millions of dollars in cash, gold, and jewelry in some kind of secret vault. Somebody told him that the cops and firemen took all the loot when the apartment caught fire, but he thinks that Lobo still has it. Anyway, Lobo got himself a good lawyer, inherited all Cole's possessions then disappeared. He came back to Nueva York a few years later, but this time he's a big man with lots of cash and contacts. He established a foothold on the upper West Side and killed off the opposition." Americo waved his empty glass at Carmen. Weadock pushed a fifty-dollar bill at her and Americo continued talking.

"About a year ago, Lopez took this area back from a nasty motherfucker named Fat Ralph Montalvo. Nobody liked Fat Ralph either so it didn't matter. Now, Lobo runs everything around here, gambling, drugs, pussy, everything. Nothing goes down without his approval. I think he's in with the Mafia guys, too."

"What do you know about Ramon Velez?"

"Not much, man. The guy is a cop and a shadow." The only time you see him is when he's driving Lopez." Americo glanced at Carmen before backing off the stool. He and Eduardo stumbled out of the social club together.

At 4:00 p.m., Weadock telephoned his office from the social club. McIntosh answered and told Weadock that Captain Guglielmo was asking for him. And a girl named Theresa called twice.

Weadock told McIntosh to get Falcone and meet at him at the Kit Kat Klub for dinner.

"Ah, Sarge," McIntosh moaned. "Alex stopped at that Italian cheese store downtown and brought back two heroes."

"You don't have to eat at the club but you have to meet me there in thirty minutes. Wait outside."

Weadock called Theresa and left a message on her answering machine.

Harrington slipped Carmen a hundred-dollar bill and then left the social club with Weadock.

Twenty minutes later, Weadock parked his gray Lincoln Continental in a taxi stand in front of Lincoln Center. He and Harrington crossed Broadway to the restaurant where

Falcone and McIntosh waited. Weadock crouched down on the passenger's side of Falcone's station wagon to talk to him. "Mr. Harrington here wants to buy you guys a gourmet dinner."

"I wish you would've told me earlier, boss." Falcone complained. "My tour's over in fifteen minutes and Jimmy's got indigestion."

"Hey," McIntosh leaned toward the window, "If Harrington's buying, I'll eat again."

Weadock looked at Falcone. "This won't take long; I just need a couple of witnesses. You'll just have to live with the overtime pay."

"But my wife is cooking a special meal for me tonight, Sarge,"

"So you ate a fat hero from D'Angelo's on your way home, huh?"

Falcone gave McIntosh a slight nudge as they exited the auto. "Big mouth."

"What?"

"Why did you tell him about the heroes, stupid?"

McIntosh responded with his Stan Laurel head scratching imitation. "What kind of restaurant is this, anyway?"

"The kind you eat at, big mouth."

A forklift shaped bouncer emerged from a dark alcove of the Kit Kat Club and looked

them over. His suit was a size too small for his muscles and he made slow mummy-like movements as he turned. Without asking a question, he back pedaled into the alcove and picked up a telephone.

"Nice suit," Weadock remarked.

Inside, a maitre d' greeted them with a counterfeit smile. He wore a well-fitted suit. "Do you gentlemen have a reservation? Oh, Mr. Harrington. I didn't see you, sir."

"It's okay, Rene." Harrington stepped forward. "These gentlemen are with me. We are going to have a drink at the bar before dinner."

"Very good, sir. I'll reserve your regular table for your party." He bowed like a Japanese houseboy and lifted a hand toward the bar.

"Rene." McIntosh twisted his mouth in broken French as he mounted one of the barstools. "Ain't that a girl's name?"

Harrington went to his usual strategic seat at the end of the bar. The bartender, also an apparent weight lifter, knew Harrington's drink. He set three glasses in front of him, pouring a double shot of Absolute vodka in one glass, orange juice in the second, and ice in the third. Harrington always mixed his own drinks.

Ten minutes later, a short thin man in an expensive suit came to the opposite end of the bar.

"Good evening, gentlemen. I'm Antonio Lopez, the owner of this establishment." He had a full head of greasy black hair, a thin mustache and more makeup than he needed to cover the scars on his face. There was no trace of Hispanic accent in his voice. He seemed more intelligent than Weadock had expected. Placing his manicured hands on the bar, he leaned forward to examine his customers more closely. He looked directly at Weadock. "Is this an official visit?"

"I haven't decided yet," Weadock said.

"I'm acquainted with Mr. Harrington, but--"

"Allow me." Harrington slid off his stool and moved down the bar toward Lopez, identifying each cop with his hand. "Sergeant Weadock, Detective Falcone and Detective McIntosh of New York finest."

Lopez kept his eyes locked on Weadock. "Francisco," he said without looking at the bartender. "Give these gentlemen a drink on the house." Lopez turned to walk away, but Weadock stopped him.

"Mister Lopez."

Lopez stopped his motion and turned.

"Can I ask you a question or two?"

"You can ask, sergeant."

"Do you own a black Limousine?" Weadock's inquiry caused the two detectives to turn their heads.

"Doesn't everyone?" Lopez shot a hard look at Harrington then focused back on Weadock. "I have two of them. Why?"

"There was a murder on Tenth Avenue a few months ago and a witness reported seeing a black limousine at the time of the incident. We think the occupants of that limousine may have witnessed this crime."

"There must be hundreds of black limousines in New York City, sergeant, perhaps thousands."

"True, but you're the only owner of a black limo, I'm sorry, two black limos, who actually knew the victim." This time Harrington's head ping-ponged with the others.

"That's absurd. Where did you get such a foolish notion, Sergeant?"

"You did know Tommy Raffes, did you not?"

"Oh." Lopez hesitated a long time before managing a surprised expression. "Was he murdered? Now I understand why he hasn't been around the neighborhood. Too bad, he was a likable boy. He did some odd jobs around here on occasion." Lopez moved his eyes to the bartender, then to Harrington, then back to Weadock. "Why would anyone murder such a useless creature?"

"Perhaps you can suggest a reason."

"Is there a problem, sergeant?"

"One of your cars may have been in the area that night."

"Well, I don't drive."

"Perhaps your chauffeur might recall seeing something."

Lopez nodded at the bartender. Moments later, the forklift-shaped bouncer ambled into the room. He showed no emotion in his face and waited without speaking.

"Dudley, this police officer wants to know if any of my limousines were in the vicinity of -- Where and when this event take place?"

"Thirty-Fourth Street and 10th Avenue on March 16th and 17th, 1992."

Dudley's eyes moved from Lopez to Weadock. "No."

"How can you be so positive about that, Dudley?" Weadock asked.

"I dunno." He looked at the two detectives and cracked a smirk. "But I'm sure I wasn't there."

"There you have it, sergeant." Lopez pouted his lips as he spread his hands. "It must have been one of those other thousands of other limousines in New York."

"Are you the only chauffeur?" Weadock asked Dudley.

"Yes, he is." Lopez answered for Dudley. "But we are so infrequently in that neighborhood and we don't keep trip logs like taxicab drivers. So you see, anything is possible and even if we were there by some remote chance and of course we were not, we didn't see anything. Did we, Dudley?"

"No, sir."

"Well." Lopez rubbed the palms of his hands together and smiled. "I am sorry that we couldn't help solve your little mystery, sergeant, but I'm meeting some people at the opera shortly and really must leave. Please stay and have a nice dinner on the house, my treat."

"Some other time, perhaps," Weadock said. "Oh, I forgot. Our witnesses gave a partial license plate number for that limo. Are your vehicles registered in your name?"

Falcone and McIntosh shot a perplexed looked at each other.

Lopez flashed an affirmative nod at Dudley and the chauffeur produced two registrations. Falcone copied down the numbers.

"A lot of high ranking members of the Police Department come here to dine, you know," Lopez said. "Lincoln Center is just across the street."

Weadock handed Lopez his business card as he looked around. "This is a nice restaurant."

"Maybe I should talk to your bosses about this matter."

"You could," Weadock took a step toward the door. "But they would only refer you back to me."

Lopez looked closely at Weadock's business card in his hand and manufactured a cheap grin. He let his gaze move from Weadock to Harrington and back to Weadock. "I think you have made a mistake, Sergeant."

"Perhaps." Weadock exited the premises with Harrington and the two detectives in tow.

Outside, McIntosh moved up nest to Weadock. "I didn't know we had a partial plate on the limo."

"We don't," Weadock, said. "I was just fishing. Everybody in the neighborhood knew Raffes was murdered but he played Mr. Innocent and why didn't he ask how Raffes was murdered? Wouldn't you?"

Harrington offered to treat the three cops to dinner at the Bull & the Bear, but Weadock dropped him at his hotel. When Harrington got out of the car, he turned to say good night to Weadock.

"This guy won't cause you any problems, will he?" Weadock asked.

Harrington moved a little closer to Weadock. "You have no idea what a dangerous man I am. Do you, Sergeant?"

KENNEDY CONFLICT

ELIZABETH KENNEDY SENSED THAT SOMETHING was wrong when she filled her tea kettle with cold water and set it on the stove. She sat at the kitchen table opposite her second son. She hadn't seen him since Christmas and wondered if she was the cause of his infrequent visits. She could feel his distress. "We don't see much of you anymore, Vincent."

"I know, Ma."

"Ever since you moved to Long Island."

"Mary Ann didn't want the kids growing up with the mutts around here."

"You grew up here. Your brothers and your sister grew up here."

"It's a long trip, Ma."

"It's not a long trip from your office to your mother's house! Is it?"

He lowered his head.

"I miss my grandsons, Vincent."

"They miss you too, Mom."

She studied her son's face as she placed a tea bag in his cup. She couldn't bring herself to tell him that she walked past his office every Thursday morning on her way to the meat market. The truth was that she had never seen the inside of a station house and had no interest in ever going inside a police building. Her husband had been a cop for thirty years and she never dreamed once of going inside the police station. She stood up, removed Vincent's jacket from the back of his chair, folded it neatly and placed it on the sofa. "Vincent, why do you suppose I'm afraid of policemen?"

He ignored her question again.

"Ma, do you know that Theresa and Charlie Weadock are living together?"

"I do."

He looked at her with disbelief.

"Michael told me."

"How come Michael didn't tell me?"

"Who's talking about me like a dog?" Michael came into the kitchen scratching his head with two hands. He had a just-awakened look on his face. He stood defiantly with his hands on his mother's shoulders facing his older brother.

"Where's pop?" Vinny looked towards the living room. "Does he know about this?"

"He's out getting his racing form and he doesn't have a clue," Mrs. Kennedy said.

"Somebody ought to tell him."

"Why?" Michael asked. "What's he going to do about it? They're in love, Vinny. They've always been in love. I think it's great."

"Where's Grandpa? I'll bet he knows about this, too."

"He's over in Chelsea Park trying to beat the Wops at bocce." Michael said. He goes there every day now. You should watch him, he's pretty good. He even speaks broken Italian."

Vinny slumped in his chair. "What a family."

All went silent as the front door opened and closed.

"What's this?" Joe Kennedy looked at his wife. "The long lost son comes to visit, must be a money problem."

"You don't have any money, pop," Michael joked.

Joe Kennedy plopped his 260 pounds into a kitchen chair and Elizabeth immediately responded with an empty cup. Joe shifted his gaze from one to the other, finally focusing on Michael. "What are you grinning about, lad?"

"Brother Vincent here has something to tell you, pop. It's really going to make your day."

"I hope it's a sure winner."

"No, Pop," Vinny said. "It's a sure loser."

"I don't want to hear about losers, keep it to yourself."

When Vinny backed off, Michael sat down pulling his father's racing form out of focus. "I'm moving out of the house, Pop."

"No!" His mother gulped.

"Sorry Mom, but I'm moving in with my new partner."

"Is he a Catholic?" She asked.

"Yeah," Vinny chuckled, "his name is Margaret."

"Margaret?" she repeated. "That's a girl's name."

"Very good, Liz." Joe shot a disappointed look at his wife. "Ever meet a boy named Margaret?"

Mumbling some barely audible words, Elizabeth moved to the stove. She retrieved the hot water and poured some into the four mugs on the table.

"Are you getting married, Michael?"

"No, mom." He rolled his eyes upward.

"Nobody gets married anymore, Liz." Joe forced a smile. "They live together to see if they like each other and get married later."

"What will the girl's parents think?" Elizabeth banged the pot on the stove as she returned it.

"They're not happy about it either, Mom," Michael said, "but we're adults and that's the way we want it."

"What he means is they're consenting adults," Vinny said, "and the parents can't do anything about it."

"Well, I hope it all works out for you, lad." Joe Kennedy focused on his racing form. "I wish you the best of luck."

"Luck, is it?" Elizabeth defended. "It's not good luck for a girl to sleep with a man without a ring on her finger."

"C'mon, Liz," Joe said, "He could be the first Kennedy to marry a cop."

"Perhaps not." Vinny grinned from ear to ear.

Michael and Elizabeth's eyes centered on Joe Kennedy's face.

"What do you mean by that, Vincent?"

"Why do you always call me Vincent when you're angry, Pop?"

"Spit it out, kid."

"When's the last time you spoke to your daughter?"

"Ah, about two weeks ago, we had a big fight, right here. She was bent out of shape over some mail my sister misplaced. She accused me and my poor dead sister of some sinister plot to ruin her life."

"She and Weadock are living together."

Joe Kennedy closed his eyes. When he opened them, he shot a loathsome glance at his wife and turned to face Vincent. "Don't tell me that lie again."

"They are. They're shacking up at her place on the east side."

Joe Kennedy covered his eyes with his hands then let his hands drop to the table with a thud. "This is your fault, woman!"

Elizabeth threw one hand over her heart and took a step back in disbelief.

"You were too soft with her."

Michael consoled his mom silently.

"So this is how she repays me." He looked to his wife for sympathy. "And all I've done for her." He lowered his face and cringed in anguish.

Elizabeth pouted in silence, proclaiming innocence with the palms of her hands.

"I'll disown her," he raged. "I won't leave her a dollar in my will."

"You don't have a will, Pop," Michael said. "You don't have a dollar either."

"I robbed her of her childhood," he cried into his coffee mug. "That's what she said to me. To me!" He raged, "I've been a good father and good provider. Have I not?" He looked at his wife.

Elizabeth Kennedy began to cry.

"Have I not, Michael?" He turned to Michael.

"You want the truth, Pop?"

Vinny grabbed his little brother by the shirt.

"Let him go, Vincent," Joe Kennedy insisted. "I'd like to hear the truth."

"We were lucky, Pop. Lucky that the old neighborhood changed when it did."

Vinny tried to stop Michael by blocking his view but Michael stretched his neck to talk around his brother. "Things got better around here when I was a kid. It was easier for me to grow up than it was for Tom and Vinny. You should have gotten us all out of here a long time ago, but you didn't. Mom would've loved a little house in Long Island, something like Vinny has now."

"We never had the money, kid."

"Yes we did." Michael walked to the kitchen window. "You blew your paycheck on booze and ponies, Pop. We knew it, we always knew it. But you were such a tough guy. No one would dare say anything to you. We could've had something." He walked back to the table. "We never even had a family car. You still don't have one."

Joe Kennedy lowered his head and took the full force of his youngest son's wrath because he knew Michael was right.

"Mom still hangs the wet wash out the back window; you could've got her a dryer or something."

"All right, Mike," Vinny said.

"No, it's not all right." Michael pushed Vinny's hand away. "I don't think Charlie Weadock is a bad guy. I'm glad they got together again."

No one spoke for a few moments and Michael continued. "Tommy's my oldest brother but he screwed up his own life. He was--"

"Hold it, Mister," Joe interrupted. "I don't wanna discuss Thomas in front of your mother."

"Why, Pop? You think she doesn't know what's going on here? She reads a book a week and all the newspapers and magazines she gets her hands on. She knows more about what's happening on this planet then all of us put together."

"I think you better leave, Michael. Don't wait till next week. Go now!"

Joe Kennedy was dodging the issue and Michael didn't like it. Michael was ready for a fight. He wanted all the dirty laundry on the kitchen table where they could examine it and fix it, but he backed out of the kitchen slowly until he hit the bedroom door. He waited a long time for his father to continue the argument, but Joe Kennedy avoided eye contact with his youngest son. Michael turned and went upstairs to his small bedroom.

The ten-by-twelve bedroom became his when Vinny moved out six years earlier. It was a kid's room, small and private, and had a door he could lock. He would miss it, but it was time to move on with his life. Michael lay back on his bed and the room came alive with memories. He wasn't sorry for ranking out his father in front of the family. He deserved it. It was something he wanted to do for years. Now it was done and he still felt the pain of his father's silent rejection. He had always wanted his father's love, but it never came. Joe Kennedy favored his oldest son Tom, and later, Vinny. Michael was frequently left out of things. He never measured up to his older brothers in his father's eyes, and now he would stop trying.

He looked out through the airshaft window at Muriel Crawford's bedroom in the next building and smiled. He wondered if she knew that he watched her undress from the darkness of his room.

All of a sudden, Vinny's frame filled the bedroom doorframe. "What are you going to do now little brother?"

"I'm moving out." Michael pulled a ragged gym bag from under his bed and began stuffing it with socks and underwear. "I should've done it a long time ago."

"You mad at me?"

"No."

"Yes you are."

"Okay, so I'm mad at you."

"Because I gave up Theresa."

"No, because you gave her up twice."

"C'mon, I was just looking out for her."

"You enjoy this, don't you?"

"This has nothing to do with Theresa. I just hate her boyfriend."

"Why, because Pop hates him?"

"Yeah, for that and for what he did to Tom."

"Vinny, Pop actually liked Weadock until you blew the whistle on him. Why did you do that? You weren't that much of a shit head as a kid were you?"

"I made a mistake. I was sorry about it afterwards, but I couldn't take it back. It was half-true anyway -- they were burning up the beach. I just made up the part about the orgies and the beer."

Michael continued packing in silence.

Vinny continued. "A uniform cop, who knew Pop, caught Bobby English and me drinking beer outside Joe's Clam Bar. He said he was going to tell Pop. I thought if Pop was angry with someone else he wouldn't kick my ass. It turned out that the cop never gave us up."

"Why don't you tell that to Pop now?"

"Why?"

"It might make things better for them."

"I can't do that."

"Why not? You told me. Now tell him."

"What difference does it make anyway? None of this excuses him for what he did to Tom."

"Vinny," Michael struggled to close the gym bag, "why don't you ask Tommy what really happened. He's your big brother, too. Maybe he'll tell you the truth."

Michael jammed an unfinished paperback into his jacket pocket and raked the room one more time with his eyes.

Downstairs, he gave his mom a bear hug and a kiss and paused at the front door waiting. Waiting for his dad to say something, anything. He closed the door and left without another word.

Vincent Kennedy returned to the kitchen and sat opposite his father. "He didn't mean what he said, Pop."

Joe Kennedy brought the coffee mug to his lips, but didn't drink. He held the cup steady with two hands and peered over the rim at his second son. "He meant every word of it, Vincent -- and he was right."

"C'mon, Pop."

"No. He was right, Vincent. It took a lot of guts for that little shit to tell me off. I never thought he had it in him. He's got toughness in him that I never saw and I admire him for speaking his mind. He's a grown man now, and a better one than me."

Locked in silent thought, Vinny Kennedy stared at the closed front door. *A better one than me, too.* He thought.

WOLFING

USING HIS FINGER AS A FOCAL POINT, Professor Ferreri strolled along his wall-to-wall bookcase searching for his signed copy of *Silent Spring.* When he found it, a dreadful fear swept over him. *Somebody had shuffled his books. A stranger has been in his house.*

The rattling sound of the basement boiler door, a sound he had ignored for years, suddenly reached his ears. Then a gust of wind blowing against the back yard door sent a shiver through his body. He picked up the telephone to call Sergeant Weadock and put it down in the same motion. *What could I tell them? Someone has moved my books."*

He sat at the kitchen table for a long time, nibbling at a cold dinner and straining his eyes and ears to detect any new sounds. The staircase leading to his bedroom seemed darker than usual. Even the hardwood steps of the old house responded to his softest movement.

Later, he rummaged through his jacket pockets for Weadock's business card. Holding it in his hand, he dialed the number. When

Weadock answered, Ferreri told him that someone had been in his house. Nothing was missing but he is certain that someone had been there.

An hour later, Charlie Weadock's frame faded into the dark alcove outside Ferreri's brownstone. An inside chime sounded when he pushed at the illuminated doorbell. A window curtain moved aside and the professor pressed his bleached face against the glass. Two locks and a heavy bolt were thrown before the door swung open.

Ferreri encouraged Weadock into the house with a pulling handshake. "Thanks for coming so quickly." He piloted Weadock through a narrow corridor that ended at the living room. Flames from a lighted fireplace bounced off the walls filling the room with warm shadows. The smell of strong coffee somehow overpowered the odor of the burning wood. "Will you have some coffee with me, sergeant? I grind my own coffee beans."

"Sure, cops drink lots of coffee."

"I've been teaching night school every summer for twenty years and I've never had a problem. Now I race with the sun like a frightened vampire. I see black limousines everywhere. I'm a chiropterologist, you know - A bat expert."

"Would you like to report a burglary? I can call it in for you."

"But there's nothing missing."

"It's still a burglary."

"You told me that drug addicts in a black limousine are searching for someone who knew the newsstand victim. Well, someone has been in this house. I know this because someone has moved the books of my shelf."

"When?"

"Today. I left for school at 8:30 a.m. and returned home at 5:30 p.m."

Weadock flipped through a small notebook to find Ramon's duty schedule. Today was his regular day off.

"The average burglarized house looks like a bomb exploded in it. What makes you so sure that someone has been here?"

"I live alone. I do my own cooking and cleaning. The disturbances may have been minor but someone was in here."

"Alright."

"Isn't that a robbery?"

"No, you can't rob a house. When someone steals from a building, it's called a burglary."

"I've been teaching policemen most of my life and I don't know the first thing about law. I'm just a useless old scientist."

"Don't be so hard on yourself, Professor."

Ferreri set out two cups and saucers of fine china and poured the coffee. "I think I'm an excellent judge of character, Sergeant and I desperately need your advice in this matter. You spoke to me about confidentiality the other day when you came to the school and I feel that I need some of that, right now."

Ferreri divulged his true encounter at the newsstand on the night of the murder. "If the murderers are looking for drugs, I have nothing to fear because I have no drugs." Ferreri stood up and walked to the window. "But if they are looking for money--"

Weadock waited for him to continue.

"The night Happy got sick, he gave me a locked suitcase and asked me to take it home and bring it back the next day. He was going to the hospital and didn't want to leave it in the newsstand overnight. I didn't know what was in it and I don't think he did either. But I have it now and I'm not giving it back."

"How much money are we talking about, professor?"

"It was given to me legitimately and now that the donor is deceased, I'm keeping it."

"How much money?"

"I haven't counted it, but it's a lot."

"Is it here?"

"No, but it's in a safe place."

"Do you have a gun?"

"God, no. I'd probably shoot myself with it. Do you think I need one?"

"I'll give it to you straight, Joe. If you give the money to the city you'll probably never see a dime of it, but it might be better for your health."

The Professor began pacing the room again. "I knew this would happen."

"You might also give it up and still become a victim."

Ferreri gave Weadock a hard look.

"The killer or killers might get pissed off about losing the money and waste you anyway."

"What do you think I should do?"

"I can't tell you that."

Ferreri flopped in a huge easy chair.

"This I know. If you surrender the money, the media will find out, they always do and they'll be in your face. They'll be outside this house every day until a better story comes along. They'll be asking a lot of personal questions. On the other hand..." Weadock crossed the room to examine a small sculpture on the mantel. An ape contemplating a human skull. "You're dealing with diabolical characters here." Weadock kept his eyes on the statue. "And I think they have your name and address."

"How did? What should I do Sergeant Weadock?"

"How did the police get your name?"

"I gave it to the cop at the newsstand."

"Anyone else?"

"No, Detective Marini called me and asked me to go to the station house."

Weadock made some notes on a small pad. "You could disappear for a while."

"You're joking of course."

Weadock turned up the palms of his hands. "Why not, you have this extra money. Take a vacation, a long one. Disappear for a couple of years. Come back when everybody's dead. Better yet, don't come back at all."

"Perhaps you're right." Ferreri scratched the back of his head. "I never had a real vacation."

"May I call you from time to time for an update?"

"Sure, get yourself a cell phone and I'll call you every once in a while and tell you what's going on here."

After Weadock left, Ferreri sauntered between his bed and the front windows for hours. The headlights of passing cars continually crept across the ceiling. Later, the soft chimes of his grandfather clock awakened him at every hour on the hour.

Twenty blocks to the north, Antonio Lopez ordered his chauffeur, Dudley, to park outside the Market Diner. "Go and get something to eat."

"I'm not that hungry, boss."

"Yes you are, come back in twenty minutes."

Dudley obeyed, moving his android-like mass into the diner. As the door closed behind him, Ramon appeared at the limousine's window like an apparition in a nightmare. He even startled Lopez. Lopez unlocked the door and the two creatures studied each other in the dim light. Lopez leaned toward Ramon. "Well?"

"It wasn't there, Poppy." Ramon lowered his head. "I searched the house for three hours. I looked in every room. It's not in the house."

"It must be there! Go back!" Lopez pushed himself back into the soft leather seat and no one spoke for a while. "Maybe the newspaper man lied."

"He didn't lie, Poppy. He was in a lot of pain. He said a professor took the bag home and Ferreri's the only professor involved."

"You must find it or..."

"Or what?"

"Or perhaps you don't have to look for it."

"Poppy, Poppy."

"Why do you call me that? You think I'm your father?"

"You're the only poppy I have."

"Perhaps." Lopez glanced at his watch. "But I have a slightly stronger affection for my money. You'll have to interrogate this professor. Show him some of your toys, but remember that he can't tell you where the money is if he's dead. I have to stay clear of you for a while. I see Detectives everywhere, I think they are following me and a sergeant from IAD is dogging the shit out of me."

"Weadock?"

"You know him?"

Lopez held up his card. "He came to my club last night."

"Why would he come to you?"

"How the fuck do I know? He knows that the rodent worked for me and he knows that I have a black limousine. He has a witness who saw half my license plate number."

"He's lying. I read all the complaint reports and there's no plate number. He doesn't know anything. But how did he know about you?" Ramon let his eyes sweep the area outside. "How did he connect you with the rat man?" Ramon grinned. "He fucked up, you know. He follows me all the time, but he's not here. If he was, he'd have us right now."

"He knows about you and me?"

"He knows nothing."

"JJ was with him."

"The Irish from the West Side?"

"Yeah."

Ramon laughed. "I guess we can't meet in public anymore."

"This is not funny. I don't need this shit," Lopez poked his finger hard into Ramon's chest, "and I don't like this sergeant either. You must have fucked up somewhere. Why don't you use a knife or a gun like everyone else?"

"Don't worry, Poppy." Ramon put his hand on Lopez's shoulder. "Ramon will fix everything."

"Whatever you fix, don't implicate me. You fucked up somewhere. This sergeant has his mark on you and now he knows about me. You must do everything normal for a while."

Ramon touched him and shrugged.

"Don't be stupid, kid." Lopez pushed Ramon's hand away. "And make no mistake about me. You know me too well."

"But you're my only family now, Poppy."

"All future contacts between us will be through Dudley."

"But--"

"But nothing."

"But I do everything for you, Poppy," Ramon begged. "You and me togeth--"

"Enough!"

"Poppy."

"What do you want from me? What do you want me to say to you?" Lopez felt inside Ramon's coat. "You're not wearing a wire, are you?"

Ramon pushed Lopez's hand away. "No wire."

Lopez reached around Ramon as if to embrace him, but it was just a ruse to feel for a wire.

Ramon recoiled like a cobra. "What are you doing?"

"You disappoint me, kid," Lopez continued. "You once had finesse, but now, you can't even find my money. You're too stupid. You think you're James Bond, but you're really just a dumb junkie. You beat those people to death before they told you anything and this sergeant who follows you, he's no fool. I've seen his type before. He's a hunter. He'll keep coming for you and me until he gets us or we get him."

"See, you need me to protect you, Poppy."

"Dudley will protect me now and stop calling me poppy. I'm not your father. Your father was a bum and your mother was a whore. Stay the fuck away from me until this shit is over." Lopez reached over and opened the door.

Ramon reluctantly faded into a dark alley. He watched the limousine until Dudley returned and drove off into the night. He felt betrayed and alone. He thought about his real father, the plumber.

Four hours later, Ramon slithered through Lopez's luxury apartment like a hungry snake.

Hearing a soft voice, Lopez folded the white satin bed sheets back and sat on the edge of the bed. As he reached for the lamp on the night stand, a brass tube flashed before his eyes and came crashing into his face. He wanted to scream for Dudley, but the dark presence was too powerful. He thought it might be a nightmare until he saw the blood on his white silk pajamas.

"Shh," the voice said.

Lopez turned to summon Dudley from the apartment down the hall, but a powerful hand covered in plastic held his mouth. The glimmer of the frightful brass pipe flashed before his eyes again and struck him in the throat. He saw blood again and knew it was his blood. He dropped to the floor on all fours as the room carouselled around him. Ramon ripped the silk garments from his body leaving him naked on the floor.

"Open the vault!" Ramon ordered. "You're not my poppy anymore, you are my lamb."

Unable to speak, Lopez pleaded with his eyes but Ramon lashed at him again with the icy weapon. This time it hit him above the right eye. Ramon waved his cruel weapon like a maestro at the opera. "Open the vault, now and I won't hurt you anymore."

Lopez leaned on the huge bronze statue and inserted the key that dangled from the gold chain around his neck into the dog's mouth. He turned it and the vault opened.

Ramon twisted Lopez's frail body over the statue and rammed the pipe into his anus. Lopez went up on his toes and squirmed like a pig. His muffled screams quickly fell silent as Ramon rammed the weapon deeper into Lopez's body.

Ramon dragged the dead body to a white leather sofa and sat it up like rag doll. Lopez's barren eyes saw nothing as Ramon filled four large plastic bags with the contents of Lopez's vault. Ramon left as quietly as he came. Downstairs he tossed Lopez's loot into the trunk of his Cadillac and drove to the Fifth Precinct.

THE WOLF IS DEAD

BY JULY 1, 1992, EVERY COP in the City of New York had heard of the Plumber Murders and newspaper reporters were calling the Mayor's office for information.

Police Officer Juan Figaroa of the 28th Precinct was the first cop to arrive at the Lopez crime scene. He immediately telephoned the Homicide Task Force. Thirty minutes after that Kennedy and Marini were standing in front of the building on 110th Street.

Weadock and Falcone arrived at about the same time and the foursome pushed their way past a camera crew that was blocking the front door. Kennedy led them single file through a swarm of media people to the stairwell and elevator door. A veteran cop posted there looked them over and stepped aside to let them pass. "Get these people out of the building, Officer!" Kennedy ordered, "This is a crime scene."

In the top floor hallway, two detectives from the 28 Squad took turns firing questions at Dudley, the bodyguard.

A forensic team was already measuring and photographing the crime scene in the background. Dudley leaned around one of the detectives and pointed at Weadock. "That guy was at the restaurant last night. He threatened Mr. Lopez."

Kennedy grinned at Weadock. "You knew this victim too?"

"I met him for the first time last night."

"You didn't give him a business card, did you?"

Weadock raised his eyes.

Kennedy walked down the hallway shaking his head and mumbling to himself then turned to look at Weadock. "What the fuck is going on here?"

All conversation in the hallway seemed to stop. Kennedy moved closer to Weadock lowered his voice. "I invited you here because I thought you could help bu--"

"I can help." Weadock walked down the hallway to an unoccupied spot near a window and waited.

Kennedy followed. "How come all these dead guys have your business card?"

Falcone and Marini watched as their two bosses argued at the end of the hall. An appropriate bolt of lightning flashed behind them in the dark morning sky.

"Don't bullshit me, Kennedy." Weadock poked a thumb at himself. "I know that you know the name of my subject, *and*, you also know his connection with that piece of shit in there."

"Is that a fact?"

"Yes, that's a fact. I don't even want to know how you know or how you got the information. I might have to act on that."

"Listen Pal, this is a murder case. Who gives a fuck how I got some bullshit information?"

"Somebody from your crew compromised my investigation."

"Well, I'm going to pick up your boy anyway and sweat his ass."

"You'd better check with the DA first."

"Fuck the DA! I don't work for him."

Outside, another bolt of lightning flashed again. This time a loud crack of thunder clapped close to the two sleuths and they stopped arguing.

Marini and Falcone waited for round two to begin, but Weadock backed off to stop the conflict.

"Alright, I'll tell you everything if you calm down." Weadock pointed his two index fingers at Kennedy as if they were smoking guns. "It just so happens that I've been ordered to tell you everything about my case against Ramon Velez and close it forthwith.

Kennedy exchanged glances with Marini and waited.

Weadock took a step away from the raging storm outside. "I have a CI who overheard Police Officer Ramon Velez telling this guy, Lopez, how he killed that drug dealer in 1990. This happened on Avenue B and 3rd Street. The CI identified Velez by photo show-up and that's it, that's all I have. The CI is a former drug dealer himself and not totally reliable. I went to see Lopez last night on a fluke. A fishing expedition for information."

Kennedy kept his eyes on the torrential raindrops pounding against the window. "Okay, is there any evidence? Any witnesses? Anything I can use in court?"

"No, Velez has an impeccable record, not a single complaint in five years. He has a wife, a kid and an honorable discharge from the Marine Corps. At the outset of this case, we followed him every day for a month and got nothing. He went straight home every time."

"I know."

"So, you *do* know."

"You going to work with me on this, or not?" Kennedy asked. "I don't give two shits for your secret cop investigations. If this Velez guy is our killer, I just wanna nail the motherfucker."

"Lieutenant," Marini called, "forensic is finished and the ME wants to take the body."

Weadock moved toward the apartment and Kennedy stopped him with a hand. "Before we go inside, I have a news flash for you. Everyone in my family knows about you and Theresa."

"Everyone?"

"Yeah, and one of them is giving her a real hard time."

"Is that one person you?"

"No, it isn't me. I made a mistake about you and her when we were kids, but that was a long time ago and I'm sorry about that but If it's okay with you, I'm ready to bury the hatchet right now."

"That's very nice of you, Vinny." Weadock looked at the rain now lashing the window with hard drops. He took a deep breath, turned his face toward Kennedy and extended an open hand. They shook hands and Weadock sensed genuineness in Kennedy's grip. Their eyes locked and Weadock leaned closer. "Okay, I believe that you're doing the right thing for your sister. Now, I'll do something for you. There's a kite in my office concerning a plain-clothes lieutenant. It's not my case but it concerns an unknown lieutenant who is jumping a female cop at the midtown Marriott Hotel on Broadway."

Kennedy turned and glanced at a rush of heavy rain hitting the window.

"Perhaps you know this lieutenant?"

The color drained from Kennedy's face.

"This anonymous complainant turned out to be a desk clerk at the hotel working the midnight to eight shift. He alleges that this police couple are regular customers. Weadock continued. "The clerk has been identified and interviewed and stated that he has nothing against free sex, but he doesn't like providing them a free room. He was unable to identify the couple but gave a description of them. My captain is on standby for the next visit. He wants to grab them in the rack."

Kennedy faltered against the wall next to the window like a flat tire. He tried to appear normal, but he was devastated by Weadock's statement. His life and career flashed before his eyes.

Outside, another clap of thunder rumbled loudly. Kennedy knew that he was that lieutenant. He also knew that Weadock had just handed him back his life. The man he had unjustifiably hated for most of his life had just saved him from a catastrophe. His police career and family life would have gone down the toilet just like his older brother's before him.

Weadock began walking up the hallway toward Falcone and Marini. "Coming, Lieutenant?"

"Lieutenant," Marini called, "they found a pair of plastic gloves in the basement garage."

"Yeah, yeah," Kennedy said. He shook off his dazed expression and walked down the hall. "Let's have a look at this crime scene." He paused, halting Marini in the hallway and urging Weadock to go into the crime scene first. "I'd like your opinion on this, Sergeant."

"Thank you, Lieutenant."

Kennedy followed Weadock into the room and Falcone followed Kennedy. Marini and Falcone exchanged dumbfounded expressions. "I thought they were going to duke it out in the hallway." Marini said.

The room had the smell of death to it. A track of dry blood ran down the white leather sofa and spilled into a pool of blood on the floor. Lopez's frail naked body reminded Weadock of the documentaries he had seen on TV of the death camps. Lopez's body was chalky white on top and dark purple at the bottom. He didn't look like the same person Weadock met at the Kit Kat Club. The murder weapon was still jammed into his body.

"Was this guy your only lead, Charlie?" Kennedy asked.

"We can't talk here." Weadock nodded at the uniformed cops nearby.

"My place or yours?"

"There's Blarney Rock Bar on the Avenue. How about lunch?"

"Only if I can pick up the tab."

Falcone and Marini gawked at each other again.

Fredric Deutsche, an attendant from the medical examiner's office, began clapping his hands in the air. "Gentlemen, gentlemen. In order to bag this body properly, I may have to remove his plumbing. Anyone care to observe?" Donning a pair of surgical gloves much like those used by the perpetrator, Deutsche rolled the corpse to one side and tugged slightly on the pipe but he decided to leave it in place. He marked the pipe for identification, tossed the bloodstained clothes and bedding into another clear plastic bag and sealed it. Then wiped his hands on his shirt.

"What's the official cause of death, Freddie?" Marini asked.

"You'll have to wait for the autopsy like everyone else, Detective. But I'd say that large crack on the top of his head had something to do with it." Deutsche went around asking everyone present if they were finished with the body. He also invited them to come downtown and watch the autopsy. No one accepted.

Detective Diaz of the 28th Squad nudged Falcone aside and stared into the empty vault. "Fancy safe, huh?"

Weadock crossed the room to see the vault. He examined the bronze figure on the top of it. "Cerberus."

"What?" A perplexed Diaz looked at him.

"Cerberus," he repeated. "A mythical three-headed dog that guarded the gates of hell."

Kennedy smiled and shook his head. "Where do you get that shit from, Charlie?"

"Greek mythology."

"Okay, people!" Kennedy turned to the detectives in the room. "This is what I want. Knock on every door in the building. Keep a list of the tenants who don't answer. Make another list of people who have cars in the basement garage. I want a detailed interview on the bodyguard and interview the building staff, especially the people working the midnight shift last night."

"I'm going to need some help." Marini said.

"I don't want any duplication, Jerry. It's the 28 Squad's investigation. Just help them where you can, bring me copies of all their five's and fill in the blanks." Kennedy turned to check with Weadock. "Did I miss anything, Charlie?"

"There was a camera in the elevator. Perhaps there are more."

"See? I knew I had a reason for bringing you up here." Kennedy turned to Marini, "Check with building security. Get a copy of all their surveillance tapes for the past twenty-four hours. How many, their locations, who monitors them. I'll call the office and get you some help. Sergeant Weadock and I are going to lunch."

Detective Diaz stopped Kennedy with his hand. "Anything you want me to tell Lieutenant Sachs?"

"Yeah, tell him I'll be back. I have to confer with these guys first."

Diaz turned to Marini and hit him with an irritated glance. "How come your boss has an IA team with him?"

"I don't know." Marini threw up his shoulders. "They think the perp is a cop."

"A cop? No way!"

The storm had chased most of the media from the scene. Some waited like vultures in cars and vans. A few others crowded under the umbrella of a hot dog peddler at the street corner. Kennedy nudged a few aggressive reporters aside when they rushed him. "No comment, no comment." He waved his hands at them and headed west with Weadock and Falcone.

The Blarney Rock Bar was a neighborhood hangout and fast food station for the local alcoholics. Half a dozen residents and two men in Con-Edison uniforms sat at the bar. Falcone went to the pay phone on the wall and Kennedy and Weadock ordered corned beef sandwiches at the hot food counter. They found a table in the rear and a twenty-year-old waitress who looked forty came to their table to take their drink orders. Kennedy ordered a scotch and soda and Weadock asked for a light beer.

"What, no silver bullet?"

"It's too early in the day; even for me."

Falcone came to the table and leaned over his boss's shoulder. He told him that Ramon worked a 4PM to Midnight tour last night and doubled back for a day tour court appearance. He ogled Weadock's corned beef sandwich and headed for the lunch counter.

The waitress delivered their drinks then went to a table in the rear. She lit a cigarette and let it dangle from her lip as she thumbed through a magazine. Falcone came to the table and Kennedy waved at the waitress for another round. She put her

cigarette in the ashtray next to one that was still burning.

"I think this cop is our assassin." Weadock said. "I can feel it, but I can't prove it."

"You read Greek Mythology?" Kennedy narrowed his eyes on Weadock.

Weadock nodded.

"You are one strange bird, Weadock."

He nodded again.

"Ramon Velez." Kennedy drained what was left in his glass. "Let's talk about him. I'm not ready to blame all this shit on a cop. Especially one with a totally clean record and neither is my boss."

"Okay, Detective Lieutenant Kennedy. How did the killer get so close to his victims? Do you think they just stood in front of him while he bludgeoned them to death? Not one of the victims showed signs of resistance. None of them had any fight marks on their faces or hands. There were no signs of resistance and most of victims were street smart junkies."

"What's your point?" Kennedy asked.

"The victims either knew the killer or he was someone they trusted. Someone who could walk right up to them without signaling a threat. It all fits. Once he identifies himself as a cop, they probably relaxed. Nobody expects to be murdered by a cop. Not even a junkie."

Kennedy pondered Weadock's statement, but did not respond to his argument. "Tell me about the Marriott."

"Forget about that, that's history if you stay clear of it."

Kennedy pointed to his empty glass when the waitress passed.

"Who's the one person at a crime scene that no one suspects?"

"Who?"

"The policeman."

Kennedy shrugged.

"And who did the CI say committed the 3rd Street murder? A policeman." Weadock continued. "Who came to the Terminal Hotel on the morning of the Hansen murder?"

"A Detective!"

"Okay." Weadock pulled a handful of papers from his pocket and flipped through them and pulled one out. "Here, look at this DD5. This witness, Dietrich Tesslar," Weadock tapped on the report, "was interviewed by Detective Coyle from the Ninth Squad a day after the Hansen's murder. Your guys just picked up all the fives and added them to your case folder. We reviewed them last night." Weadock handed the work sheet to Kennedy and the lieutenant read the worksheet while Weadock continued talking. Weadock motioned to Falcone to take out his badge. "Tesslar told

Detective Coyle that he was watching the late show on TV in that small office on the main floor of the Terminal Hotel when a Detective came up to him. He said this Detective had a badge just like this one." Weadock tapped on Falcone's shield. "Tesslar also said that this detective told him that he was there to notify Hansen about his burglarized newsstand but Detectives don't make notifications, do they?"

"No."

"And the only Detectives who knew about the busted up newsstand at the time of Happy's murder were your guys. Tesslar also said he told this detective Hansen's room number and went back to watching his movie. He didn't find out about the murder until he came back to work the next day. He probably assumed that the detective who came the previous night was the one who found Hansen's body. Since your guys discovered the body five hours later, this alleged detective had to be the killer."

"So how come Velez is not in handcuffs?"

"Coyle didn't know about Velez, he assumed it was just one of the other Detectives working the case. Tesslar was never shown a photo of Velez."

"So let's show him one now."

"We can't find him. He hasn't come to work and his landlord says he hasn't been home either. He checked his apartment. All his stuff is there but no Tesslar."

"So, you have nothing,"

"And now you know I have nothing. Would you arrest Velez?"

"How can I?" Kennedy asked. "If the DA won't indict him for *you*, he won't do it for me either."

"Bergermeister is the DA on my case. He's trying to get some drug dealer who is doing fifteen to life, to cooperate. If this guy turns on Velez, Bergermeister will indict him for the Cruz murder but so far it's nothing doing."

"I'm sorry, but I still can't buy the idea of a cop murdering all these people on his way to work."

"Maybe he's a psycho," Falcone said.

"Okay," Kennedy said, "what's his motive? Drugs? Most of the victims were drug dealers and any drugs they had were still at the scene of the crime. Money? Money or property was never taken."

"Until now."

"That's speculation. Lopez's safe could've been empty and burglary doesn't fit the plumber's MO. My guess is the bodyguard

emptied the safe when he discovered the body. Then we're back to why Lopez was murdered."

"I don't know." Weadock waved his empty bottle at the waitress, "Why were any of them murdered?"

Kennedy turned to Falcone when Weadock headed toward the men's room. "Is he like this all the time?"

"Worse." Falcone slugged his beer. "I don't know what he's talking about half the time but I'll tell you this. I've been in the Internal Affairs business for almost twenty years and he's the best I've ever seen." Falcone turned to look at the men's room door in the rear. "I wouldn't want him investigating me."

"I guess I have to fine this Tesslar guy now."

THE FOURTH OF JULY PARTY

MICHAEL KENNEDY LEANED BACK in a soft cushion chair and squinted at the Sun trying to find its way through the leaves of a century old willow tree. "This is a real *Gone with the Wind* tree, Charlie. How'd you ever find it here in a Brooklyn back yard?" The tree's long branches stretched down to touch the ground like hanging ballerinas and covered the whole yard with cool shadows.

"It kind of found me, Mike." Weadock examined the huge tree as he reached for another beer. "I bought this place from a police Sergeant named Peter Donato. He was a first line supervisor at the 71st Precinct and a good friend and mentor to me during my first years on the job."

"Never met him."

"He retired long before you joined the force. Peter Donato was the perfect cop, a good cop. He gave thirty-five years of his life to the people of New York. All of it on patrol duty. He had one child, a son, Dominick, who was killed Viet Nam. He was about my age when he died. Pete and his wife kind of adopted me. They treated me like

I was their own son. When he retired, they moved to Florida for health reasons and they insisted that I buy this house from them. I guess it was their way of keeping it in the family."

"Well, we like it. Maggie and I are sharing a small apartment in Stuyvesant Town but there's something about a house that binds a family together. Perhaps we'll find one like this someday."

"I'll give you the first shot at it if I ever move."

Margaret Dolan nudged a kitchen curtain aside to peek at the two men in the back yard. "It was nice of you to invite us, Theresa."

"I'm glad you accepted. Charlie doesn't have many police friends because of his internal entanglements."

"Michael likes him."

"So do I," Theresa said.

Margaret smiled. "Me too."

Margaret sliced a tomato for the salad. "Michael thinks your family is breaking up."

Theresa uncorked a bottle of red wine and centered it on the table next to a solo candle. "He may be right. They're all kind of confused right now"

Dinner conversation revolved around Maggie. She survived a head on collision that killed both her parents and her baby brother. She was four years old when she came to live with her Aunt Ellen and Uncle Joe in New York City. Aunt Ellen had her own problems, four children and an alcoholic husband who began touching Maggie in the wrong places. Aunt Ellen signed the papers and Maggie joined the US Army at 17. She did three years as an MP in England and became a New York City police officer at twenty-one years of age.

After dinner, Weadock led Michael up an escape ladder to the roof. "Your sister says you're both in trouble with your family."

Michael raised his shoulders with indifference. "You know the Irish; I don't have to tell you about them."

"Was it because of what I did to Tom?"

"No…well--"

"They must like Maggie. She's a cop and she's Irish."

"They know we're living together, but they haven't met her."

"Don't worry; it'll work out in time."

"I don't know. I came down pretty hard on the old man. I blamed him for everything that went wrong, even the stuff about Tom. My mom and Vinny were there too."

"I see Tom at the Ranger game once in a while. He waves at me. He doesn't seem to be angry about our encounter."

"He's back with his family, you know?"

"Theresa told me. She says Vinny had something to do with that."

"Vinny's a changed man. All of a sudden he's the family poster boy and peacemaker. He invited us to his house for a family barbecue on August 18th."

"He asked us too."

"Are you going?"

"Are *you*?"

"I guess, are you?"

"It's up to your sister."

Michael called Margaret for two beers. "Theresa told me that you're going to testify at the Mollen Commission Hearings."

"Next month."

"Why you?" Michael asked.

"It's a long story."

"A secret?"

"No," Weadock leaned back against the cold chimney, "I locked up this cop in the Ninth Precinct for selling cocaine."

"Baker?"

"You heard?"

"That kind of news travels fast. Most of the guys I hang with say you should have gotten him sooner."

"I didn't get him sooner because none of the guys that you hang with came forward with the information."

Michael shook his head in agreement. "It's tough for a cop to turn in another cop."

"That's the purpose of my testimony, Mike. Cop's can't supervise cops."

"This commission is not very good for morale."

"It's going to get worse. They're going to expose a whole gang of criminal cops on national TV. Not cops like Baker. Baker was a good cop until his frequent exposure to drugs made him a junky. This cop, Dowd, and his gang are going to admit to committing all kinds of crimes on national television. Dowd and his pals did what they did for profit and they're going to blame guys like you for allowing them to do it."

"Are you going to say that on television?"

"I don't know, the more I talk to them, the less confidence I have in what they're doing. Now they want me to testify as the expert witness on corruption. They want me to put my suggestions in writing."

"Will you?"

"Nine pages of it."

"I wouldn't trust them, Charlie."

"Perhaps you're right. At first they merely ask me to testify about the IAD foul up in the Baker Case, Now they want me to testify as the department's expert witness on police corruption. They're trying to show that the NYPD or any police organization cannot clean up its own garbage."

"Why did they pick you?"

"I guess because I was the sergeant who supervised the Baker case."

"That's right, a sergeant who would have made a great PC."

"Ah."

Michael felt that Weadock didn't want to talk shop anymore and changed the subject. "Vinny told me how you helped him out."

"How was that?"

"You know, warning him about that investigation at the Marriott Hotel. The guy turned over completely. He's a different person. He broke up the affair with Detective Ferguson and had her transferred to Staten Island. And he's been going home every night. You did a good thing, Charlie Brown. You're my hero."

"Your brother, Vinny, has a big mouth."

"I didn't think you'd ever compromise an investigation."

"You're right, I wouldn't."

"But you did."

"I lied."

"What?"

"I invented the whole story."

Michael's lips separated in silence.

"Your sister was at Morgan's bar one night when Vinny and his girlfriend got drunk. When he went to the head, Detective Ferguson began bragging to Theresa about the free Marriott Hotel suites she and your brother were sharing. Theresa didn't want Vinny following in Tommy's footsteps, so I dropped the bomb on Vinny. Now, spit and seal your lips forever, my friend."

"You're a strange bird, Charlie Weadock."

"That's what you're brother said."

"That's what everyone says."

When night fell, the girls brought some Irish coffee to the roof and settled down for a postcard view of the Universe and the Manhattan skyline. The Verrazano Narrows Bridge and the Statue of Liberty were visible in the harbor, the Twin Towers in lower Manhattan and the Empire State building in midtown were lit up like Christmas trees and the fireworks exploded over the East River at 9:00 PM as scheduled; lighting up the night sky. The two couples Leaned back against the cold bricks and watched the spectacle light show in awe.

Charlie Weadock watched the fireworks change colors on Theresa's face. The bright flashes of light fell softly on her cheek.

Theresa moved closer to him. "I don't know what I would have done with my life if I hadn't found you again."

Their lips came together. Their kiss was far more explosive than the pyrotechnic display above them.

A NICE ITALIAN RESTAURANT

TWO DAYS LATER, AT THE REQUEST OF JJ HARRINGTON, WEADOCK ENTERED A SMALL, unassuming Italian restaurant on Manhattan's Lower East Side and half a dozen men in casual attire sitting at a large round table in the rear, stopped talking to look him over. Weadock knew immediately that he was in a FAMILY restaurant.

Sitting alone at a table near the bar, Harrington waved at him and the men in the rear continued their conversation. An elderly Italian waiter came from behind a small service bar to bring Harrington his drink. The waiter pulled out the chair next to Harrington and waited for Weadock to sit down.

"Giuseppe, give my friend a vodka martini, straight up with olives." Harrington began rummaging through a worn leather attaché case, pulling a frayed letter from the satchel. "Here, read this and tell me what you think."

"I don't have time for this, Jay."

"This is important; it's from the president of a Canadian Fish Company."

Weadock peeked over the letter in his hands to scan the restaurant. Each of the smaller was tables was topped with red-and-white checkered tablecloth and an unlit candle. There were no other customers present. "I've got to be somewhere else by nine o'clock."

"You know what I like about you, Sergeant Weadock?"

Weadock waited in silence.

"You're not afraid of anybody. You come to meet me anywhere, anytime. I could be in the nucleus of high society or in the trenches of degradation, but you always come when I need you. You're my only true friend, Charlie Weadock. I made you the beneficiary of my will, you know. When I die, you get my entire estate."

Weadock shook off Harrington's accolades with a smile, but he couldn't help wondering what the old man was really worth. He was the only person Weadock knew who carried more than a thousand dollars in pocket money.

Giuseppe came to the table with one glass and a bottle of red wine. "This is on Mr. Piney. It's his private stock." He popped the cork, poured a half-inch into Weadock's glass and waited.

Weadock let the wine roll slowly around in his glass. Sniffed the aroma, and then drank. "Excellent."

Harrington watched the aging waiter as he filled Weadock's glass to the rim.

"Who's Mr. Piney?"

Harrington nodded at the group in the rear. "He's the owner of this establishment, and an old friend."

"Mr. Piney is a member of which family?"

"He's just a businessman like me."

A few minutes later, Giuseppe brought the house specialty to Weadock's table. A dish of veal and shrimp oreganato. "Bon appetite, gentlemen."

As Weadock and Harrington ate dinner, two men entered through the front door and waited. The shorter of the two men had slick black hair and wore a sharkskin suit without a tie. He shifted his eyes between Weadock and the men in the rear. He had the flat nose of a punched out prizefighter and bobbed his head to one side with a frequent nervous tick.

The second man, dressed in work clothes, was apparently Irish and completely detached from his surroundings. The sharp dresser took a cue from the rear and walked the length of the restaurant alone. He bowed low to whisper into an older man's ear.

Sharp Dresser's hands moved in silent uncoordinated gestures.

Weadock resolved that the man listening to Sharp Dresser was Mr. Piney. Piney continued eating his dinner as he listened. He never turned his head to look at the man talking to him. Sharp Dresser returned to the front of the restaurant, held a brief conversation with the Irishman, and they both walked to the rear. The man sitting next to Piney stood up, relinquishing his seat to the Irishman.

"Jay, what's going on here?"

"Business. Lots of business is conducted here. This restaurant has been with the same family for a hundred years."

"I'm sure it has, it reminds me of the place where Michael Corleone wasted two guys in a movie."

"I know that place, it's in the Bronx. Would you like to eat there sometime? They have great-"

"You *know* what I mean."

"I have old friends here and the food is marvelous," Harrington continued. "How do you like the food?"

"The food is great. The wine is great, but I get the feeling I'm being analyzed."

"Don't worry, they've never had any trouble with the law here and they sweep the place every day for bugs. Oh, I almost forgot. I stopped at that Social Club last night to conduct a little business and Carmen said that the Spic came in and asked about me. He mentioned my name."

"Who came in?"

"The guy you put me on - Ramon."

Weadock narrowed his eyes with concern, "What did he say?"

"He asked her if she knew me. She told him I was a banker who did business in that neighborhood on Monday afternoons. He left the club without having a drink."

"Why would he ask about you?"

"I've been asking about him, haven't I? I put the word on the street for information about him."

"You better watch your ass, old man," Weadock warned. "Stay out of that place for a while and if you meet this guy on the street, don't let your guard down because he's a cop."

"You think this punk scares me?"

"He scares me. This guy is a psycho."

"Fuck him." Harrington leaned towards Weadock. "I'm a psycho too."

Weadock pulled a copy of Ramon's ID photo from his shirt pocket and slid it across the table in front of Harrington. "This picture was taken about five years ago."

"I've seen this guy." Harrington moved his gaze to the ceiling. "Where the fuck did I see him? I don't know, but I've seen him and it wasn't in Spanish Harlem."

Weadock liked Harrington when he was sober. When he was razor sharp, intelligent, and charming but that was rare. Harrington was an incurable alcoholic. He drank constantly, becoming progressively unpleasant with each new drink, occasionally transforming himself into the dreadful Mister Hyde. This was when he was most offensive and most vulnerable.

Suddenly, the Irishman stood up, bent over with his hat in his hand, and kissed Piney's ring as if the old man was the prince of the church. Guiseppe followed the two men to the door and locked it when they left the premises. He stopped at their table to clear the dishes and Harrington ordered another drink. Weadock ordered an espresso.

Guiseppe came back with double espresso and a bottle of anisette. He filled Weadock's wineglass.

"Grazie," Weadock said.

Guiseppe nodded.

Weadock and Harrington had reached that placid area of inebriation where men talk about private things.

Harrington sensed some anxiety in Weadock's face. "Don't worry about me, kid. I know what

I'm dealing with here. This psycho of yours has no idea what a dangerous son-of-a-bitch I am."

"Jay," Weadock twisted a lemon peel and dropped it into his espresso, "this guy may have killed a dozen people. I think he killed Lopez and you know what a bad guy he was."

"Lopez trusted too many people. I don't trust anyone… except you, sergeant darling. I trust you."

Weadock splashed a shot of anisette into his espresso and emptied the cup in one swallow.

Harrington turned to order another espresso.

"No." Weadock locked eyes with Guiseppe. "I have to drive home, but tell the Don that I saved this last glass of his excellent wine to toast his good health."

"Well." Harrington sat up in awe.

Giuseppe shuffled to the rear and whispered Weadock's message into Piney's ear.

Weadock drank and Piney responded with a smile and an affirmative nod.

"Well."

"Can I drop you someplace, Mr. Harrington?"

"Thanks, but Frankie the Hand is coming for me." Harrington had chosen Charlie Weadock to be the son he never had and he was grateful for all their brief encounters.

A genuine thrill of fatherly pride flowed through him when the Don nodded with approval. The one thing that cut him deep was Weadock's restriction on their relationship, it was strictly business. Weadock kept the old man out of his private life. Harrington wanted more, but understood the rules that applied to CI's and played the game. He carried Weadock's home phone number in his wallet for years, but never used it.

"Frankie the Hand?" Weadock looked puzzled.

"You met him at the Bull & Bear."

"The midget with the hearse?"

"Frankie is a tough piece of work. And he has a mint Cadillac limousine."

"C'mon, the car's older than him."

"He has a license to carry, and he's my chauffeur and bodyguard tonight."

Weadock grinned silently.

"Your money is no good here." Harrington waved when Weadock pulled out his wallet. "It would be an insult."

"I'll leave a tip."

"I gave Giuseppe fifty bucks before you got here and I'll give him another fifty when I leave."

"Well." Weadock stood up. "Watch your ass, old man."

Twenty minutes later, Weadock parked in front of the oval building on Third Avenue and Fifty-Third Street. Waiting for Theresa to come out, he slumped in the seat. The digital clock on the dash board read 8:50 p.m.

Routine surveillance habits urged him to check his mirrors. Looking in the rearview mirror, he noticed a man in black clothing just inside the subway entrance on the corner. When he stepped out of the car to get a better look, the figure had vanished. He locked the car and scrambled toward the subway station. The ghostly figure could have only gone down the steps. No one else was in the area or on the subway stairs but he could hear footsteps below. He followed the sounds down to the next level only to find two homeless bodies already covered with cardboard for the night and a lone black man in the token booth. The subterranean cavern was quite silent with a steady cool breeze coming from the tunnels below. He quickly walked through the subway tunnel to the West side of Third Avenue and climbed the staircase steps to the street.

The immediate area was vacant so he went back down, showed his badge to the token booth clerk, and questioned him. The clerk said he had dozed off and saw nothing. Weadock returned to his car and leaned against the cool metal, he wondered if he had drank too much wine with Harrington or had it been an actual visit from the monster.

His troubled expression changed as Theresa came through the revolving front door with a load of homework in her hands. She pushed through the door with her shoulder.

Outside, a gust of wind blew a few strands of her hair in her face. She puffed them aside by extending her lower lip and blowing hard. She smiled when she saw him. Her face beamed with radiance and inner happiness. She was oblivious to everyone but him as they kissed. Taking her attaché case, he scanned the area again. She hugged him close and remained in his safe grasp for a long time.

Two young secretaries chuckled as they walked around them.

"The whole building will know about us tomorrow." she said.

THE HIERARCHY

WEADOCK AND GUGLIELMO WERE ORDERED BY THE CHIEF OF DETECTIVES to attend a Task Force Conference at the Midtown Precinct South the next day.

Irked by Weadock's lack of zeal to attend the top brass meeting, Guglielmo waited in the precinct hallway outside the squad room for Weadock to arrive. He appeared at 9:55 AM and they entered the crowded squad room together.

"Don't start any trouble here, Charlie. If the Chief wants any input from FIAU, I'll give it to him."

Guglielmo crossed the room to engage a colleague in a one-sided conversation about the futility of detectives. Captain Pinsky pretended to listen to Guglielmo's small talk but his attention was somewhere else in the room. Guglielmo's pointless laughing agitated Pinsky more than his cutting remarks about detectives so Pinsky finally walked away.

Guglielmo actually held a position of great power in the NYPD as Chief Whalen's top advisor on corruption, but he had no idea how to use that power. He was just a nervous cop who laughed inappropriately after every remark made to him. He was also quite rank conscious, snapping to attention as the Chief of Detectives entered the squad room.

Chief Lazarus, in his mid-sixties, was still a forceful and charismatic personality. His fifteen years as a super chief made him a powerful entity in the Department. He had a knack for matching names and faces, a talent that helped catapult him to the top ranks of the NYPD.

Lazarus made his way into Kennedy's office and sat in the squad commander's chair. He whispered to his aide, Inspector John Flynn who began pushing chairs into the room like the house waiter.

Weadock felt that he was the leader of a covert investigative team and it was wrong and unnecessary to expose his identity and purpose to so many other cops. Cops he made someday have to follow. Lieutenant Kennedy came up next to Weadock and handed him a container of coffee. "I hope I didn't leave anything personal on my desk." He stared at the crowd around his desk.

"What's this all about, Vincent?"

"Beats me." Kennedy dipped his head at the chief. "He usually waits until Christmas to let us kiss his ring and his ass."

"Why, Vincent." Weadock turned to examine Kennedy's face, "Have you no respect for the hierarchy?"

"Ah, I heard he's writing a book and wants to use this case for the last chapter."

"Optimistic, isn't he?"

"If we solve this mystery, he gets a great finish in his book and retires with a fat monthly check. And the PC and Mayor will get a lot of great press."

"And if we don't?"

"If we don't solve it, you or more likely I, will take the rap for it."

"What kind of guy is he?"

"The Chief?"

"Yeah."

"My grandfather would say that he could be easily spotted in a naked lineup."

"No balls, huh?"

Kennedy nodded.

"How is the old sergeant?"

"I haven't seen him in a long time. Michael tells me that he hangs out at Chelsea Park and plays bocce ball with the wops."

Weadock laughed.

Inspector Flynn stuck his head out of Kennedy's office. "Are the people from FIAU here?"

"Here, sir." Guglielmo waved an arm high in the air and began pushing his way through the crowd. Weadock followed him. Flynn waved at Kennedy and Kennedy nodded at Marini. They moved into the small office. Detective Marini, the only non-ranking officer in the room, managed to close the door.

Chief Lazarus stood and swept the room with his eyes. "I came here directly from the Commissioner's Office. This investigation has mushroomed into an ugly mess and he wants it solved. It's my understanding that the body count is now ten. Is that correct?" He turned to Flynn.

Flynn nodded.

"Excuse me, Chief," Kennedy said, "but that's only in Manhattan South."

"What exactly does *that* mean, Lieutenant?"

"The stats we have are for the borough of Manhattan only. I sent out citywide inquiries, but none of the other boroughs have answered yet."

"Great." Lazarus shot an annoyed look at Flynn.

Flynn reacted with embarrassment and turned to Kennedy. "You think there might be more victims?"

"I don't know, Sir. Since they have not answered, it's possible."

Lazarus looked at Guglielmo. "It's my understanding that FIAU has a suspect."

"Yes, Sir." Guglielmo turned to Weadock.

"But I thought you-" Weadock stammered.

"Answer the Chief, Charlie!"

Weadock glanced around the room full of strangers before focusing on Chief Lazarus. "I would like to remind everyone in this room that the subject in my case is part of an active Internal Affairs Investigation. Under normal conditions, the details of any FIAU case would be unavailable to anyone until the case is officially closed. But due to the seriousness of the crimes involved, the Police Commissioner has authorized us to share our investigation with the Detective Division."

"You're Sergeant Weadock?" Chief Lazarus asked.

"Yes, sir."

"Is there anyone in this room who does not completely understand what the sergeant has just said?" The chief looked around the room and waited for a response but no one dared speak. "We get enough bad press just doing our jobs. They could have a field day with this one so I want a tight lid on it. If this killer turns out to be a cop, the arrest will be made by FIAU. Otherwise a Detective will make the arrest. That's the way the PC and the Mayor want it. He wants the public to know that we can clean our own house. You've all seen the Mollen Commission Hearings on TV. Right now they're dramatizing a few rotten cops whose names you all know and the public is eating it up. A lot of people think we're all in it with them and we're all going to take it on the chin for that. Just like our predecessors did twenty years ago from the Knapp Commission." Lazarus turned to Lieutenant Kennedy. "Okay, Lieutenant, tell them what we've got?"

Kennedy lectured to the group for half an hour. He began with the murder of the Perez brothers on Halloween night in 1987 and worked his way through each of the homicides to the Lopez murder. Frequently referring to his notes on the blackboard and key information provided by Weadock, Kennedy zipped through the briefing in record time and asked if anyone had any questions.

"Is there a description of the perpetrator?" Inspector Flynn asked.

"Male, Hispanic, 30 years of age."

"That's it? That's all?"

Kennedy handed Flynn the last complaint follow-up report. NO NEW INVESTIGATIVE LEADS SINCE LAST REPORT.

"I can't believe that there are no witnesses to ten separate homicides," Lazarus said.

"There are a few, Chief," Kennedy said, "but only one of them saw the killer up close and he failed to pick our suspect out of a line-up." Kennedy pointed to the blackboard. "We've interviewed every witness in every homicide several times, it's a dead end. There is no useful physical evidence; no prints on any of the weapons recovered, no prints at any of the crime scenes, nothing. We've got nothing and the DA will not prosecute FIAU's subject on nothing."

"Okay." The Chief clapped his hands. "The first meeting of the homicide task force is over." Everyone exited like the ball game was over, but the Chief stopped Kennedy and Weadock. "You two guys stay put." The chief waited until everyone was out of the room then went to the window and looked at a heavy overcast sky. "Close the door, Lieutenant." He took a three-foot wooden ruler and swung it like a five iron. "I can't hit a green with all this shit on my mind… What's your gut feeling about this, Sergeant?" He looked at Weadock.

"I'm convinced that this cop is our assassin. I also believe that he knows that we suspect him as the killer. How he found out is another mystery, but I think it's a mistake to sit on it. He might or might not kill again and even if he does it's not likely that he'll leave any new clues behind. He's methodical and I don't think we're going to catch him in the act with the pipe in his hand."

"Is that it?"

"Chief, this guy is street wise and clever." Weadock glanced at Kennedy, then back to the Chief. "For reasons I don't quite understand, he's playing some kind of cat and mouse game with us. Perhaps this is his weakness."

"Go on." The Chief leaned back in Kennedy's chair and lit the slobbered cigar he had previously chewed to bits.

"I'd like to get him into psych services for an evaluation. Perhaps a shrink can push his buttons and make something happen. He might make a mistake."

"How can you get him into psych services if he's so clean?" Lazarus asked.

"We're going to flake him," Kennedy said.

The Chief almost swallowed his cigar. "Look, you guys work out the details of your plan after I leave." He rolled his eyes past Flynn who looked at the ceiling.

"What about our other cases, Chief?" Weadock asked.

"Right now, this is your only case." Lazarus and Flynn headed for the door. "If you need any more people, call Inspector Flynn at One P.P."

"Whaddaya' mean, we'll flake him?" Weadock asked.

Kennedy moved into his chair and tapped a pen against the top of his desk. "Well, I got this idea. Tell me what you think. Velez, like a lot of cops, owns two guns, an off duty and a service revolver. They usually leave one in their locker. I'll pick the lock and steal his gun. A lost gun is automatic Charges and Specs. You get the case and do the GO15 Hearing. At the hearing you aggravate the shit out of him. That should be easy for you. When he goes wacko, you refer him to psych services for a lobotomy or something."

"You can pick a lock?"

"Sure, all good Detectives can."

"I don't like it." Weadock rubbed his head. "What if he's really innocent? Are we going to become criminals just to catch a criminal?"

"Okay, okay, it was just an idea."

"How about a prostitute?"

Kennedy slanted his head with interest. "An anonymous prostitute makes a complaint about a male Hispanic cop who matches Ramon's description exactly. She alleges that he showed her a police badge with his number on it and frightened her into giving him free sex."

"I like that one, too."

"One of the girls in my office will make the complaint."

"I may have misjudged you, Weadock," Kennedy said. "You are a tenacious cutthroat, aren't you?"

THE ALLEGATION

DETECTIVE VALERIE BISHOP HAD A TALENT for playacting on the telephone. She played a telephone game at FIAU every six months by calling one of the station houses in the Manhattan south area and alleging that one of its members made sexist, racial or profane remarks to her and insist that the named officer be reprimanded. Afterwards, she would check with the Civilian Complaint Review Board to determine if the person accepting the complaint actually reported it.

On Wednesday, July 8, 1992, she telephoned the Action Desk at IAD.

"Internal Affairs, Detective Dipietro." Beep...

"I want to complain about a pig."

"This is the New York City Police Department's Internal Affairs Division." Beep... "Do you want to make a complaint about a New York City police officer?" Beep.

"Yes... Yes, I do."

"Can I have your name, miss?"

"Sweet Gloria."

"What's your last name? Beep..."

"Sweet."

"Sweet Gloria Sweet?"

"No, fool. It's Gloria Sweet but everybody calls me Sweet Gloria."

"Address?"

"No address and no phone."

"How can we contact you if you don't give me an address?"

"I just want to report this deranged motherfucking cop to you. Are you going to accept my information or do I have to call the Mayor?"

"Is it Miss or Mrs. Sweet?"

"Miss."

"What happened?"

"About four months ago, this Puerto Rican pig picked me up on 28th Street and 11th Avenue. He had a black Cadillac with leather seats. He showed me his badge and gun and said he would bust my ass unless I gave him some free head."

"What kind of head?"

"You know, a blowjob."

"...continue."

"So I complied but he comes back last Friday night and wants another free one."

"Lots of people have guns and badges. What makes you think he's a cop?"

"He threw that badge and gun on me and I gave him head."

"You're a prostitute?" ...Beep.

"Of course, fool."

"Do you know this person's name?"

"No but his badge number is 24481, I saw it twice.

"Describe him."

"He's tall for a Puerto Rican. Good looking, but scary. My old man told me to call IA"

"When did this happen?" Beep...

"What is that noise?"

"That noise is to let you know that this conversation is being taped."

No response.

"What was the date of occurrence?"

"What?"

"When did it happen?"

"Saint Patrick's day and again last Friday about five in the morning."

"Where?"

"I told you, 28th Street and 11th Avenue."

"Both times?" Beep...

"Yep," Bishop wanted to laugh but muffled it when Weadock waved a hand at her. "I'm telling you this pig is one sick mother."

"Why do you say that, Sweet Gloria?"

"He made me hold his gun while I was doing it."

"You mean his dick?"

"No, Mister. I mean the one with the bullets in it. His dick was in my mouth."

"You better give me an address and telephone num–"

"No way, bro."

"Where are you now?"

"Working."

"Where?"

"28th and 10th."

"Wait there, I'm sending someone to talk to you."

Click.

"Hello? Hello…" Beep.

Five minutes later, an IAD supervisor telephoned Manhattan South FIAU with the details of the allegation and requested a response to the scene. Detective Falcone acknowledged the *call-out* information but there was no response.

Two hours later, weadock telephoned the IAD Action Desk and reported that he and Detective Falcone responded to the scene and questioned several prostitutes. None admitted to giving free blowjobs to police officers or holding a cop's gun during a sex act. Two of the prostitutes stated that they knew Sweet Gloria and described her as a female, black, 20 years of age with long black hair and bad

teeth, but they hadn't seen her in the area for weeks.

Due to the nature of the complaint the investigating complaint should be returned to FIAU for investigation.

Four days later the pinks *(official complaint forms)* came through channels to MS/FIAU. The base papers identified shield number 24481 as Police Officer Ramon Velez, assigned to the Fifth Precinct. IAD failed to connect Velez to the already active murder case.

Weadock telephoned Kennedy when he received the pinks and invited him to witness the GO15 hearing of Police Officer Velez on August 18, 1992 at the FIAU Office in the 17th Precinct.

"At your office?" Kennedy sulked. "Somebody might see me."

"Wear a disguise."

"Very funny. How come I'm not laughing?"

"This is a murder investigation, Lieutenant. Don't you want to solve it?"

"Listen, Weadock, it's hard for me to believe that this serial killer could actually be a cop but it's even harder for me to be associated with Internal Affairs."

"Be here by 09:30."

THE G.O.15 HEARING

THE CROWDED BACK ROOM IN THE FIAU OFFICE HUMMED WITH CONVERSATION until Weadock raised one hand and pointed to the tape recorder with the other. The room went silent and he pressed the record button. "The date is Wednesday, July 15th, 1992, the time is 0940. This is Sergeant Charles Weadock, Shield Number 1065, at Patrol Borough Manhattan South, Field Internal Affairs Unit. I am about to interview Police Officer Ramon Velez, shield number 24481, Fifth Precinct, in connection with a complaint alleged by a prostitute known as Gloria Sweet. The allegation was received at IAD by telephone. The complainant alleged that Officer Velez coerced her into an act of oral sodomy on two occasions, March 17th, 1992 and July 2nd, 1992 in the early morning hours. The complainant further alleged that on both occasions Officer Velez insisted that she hold his loaded .38 caliber revolver while she performed oral sex on him. She identified the subject officer by his shield number 24481, his physical description and a black Cadillac with black glass windows. This is a test of the machine."

Twenty minutes later, Velez's attorney, Ray Kero, announced himself at the front door and Weadock walked the length of the office to meet him. Most of the FIAU Investigators knew him as the daydreaming PBA Attorney with the big mouth who always helped himself to the doughnuts on the table but never brought any with him. Weadock advised Kero of the allegations made against Velez and walked with him to a hallway bench where Velez waited alone. Weadock and Velez silently sized each other up.

Ten minutes later, Weadock and Sergeant James Casey led Kero and Velez through the 17th Detective Squad room to a sound proof interview room that was shared by the FIAU and the Detectives. The detectives clearly took offense to having the Internal Affairs people in their office.

Velez sat stone-faced next to his waggish legal counsel and studied Weadock's movements. He knew the allegations against him were a mistake in identity or more likely a setup to see his memorandum records for the last five years.

Waiting for Weadock to set up the recorder, Kero fingered his polka dot tie in Oliver Hardy fashion. His fish like eyes bulged behind a pair of iron rimmed glasses as he scanned the room.

Weadock opened a thick manila folder and searched Velez's face. "Do you have any questions before I begin, Officer?"

"No, sir."

"Counselor?"

"No questions."

Weadock depressed the record button on the tape recorder and verified the tape's movement with his eyes. As the cassette turned, he fixed his eyes on Velez and gave his opening statement from memory. "This is an official Department investigation. It's my duty to inform you that you are required to answer questions directed to you by a ranking officer truthfully and to the best of your knowledge. Do you understand?"

"Yes, sir."

"I am Sergeant Charles Weadock, Manhattan South, Field Internal Affairs Unit. Present with me is…"

"Sergeant James Casey."

"State your rank, name, shield number and command."

"Police Officer Ramon Velez, shield number 24481, Fifth Precinct."

"Present with you for voice identification is..." Weadock turned to Kero and waited.

"Raymond E. Kero, Attorney for Stanashack, Stanashack and Cohen, representing the PBA."

"Officer Velez, are you acquainted with a prostitute named Gloria Sweet?"

"No, sir."

"Are you acquainted with any prostitutes?"

"No, sir."

"Did you ever frequent the area of 28th Street and 11th Avenue in the Tenth Precinct?"

"I don't recall, sir."

"Did you ever permit another individual to hold your weapon?"

"Maybe a range officer."

"Anyone else?"

"No Sir."

"The complainant stated that she performed oral sex with you at your insistence on two separate occasions. Is that true?"

"No, sir."

"She further alleged that on these two occasions you ordered her to hold your loaded revolver. Is that true?"

"No, sir."

"She said that you picked her up on both occasions in a black Cadillac with black glass. Do you own a car like that, Officer?"

Ramon hesitated. "Yes, sir."

"She said that the badge you showed her had the numbers 24481 on it. Is that your badge number, Officer?"

"Yes, sir."

"How do you suppose the complainant knew that you owned a black Cadillac?"

"Speculation," Kero said.

"How do you suppose she knew your shield number?"

"Speculation, again. You can't ask the officer what someone else was thinking."

"You live and work on the East Side, but this happened on the West Side. Why would you go there?"

Ramon stared directly at Weadock and gave a negative shrug.

"If you do not give a verbal answer, the machine cannot record it."

No response.

"Speak up officer," Kero said. "The sergeant tape recorder can't hear you."

"I don't know this woman." Velez looked at his attorney. "I don't know how she knows these things about me, but it's a lie."

"How could she describe you so perfectly?"

"Sergeant," Kero interrupted, "is the complainant available for cross examination?"

"Not at this time, counselor."

"If she does become available for questioning, please contact my office immediately."

"What was your assignment on March 17th, 1992?"

Velez flipped through his memorandum book and stopped. "I was off duty."

"And on July 2nd, 1992?"

He flipped a few more pages. "Off duty." Velez was sure by now that this whole show was nothing but a witch-hunt for information.

"If you could establish where you were on either of those dates this case could be closed immediately with an exonerated disposition."

"I don't recall." Ramon knew exactly what it meant and he knew exactly where he was on both occasions, but he let his mind speculate. Some cop may have used his name or perhaps it was just a mistake in identity but finally he felt some type of frame-up was in progress. *Only an asshole would use his own shield to do something wrong,* Velez thought to himself. *Weadock should be questioning Detective Santos, not him.* He looked at Weadock's gold sergeant's badge hanging from his shirt pocket, and then looked right into Weadock's eyes. "I believe I was at home on both those occasions, sir."

In an adjacent room, Falcone adjusted the hidden video camera and zoomed in on Ramon. As his face came into focus, Falcone could see the rage in Ramon's eyes.

"This is my first visit to Gestapo headquarters." Kennedy leaned against a cinder block wall to observe Ramon's icy glances through a one-way mirror. "What do you think, Alex?" the lieutenant whispered.

"This guy's a sick puppy, lieutenant. Look at him. He keeps glancing at the mirror, he knows we're here. He's a true ice man."

The locker room was dark and had the smell of armpits and soiled socks. Marini lost interest in the interview and began strolling up and down the rows of lockers until he found a familiar name tag. "Hey!" he blurted out. "Remember-"

"Shush!" Falcone hissed. "The walls are thin."

Kennedy bent over to look through the lens and Ramon turned his face to the mirror. "Are you sure he can't see us?"

Falcone nodded affirmatively as he disconnected the camera from the tripod. The interview had ended.

Kennedy continued looking at the empty interrogation room. "What do you think of Charlie Weadock, Falcone?"

"What do you mean?"

"Is he a good boss?"

"When we're in the field, he always introduces me as his partner. I'm a detective and he's a Sergeant, my boss, but I never feel it. You know what I mean?"

"How about the rest of your team?"

"They'd follow him into hell."

"Does he know what he's doing?"

"Lieutenant, he could be the PC. I mean... He's only a sergeant but he knows what's wrong with the job and he knows how to fix it. Everybody comes to him for advice. The captain runs everything passed him. Even Chief Whalen comes to our office to have private chats with him. He's the best investigator I've ever seen."

"I've heard that he goes for the throat every time."

"If you're talking about bad cops, criminal cops -- yes. If he thinks he's got a bad guy, he won't let the case go. The captain has to sneak into the back room and snatch the older cases from our files. If he didn't, they'd never get closed."

Falcone and Kennedy watched Marini wash his hands and dry his wet hands on a uniform shirt hanging from a locker.

"There are no paper towels in this place." Marini complained.

Walking between rows of lockers back to the squad room, Kennedy shook his head at the identical combination locks dangling from the locker handles. He touched each of the locks as he passed them; then paused to look back. "Some things never change, do they?"

THE FACE LIFT

AS THE VOLUME OF NEW FIAU CASES INCREASED, the Ramon Investigation got less and less attention. Observations on Ramon became boring as he led investigators on worthless journeys and dead end surveillances.

On August 10th, 1992, Alvin Baker and Oswaldo Urena pled guilty to one count of Criminal Sale of a Controlled Substance. The attorneys played *Let's Make a Deal,* and the two defendants got five years probation with no jail time. It was a tougher rap for Baker because the PC fired him as soon as he received confirmation of his felony conviction. Baker lost his job and his car. Since the car was used in the commission of a crime, the City of New York confiscated it but he and worse his family lost his pension.

The excellent videotapes and 35mm photographs taken at Ramon's GO15 Hearing became useless when the only witness to see the murderer up close at the Happy Hansen murder scene, Dietrich Tesslar, had vanished.

Professor Ferreri telephoned from Carlsbad, New Mexico and told Weadock that he had met the woman of his dreams in a bat cave. He would not be coming back to New York City.

The Mollen Commission was in its fifth week of televised corruption hearings. Every day, a procession of nefarious cops testified before the panel of five judges and the cosmos watched the show. One corrupt cop after another spun a tale of greed and misconduct in soap opera fashion. Some of them smirked as they told their repugnant stories, others cried. Still others shocked the nation and overwhelmed their own brothers in blue. The word on the street was that IAD would take the rap for failing to capture these criminals in the ranks of policemen and heads were going to roll for that failure.

The media's exploitation of these public traitors only lengthened the agony for other hard working, dedicated cops who hit the streets every day. The good cops took it on the chin from friends, neighbors and families. The rogue cops were blaming their brother officers and supervisors for allowing them to become such villains.

Theresa and Charlie watched the unfolding police drama every night on video replay TV.

"Am I going to see you on television?"

He glanced at her and returned his attention to the television. "I don't think so. They decided to use Falcone and Mister X, to tell the Alvin Baker Story. I guess the hierarchy doesn't want me to tell my version of the case."

"Who's Mister X?"

"One of my confidential informants."

"Do you think all cops are corrupt like they say?"

"Do you?" He didn't look at her.

"Well, I know some of them are good, but I trust them less and less as this show goes on."

"See," Weadock headed for the kitchen, "it's a show, nothing but Monday night at the movies. Nothing will ever come of this. We all know that the space between good and evil is thin and complicated. All those ex-cops testifying on TV are grasping for something. Shorter prison sentences, sympathy or… perhaps forgiveness. They all didn't begin as bad guys. Some are just bad and probably would have drifted into criminal activity regardless of their occupation. If they were bus drivers, they'd probably become bad bus drivers, etcetera, and etcetera."

"Attorneys, too?"

"You know what I mean." He watched the TV from the kitchen. "They found the easy money and liked it. They liked having the things that easy money could buy and went for it. There's no difference between them and any other criminal, except they were wearing uniforms and badges."

The panorama of the Manhattan skyline drew her to the terrace. "I suppose." Her gaze moved east to the darkness of Long Island. "Are we going to Vinny's party?"

"Do you want to go?"

"I asked you first."

"Who else is going to be there?"

"Everyone."

"Your father?"

"Yep."

"Your brothers?"

"Yep."

"I'd rather not go."

"Coward."

"I don't wanna deal with your family right now."

"Okay."

"But I don't want to keep you from going."

She walked to the kitchen and kissed him on the neck. "You aren't keeping me from anything. I'm with you now. I need you and I love you. My mother told me that there were men like you but I didn't believe her."

"What do you mean by that?"

"She said I would find my prince charming. A man who would listen to my needs and share himself with me. There's something in you, Charlie Weadock, that all men need but very few have."

Placing his hands on the sides of her face, he caressed the stress points behind her eyes and kissed her on the lips. His fingers moved softly over her skull and down to her shoulders.

"Where did you learn this stuff?"

His hands migrated over the muscles in her back and neck. When she turned her face him, one of those magnificent hands worked its way under her blouse. She smiled and he rolled his eyes. He was gentle and giving and began undressing her. He kissed her body in secret places. Places where no one but she and now he had ever touched. He kissed her everywhere. She tugged at his clothes as they sank to the floor. "Where did you learn this stuff, sergeant?" She whimpered in delight.

He took a deep breath. "I just make it up as I go along."

He brought his lips to her ear. "It just seems right," he whispered, "and it *feels* right." He massaged her feet and ankles, alternating from one leg to the other and worked his way to her knees and up between her legs, his hot fingers squeezing the aches from each thigh with two hands. Then higher, she lifted her pelvis to expedite the removal of her panties. Steaming with hot emotion they hardly undressed and locked their lips together. She was hot and wet and ready. She arched her body against him. Urging him forward until he was deep inside her. Afterward, they were spent and sleep came easy to them.

The next morning, they walked to the oval building on 53rd Street and 3rd Avenue. "Theresa called it the Lipstick Building," she said as she cupped a hand around his neck and reeled him in for a final kiss. It was a big wet kiss that drew loud cheers from passersby. Then she disappeared through a revolving door.

McIntosh laid his newspaper down as Weadock entered the SIU room. "You hear about IAD?"

"What about IAD, Jimmy?"

"They're out. Finished. They won't exist after October thirty-first."

"You're joking."

"Came over the teletype this morning. The Captain's down at the borough office with the Chief right now."

"Halloween, huh? They couldn't have picked a better day for it."

"The word is that all the FIAU Units will become the new Internal Affairs Bureau. Oh, yeah. Lieutenant Kennedy called about an hour ago. He wants you to meet him at Bellevue Hospital at eleven o'clock."

"Did he say why?"

"Harbor's bringing in a floater from Staten Island. He thinks it's that night clerk from the Terminal Hotel."

Two hours later, Weadock and McIntosh waited in the main lobby of Bellevue Hospital. A stainless steel door marked City Morgue opened and a group of medical students crowded into the lobby from the vaults below. The orderly leading them joked about the price of blood and body parts on the black market.

Kennedy and his two wingmen, Marini and Carbonaro, came in as the students moved into another room.

"Ever been in here before, Charlie?" Kennedy asked.

"No, but I've been to the Brooklyn Morgue."

Kennedy turned to the orderly who was saying goodbye to the students. "I'm Lieutenant Kennedy; I have an appointment with Doctor Stone. Is he here?"

"Mister Stone will be right back."

"Stone isn't a medical doctor?"

"He isn't a doctor of any kind, sir. His status as an orderly is also questionable. In fact, his status as a human being is--"

A tall, slender man in a white coat appeared. Don't pay any attention to this fool, gentlemen. I know why you're here. Please follow me."

Stone led the five sleuths down a flight of metal stairs and through a long narrow tunnel. At the end, he pushed a refrigerator-type door open and held it open with his back, revealing hundreds of dead, naked corpses dangling from the ceiling on meat hooks. A pair of steel earmuffs connected each cadaver to a rolling monorail system in the ceiling.

"This is the meat locker, gentlemen."

"We're not here for the regular tour," Kennedy said. "We just want to see the floater from Staten Island."

"Okay, Lieutenant," Stone frowned. "Come this way."

The sound of their footsteps echoed through the crypt-like passageways as they walked past several autopsy rooms. Stone flicked at the ID tags dangling from the feet of dead bodies. All attempts to mask the odor of death with chemicals had failed. Corpses filled the hallways and autopsy rooms. The body they came to view was in a stainless steel cooler. Stone pulled on the handle and the naked, uncovered body became visible.

"He was completely dressed when they fished him out of the water," Stone said. "Shoes, socks, everything. He even had his wallet. No money of course. They never have money by the time they get here. His brain and eyes were gone, Fish food, you know."

Stone smiled as the cops were appalled at the sight of the hideous corpse. This orderly seemed to enjoy his job.

"The body actually stayed pretty fresh in the cold water. We figure he was in the sea for four or five days. A piece of the skull is missing, you know." Stone turned the cadaver's head with his bare hands. "This type of injury could have been caused by a fall."

"Or a blow to the head by a blunt instrument." Weadock suggested.

"I suppose. Any other questions, gentlemen?"

Kennedy glanced at Weadock. "Is that Tesslar?"

"I don't know, I never met the man."

Kennedy put his arm around Stone and walked away. He came back with a plastic bag of clothing and personal property and waved it at Weadock. Kennedy nodded at his two detectives. "These guys checked out Tesslar's apartment this morning. He lived alone in an eight family walk-up in the East Village. They had to break into the apartment with the patrol sergeant. They searched the place and questioned everyone in the building. They came up with nada. The landlord was the last person to see him alive. That was Friday night when he went to work."

"Shit!" Weadock fumed. "He was the only witness who could have positively identified the killer. We should have protected him."

"But you said he didn't see a photo array of Velez."

"Perhaps Velez didn't know that."

Outside, Weadock took Kennedy aside.

"I think this guy is stalking your sister and me."

"What?"

"We went to Lincoln Center last week. When we came out, I saw his car parked on a side street. I'm positive it was his Caddy. I didn't say anything because I didn't want to frighten her, but his car was there, parked exactly where I would park it if I were doing surveillance. He was in a good position to see my car when we left but he was already gone when we came out."

Kennedy looked up in thought.

"It may have happened once before," Weadock continued, "near the building where she works but I'm not too sure about that one. She was working late and I met her there. I believe he's also shadowing one of my informants, a CI I sent up to Spanish Harlem to get info on him."

"What do you want do about it?"

"I don't know. I can't keep my case open like a homicide. The DA and my boss have been pushing me for six months to close it. I think they're waiting for the Mollen Commission to close its doors. You, on the other hand, can follow this monster around until he dies. Homicides are never closed, am I right?"

"That's right, but I don't like what you're telling me and I think you should tell her what's going on. It's better if she knows."

"I'm with her all the time. I walk her to work and pick her up at night."

"All the time?" Kennedy raised his voice. "My sister? You're with my sister all the time?"

"It's okay." Weadock patted Kennedy on the shoulder. "Like it or not, I'm going to be your brother-in-law."

"Well, brother-in-law, lets figure out what to do with this psycho?"

PUBLIC TESTIMONY

DAY AFTER DAY, A CAVALCADE of criminal cops attesting to their dishonorable and shocking behavior came into living rooms of citizens everywhere. Two things became obvious to viewers. The Internal Affairs Division was the main target of the Commission's Investigation *and* the police were unable to police themselves.

On Friday of that week, an ominous figure wearing a black hood entered the court-like arena and Channel 13 recaptured the now sagging public attention. Only those closely associated with the Alvin Baker case knew the real identity of this witness. A rumble of noisy curiosity and awe swept through the chamber when the witness first appeared in the doorway of the New York Bar Association. All eyes and ears focused on the fat man with the raspy voice. CI 13737 treaded his way through a barrage of photo flashes to the witness table. The eyes within the dark hood darted around the room with audacity. He lowered his huge frame into the witness chair and an unseen smirk formed on his face under the black hood.

Introduced as Mister X, Heckle raised his right hand and swore to tell the whole truth and nothing but the truth.

"I'm a confidential operative working for various government agencies," he said.

"Such as?" Assistant counsel Sarah Ginsberg prodded.

"FBI, DEA, ATF, NYPD."

Ginsberg turned to face the judges and began her puppet show. "Your Honors, this witness is a registered Confidential Informant with an impressive record of felony convictions." She pulled all the right strings from her chair at the attorneys' table and Mister X merely responded to her questions.

The man in the black hood told of his long association with rogue cops. "I hung out with cops who used and abused drugs. They were my friends, we partied together. We bought and sold drugs… and other stuff."

"What other stuff?" Ginsberg probed.

"Guns."

"Tell the court about your association with IAD."

He adjusted the itchy, black hood that kept inching up his lower lip as he spoke. "I went to IAD to identify a hit man and they treated me like shit."

One of the judges leaned forward. "Can you be more specific about the allegation without using profanity?"

"Sure, judge. I told my boss at ATF about a cop who kills for drug dealers. She sent me to IAD."

"What happened to the allegation?" Ginsberg urged.

"I don't know. IAD said he wasn't a cop."

"Mr. X, do you know if any other investigative agency received your complaint?"

"Yeah, Manhattan South, FIAU. A couple of months later, a sergeant and a detective came to see me with the same information. They found this cop in three days."

"When did you report the criminal activities of Officer Baker to FIAU?"

"About a month after I began working for FIAU."

"But you were working for various law enforcement agencies for over two years. Why did you wait so long before reporting Alvin Baker to the police?"

"Well, ya' see -- I was with the bad guys for a long time and didn't trust anyone."

"Mr. X," a judge leaned forward, "How did you come to be employed by the FBI?"

"They caught me transporting drugs. I agreed to work for them, and they dropped the charges. Then some of the other good guy organizations heard about me and hired me to work undercover for them. I became a regular CI for them all. I helped them make cases and testified in court against hundreds of felons."

The judge leaned back.

"Judge," Mr. X continued without being questioned, "I'm a street person, you know?" He turned to face the television camera. "In my business, you can't trust anyone. There's no way a CI can survive on an informant's paycheck and when it comes paying for information, the NYPD was the cheapest."

"Were all your police acquaintances dishonest?" Another judge asked.

"The cops? Not all of them, some did drugs; some sold drugs and ripped off a lot of dealers. I was right in the middle of this sh.. stuff. The cops I knew were bad, judge. They held a lot of black and blue sessions. They even snitched on their brother cops by telling me about impending raids. Then I'd warn the dealers. The dealers would pay me for the info and I'd pay the cops."

"You worked both sides of the fence?" Attorney Amato implied.

"I did what I had to do to eat and pay the rent."

"If Officer Baker was your friend, why'd you give him up?" Ginsberg asked.

"The sergeant from FIAU did the right thing by me and my… partner. He didn't jerk us around like IAD or the Feds. He was straight with us and offered to help us clean up our act, so we could live the good life. He offered us a chance to start over in another state. So we gave him Baker. We didn't have to do it; he didn't ask us for anything. Baker was our friend, but he was also a bad cop."

"Excuse me, Mister X." One of the other judges leaned forward in his chair. "What is a black and blue session?"

"That's when you get your butt kicked for information."

The enlightened judge nodded at Miss Ginsberg.

She continued. "Did there come a time when you purchased a quantity of drugs from Alvin Baker under the supervision of the FIAU?"

"Three times. We made three buys with him."

"What was the main thrust of the Baker investigation?" Ginsberg rephrased the question when Heckle fumbled for an answer. "You mentioned a barbecue."

"Right, everybody was invited to Baker's barbecue. It was B-Y-O-D, Bring Your Own Drugs."

Ginsberg urged him to continue.

"I mean... you could buy the product there, but it'd cost a lot more. The party was set for July Fourth weekend and a lot of drug dealing cops were coming."

"After you made the first buy on May 13th, 1992, did FIAU investigators make any attempt to arrest Officer Baker?"

"No, Ma'am."

"And approximately twenty-two days later, on June 4th, 1992, you were involved in a second controlled buy of narcotics with Officer Baker?"

"Yes, Ma'am."

"And at that time were there any indications that Officer Baker would be arrested after that buy?"

"No, Ma'am."

"When did you think Officer Baker would be arrested?"

"I was told by the FIAU Sergeant that Baker would be arrested at the Fourth of July barbecue with all the other cops who attended. My brother and I would be arrested, too, but that was just for show."

Ginsberg glanced at the judges before turning to face the camera. "Exactly ten days after that second drug buy, Officer Baker contacted you and requested a third purchase of drugs. Is that correct, Mr. X?"

"Yeah."

"What did you do?"

"I called the FIAU Sergeant and he set up the third buy."

"And was there any indication at that time that Officer Baker would be arrested?"

"No."

"So, when did you first learn that Alvin Baker would be arrested?"

"The morning of the third buy."

Ginsberg turned again to face the judges. "And how did the FIAU investigators feel about arresting Baker at that time?"

"They were pissed; they said their hands were tied. They had orders."

"And what effect did the arrest of Alvin Baker have on the Fourth of July party?"

"It was over, finished."

"So..." Ginsberg walked back to her table and leaned on one hand, "precisely seventeen days before the planned barbecue party in Staten Island where dozens of corrupt cops were to be arrested," she pounded the table with her fist, "the whole investigation came to a sudden and abrupt end."

"That's right."

When the clamor died down, Judge Mollen leaned forward. "Mister X, do you know who gave that order to arrest Alvin Baker?"

"No, no sir. I don't."

On Thursday, August 18th, 1992, the melodrama continued with one more partly disguised witness. First Grade Detective Alexander Falcone made his way to the witness chair. His identity concealed by a wide brimmed hat, Falcone entered a makeshift wooden cubicle and settled into a witness chair. Only the five judges and the two Commission attorneys could see Falcone's face. But public interest, once again aroused, zeroed in on the mysterious witness box in the center of the chamber. A faceless cop with an oversized hat and a turned-up collar promised new thrills to the hearings.

"Did you participate in the FIAU investigation against former Officer Alvin Baker?"

"Yes."

Later, Theresa and Charlie watched a video replay of Falcone's testimony. Falcone just responded to Ginsberg's puppet strings questions and merely filled in the blanks.

"I should have been there," Weadock sulked. "I was responsible for that investigation. I supervised it, I made it happen… I should have answered for its failure." He walked away from the TV in anger. I would have given them all up."

"That's why you weren't called to testify. You can't change any of it now, Charlie. You might as well just watch the show."

He came back and they watched Falcone being led through a series of planned questions. This time, Ginsberg's assistant, Paul Amato, extracted the responses he wanted with laser beam accuracy. The public heard what the attorneys wanted them to hear and no more. Now he knew why the commission had moved him to the back burner.

Falcone was a good detective, but Ginsberg and her sidekick, Amato, were great attorneys. They dramatically navigated Falcone's testimony to focus on their objectives. They used colorful, ingenious charts to show how dozens of corrupt cops escaped punishment. They showed that a direct order from the IAD led to the blown investigation. They made good points, but no one was held accountable. No heads rolled off the block as expected. The order for the premature arrest of Alvin Baker was swept under the rug.

"Who in IAD gave the order?" Weadock yelled at the television set. "And who gave IAD their orders? How far up the ladder did it go?" He turned to Theresa. "Why aren't they asking these questions? Did the PC know? Did the Mayor know? Who's responsible? Why were

there no questions about Ramon? Didn't anyone care about a killer cop?"

The Public hearings on corruption continued for several more weeks, but most of the public lost interest and switched back to the regular fiction cop shows on TV.

A COP IS DEAD

AT ABOUT 2:45 AM ON WEDNESDAY MORNING, Frankie "The Hand" Casarino glanced into the rearview mirror of his limo for the third time in as many blocks and saw something disturbing. He was driving north on an almost empty Avenue of the Americas. After passing Radio City Music Hall a loose tail became visible in the bright lights of the theater behind him. Frankie made a left turn at 57th Street and the dark auto turned with him and followed. "Somebody is shadowing us, JJ."

Harrington struggled to raise his inebriated body from its cushy slouched position and peeked back through the rear window. "Are you sure, Frank?"

"I've been an off the record chauffeur for half a century. Don't you think I can spot a tail? This guy is good, but he isn't *that* good. Looks like a black Caddy to me."

"Son-of-a-bitch!" JJ slapped at the seat between them.

"You know who it is, don't you?"

"Perhaps." Harrington leaned forward. "Drop me off at my hotel. Then go around to the back entrance and pick me up again. I want a closer look at this guy. It could be somebody who wants to kill me."

When Harrington entered his hotel, Frankie drove around the block and picked him up again. Then the two crusty old-timers made their way back to 57th Street to a parking spot opposite the Green Parrot Discotheque, a place where Frankie's limousine blended easily with the other limos and taxicabs waiting for the disco crowd to come out. The black Cadillac Eldorado remained idle in front of the Henry Hudson Hotel.

"I'm not sure," Frankie said, "but I think he latched on to us when we left the topless joint on Murray Street. Why does this person want to kill you, JJ?"

"My friend, Sergeant Weadock, has envisioned my untimely demise by this police dude."

"This guy is a cop and he wants to kill you?"

"Apparently."

"Why don't we kill him first?"

"He's a cop. Sergeant Weadock says this cop following me is a hit man for the Spanish Mafia. I guess he's angry because I'm sticking my nose into his business."

"I can understand that."

Harrington glanced at his friend.

"Let's stay with him for a little while?"

"Whatever you say, boss?"

Thirty minutes later, the Black Cadillac moved off, Eastbound on 57th Street. They followed. The car moved like a model electric train at low speed, smooth and slow. It traveled across Manhattan Island and parked on East 55th Street and 1st Avenue.

Ten minutes later, a man in black clothes opened the trunk of the car and studied its contents for several minutes. Harrington focused on him from a distance. It was indeed Ramon Velez. He removed a large gym bag, closed the trunk and disappeared into the shrubbery of an apartment house. Harrington hawked him like one predator watching another. Sliding down into the soft leather seat again, Harrington stretched alley cat-style and looked to his left. He saw Charlie Weadock's Lincoln parked in a bus stop on the corner. "Something is very wrong here, Frankie." Harrington bailed out of the limo to closely inspect the Lincoln. When he saw the police plate in the front window, he ran to a telephone booth on the corner and dialed the FIAU Office. When no one answered, he dialed 911.

"Hello," a mousy female voice answered, "police operator 365, what's your emergency?"

"I need to contact Sergeant Charles Weadock of Manhattan South Field Internal Affairs and I don't know his pager number."

"Sir, the number for Internal Affairs is 718-555-4321."

Harrington pushed a quarter into the slot and dialed the IAD Action Desk.

An annoyed detective said he would contact Sergeant Weadock through the Manhattan South Borough Headquarters Command and disconnected the call. Harrington turned to his driver who had now moved the limo up to the telephone.

"You have any quarters, Frank?" Harrington began shifting wads of money from pocket to pocket searching for change. "Never mind. Do you have a gun?"

"You know I don't carry anymore, JJ."

Listening to the uproar in the street outside, the night doorman, Juan opened the front door to investigate.

Harrington spotted him and ran for the door. Juan tried to close the door, but Harrington got a foot in the breach. He asked Juan for quarters, but Juan only threatened to call the police.

"You know Sergeant Weadock?" Harrington's eyes centered on the doorman.

Afraid to answer, Juan continued closing the door.

"The policeman who owns that car." Harrington grabbed the frail Hispanic by the collar and pulled his face against the glass. His iron grip tightened when Juan didn't answer. "*That* car!"

"Jes, jes, he lives here now."

"Well, get him on the phone!" Harrington pushed the little man backward. "And tell him that JJ Harrington and Frankie the Hand are downstairs."

"But sir, it's four o'clock in the morning."

"This is a police emergency. Do it now!"

"Frankie who?"

"Harrington, JJ Harrington!"

"You're the police?"

"That's right, I'm a chief Inspector!"

Juan came to attention.

Theresa answered the phone with a yawn. "Yes?"

"Miss Kennedy?"

"Yes?"

"This is Juan, the night man. I'm sorry to annoy jou but there's a Police Chief down here demanding to speak with the sergeant."

"Hold on," Theresa stretched across the bed and tapped Weadock with the phone. "It's for you, Charlie. It's one of your men."

"Hello?" Weadock answered.

"Good morning, Sergeant Weadock." Harrington articulated in his normal suave manner.

Weadock recognized his voice. "Are you out of your skull, Harrington?"

"Listen to me carefully, Sergeant. The spic you are after is in the bushes outside this building right now."

"What?" Weadock changed his demeanor quickly.

"The spic! The spic!" Harrington yelled into the phone and Juan backed away with a wounded expression. "The guy you sent me to find in Spanish Harlem. The one who's killing everybody, he's outside this building in the bushes."

"Wrong." Frankie had followed Harrington into the building and now tapped Harrington on the shoulder. He nodded at the CCTV screen in front of them. "He's in that elevator."

"Now he's in the elevator," Harrington repeated, "and he's going up!"

"Let me talk to Juan."

"Jes sergeant!" Juan snapped to attention when he put the phone to his ear.

"Juan, is there anyone in the elevator?"

"Jes, a man. I don't know him. He didn't come in through the lobby."

"What does he look like?"

"I can't see his face but he has a large bag."

"Tell me what floor he goes to."

Juan handed the telephone receiver to Harrington and ran to the elevator banks where he could watch the floor indicator lights. The elevator stopped on the twentieth floor.

"The top floor!" Juan yelled.

"He got off on the top floor." Harrington repeated into the phone.

"The roof?" Weadock shot a perplexed look at Theresa. "Is there a staircase to the roof?"

Theresa raised her shoulders.

"Jay!"

"Yes."

"Tell Juan to call 911 and report a prowler on the roof. When the cops get here, send them to the roof." Weadock began dressing as if the building was on fire. "Get dressed quick!" He shot an order at Theresa and the look on his face convinced her that it was no drill. She was sure he meant business when he pulled the Walther PPK from its holster. "Stay here!"

"What's wrong, Charlie?" she pleaded.

"There's a bad guy in this building who wants to hurt us." Weadock nudged open the front door and peeked into the hallway. "I think he went to the roof." Weadock stepped out into the hallway and looked back at Theresa. "Lock this door and don't open it for anyone but me."

"Be careful." She closed the door and watched him through the peephole until he disappeared. She bolted the double lock.

Weadock moved down the corridor to the stairwell door and pushed it open. The cinder block walls were cold and damp to the touch. He released the safety on his automatic and held it close to his body. He kept one round in the chamber and seven in the clip and patted the extra clip in his jacket pocket. Listening for the slightest sound, he started up the stairs.

The latch on the roof door dangled in the open position. It was visible the moment Weadock reached the top floor landing. To avoid making a silhouette target for his opponent, he unscrewed the light bulb at the top of the stairs and pushed against the metal roof door until it swung open. The door was worn but silent. Straining his ears and eyes for any sound or movement, he stepped out onto the roof. It was pitch black, save a little illumination from the nearby skyscrapers. The surface was covered by millions of crunchy little pebbles and his first step sent a loud signal across the roof. He readied himself for a response but none came. Listening for footsteps, he stood motionless, hardly breathing until the spring-loaded hinges on the roof door caused it to slowly close behind him.

He reacted quickly to the sound of the elevator cables turning behind him but continuing to cross the roof. Several globe shaped air vents turned silently in the mild wind and a lone siren could be heard far off in the distance. A strange squeaking noise came from the southwest corner of the roof and he moved toward it. He took about ten steps when the roof door suddenly burst open. It slammed against the wall with a loud bang. The sound ricocheted into the night.

Weadock thought he was dead meat and instinctively spun around hoping to get a shot off before he was killed. He raised his gun to eye level. It was exactly the way he had practiced at the police pistol range, but somehow, some unknown force, deep in his gut stopped him from taking the shot and Harrington's paralyzed frame came into focus.

The old man stood in the roof doorway with his mouth open and his eyes gawking down the barrel of Weadock's gun. He threw his hands up in an act of surrender. Weadock signaled to him with his free hand that it was all right and to remain quiet. He lowered his weapon to the ready position and continued advancing to the strange noise. All of a sudden, he saw it. A heavy one-inch rope, one end tied to an air vent pipe and the other end draped over the edge of the building. The rope disappeared into the dark night above Theresa's balcony. No one was on the rope and Weadock bolted passed Harrington knocking the old man on his butt. Weadock raced down the stairs, three or four steps at a time, stumbling, falling but persisting.

Theresa heard clicking noises at the terrace door and turned to see the dark shape on the terrace. Her first inclination was to scream, but she held it back. She wanted to run for the front door when the lock on the patio door snapped and the frightening figure stepped into the living room. He wore a black hood with eye cut outs like Mr. X at the hearings. He hadn't detected her and she quietly stepped back into an open closet and closed the louvered doors. She could see the dark shape through the open slats. His movements were powerful and deliberate. His dark eyes were deep inside the ski mask. They flashed with a demon-like blankness as he moved toward the closet. He held a menacing weapon in his hand and massaged it with gloved hands.

Her fear was too much to contain. She made a noise and his eyes blazed in her direction. When he reached for the closet, she cried out, "Charlie!"

At that very moment, Weadock hit the apartment door at full throttle. The door flew off its hinges and he tumbled into the living room on top of the damaged door. His gun flew out of his hand.

Ramon whipped around to face Weadock. Their eyes locked like two boxers. Clutching a painful shoulder and an empty holster, Weadock got to his knees in time to block Ramon's first slash to the head, but Ramon struck again. This time Weadock caught the pipe with his left hand and held on to it. Ramon yanked on the pipe to free it from Weadock's grip and pulled Weadock to his feet. The two men hit the walls like bulldozers, obliterating the furniture with their power. Weadock drove his fist into Ramon's face with furious velocity. Then nailed him with a solid right to the head. Ramon staggered backward and Weadock rushed at him, hammering his fists into the black mask again and again but his opponent refused to relinquish the pipe. They crashed into the walls again and again. Both fell on a coffee table. Ramon managed to free one hand and hit the sergeant in the head with the pipe. Stunned by the blow, Weadock fell back. Ramon paused to survey the blood on his hand. It was his own blood - he was bleeding badly under the ski mask. He cocked his arm to give Weadock the coup de gras, but Theresa came up behind him swinging her nine-hundred dollar Minolta. The camera shattered against the back of Ramon's head and he fell forward on Weadock. She began back peddling when Ramon sprang to his feet trying to grab her.

He lunged for her and missed. She ran for the bathroom, slammed the door closed and turned the door lock. Ramon hit the door with the force of a head-on collision. She fell backward against the medicine cabinet and the mirror shattered exposing the contents. Somehow the bathroom door hinges held and kept the door between them. She tore through the open medicine cabinet for a defensive weapon and armed herself with a can of hair spray. Ramon hit the door again and it flew open. She twisted the nozzle so it was pointing in the right direction and hid the aerosol can behind her body and

hoped it wasn't empty. He raised his pipe to strike at her but hesitated when Weadock screamed her name. She raised the can to eye level, pointed it at his eyes and pushed the button. The hooded man screamed in pain as the chemicals hit him flush in the eyes. He swung the pipe in blind rage and it crashed through the tile on the wall. Theresa staggered backward into a sitting position on the toilet. Theresa grabbed a jagged piece of the broken mirror plunged it into Ramon's hand. He dropped the pipe and fell backwards holding his wounded hand. He rubbed at his burning eyes with his good hand and continued clutching for her with the other. She was trapped. She squared her shoulder at him and charged. Bouncing off his hard frame, she crashed into a bedroom dresser and fell to the floor.

Ramon ripped the hood from his head and wrapped it around his bleeding hand. His fingers were numbing and Weadock was struggling to get up. Ramon looked for an escape route and moved slowly and deliberately to the terrace.

Weadock saw his gun and dragged himself to it. He brought the gun up to fire, but Ramon was gone. Weadock called Theresa's name and she called his name back. An inner rage drove him to the terrace and he pointed his

weapon at the dark shape on the rope. He knew he couldn't allow Velez to escape. He knew it would never be over as long as Ramon was alive. He took aim but suddenly the rope gave way and the dark figure fell like a sack of cement. His eyes on Charlie Weadock and his arms outstretched like a falling cross, Ramon Velez fell twenty stories to the ground and never uttered a sound.

Pushing his gun hand aside, Theresa dropped her head on Weadock's chest. "You okay?"

A sigh of relief swept over his face. "Oh, yeah." He put his arms around her trembling body. "Are you hurt?"

"No."

They stood on the terrace in each other's arms as a glimmer of daylight broke on the horizon.

Harrington stuck his smiling face into the apartment. "Breakfast anyone?"

"Stay right there, Mister." Weadock fished around the rubble for the telephone and punched 911.

"Police Operator 927, what's your emergency?"

Weadock gave the operator his shield number and asked for the patrol sergeant, the duty captain, emergency service, an ambulance and detectives. "Tell them the perpetrator is dead."

"What? What was that?"

He repeated the message again slowly before dropping the telephone.

Harrington retreated to the hallway, pushing a few nosey neighbors aside.

"Where are you going?" Weadock asked.

"I might as well get some bagels and lox. Looks like it's going to be a long night."

"What happened up there?"

"Beats me," Harrington shrugged. "You told me to stay out of the way and I did."

"The rope must have broken and he fell."

Turning his palms up with a shrug, Harrington reached for the lobby button and pushed. "They don't make rope like they used to, do they sergeant?" The doors closed.

Twenty stories below, two sanitation men were collecting the garbage. Slamming garbage cans against the truck in a zombie-like fashion, they failed to notice the dead body laying thirty feet away from them. Most of the residents ignored the noise and the garbage truck moved along.

Harrington ambled pass the heated argument going on between Frankie and Juan about

Puerto Rican statehood and made his way outside to Ramon's body. Approaching it like a golfer sizing up a long putt, Harrington's eyes became fixed on the set of gold keys near the mangled corpse. With a somewhat nauseated grin on his face, he picked up the keys and headed for Ramon's Eldorado. Wondering why Ramon spent so much time by the trunk of his car, Harrington popped the lid and unzipped one of the two huge gym bags in the trunk; then closed it immediately. He closed the trunk quickly when Frankie approached him.

"My good man." Harrington urged Frankie back to the limo. "I know its long past your bedtime, but the sergeant wants us to talk to the police when they get here. So you run down to that bagel shop on Second Avenue and pick up six dozen bagels. Get some lox, some butter and cream cheese and bring it up to the sergeant's apartment."

"This is going to cost you extra, JJ."

Harrington handed Frankie a hundred-dollar bill and Frankie left. Harrington removed the two heavy gym bags, closed the trunk and tossed the keys at the body. He flagged a cab and left the scene.

About an hour later, Harrington returned to the apartment building and found it

surrounded with blue and white police cars. He had the look and demeanor of a police chief and no one questioned him as he boldly moved through police lines saying Chief Harrington. He took the elevator to the sixteenth floor where a baby-faced rookie holding a container of coffee and a bagel stopped him.

"Can I help you, sir?"

Harrington took a step closer to the officer. "I doubt it."

"Do you know Sergeant Weadock?"

"No Sir."

"Well, find him and tell him that Chief Harrington is here."

"You're Chief Harrington?"

"That's correct, Officer. The same Chief Harrington who paid for that bagel that you are now eating."

"Are you a cop?"

"Do I look like a cop, Officer? I'm seventy-one years of age and I've never had a girlfriend."

"What?"

"Do you know the definition of buffoonery?"

Weadock came out of the kitchen in response to Harrington's loud mouth and pulled him inside the apartment by his tie. "Where have you been?"

"I needed a little nap and--"

"That's a lousy tie, Jay."

"You really like it?"

"C'mon."

"You know, Sergeant, I was on my way home when all this nasty shit unfolded. I didn't have to come here to save your ass."

"All right, all right, I owe you one. Now take a seat in the kitchen next to your friend, Frankie and tell the nice captain with the green tie exactly what you saw and heard today."

"I finally get to talk to a captain." Harrington rubbed his hands together. "I might even be recognized some day for all the contributions I've made to the NYPD."

Weadock pulled a chair out for Harrington and placed his hands on the old man's shoulders. "Gentlemen, this person is a registered Confidential Informant. He was assisting me with one of my cases when the incident occurred. I ask you to protect his identity by referring to him in your reports as CI 39. He and his driver alerted me that the burglar was in the building. He was here when the burglar fell. He is also an incurable alcoholic, so if you have any questions to ask him do it now while he is sober."

"Did you see this man fall from the building?" the duty captain asked.

"What man? What?"

Kennedy and the Duty Captain whispered something to each other and the Captain continued with his questions.

"Where were you when the burglar fell from the building?"

"Captain, if I didn't see the burglar fall, how would I know where I was when he fell." Harrington turned to Weadock. "Is there a school of buffoonery where all these Capt--"

"Just answer the Captain's questions, Jay," Weadock said.

"Sorry Captain, but I'm seventy-one years old and I never had a-"

"Jay!" Weadock interrupted. "Tell the captain what happened from the time you spotted Velez until you came down from the roof."

Harrington reached for a bagel. "Okay, the spic was following Frankie and me for about twenty minutes but we reversed the tail and we followed him. He thought I went home but we followed him here. That was about four o'clock this morning."

"The spic?" The Captain looked around.

"He means the burglar, Ramon Velez," Weadock said.

"That's right, Captain. I called Sergeant Weadock on the house phone in the lobby when we," Harrington waved at Frankie. "seen this

Velez character on the security camera go up to the top floor in the elevator. I told Sergeant Weadock and he went to the roof after him. I also went up to the roof to help him but when I opened the door the sergeant here pointed his gun at me. Me! He pointed his gun at me, the man who saved his life many times. But he didn't shoot me. He looked over the edge of the building. Then he ran past me and down the stairs. That's when he knocked me down and I sustained an injury that I hope the NYPD will compensate me for in the future… Are you writing this down, Captain? Anyway, I was able to get up and followed the Sergeant downstairs."

"That's it?"

"Yes. Is there any lox left? I like lox with my cream cheese bagel."

"Did anyone touch the rope?"

"What rope?"

"Did you or the sergeant touch the rope?"

Harrington shot a puzzled look at Weadock. "What rope?"

Weadock stood up to leave. "Velez lowered himself down here on a rope."

"Oh, that rope." Harrington shrugged. "No."

"Where were you when Sergeant Weadock broke into this apartment?"

"Coming down the stairs. I'm not as fast as I used to be, Captain. It took me a lot longer to get down here but I heard him crash through the door. That must have hurt because it was a strong door."

"Did you know that the alleged burglar was a cop?"

"I knew that the cop had a black Cadillac Eldorado, but I never met him formally. I didn't know that the cop was a burglar. Frankie spotted the Eldorado first"

"When was that?"

"I just told you." Harrington filled his mouth with a bagel and muffled his answer. "We shook his tail at the Henry Hudson Hotel and followed him here. He led us here. I didn't know the sergeant was living here, but I know his car and saw it outside."

Harrington was a great witness when he was sober. He protected his relationship with FIAU like a patriotic prisoner of war and told the Captain only what they needed to know.

Lieutenant Kennedy leaned across the table. "Where's the Cadillac now?"

"It's outside the building where Velez left it," Harrington said.

"Miss Kennedy." The captain looked at Theresa. "Did the perpetrator say anything to you?"

"Nothing."

"All this damage and he said nothing?"

"Not a word."

"Strange."

"This was a strange individual, Captain." Harrington leaned toward the captain. "He fell twenty stories and never cried out."

"How did you know that, Number 39?"

Harrington pointed at Weadock. "He told me."

Weadock now suspected that Harrington was on the roof when Ramon fell, but he nodded at the duty captain. "That's right Captain."

Kennedy glanced at his sister's fatigued face and tugged on Lieutenant Noonan's arm. "Can we move this investigation to the station house?"

Noonan, the 17th Precinct Squad Commander, was the first to slide off his chair and stand up. "I'll check with the crime scene people."

Kennedy began prodding the other cops out of the apartment.

"Would you like some extra bagels, Captain?" Harrington asked.

"No thanks, Number 39." The duty captain turned to Kennedy. "Did anyone interview the doorman?"

"I did, boss." Noonan answered.

"How about the garage attendant?"

"It's a park & lock thing, no attendant but there are two security cameras in the garage."

The Duty Captain followed the others out the door. "Who has the DOA's property?"

"It's at the station house," Noonan answered again. "The body went to Bellevue and his car will go to the White Stone Auto Pound."

Theresa leaned against the kitchen doorjamb. "What a mess."

Weadock crossed the room and pinned her against the wall. "Is there anything left to eat?"

"You want to eat?"

He kissed her gently. "You make me hungry."

Her smile was short. "Is it over, Charlie?" There was still a touch of fear in her little girl's voice.

"It's over now." He scooped her up like a bride and carried her to bedroom. "You better pack a bag for about a week. This place is a crime scene now and you need a new door. We might as well go to my house in Brooklyn."

THE COVER UP

SOMEWHERE IN WEADOCK'S HOUSE, his pager sprang to life waking Theresa from a menacing nightmare. She made no attempt to remember her dream and snuggled closer to her mate. "Don't they ever leave you alone, Charlie?"

It seemed as if only minutes had passed since they fell asleep, but the sun was high enough in the sky to cause Weadock to shade his eyes from its rays. He found his pager and telephoned his office.

Falcone answered his call. "The PC and a couple of chiefs are in the squad room down the hall. Lieutenant Kennedy came into our office and said they're asking for you."

Kennedy waited outside the station house. Every few minutes, he paced a hundred feet to the corner and back to the station house door, occasionally stopping to drum his fingers on the precinct doorjamb. He was tempted to telephone Falcone again when he spotted Weadock crossing Third Avenue. He walked to the corner again to meet him.

"What's up?" Weadock asked.

"We conducted a search of Velez's apartment and recovered four identical pipes."

"That's good."

"We found two more in the trunk of his car."

"Good."

"And, of course the one that he used on you and Theresa in her apartment."

"Very good."

"No," Kennedy lowered his head. "Not even good."

"There's a problem?"

"Yes."

"The PC is going to shit-can your case."

"What part of it?"

"All of it."

"You're joking, right? This guy killed a dozen people, Vinny."

"You don't know that for sure."

"They want to bury this with Velez?"

"I guess."

"There are probably more victims, you know."

Kennedy stared up at the squad room window.

Weadock turned, walked five feet and turned again. "What do they want us to do?" Weadock raised his voice. "Make this guy a fucking hero?"

Kennedy remained mute.

"I don't believe this." Weadock shook his head. "I don't fucking believe this!"

"Charlie," Kennedy moved closer to Weadock, "you said it yourself. The DA doesn't have a case."

"That was before he tried to kill your sister and me. Now he has witnesses and evidence."

"No, he doesn't."

Weadock looked up at the second floor windows. "Who's up there?"

"Your boss, your chief, my chief, their chief, the PC, and some guy from the Mayor's office. They're all there. Lots of chiefs and no Indians."

Weadock nodded at an Eyewitness News van parked down the block. "What about them?"

"The Mayor will handle them."

"Is he here, too?"

Kennedy shrugged.

"Are you going along with this?"

"There's a lot of pressure on me, Charlie."

Weadock turned to enter the station house, but Kennedy held his arm. "Chief Brennan has all the evidence. All the pipes, Velez's phony Detective badge, everything we found at Velez's apartment, and everything from Theresa's building - everything."

Kennedy and Weadock cut a path through a herd of reporters in the main entrance and weaved their way up to the squad room.

Captain Guglielmo broke away from Chief Whalen and made his way to Weadock. "Come with me," he said and escorted him to Lieutenant Noonan's office. Without knocking, Guglielmo pushed the door open.

Weadock recognized the two men inside. The Commissioner was a lot shorter than he appeared on television. Super Chief Tom Brennan was 6'4" and had a number of rude nicknames including Bigfoot.

"I'm Captain Guglielmo, the Commanding Officer of Manhattan South FIAU, and this is Sergeant Weadock."

"Thank you, Captain," the PC said. "Do you mind waiting outside?"

Both men turned to leave, but Chief Brennan stopped Weadock. "Not you, Sergeant." Brennan glanced at Commissioner Karp. "Sit here where we can talk."

Weadock sat in the chair and Brennan sat on the edge of the Squad Commander's desk. "Sergeant Weadock, you did a fine job with this investigation. The Commissioner and I both agree that someone with your talent should be a detective squad commander. How do you feel about that?"

"I have no interest in becoming a detective, Chief. I turned it down twice."

The PC registered a confused expression on his face and took over the conversation. "Look, Sergeant, the Mayor is under a lot of pressure right now with these public hearings and everything."

"I thought the hearings were his idea."

"They were." Brennan and the PC studied each other's puzzled expression.

"But," Karp shot out, "this is not the time for some alleged police scandal."

"Alleged?" Weadock asked. "This guy tried to kill me and my fiancée."

"We don't know that for sure." Karp looked at Brennan.

"That's right," Brennan said, "the individual who attacked you wore a mask and no mask was found at the scene."

"It was Velez," Weadock insisted.

"Did you see the burglar's face?"

"No."

"Did your fiancée see his face?"

"No."

"Then how can you be–"

"It was *him*."

Brennan went to the door and waved at Lieutenant Noonan. Noonan came into the office. "Lieutenant, did any of the witnesses at the apartment house see the perpetrator's face?"

"No, sir."

"Were any weapons recovered at the scene?"

"Only Officer Velez's revolver, it was found on the roof of the building."

"Were there any blood stains on it?"

"No, sir. It was loaded and clean."

"Thank you, Lieutenant."

Noonan shrugged at Weadock as he left the room.

"This guy killed a dozen people, Commissioner," Weadock said. "You know it and I know it."

"No, we don't know that for sure," Karp, said.

Brennan sat down next to Weadock and softened his tone. "Most of the victims were junkies."

"One was a judge, one was a councilman and two were friends of mine. They weren't junkies."

The PC walked to the door, staring at the Detectives in the outer office. "I know all this."

"Listen lad," Brennan said, "it's like the boss says, it's a bad time for all cops. Every good cop on the street is taking a beating for what those corrupt cops are saying on

TV. What do you think a scandal like this is going to do for them?"

"How does this involve me?"

"You close your case and go home," Brennan prodded.

"Is that what you want, Commissioner?" Weadock waited for the Commissioner's answer.

Brennan tried to lead him off in another direction but Weadock insisted on an answer from the PC.

Karp knew the Mollen Commission's axe would strike him, but they couldn't blame him for corruption that took place during his predecessor's time in office. He could only be held accountable for what was happening now, and this Velez business would surely end his professional and political career. He turned to face Weadock. "Yes, this is the way I want it. I want to protect all the good cops. I intend to make sweeping changes in Internal Affairs so that this kind of mismanagement doesn't happen again, but I can't do that if I'm not the PC. And this torpedo will end it for me."

"It's not right."

"It's necessary."

"What kind of changes?"

"What?"

"What kind of changes would you make?"

"Uh, I can't give you all the details now, but something like the stuff you sent to the Mollen Commission."

"You knew about that?"

Karp shrugged his shoulders.

"Nothing is sacred, is it?"

Karp didn't answer.

"What exactly do you want from me, Commissioner?"

"Close your case against Velez and you and your team make no comments to the press about it," Brennan said.

"Killed in the line of duty?" Weadock laughed. "You're going to give this psycho-animal an Inspector's funeral? Weadock began laughing uncontrollably.

"Are you okay, Sergeant?" the Commissioner asked.

"Is the Mayor in on this, too? What am I saying? He's a politician, isn't he?"

"What does that mean?" Karp asked.

"Look, lad." Brennan smiled, "you can't hurt Velez now. He's dead. Nothing can change that."

"What about the DAs office? They're not going to stand for this, are they?"

"Let his Honor handle the DA," Karp said.

Chief Brennan stood up. "I'm giving you a direct order, Sergeant. Close the Velez case as Unfounded and do it now."

"Yes, Sir," Weadock left the room.

Two hours later, Kennedy left the 17th Precinct squad room and walked thirty feet down the hall to the FIAU office and found Weadock in his office. "You read all those books?"

Weadock ignored the question and the stacks of books piled on Weadock's windowsill. "What's happening in there?"

Weadock turned to look out the window. "You know what happened."

"You have anything to drink in here?"

"Do we have any evidence, Alex?"

Falcone pulled a full bottle of Johnny Walker Black Label from his bottom desk drawer and walked it to Weadock.

Weadock cracked the seal and poured three fingers into two coffee mugs.

Kennedy sipped the warm liquid and nodded in the direction of a plastic human skull wedged between Weadock's books. "Anybody I know?"

"He's everybody." Weadock answered without turning around. "He's man."

"C'mon, Charlie. We only have this one bottle."

"I can fix that." Weadock spun around in his chair and grabbed his jacket. "The lieutenant and I are going to Harglows for lunch."

Harglow's Pub was unique for a police watering hole. Most cops avoided bars frequented by Internal Affairs people, but Harglow's became an exception. Even the bartender, Tiny, was an ex-cop.

Happy hour was a long time off when the two sleuths mounted stools at the back of the bar. Cops always sat in the rear for strategic reasons. Tiny made Weadock a martini that only the steadiest of hands could lift without a spill. Weadock bent his head to take the first sip. He looked at Kennedy. "Well?"

"Brennan closed out all the murder cases with a master Five. Based on all the pipes we found at Lopez's apartment it was concluded that Lopez was the plumber."

"Beautiful, fucking beautiful. They're going to frame the wolf."

"He was a piece of shit anyway," Kennedy said.

"I'm going to pack it in."

"What? Quit?"

"I never liked being a cop anyway."

"C'mon, you loved it. What are you, crazy?" Kennedy got wild. "Don't quit over this bullshit!"

"It's not only the job. My life is moving too fast. I don't know where the last five years went. Even you said I was burnt out as an investigator."

"So do less work," Kennedy suggested.

"That's what an old-time cop told me when I first came on the job."

"It was good advice."

"No, it wasn't good advice, but I was naive and proud and wore my uniform like a suit of armor. I walked into dark alleys alone. I chased the big guys off the corner and my feet hurt. My feet always hurt. I asked an old-timer what I could do about it. He told me to walk less."

"C'mon, Charlie." Kennedy swallowed the scotch in his glass. "I admit I hated your guts when this case started, but I don't feel that way anymore. I learned a lot working with you. You're the kind of boss this job needs. Don't let those assholes run you off."

"That's very nice of you, Vinny."

"Even that thing with my brother. I knew all along you were only doing your job, but I couldn't accept it."

"It's not only the job, Vinny. It's me."

The bartender filled their glasses and tapped on the bar indicating that the round was on the house.

Spinning his ice cubes with a finger, Vinny licked the off the excess. "The world is passing us all by."

"Ha! You're beginning to sound like me now."

Two hours later, Falcone and McIntosh filtered into the bar with the lunch crowd and sat next to their boss.

"Well?" Weadock said.

"It's done," Falcone said. "Guglielmo took the Ramon Case folder downtown an hour ago."

No response.

"He said I could continue being a First Grade Detective if I kept my Maltese mouth shut."

"That was nice of him."

"Yeah," Falcone flicked his head at McIntosh. "He promised everybody a promotion."

"Yeah," McIntosh said. "He's acting like he won an election or something."

Weadock looked at Kennedy. "Perhaps he did."

"The PC made a statement to the press," Falcone said. "It'll be on the six o'clock news."

McIntosh sat down. "The word in the office is you're going to be a Detective Squad Commander."

Weadock began laughing.

"That wouldn't be too bad," Kennedy said.

"It's not going to work," Weadock said. "There was a time when I thought I could make a difference, but that time is long gone. Most of the cops on patrol think Internal Affairs investigators are scumbags but they don't have a clue about who the real scumbags are, do they?"

"Let it go, Charlie," Kennedy urged. "A sergeant working as squad commander gets lieutenant's pay and it's a chance for you to get out of IAD altogether."

McIntosh turned to Falcone. "We're going with the boss, right?"

Weadock stood up. "Right now, I'm going home."

THE FUNERAL

There was no wake for Ramon Velez. His body remained at the city morgue until the Patrolman's Benevolent Association claimed it.

On September 7th, 1992, every station house in the City of New York flew its flag at half-mast to honor a fallen hero. Six uniformed police officers wearing white gloves shouldered an inexpensive casket out of a local Manhattan church on 114th Street while a lone trumpeter played taps.

Hundreds of police officers from all over the country came and stood at attention in front of the old neighborhood church as the Emerald Society Bagpipes played a slow beat.

The PBA found and flew Ramon's wife and kid in from the Dominican Republic where they had been hiding for three years. She refused to come until the PBA faxed her a copy of Ramon's death certificate and told her she was entitled to an estimated eight hundred thousand dollars in line-of-duty death benefits.

Charlie Weadock watched the sad commentary on TV and felt for the honorable individuals in uniform who came such long distances to honor the creature. All they knew was that a brother officer had died in the line of duty and they were proud to be there.

As the TV camera panned the noble faces in uniform, Weadock toyed with the idea that the police brass may have been right to bury the truth. As far as anyone knew, this police officer had made the supreme sacrifice. It was great press for the Nobel cops and took some of the media heat off them for a while. *Who am I to stain these cops with accusations of dishonor? Who'd believe me, anyway?*

THE BANK DROP

ON THURSDAY, SEPTEMBER 9th, 1992, Jeremiah Joseph Harrington entered the storefront office of attorney Bernard M. Hoffman. Hoffman and Harrington frequented many of the same watering holes, but Hoffman never once picked up the tab when he and Harrington were there together. Harrington was on time for the 10:30 appointment that he made in haste the day before.

Hoffman's long time secretary, Joyce Kowalski, ushered Harrington directly into Hoffman's back office.

"Is it done?" Harrington asked.

"Are you sure about-"

"Christ sakes, Bernie." Harrington rapped on Hoffman's desk with his cane. "Did you do what I asked?"

"Of course, of course I did." Hoffman rearranged the documents in front of his client. "Just sign these pages and this character, Charlie Weadock, gets all your worldly possessions when you go to that big tavern in the sky."

Harrington affixed his unique signature to the pages and Miss Kowalski and Mister

Hoffman signed as witnesses. "There." Hoffman leaned back in his soft chair. "It's done, I feel better now."

Hoffman stood. "Does that include that Tenth Century Chinese tapestry that I have always admired?"

"You can have that piece of shit as part of your fee."

"Thank you, Mister Harrington but I thought you had some living relatives in Florida."

"They're all dead as far as I'm concerned."

"Tell me, J.J., how much are you really worth?"

"Mister Hoffman," Harrington turned his chair to examine the room. "You're a shrewd attorney and a good judge of human strengths and weaknesses when you're sober, and we have a lot of similar traits. Why do you think I picked up your bar tab all these years. Do you think I'm stupid?"

Hoffman cringed with doubt.

"Let me rephrase that somewhat. Do you ever listen to my babbling? I mean really listen to me?"

Hoffman yielded with a negative nod.

"Well, this lad comes to me whenever I call him, whether I'm in trouble or not and no matter what penthouse or shit hole I happen to be occupying at the time. He comes and tolerates my drunken, lunatic antics and he's the only person who ever lent me money. I never needed money, but occasionally I'd ask people for a loan just to get a response. Two years ago, he loaned me a hundred bucks and never once asked me to pay it back."

"Maybe he forgot."

"No, he doesn't forget anything."

"Why do this now, J.J.? What's the rush?"

"When I was in the hospital two months ago, he was the only person who came to see me. I've been in and out of five hospitals in the past five years. They all say the same thing. Stop drinking or stop living."

"So why don't you take better care of yourself?"

"You just take care of my boy." Harrington tossed an envelope containing fifty one hundred-dollar bills on Hoffman's desk and left.

After making a quick stop at his hotel, Harrington crossed 57th Street to the Chase Manhattan Bank. This was the eighth and final trip to his four large safe deposit boxes. All his Chase Manhattan Bank accounts were now in his and Charlie Wedlock's names. Harrington followed an aging bank guard into the vault. "Do you ever go out for lunch, Marty?"

"I'm afraid not, Mister Harrington."

The old guard waited at the door while Harrington stacked the last of the cash he found in Velez's car into one of his safe deposit boxes. He estimated about twelve million dollars in U.S. currency and several million more in stocks, bonds, gold coins, diamonds and other valuables. He left a set of the safe deposit box keys and a personal note in a sealed package addressed to Charlie Weadock with Hoffman. The note read:

Dear Charlie Weadock,

I invested that hundred dollar bill you loaned me in 1990 into various endeavors. That money plus interest is stored in my bank accounts and in these safe deposit boxes, I thank you for the time we spent together and I leave all my worldly possessions to you, the son I never had.

Jeramire Joseph Harrington

Harrington fenced what seemed to be Lopez's collection of jewelry for three hundred thousand and kept that cash is the hotel safe at his new residence, the Waldorf Astoria.

THE BARBECUE

CHARLIE WEADOCK TOSSED A SMALL TRAVEL BAG ON THE REAR SEAT OF THERESA'S MERCEDES BENZ and leaned against the front fender. He watched her as she left the building; she greeted an elderly neighbor and a member of the building staff. She was radiant, her ponytail bounced with each step and when she reached him, she was somewhat suspicious of the happy grin on his face. He pulled her close and kissed her.

"What?"

He handed her a lone yellow and orange September leaf that he found on the windshield, licked his lips and flapped his eyebrows.

"You're not thinking about sex, are you? You promised to behave today."

"Does anyone know that we're leaving New York?"

"Nope." Her eyes widened. "I thought we'd tell them sometime after we settle down."

They drove south through the Manhattan streets and Weadock paused to glance at the Terminal Hotel on the Bowery. He turned left at Canal Street and drove over the Manhattan Bridge into Brooklyn. They stopped at Junior's Restaurant on Flatbush Avenue and bought a large strawberry cheesecake, two containers of coffee and one bagel with cream cheese and jelly before boarded the Belt Parkway to Long Island.

"Are you ready to meet the family?"

"I already know most of them. Some of them will accept me, some won't. I can live with that."

"You can, huh?" she teased.

"I'll just mingle. I'll mingle at the barbecue and I'll mingle at the wedding."

"What wedding?"

"Our wedding."

"What makes you think I want to marry you?"

Weadock pulled into a service area near Kennedy Airport and stopped. He twisted his body to face her. "You must marry me. I love you and I need to see you and touch you every day. We have something very special. You and I, something magical. We always had it. Something that few people ever get to experience." He reached for her and she slid across the seat into his arms.

Twenty-six Cherry Hill Lane was a two story white house with green shutters. All the houses on Cherry Hill Lane were white with green shutters, but only one had a dozen cars double parked in front.

Michael and Maggie got out of their car and greeted them in front of the house. "We waited for you," Michael said. "We didn't want to be the only outcasts to show up."

Mary Ann Kennedy met the foursome at the front door and led them to the back yard. Vinny Kennedy stood in front of a crudely built brick barbecue flipping hotdogs and burgers. The barbecue had been built on the wrong side of the yard and a steady stream of black smoke floated past the kids in a small above ground swimming pool.

Several women, all talking at the same time, maneuvered themselves around a table full of food. The men grouped themselves into a tight circle around a keg of beer. Michael led them to an empty bench in the rear.

Elizabeth Kennedy broke from the crowd and headed for her daughter.

"Mom," Theresa threaded her hand through Weadock's arm, "you remember Charlie Weadock?"

Mrs. Kennedy looked deeply into Weadock's eyes as if attempting to read his inner thoughts. "I do," she said with a stone face. "I'll bet he doesn't remember me."

"I remember you, Mrs. Kennedy," Weadock grinned, focusing on her face. "It's easy to see where Theresa gets her good looks." They continued to study each other's faces. Theresa became anxious. Michael and Maggie waited for something to happen. Finally, Weadock smiled.

Mrs. Kennedy followed with a suspicious grin of her own. Then she gave in to a hearty laugh. "It's plain to see that you've inherited your father's blarney, Charlie Weadock."

Theresa brushed the loose strands of hair from her face and let out a sigh of relief. She hugged her mother and tugged her away for some female talk.

Vinny Kennedy saw Theresa and his mother walking away and made his way over to Weadock. As he left the crowded bar area, some neck stretching occurred to see the guest from IAD.

"I'm glad you came, Charlie," Vinny said. "You guys wanna take a turn in the pit? The kids eat a lot of burgers and dogs."

Weadock and Michael looked at each other and followed Vinny to the barbecue. Weadock knew the men near the beer keg were talking about him. Vinny walked off and Michael studied Weadock's expression.

"Most of those guys are in the Bureau."

"I know who they are, Mike." Weadock began placing hamburgers on the hot grill in rank order. "They don't bother me."

Michael Kennedy scanned a row of rubber stamp houses across the street. "What do you think of East Cup Cake?"

Weadock backed away from the smoke. "Too long a trip to make every day."

One of the detectives took over the grill and they walked toward the bench where Maggie sat alone.

"I'm pulling the plug, Mike."

"What are you talking about?"

"I'm resigning," Weadock announced.

"You're kidding."

"No."

"That's crazy, man. All the guys I know want to be cops."

"I wanted to be a cop too, Mike, but I've made up my mind. Your sister and I are getting married and we're moving to the West Coast."

"What the hell are you going to do there?"

"I'm going to teach Criminal Justice at a small town college and write a few books."

"C'mon, Charlie. There's no action being a teacher. You'll never last."

"That's what your sister says." Weadock stared at the crowd of detectives across

the yard. *No bad guys to chase? No cases to solve. Michael might be right.*

"This can't be true, Charlie? Tell me it's not true"

"We're going. I'm going to be Professor Weadock with weekends and summers off."

"That is bad news, Charlie."

"C'mon, you can visit us anytime."

"I thought you were going to take some of the heat off me here."

"Look, I thought I could really change the system but it's a totally lost cause and your sister wants out of corporate law." Weadock concentrated on Theresa's face as she crossed the yard and somehow he knew that everything was all right between her and her mother. Theresa had that kind of natural beauty that stays with a woman into old age. The afternoon sun fell on her face like a renaissance painting.

"I told my mom everything," she said.

"And?"

"She's delirious!" Theresa shouted with joy, wrapping her arms around Charlie.

"And your dad?"

"No," she sulked.

"Well," Mike stretched his neck to see around Weadock, "Pop is here now; he's over there with Tom and his family."

"They're back together!" Theresa ran off to greet them.

Mike shrugged. "Tom's wife is giving the big guy another chance. He's been straight for a couple of years now and owns his own bar."

About an hour later, Joe Kennedy sauntered through the crowd and made his way to the bench where Theresa and Charlie were sitting. "I'd like to have a word with himself, daughter," Joe said.

Theresa moved to stand, but he put his hand on her shoulder and held her down. "No, I want you to hear what I have to say."

Theresa sank back down against Charlie.

Joe Kennedy looked up, down and away. His eyes shot between them and he began talking about the other guests. He was searching for the right words. "What I want…" He began to breathe heavy. "What I want to say is…" His eyes watered and he stammered. Dropping his gaze to the ground, he forced words past his quivering lips. "My wife says you're to be married." He focused on Weadock. "I won't let my daughter walk down the aisle alone. I ask you to forgive me. I mean… I ask for permission…"

Neither Charlie nor Theresa anticipated this response. Their mouths opened as they turned to each other.

Joe Kennedy lowered himself to the bench. "Thomas has told me everything."

"its okay, Daddy." Theresa put her hand on her father's shoulder.

"Tommy never wanted to be a cop, you know. He did it for me. He was the oldest and I pushed him to it. I pushed him too hard. I pushed all of you too hard. Just now my son cried on my shoulder like a baby." Joe Kennedy, the iron man of the force broke down and wept. "He told me how he was all alone and how he got involved with the drugs. He lost himself and his family because he was afraid to come to his own father for help."

Theresa started crying.

"All this happened before that incident with himself." He nodded at Weadock. "When my Tommy lost his job it was just another hard pill for him to swallow and an even harder one for me. But Tommy was stronger than I thought and he straightened his life out. He did that without my help. Now, I have to set things straight." He sobbed, "I don't expect forgiveness for the things that I've done, but I tell you both, here on this spot -- I am sorry. I'm sorry for the trouble I caused you both." Joe Kennedy peeked toward the house to see if anyone noticed his display of weakness. He dried his eyes on his shirtsleeve and waited with a puppy dog pout for a response.

Theresa and her father turned their sad faces to Weadock and he made the right response: "Okay, you can give the bride away."

EPILOGUE

DURING THE THREE YEARS FOLLOWING CHARLIE WEADOCK'S departure from the New York City Police Department, the NYPD received more than six thousand allegations of serious police misconduct.

Those six thousand allegations resulted in the arrest of nine police officers; only two of the nine officers were convicted of a crime. None of them actually went to prison…

ABOUT THE AUTHOR

Kenny Ferguson served in the US Air Force and worked for the New York City Police Department. He is the director of security for a large building materials company in New York City. Ferguson lives in Metuchen, New Jersey, with this wife. This is his fourth book.

CPSIA information can be obtained at www.ICGtesting.com
Printed in the USA
BVOW04s0922130315

391482BV00003B/5/P